LEGENDS

TALES FROM THE
ETERNAL ARCHIVES #1

EDITED BY
MARGARET WEIS

with Janet Pack and Robin Crew

DAW BOOKS, INC.
DONALD A. WOLLHEIM, FOUNDER
375 Hudson Street, New York, NY 10014

ELIZABETH R. WOLLHEIM
SHEILA E. GILBERT
PUBLISHERS

Copyright © 1999 by Tekno Books, Margaret Weis,
Janet Pack, and Robin McGrew.

All Rights Reserved.

Cover art by Jean-Francois Podevin.

DAW Book Collectors No. 1111.

DAW Books are distributed by Penguin Putnam Inc.

All characters and events in this book are fictitious.
Any resemblance to persons living or dead is
strictly coincidental.

If you purchase this book without a cover you should be
aware that this book may have been stolen property and
reported as "unsold and destroyed" to the publisher. In such
case neither the author nor the publisher has received any
payment for this "stripped book."

First Printing, January 1999
1 2 3 4 5 6 7 8 9

DAW TRADEMARK REGISTERED
U.S. PAT. OFF. AND FOREIGN COUNTRIES
—MARCA REGISTRADA
HECHO EN U.S.A.

PRINTED IN THE U.S.A.

WHICH LEGEND WOULD YOU LIKE TO HEAR?

The Eternal Archives. They have been described as the "imperishable chronicles of all creation, past, present, and to come." It is here that the complete histories, legends, and tales of all cultures and civilizations are stored. The mysterious Masters have appointed the Guardian of the Light to be your guide as you and the other Seekers of Knowledge quest for the wisdom contained within. . . .

"Bast's Talon"—Into what figure should the huge limestone outcropping close to Pharaoh Khafre's new pyramid be transformed? An obelisk, a great snake, a giant bird? The cat goddess Bast has her own ideas. . . .

"Silver Thread, Hammer Ring"—John Henry is a steel driving man, who can drive more steel than any nine men can. But can he beat a man with the head of a bull in a contest to drive a tunnel straight through a mountain, while visiting the gates of Hell along the way?

"Ninety-Four"—The U-boat Ninety-Four seems charmed, sinking more Allied ships than any other WWII submarine. Is it due to the mysterious Fraulein out in the deep sea water who speaks so sweetly to the Kapitänleutnant?

LEGENDS

More Imagination-Expanding Anthologies Brought to You by DAW:

BATTLE MAGIC *Edited by Martin H. Greenberg and Larry Segriff.* From kingdoms saved by the power of a spell, to magicked weapons that can steal the souls of countless enemies, to lands and peoples destroyed by workers of dark enchantment, here are adventures to capture your imagination and hold you spellbound till the final victory has been gained. Let such masterful conjurers of the fantastic as John DeChancie, Josepha Sherman, Rosemary Edghill, Jane Lindskold, Mickey Zucker Reichert, and Julie Czerneda carry you off to distant battlegrounds where heroes face their greatest challenges.

WARRIOR PRINCESSES *Edited by Elizabeth Ann Scarborough and Martin H. Greenberg.* From a young woman burdened with the responsibility for a magical sword . . . to a pharaoh's daughter gifted by the gods . . . to the most unusual reincarnation of Arthur . . . to a barbarian princess who can outbargain an Empress—here are all-original tales of powerful women ready to fight for what they believe in, unforgettable yarns by such top fantasists as Morgan Llywelyn, Jane Yolen, and Elizabeth Moon.

CAMELOT FANTASTIC *Edited by Lawrence Schimel and Martin H. Greenberg.* Arthur and his Knights of the Round Table live again in these original and imaginative tales set in that place of true enchantment—Camelot! Let such heirs to the bard Taliesin as Brian Stableford, Mike Ashley, Nancy Springer, Rosemary Edghill, Gregory Maguire, Ian McDowell, and Fiona Patton carry you away to this magical realm. You'll find yourself spellbound by stories ranging from the tale of young man caught up in the power struggle between Merlin and Morgan le Fay, to that of the knight appointed to defend Lancelot when he's accused of committing adultery with the queen.

ACKNOWLEDGMENTS

Introduction © 1999 by Katherine Kurtz.

Prologue © 1999 by Margaret Weis, Janet Pack, and Robin McGrew.

Why There Are White Tigers © 1999 by Jane M. Lindskold.

The Theft of Destiny © 1999 by Josepha Sherman.

Final Conquest © 1999 by Dennis L. McKiernan.

The Wisdom of Solomon © 1999 by Kristine Kathryn Rusch.

Bast's Talon © 1999 by Janet Pack.

Wisdom © 1999 by Richard Lee Byers.

The Last Suitor © 1999 by Kristin Schwengel.

Two-Fisted Tales of St. Nick © 1999 by Kevin T. Stein and Robert Weinberg.

Kings' Quest © 1999 by Mickey Zucker Reichert.

Silver Thread, Hammer Ring © 1999 by Gary A. Braunbeck.

Memnon Revived © 1999 by Peter Schweighofer.

The Ballad of Jesse James © 1999 by Margaret Weis.

Legends © 1999 by Ed Gorman.

The Wind at Tres Castillos © 1999 by Robyn Fielder.

Ninety-Four © 1999 by Jean Rabe.

Hunters Hunted © 1999 by John Helfers.

Precursor © 1999 by Matthew Woodring Stover.

"Dearest Kitty" © 1999 by Brian M. Thomsen.

Last Kingdom © 1999 by Deborah Turner Harris and Robert J. Harris.

Contents

INTRODUCTION
by Katherine Kurtz

WHAT is it that we mean when we speak of the Eternal Archives? For most readers, the term is likely to conjure vague impressions of something akin to that great cosmic ledger book to which Saint Peter is sometimes said to refer, when deciding who may pass through Heaven's pearly gates: a list of good deeds and bad, for every individual who has ever lived—or will live.

This image perhaps can serve as a starting point, but it captures only a tiny and simplistic part of what these records are. In more esoteric terms, they are often called the Akashic Records—which is a term probably even more alien to most readers. Rudolf Steiner, the founder of Anthroposophy, used this terminology when he explored the concept in a series of essays called "From the Akasha Chronicle." And here, we begin to get to the heart of what we are talking about, when we speak of "Eternal Archives."

Akasha comes from the Sanskrit, and might be defined as "the mixing bowl of the Elements," the totality of the four basic Elements of Air, Fire, Water, and Earth, plus their mutual interaction. In more Western terms, *Akasha* might be reckoned as the Alchemical Quintessence, that Allness that contains the four Elements and also encompasses their essential distillation as a fifth, all-pervading Element, which is more than the sum of its parts. This all-pervasive nature of *Akasha* means that it receives impressions of all energy movements—physical, mental,

1

and spiritual—and retains this information, rather like the iron particles on magnetic media such as floppy disks and cassette tapes. In a sense, *Akasha* is proto-matter, the very breath of the Ruach which moved upon the primeval waters and brought forth life.

Not only does *Akasha* receive impressions from the past and present (which is always becoming the past, from our human perspective, since we view time as linear), but it is said to receive impressions from the future. Taken in this sense, *Akasha* may also be viewed as Timelessness, a dimensionless point outside our planetary time-frame, in which past, present, and future exist simultaneously. Accordingly, we might liken *Akasha* to bands of timelessness, like extended black holes, in which time, as we know it, is suspended.

By extension, *Akasha* becomes an infinite fount of universal wisdom into which it sometimes is possible to dip and retrieve certain (hopefully useful) information, depending on the skill of the one who dips and the efficacy of the dipper itself to contain that information and bring it back into human perspective, within time as we know it. Is such information "real?" That depends on your definition. Perhaps we might treat it as Sir Adam Sinclair, of the Adept universe, treats information purported to come from memories of past lives: it may be precisely that; or it may simply be material brought up from the unconscious and framed in terms of "memories" of past lives. But if it's useful, we treat it "as if" it were real, and proceed accordingly.

The most usual Western image for such a storehouse of knowledge is a vast library or archival hall, wherein are stored an infinite number of great volumes containing all our past, present, and future. (Usually, those records having to do with the future are not accessible to the seeker, though there have always been those among us who are gifted—or cursed—with the ability to see at least portions of what is to come.) In earlier times, these volumes might have been clay tablets or papyrus scrolls. Sometimes they appear as ancient vellums of varying degrees of decrepitude, bound up with colored cords. More often, the information resides in finely tooled leather-bound volumes, stamped with gold—the epitome of every book-lover's dreams. Nonliterate seers often "saw" material in mirrors or windows; and in these days of cyber-information and electronic storage media, "windows" may well prove the medium whereby some seekers will access at least some of these records.

But these are only images and analogies. And as for accessing the Eternal Archives—the methods vary with the culture and spiritual enlightenment of the seeker. For most, brushes with the Eternal Archives will usually come randomly, during sleep, with varying amounts of information retained upon awakening—and with interpretation wide open, as everyone who has ever tried to interpret a "dream" will agree. Those with the discipline of training in esoteric matters may attempt to seek out such information by means of meditation or a trance state, both of which are altered states of consciousness somewhat akin to sleep. Some would say that the relatively recent phenomenon called "channeling" is another means of tapping into *Akasha,* by making a connection through some discarnate spirit intermediary. The bottom line is that what we "know" about the Eternal Archives is more a matter of intuition—or *gnosis,* if you will—than of pure, quantifiable knowledge in a scientific sense—though that does not make such knowledge any less "real."

One final thought regarding the Eternal Archives: However we may access these archives, and whatever form they may take, more often than not, there will be a "librarian" or other archetypal guardian or guide within the precincts of the Hall of the Archives, usually of a more highly evolved nature than commonly encountered, who will assist the honest seeker, at least to the level that he or she is ready to receive such knowledge. Such a guardian awaits you, within the pages of this anthology, to offer glimpses into the *Akasha,* with some insights into our past, our present, and even our future— new perspectives on some of our hidden history as a species and perhaps of our destiny.

With these ideas in mind, I invite you to enter the outer precincts of the great Hall of the Eternal Archives, those "imperishable chronicles of all creation, past, present, and to come," as Sir Adam might describe them, whose vaults as "as infinite as the mind of the Absolute. . . ."

PROLOGUE

THE Seekers of Knowledge, old and young, women and men from the diversity of Earth's cultures, cross the boundaries of time and space toward their goal. A few are aware they've passed these barriers and look about them curiously, trying to see through the mist swirling around them. Others, too wearied by their journey to be interested in their surroundings, focus on putting one foot in front of the other and continue onward. Each of them has come searching for wisdom beyond normal means to obtain.

Though they pass close to one another, each Seeker thinks he or she is alone. The mist dancing about them effectively separates the individuals on their unique paths, chosen for them by the Walker of Two Worlds. This guide, also known as the Guardian of the Light and the Master of the Archives, is the personage appointed by the hidden Masters to show Seekers the way to the Eternal Archives.

The swirling mist, seemingly alive, parts suddenly, revealing stone stairs leading to a massive door. One by one, Seekers climb the gentle ascent and touch it. The door swings open, allowing each individual entry into an ancient structure that is beyond time. This is the Hall of Memory, also known as the Akashic Archive, the Lists of Time, and the Eternal Archives. The portal opens to reveal an immense, beautiful hall with vaulted ceilings. Arched windows look out upon the sea of infinity. The Seekers gather here, waiting, accompanied by the ever-present mist.

A column of golden light forms in the midst of the group. It wavers, coalescing into a tall figure that floats above the floor. The being is dressed in a hooded golden robe girdled at the waist with a belt of luminescent spheres of diverse hues. One radiates like a sun seen from a distance; another is the soft blue-green of water. Black, russet, citrine, and olive curl around one another in a third. A fourth gleams with the orange-reds of young fire. Others are partially hidden, their colors unclear.

The Seekers turn toward the being. They cannot see features beneath the hood, but they all share the impression the powerful Guardian is studying each one of them.

"Welcome."

To some Seekers, the figure's voice sounds as if it comes from the surrounding mist. To others, words form within their minds. A few hear a male's deep baritone, others the lighter tones of a female. Several Seekers apprehend a melody that provides distinct images.

"You who have striven long and hard to reach Knowledge will soon have your heart's desire. First, refresh yourselves."

The Walker of Two Worlds sweeps his arms to both sides and a large round table with a central hole forms about him. Comfortable chairs surround its periphery. The Seekers find places; as they sit, goblets appear before them.

"Drink, and regain your strength."

The Seekers raise their goblets and tip the amber draught into their mouths, surprised to find their fatigue vanishing as they swallow the liquid. Their minds sharpen, their bodies straighten. No matter how much nectar they need to satisfy their thirsts, the goblets remain half full. The Guardian waits until the last member of the group is sated.

"When you drink again, I will open the Way to answer your questions. Consider well what you wish to learn in the Eternal Archives. Then drink, and know. When your time in the vaults is over, return here to the table. When I release you from this Hall, journey back to humankind as messengers bearing information no one else owns. Use it wisely."

Each Seeker gazes thoughtfully into his or her cup. Finally, one individual lifts her goblet and drinks.

The Walker of Two Worlds nods. It is time to give hidden knowledge to the world of man.

The Guardian scrutinizes the Seekers seated around the table. A number wear contemplative expressions, obviously still considering their questions. One woman raises her head and regards him with suppressed eagerness: she is ready to enter the Eternal Archives and find the answer to her quest. The Guide nods to her, pointing two fingers at her body as she pushes her chair away from the table and stands. Golden light streaks from his hand. Its thread touches her throat, impelling the woman to turn and walk to a doorway at the side of the room. Beyond it swirls the living mist. She hesitates only a heartbeat, then steps into grayness.

The mist exists no longer. Wondering, the woman walks beneath an archway of enormous peacock plumes into a corridor inlaid with crimson-and-gilded tiles. At its end stands a huge door painted with red enamel, incense smoke wreathing it from two burners set into the doorposts on either side. Gingerly she approaches and touches the portal. It swings open, allowing her to discover:

WHY THERE ARE WHITE TIGERS

by Jane M. Lindskold

SOON after P'an Ku hatched from the Cosmic Egg, he decided that he needed help resolving Universal Order from Chaos. This was a reasonable decision as his hands were busy holding up the top half of the Eggshell, while his feet were braced against the bottom half. To complicate matters further, P'an Ku was growing at the rate of ten feet a day and knew that he would continue doing so for the next eighteen thousand years.

Limited prescience may be one of the purviews of divine principles, but it isn't always encouraging.

Now, immediately following the hatching of the Cosmic Egg, some ordering had begun. The heavier elements of the Egg had drifted downward and were resolving into the Earth, while the lighter elements floated upward and were becoming the Heavens.

P'an Ku blew on the parts that hadn't decided whether to fall or rise, and from them resolved five creatures: the dragon, the phoenix, the tiger, the tortoise, and the chi'lin. These looked much as they do today, with one major exception. They were a uniform muddy gray, for color had not yet been created from the particles contained within the Egg.

"Folks," said P'an Ku, "I have a bit of a problem. Chaos is giving way, but without help, Order is going to take a while to . . . well . . . organize."

(Remember, language was just getting started then. P'an Ku was making it up as he went along).

"Now," he continued, shifting slightly to adjust to his newest growth spurt, "my hands are full. I need you to help Order along."

Five heads—one feathered, two scaled, one furred, and one horned—nodded, thus creating harmony. Then the Dragon said:

"Any suggestions where we should start, O-Source-of-Divine-Breath?" (In this way the Dragon created both questions and subtle flattery.)

P'an Ku considered. " 'Where' is a very good question, really, when you think about it. Right now we have two designations: Here and Not Here. I think we should start with finding out what else is out there."

"Excuse me," said the Tortoise. "Most of the others here have wings, but I am a rather short-legged, heavy-bodied type of person. How shall I go about finding what is out there in the Not-Here?"

P'an Ku considered. What the Tortoise had said was true. The Dragon, the Phoenix, and the Chi'lin could all fly, but the Tortoise and the Tiger could not.

Without voicing his intention, P'an Ku blew upon the Tortoise, but since she was turning to speak to the Chi'lin, his breath fell upon the back of her shell rather than on the side. Instead of creating wings, as P'an Ku had intended, his breath resolved into a sixth creature: a serpent, firmly fastened to the Tortoise where her tail had been.

All of them stared, including the serpent.

"Well, hello," the Serpent hissed softly. "This is a surprise."

"Uh, yes," admitted P'an Ku. "I was attempting to give the Tortoise wings."

"Messed up a bit, didn't you?" said the Serpent, twisting about to get a good look at the Tortoise who craned her neck back in return, amazed at the sight of her tail given life and mind of its own.

"I . . . uh," P'an Ku was saying when the Tortoise interrupted.

"Not at all. I was rather nervous about going out into the Not-Here by myself. Now I'll have company."

"But what about flying?" the Tiger prompted, since he was rather interested in this matter himself.

The Tortoise gave a few experimental spins to her elongated tail and the Serpent began to spin like a propeller.

"I think we can manage," she said cheerfully. "The Serpent will push, and I will swim. We won't be swift, but we'll be steady."

The Tiger looked at his own tail thoughtfully. Then he flexed his legs, noticing for the first time how strong and springy they were. Earth and Heaven weren't as far apart then as they are today, so distances—both horizontal and vertical—weren't as great a problem.

"If your Excellency doesn't mind," he said, "I think I can do without flying. I'll stay on my own four feet, and if I come to a tough spot, I'll jump."

P'an Ku nodded, secretly rather relieved. "Very good. Now all five—that is, all six—of you go explore. Find out what the Not-Here contains."

Then the five (we'll stick with five, since the Tortoise and the Serpent were inseparable) launched off into the drifting matter surrounding P'an Ku. They made no effort to stay together, since their goal was to learn as much as possible about what was taking form. Nor did they hurry back, for there was much to discover. When P'an Ku grew lonely, he called them back.

They heard his call, though the Universe had grown taller by some fifty feet since last they gathered around the one whose breath had created them out of the new matter. One by one they returned: first the Dragon, then the Chi'lin, then the Phoenix, and lastly, one leaping and bouncing from cloud to cloud, one chugging along propeller-driven through the void, the Tiger and the Tortoise.

"What is out there?" asked P'an Ku.

"I have seen brightness and darkness," said the Tortoise. "It has many shapes, some smooth, some rough, some round, some angular."

"Some," added the Serpent, not to be left out, "combine smoothness and roundness, or roughness and angularity. It is quite amazing."

"Sounds!" sang the Phoenix, fluttering her wings. "Splashes and gurgles, clunking and bumping. All matter talks, filling what was empty with noise."

"Tastes!" proclaimed the Dragon, flicking out his long tongue. "There are tastes. Salt, sour, pungent, bitter, sweet. Even when my eyes are closed and my ears are plugged, the Universe proclaims itself."

"Smells!" added the Chi'lin, in a voice light yet strong. "They are like tastes but more varied. The variations in pungent scents alone is a wonder and a delight."

"Solid matter," growled the Tiger licking the pad of his left front paw. "Shapes strong enough to push against, to wear the skin from my tired feet. What the Tortoise sees as mere curiosities are hard reality."

P'an Ku thanked them before sending them to explore once more. This time he waited until he had grown a hundred feet taller before calling them back. Once again they returned. This time the Tiger, limping a bit as he leaped from cloud to cloud in order to mount level with the giant's head, arrived the last of all.

P'an Ku listened as the five told him about color, about oceans, about growing plants and scampering animals. With his head so high above the ground, these were a greater wonder to him than the sun or the moon or even the myriad stars. He listened eagerly to their descriptions, but above all these wonders, one thing caught his attention.

"Chaos is indeed forming into matter, but Order is slow to impose itself. Each time one of you tells me what you have found you must give a long account of how you reached that point. I think we must agree on designations for direction."

Nodding her single-horned head, the Chi'lin spoke sweetly, "The Earth is a great square, laid out beneath the spreading canopy of Heaven, flanked on all sides by water. Since a square has four sides, we need four directions."

All agreed and so the four directions were designated North, East, South, and West. Mountains were set in each of these points to mark them. They remain in place to this day, as anyone who has heard of the Holy Mountains most certainly knows.

"We need one other designation," growled the Tiger. "P'an Ku is becoming so large and the Earth and Heavens are spreading so wide that I had trouble finding my way here when he called. Let us place another mountain between his feet and call it the Center."

The other creatures, all of whom could fly and so could see P'an Ku through the uncluttered reaches of the Sky, did not really need this last designation, but they took pity on the Tiger and agreed to set another mountain in the center of the square.

"With the addition of Up and Down," chirped the Phoenix, greatly satisfied, "we shall always know where we are going and be able to tell each other where we have been."

Everyone agreed and then they went on their ways, meeting whenever P'an Ku called.

The Tiger was less than happy with how everything was developing. Now that the Universe was growing larger, he could see less of it. Moreover, he lived in fear that something important would be decided without him, for he was always the last to arrive at a meeting and he knew that P'an Ku could be impulsive.

The Tiger's fears were confirmed when he arrived last for a meeting to learn that P'an Ku had decided that a new general designation was needed.

"There are so many opposites," P'an Ku explained. With his head in the clouds as it was, he had much time for lofty, abstract thoughts. "Perhaps because the Cosmic Egg had two halves. It would help if we could sort things by category: hot or cold, male or female, dark or light. See what I mean?"

The Tiger did indeed see, he even agreed, but he was less than happy to learn that P'an Ku had named the Phoenix and the Dragon as keepers of the twin concepts of Yin and Yang.

"They got there first," P'an Ku explained apologetically. "I had the time to sort ideas out with them and they agreed to take charge."

"I just bet they did," growled the Tiger to himself, and from that moment he became ambitious. It was clear to him that the next thing to be parceled out would be the four Directions.

"All I need," he grumbled to himself as he bounded from cloud to cloud on his way down to Earth, "is to be late for the next meeting. I'll come climbing up there, my paws aching, and P'an Ku will say: 'Oh, I'm so sorry, Tiger, but there are only four Directions and since you weren't here . . .'"

He snarled at the image, feeling as put out as if the event had already happened. The Tiger decided he needed to be the first one there when P'an Ku next summoned his agents. The best way to do that, of course, would be to arrive unannounced and prompt old Head-in-the-Heavens to call the others.

However, that wouldn't guarantee that Tiger would be granted one of the Directions for his own. The only way to be certain of that would be to make sure that one of the Five was late—or better yet, didn't arrive at all.

"How to do that?" mused the Tiger, pausing to sniff a flower. "I don't dare brace the Dragon. He's bigger than me and, now that he has been designated the Emblem of Yang, he's twice as important. Of course, that applies to the Phoenix as well, and she has a very sharp beak. Oh, my. . . ."

He considered further, wading into a river and admiring a flashing school of little silvery fish.

"That leaves the Tortoise and the Chi'lin. The Tortoise has two heads. She's growing wise from talking to herself all the time. Cunning, too. There's no way to sneak up on her—literally or figuratively. So only the Chi'lin remains."

Thinking about the Chi'lin, the Tiger felt encouraged. (It didn't hurt that the cool waters of the stream were soothing his abraded paws). Although able to fly, the Chi'lin was the least formidable of the Five.

Alone among the Five, the Chi'lin lacked claws, even small claws like those of the Tortoise. She possessed hooves instead. Nor did she have fangs or a sharp beak or an extra head. The Chi'lin's single horn was soft, not hard. Her tail was long, like that of an ox. Contemplating the many vulnerabilities of the Chi'lin, the Tiger felt heartened.

"I won't hurt her," he assured himself. "I'll just delay her long enough for me to climb up to P'an Ku, put my proposal to him, and get him to summon the rest."

The Tiger spent the next several days planning, and the longer he planned, the more he realized what would need to be done if he wasn't to be slighted.

"There are four seasons," he said to himself, "so someone is going to get left out when those are divvied up. There are elements, too, and colors. Of course, there are more of them so something will be left for the Chi'lin. The Center remains, too. The Chi'lin can share that with P'an Ku."

So reassuring himself that he was not intending to cheat the Chi'lin out of every honor, the Tiger laid his plans.

The Chi'lin was a social soul. She also had a liking for fine jade. The Tiger knew that she would come by to visit before too much time had passed. When she did, he would have his trap prepared.

"Hello, Tiger!" called the Chi'lin, soaring down from the sky, then trotting briskly along the rocks at the base of the Holy Mountain at the Center. "You haven't gone too far!"

The Tiger hadn't, for after he had caught the Chi'lin, he would need to reach P'an Ku's ear as soon as possible. He also knew that P'an Ku wouldn't be able to see what was going on in the shadow of the mountain that rested between his two spread feet.

"No," he replied, making his voice sound welcoming and excited. "I have made a great discovery. It has kept me here ever since. I think you'll like it. Do you want to see?"

"Of course!" said the Chi'lin.

He led her to where he had heaped a great pile of jade boulders in a hidden grotto. These were boulders such as carvers of today only dream and were exceptional even at the dawn of creation.

Some were five times as large as the Tiger himself. Others had broken open to show the pure stone within, the exposed slices were as clean and bright as if they had been polished. There were all colors of jade: deep green imperial jade, white jade, pink jade, orange jade, moss-in-snowjade. The Chi'lin was delighted and pranced up and down between the boulders, inspecting the hoard with innocent enthusiasm.

Meanwhile, the Tiger padded to where he had hidden a lever beneath a carefully stacked pile of jade boulders. When the Chi'lan stopped to examine a particularly fine piece of moss-in-snow that he had placed to tempt her to that very spot, the Tiger stepped on the lever. The boulders rolled, pinching the Chi'lin's long oxtail firmly between them, holding her as fast as if she had been chained.

"Ouch!" she cried, trumpeting in the fashion of a horse.

"Are you hurt?" asked the Tiger, truly concerned, for if she was he would have to let her go.

"No," she answered after a moment, "but my tail's stuck solidly between these boulders. I can't seem to tug it loose!"

The Tiger made a great show of trying to set her free, all the while moving other rocks into place so that she would be more firmly held.

"I can't get you loose," he said after a while. "I need help."

"None of the others will be close," moaned the Chi'lin. "They will have gone exploring in the farthest reaches of the four Directions. Every day when P'an Ku grows, new things are revealed and everyone wants to be the first to see them."

"I know," growled the Tiger, sounding more angry than he had meant, for he greatly resented that he could not reach these distant places as easily as the flyers could.

The Chi'lin took the anger in his voice as directed toward her predicament and shook back her mane bravely.

"I know what you can do," she said. "We are at the base of P'an Ku's mountain. You can climb up to him. Then he can bend down and loosen the stones that hold me."

"What a good idea!" the Tiger said, delighted that she had voiced what he most wanted to suggest. "And if he cannot bend without dangerously lowering the Eggshell, he can call the other three. They are certain to come and help."

"I'd forgotten about the Eggshell!" the Chi'lin admitted. "Yes, P'an Ku certainly needs to call the others. Climb up to him, Tiger. I'll be so happy when I hear his call, for I'll know that our friends are coming."

Feeling rather guilty, the Tiger touched noses with the Chi'lin, then began his climb to P'an Ku's head. As he climbed, first up the mountain, then to where he could tread on mist and cloud, he forgot his guilt, feeling instead anticipation and a certain sense of righteousness.

"This is the only way I am sure to get my due," he muttered to himself. "Even the Chi'lin would understand."

When he reached P'an Ku, the giant was pleased to see him.

"Tiger," he boomed. "I've been thinking about you."

"Oh?" asked the Tiger, somewhat taken aback.

"Yes. I've been thinking. The Earth is becoming full of Beasts. They will need someone to make laws for them, to give them Order. You spend most of your time on the ground . . ."

"That I do," the Tiger muttered.

". . . And so I thought you would be the best one to rule over them. What do you think?"

"I would be honored," the Tiger admitted.

"Then consider it done," said P'an Ku.

For a moment, pleased with his new designation, the

Tiger considered telling P'an Ku about the Chi'lin's problem and going to free her without asking for more. Then the little voice of his ambition whispered to him:

"What if this is just a sop? Perhaps P'an Ku plans to make the others the Guardians of the Directions and all the rest. Then you would be left the least of the Five, a mere vassal, ruling Beasts, but with no Honors given to you."

The Tiger lost all desire to hurry back to the Chi'lin. Instead he began the speech he had practiced so many times, adapting it a little to new circumstances.

"Great P'an Ku," he said, "what you have just done for me has given me an idea."

"Yes?" rumbled the giant.

"Just as the Beast need a ruler, it seems to me that the portions of the expanding universe need their Guardians. Once it was enough that we designated the Directions, but now each of the four quarters is larger than the entire Universe was at that naming. If each quarter had its Guardian, then Order could be better given. As it is, after each meeting the other four rush to see what the expanding universe has revealed. I am somewhat slower, so perhaps I alone have a realistic view of how large the universe has grown."

P'an Ku laughed. "I, too, have a very good idea of how it has grown. I can no longer see my hands and I have forgotten what my feet look like. Still, your thoughts are similar to ones that I have had."

I thought so, thought the Tiger, *and you meant to leave me out.*

Aloud he said, "Then summon the others so we can organize things immediately."

P'an Ku sighed. "I don't wish to summon them too quickly. Bide with me a time. Perhaps between us we can create an initial order. Then there will be less need for debate."

The Tiger couldn't have been happier. In his mind, he had already divided things neatly. Now all he had to do was share his conclusions with P'an Ku in such a fashion that the giant wouldn't realize how much planning had already been done.

"There are four directions, each with its mountain," the Tiger began, "and four seasons."

"Yes!" agreed P'an Ku. "I thought to divide them thus: East and Spring; South and Summer; West and Autumn; North and Winter."

"That makes perfect sense," said the Tiger. "Center, of course, remains, but there is no Season to match with it. I suppose . . ."

Never mind that for now," P'an Ku said impatiently. "First let us order the basics. There are five elements. They should be easy to assign."

The Tiger nodded. "Summer is hot, so Fire is obviously its element. By the same logic, Winter should get Water, for water is cold."

"Good," said P'an Ku. "Wood goes well with Spring, for that is when trees come to life. West . . . hmm . . . Metal or Earth?"

"Earth," the Tiger said firmly. "For Autumn is when the Earth gives her fruit. That leaves Metal for the Center."

"I like it," P'an Ku said eagerly. "Now, there are three primary colors: red, blue, and yellow. Then there is black which is no color. What should the fifth color be?"

"How about white?" the Tiger said. "It is the blending of all colors."

"It is a dangerous color," P'an Ku said, somewhat worried, "for it is the color of death, when there is no blood left in a body or sap in wood."

"It is also the color of bright light," the Tiger prompted, "and the color of polished metal."

"True," said P'an Ku. "Then since white is the color of metal, it should go to the Center. Blue, of course, belongs to the Spring."

"Not to Water?" The Tiger asked.

"No, we have given Water to the North. Blue is too warm a color for Winter. Besides, deep water is black. Blue for Spring. Black for Winter. Yellow for Autumn."

"That sounds very good to me," said the Tiger.

They worked out a few more details, such as appropriate tastes, fixed stars, and flowers for each of the Five realms, but it was not until the advent of humans that the designations grew very complicated, embracing animals, qualities, and opposing designations as well.

When P'an Ku next spoke, the Tiger had reason to feel that he had acted poorly indeed toward the Chi'lin.

"Since you alone do not fly," said P'an Ku, "you, of course, are the ideal Guardian for the Autumn, since Autumn is the season of the Element of Earth. What do you think?"

"I'd be honored," said the Tiger, for this was the role he had desired above all the rest.

Guilt nipped at his tail, but it was too late for him to tell P'an Ku about the trapped Chi'lin. It would look strange that he hadn't spoken sooner, maybe even thoughtless. Perhaps P'an Ku would take his new honors from him as a punishment. So the Tiger shook off his guilt and repeated.

"I would be honored, sir."

"Then so be it," said P'an Ku, and with his words the Tiger felt a tingling upon him and his coat, which to that point had been the featureless gray of early creation now became a brilliant yellow barred with black.

"Striking!" congratulated P'an Ku. "I can't wait to give the others their designations."

He called out the summons, nearly deafening the Tiger who hurriedly clapped his paws over ears folded tight against his head.

"Sorry about that," muttered P'an Ku.

The Tiger, who saw P'an Ku's lips move rather than actually hearing the words, nodded.

"I accept your apology," he said.

They talked of this and that until the Dragon and the Phoenix arrived. The other two were suitably amazed and (so the Tiger thought) more than a little envious at the brilliant color of the Tiger's fur. The Tortoise and Snake arrived just as P'an Ku was starting explanations.

"Where is the Chi'lin?" asked the giant, noticing her absence for the first time.

"She must have flown far," the Dragon said, a bit impatiently. "Tell us more about how the Tiger got his color!"

Last son of primal Chaos that he was, P'an Ku was easily distracted. He rattled on, talking about affinities and interrelationships. This led to a discussion on the cycle of creation and destruction between the five elements themselves.

"So you see," P'an Ku concluded. "No one element is supreme. Wood weakens Earth. Earth blocks Water. Water extinguishes Fire. Fire melts Metal. Metal chops Wood. It's all very neat."

"What about Air?" asked the Phoenix, gently beating her long-feathered wings. "It feels like an element to me."

"No," said P'an Ku with a decisive shake of his head. "Air isn't an element. It is either the last remnant of Chaos or the first manifestation of Order, but it doesn't enter into the cycle of creation like the others. It isn't solid enough."

He looked around him, then. "Where's the Chi'lin?"

"Perhaps she didn't hear you," suggested the Tiger. He'd kept fairly quiet during the previous discussions, feeling that his position was safe.

"She does like to venture hither and yon," said the Tortoise and the Snake hissed agreement. "Call her again."

P'an Ku did this. Then he turned eagerly to the others. "It occurs to me that three of you are present and that three seasons are ready to be assigned Guardians. Shall we begin?"

The other three might have waited, but by then they had been covertly studying the Tiger's resplendent coat and wondering what *they* would look like if they had color. Secretly, no one wanted to be assigned the Center, which not only didn't have a Season, but whose Color was White. Not only was white a color of mixed omens, quite frankly, it was boring.

"Yes," said the Dragon, flexing his four-clawed feet. "Let us move on. The Chi'lin will certainly be here soon and will need to have everything we have already discussed explained to her. Why should we be delayed from our duties?"

P'an Ku nodded. "Very well. Dragon, I thought to assign you the role of Guardian of the East. Your season shall be Spring, your color Blue, and your element Wood."

"That sounds good," agreed the Dragon.

"Then let it be so," proclaimed P'an Ku.

The giant must have been getting a taste for flashy effects. Instead of the Dragon merely turning color to indicate the assignment of his new duties, as had happened with the Tiger, a flash of blue lightning heralded a shower of spring rain which washed the Dragon in his new hue. When the rain ceased, the now resplendently azure Dragon raised the branch of plum blossoms that had sprung to life in his right forepaw and bowed with humble majesty.

"Wonderful!" cheered P'an Ku. "Now it is your turn, Phoenix, for Summer follows Spring."

"Summer!" sang the Phoenix. "Then you mean me to be the Guardian of the hot South whose element must be Fire and whose color must be Red!"

Laughing loudly, for the bird's joy and enthusiasm was contagious, P'an Ku took a deep breath. When he exhaled, bright fireworks exploded in the air around the Phoenix. The sparks that touched her feathers burned away the primordial gray, replacing it with brilliant red. A final fireball resolved into a delicate orchid that the Phoenix seized in one claw as a monarch would a scepter.

"Bravo!" muttered the Tiger sarcastically, just a wee bit jealous that he hadn't been provided with such an elaborate investiture. No one heard him for the Tortoise and the Snake were clearing their throats nervously.

"That leaves the North for us, right, P'an Ku?" asked the Tortoise.

"Yes," the giant agreed. "North from which comes Winter, but which is also the realm of the life-giving element of Water. The color of the North is black, but not the black of obscurity and darkness, the black of depth and insight. Since the dawn of creation, you two have consulted with each other on many matters. Thus, you may be the wisest of any living things. Black is appropriate to you."

The Tortoise cheered up, and even the Snake looked pleased.

"That sounds pretty good, P'an Ku."

"Yesss. Thank you."

P'an Ku grinned and exhaled once more. An ocean of dark mystery appeared around the Tortoise. Its waves lapped her shell and scales, dyeing them a shining, polished ebony. When they receded, a graceful bamboo stalk, young and delicate, rested between the Tortoise's front feet.

"Delicious," she said, sampling it. "I am quite pleased."

"But where," chirped the Phoenix, preening her bright red feathers, "is the Chi'lin?"

Ambition is a curious thing. Once fed, it grows hungry rapidly, rather than remaining satisfied. So, while the others had been receiving their responsibilities, the Tiger had begun eyeing the portions set aside for the Chi'lin.

"Perhaps," he said to P'an Ku, knowing that he was being unfair, "the Chi'lin no longer cares to come to these gatherings. What other reason could there be for her continued absence? She can fly, after all. If she has become so inattentive that she no longer answers your call, P'an Ku, what type of Guardian would she be?"

Only the Tortoise, who had spent many hours talking with the Snake, heard anything but logical reason in these words. To the Phoenix and the Dragon, the Tiger's words made perfect sense.

The Tortoise didn't speak up, however, for she was still coming to terms with the grave responsibilities of being the Guardian of the North, protector of both freezing Winter and life-giving Water.

All she did was turn her black head to trade glances with the Snake. That cunning one hissed "Yesss, strange . . ." so softly that no one but the Tortoise heard.

"Well, Tiger," said P'an Ku, "you have a point. I could keep these responsibilities for myself, of course. I am at the Center, though it is long since I saw the Central Mountain and I am somewhat tied down by my responsibilities."

Tiger took advantage of the giant's concern.

"Let me help you," he said quickly. "Whenever we have one of these meetings, I must climb the Central Mountain. You can stand in as the Guardian of the Center, but I will deal with those things that need running about, such as administering the element of Metal and the color White and suchlike."

"That is very generous of you," said P'an Ku. "Can you take on so much more? Already you are the King of Beasts and the Guardian of the West."

"These responsibilities make me all the more able to help you," the Tiger said quickly. "I can have the Beasts run errands for me or bring me news."

None of the others were terribly interested in taking on the Chi'lin's portion. The Phoenix and the Dragon already felt they had too much to do. The Tortoise thought that the same creature could not administer both Black and White, Water and Metal. Besides, the more she wondered, the more worried she became about the Chi'lin and the less she wanted anything to do with that one's disenfranchisement.

Thus the Tiger became the Guardian of all the qualities that had been given to the Center. His coat did not change color, since he preferred shining yellow to flat white, but he gained in importance and honor.

When the meeting ended, the Tortoise made as if to fly off to her new holdings in the North. What she really did was fly a short distance toward the North, then double around and head back to the Central Mountain.

"Have you kept the Tiger in view?" she asked the Snake.

"I have," replied that one. "His bright coat makes him easy to see against the white clouds and green trees. He has gone down the Central Mountain. However, rather than heading to the Holy Mountain of the West, as we might have expected, he has vanished into a grotto at the mountain's base."

"Curious," said the Tortoise. "Shall we see what is so interesting there?"

"I have my suspicions," hissed the Snake.

"So," said the Tortoise, swimming steadily along on the air currents, "have I."

They arrived and found the Tiger, glorious in gold, talking to the Chi'lin. His account twisted fact, but stayed close enough to reality that the Tortoise was impressed.

"So, as you can see," the Tiger concluded, "I tried to get the other Three to come with me, but they were so eager to hurry off to their new domains that they couldn't be bothered. However, I am now the King of Beasts, so I can summon my subjects and we'll have you out in a trice."

The Chi'lin was so pathetically grateful for the Tiger's promised help that the Tortoise, phlegmatic soul though she usually was, became furious. Coming out of her hiding place like a blast of Winter wind, she confronted the Tiger.

"Told us all!" she said, advancing on ponderous feet. "Begged us all to help! Oh, yes!"

"Yesss . . ." echoed the Snake mockingly.

Words escaped the Tiger in the first shock of discovery. The Tortoise snapped her beak at him.

"Pitiful!" Then she glanced over at the Chi'lin, knowing that the Snake would watch her back. "Are you hurt, sister?"

"No," replied the Chi'lin in a whispery voice. "My tail is pinned securely between two boulders."

"I can get you out," the Tortoise said, pushing with one shoulder, proving that her shell was good for more than keeping the rain off her head. "Then we will fly to P'an Ku and tell him what has transpired. Hopefully he can return to you some of the honors the Tiger has usurped."

At the mention of flight, the Tiger growled resentfully, but when the Tortoise set about freeing the Chi'lin, he padded over and put his own shoulder to the jade boulder.

"Ah well," he muttered. "It was too good to last."

"Communication seems to be the problem here," said P'an Ku, a trace of sorrow in his voice. "Tiger, why didn't you tell me you wanted to fly?"

"I," the Tiger glanced at the Tortoise, "didn't want a Snake in place of my tail."

P'an Ku colored. In all four corners of the world, creatures stopped to marvel at the beauty of the sunset.

"There may be something to that," P'an Ku said gruffly, "though the Tortoise doesn't seem to mind."

"I don't," she said. "I rather enjoy the company."

"And you, Chi'lin," asked P'an Ku, "how do you feel about these matters?"

"I'm not happy," she said, "but the Tiger was careful not to harm me. He is ambitious, but not evil, and that ambition has brought about its own discovery."

P'an Ku brightened at her words (and dawn came early, with the sun rushing to catch up with the light).

"You are generous of spirit and kind of heart, Chi'lin," said he, "and your words have given me the answer to my dilemma.

"Tiger," continued the giant, "as I see it, your problems came from resentment that grew when you had to run when others flew."

"My paws hurt," said the Tiger reasonably, "and I was always late."

"These meetings *are* ceasing to be practical," agreed P'an Ku. "Therefore, I will set the Chi'lin over you all. I give her the winds to carry her messages. Air is not among the five elements and is free from the cycle of destruction and creation that we designed earlier. Thus, she will be the most powerful of my creatures and the most honored."

At his words, the Chi'lin glowed with a pale light. Her coat was no longer the flat gray of no-color, but a mixture of all colors tastefully arranged. Her soft fur stirred in a wind none of the others felt as her minions greeted her.

P'an Ku looked very satisfied and continued. "Moreover, the Chi'lin alone will have the power to punish good and evil. The innocent will be spared, but the guilty will be destroyed by a single touch from her horn."

"That," said the Tortoise with a satisfied smirk at the Tiger, "should keep *you* in line."

But the Tiger had no attention to spare for the Tortoise. P'an Ku was speaking to him.

"As for you, Tiger," said the giant, "you have taken much upon yourself. You are both Guardian of the West and the King of Beasts. In usurping the portion meant for the Chi'lin, you may have taken on more than you intended. Have you forgotten how we discussed that the color white represents death and so is a great responsibility?"

The Tiger had in fact chosen to overlook this in his

eagerness to take on honors. "I might have done so, sir," he admitted.

"And I suppose you didn't consider that although metal represents wealth and prosperity, it can also be both reason and means for furthering conflict."

"I hadn't really thought about it that way," the Tiger said morosely.

"We can't have you forgetting," P'an Ku said. "Therefore, I decree that your fur shall bear the white color of death to remind you of the weight of your responsibilities."

The Tiger gasped, for he was very proud of his shining black and yellow fur, but P'an Ku's will was carried out in a breath.

"White and black doesn't look bad at all," comforted the Tortoise, who, now that the Chi'lin had her due no longer felt any resentment toward the Tiger. In fact, she secretly admired his boldness.

"Handsome, even," soothed the Chi'lin.

The Tiger, realizing that he had lost little and kept much, bowed to the ladies.

"Thank you. I am honored."

To show that he truly meant what he said, the Tiger turned to P'an Ku.

"It seems to me that the Tortoise and the Snake deserve recognition for their deeds. Not only have they prevented my ambition from leading me into evil, but they have also rescued the Chi'lin. I suggest that from this day forth the Tortoise and the Snake be called 'The Black Warrior,' as a tribute to their valor."

P'an Ku laughed loudly (and in the four corners of the Earth creatures scurried for shelter).

"Tiger, that is wonderful! Let it be so, and let you remember that generosity toward others brings its own rewards."

The Black Warrior looked eye to eye with herself and, despite a certain tendency toward cynicism, felt rather pleased.

"Chi'lin," thundered P'an Ku, "set loose the winds to carry my new dictums to every creature on the Earth."

When this was done, he bid them farewell. It was the last time the Tiger met the giant face-to-face. The climb *was* getting prohibitive.

* * *

P'an Ku's dicta held even after eighteen thousand years had passed, and, grown taller than any creature should be, the giant was released from holding apart the halves of the Cosmic Egg.

Only the Central Mountain remains to mark where P'an Ku stood when the Egg first split in half. Where he has gone, no one knows—no one except possibly the Chi'lin, who isn't telling.

As for the White Tiger, he carries out his many duties with great care. Not without cause did mankind grant the Tiger the quality of benevolence, when in later years it added its own designations to those given by P'an Ku.

There are times when the Tiger has his doubts about how benevolent he feels. What he knows for certain is that having twice the responsibilities of any other Guardian leaves him with very little spare time.

Somehow, he didn't anticipate this when, with sore paws and aching vanity, he set out upon the road of ambition.

* * *

Author's Note: Due to the Burning of Books in 213 BCE, what remains of Chinese creation mythology is fragmented and, according to some scholars, based more in the justifications of later theological systems than in belief. Therefore, in this tale, I have felt comfortable merging material from several different stories. However, I remain faithful to certain aspects of Chinese mythology, most importantly that the Chinese cosmological system conceive of five, not four, elements; that Air was not considered one of these elements; and that the White Tiger of the West has an overabundance of responsibilities.

The next Seeker chosen by the Master of the Archives can hardly keep her excitement in check as his presence singles her out. Although still relatively young, this woman has thick salt-and-pepper hair cascading down her back. Crinkly lines at the corners of her lips and eyes show her love of laughter. The incredible length of her journey to this hall is buried beneath her irrepressible energy. All the problems and difficulties she surmounted are over: now is her time to assimilate the knowledge she's desired for so long.

The golden light touches the base of her throat. Springing out of her chair, she heads immediately for a portal barely showing through the mist. Entering, she finds a corridor lined on both sides with ancient wooden doors. Walking past those, she pushes open the one bearing letters of liquid gold spelling out:

THE THEFT OF DESTINY

by Josepha Sherman

NOW, here is a tale long hidden by the gods themselves, so that humankind might not know how close they, and all creation, once came to utter horror, utter loss. . . .

Enlil, God of Air and keeper of the Tablets of Destiny, those magical tablets of Power on which was written all that was, all that is, all that would be, stood in the gateway of his palace, its inlaid bricks gleaming blue and gold in the mountain sunlight. Today, Enlil had the seeming of a mortal man of middle years, one in the utter peak of life and contentment, and his robes glittered with cloth of gold, the fringes rippling gently in the morning breeze.

Right now, he thought, at peace with himself and his lot, all life, mortal and Other, was surely splendid, everything perfect and in its place.

Was it, though? Enlil straightened in sudden surprise, frowning slightly. Here came his children climbing up

27

the mountainside, his four fine young sons and daughters, but with them came . . . what? What had they found? Something living, yes, but like nothing else he had seen. Laughing and chattering with excitement, the youngsters were bringing the . . . being up here for their divine father to examine.

"See what we have found!"

"What is it?"

"Where can it be from?"

The creature had, at first glance, looked only newly hatched, but it had already grown, as was the way with magical beings. And if it had not been huddling in such seeming submission, Enlil thought, it would have towered over them all. Both wild and terrible to see, it was great eagle and lion mixed madly together, with a beak that looked strong enough and sharp enough to bite through twelve coats of mail at once, and talons like so many cruel knives. Its eyes were hot yellow, savage as the desert sun—but they were not, for all that, for all else, the eyes of an unreasoning beast.

"Who are you?" Enlil demanded of it.

"I am Anzu," the creature replied. Its voice was fierce as an eagle's cry, but its head was bowed politely. "I am here to serve you. Pray command me."

"Wait," Enlil told it.

Trying not to show unseemly haste, the god strode off into the great chamber that held the Tablets of Destiny. As he reverently unwrapped them from their fine woolen sheathing, the chamber blazed with sudden golden light, but Enlil, used to such splendor, never even blinked. Quickly, he searched in the Tablets for any trace of Anzu.

Nothing! Not even the slightest of hints!

Enlil hesitated thoughtfully, then wrapped the Tablets neatly up again. This Anzu must be a newly created creature, at a guess something spontaneously spawned from the wild magic of the mountain rivers and rushing winds. Such beings sometimes did spring into existence. And they could, indeed, prove quite useful—always presuming, of course, that they were tamable.

Yes. Ah, yes. Best to put this creature's undeniable strength to work in the cause of Good right away!

Rejoining the others, Enlil told Anzu, "I have decided. You shall, indeed, serve, even as you wished. In fact, you shall be a Guardian. You shall help me guard the Tablets of Destiny."

He told himself that what he saw was a look of pleasure crossing that savage face. But just in case, Enlil bound Anzu to truth and honesty with words that would mean death to the being if broken.

"Well and good," Anzu said, and swore the vows without a word of complaint, then purred like a great cat. "I am content."

So it seemed. And in the days that followed, Enlil told himself that he had made a wise choice. For all his size and strength, Anzu did make a docile, utterly obedient servant. He crouched, strong and steady, just outside the chamber of the Tablets, letting no one pass save Enlil. Bit by bit, Enlil's suspicions faded and his trust began to grow.

And all the while, Anzu seemed most utterly content.

Content! Anzu thought with a silent snarl. *Oh, I act most charmingly content, yes. But all the while, all the while, he, that Enlil, that so proud and good Enlil, parades about before me in all his godly splendor. All the while, he lets me see the golden splendor of the Tablets but never, ever lets me touch them with the smallest of my talons.*

And Anzu brooded, and Anzu dreamed. Once he risked asking, "Great One, why is it only you who dare touch the Tablets of Destiny?"

Enlil smiled—a patronizing smile, Anzu thought. "They are my rightful charge, good Anzu. Therefore, they do not harm me."

"Harm!"

"Yes, Anzu, even the gods could be harmed by such Powerful artifacts! Indeed, madness lies within their strength—for too much clear sight of past and future *is* madness." Enlil paused, shaking his head. "They would destroy you, Anzu."

"They are not for such as me," Anzu agreed softly.

But when Enlil had left, Anzu looked after him and thought, *Are they not? Was all that not just words to*

*keep the inferior being safely in his place? Patronize me
while you may, Enlil. I will have the Tablets, yes, and
with them, all the power of the gods.*

He waited with the slow, cautious patience of the lion
stalking its prey, knowing that Enlil had grown compla-
cent as only one can be who has never been crossed.
And . . . yes! Enlil entered the ritual Bath of Purification,
alone and off guard, leaving Anzu by himself before the
chamber of the Tablets of Destiny, sure that he need
not watch over his trusted Guardian.

Oh, fool!

Anzu snatched up the Tablets of Destiny, spread his
mighty wings, and soared away.

"Mine!" he shrilled, and his shriek echoed and re-
echoed throughout the mountains. "The powers of the
gods are mine!"

Behind him, below him, he heard Enlil's cry of despair, and Anzu laughed.

There on Enlil's mountaintop, in a flat open circle of
plain white stone, the gods held a frantic council: Many
voices, much noise.

"Enough of this!" Enlil cried. "Who will go after Anzu?"

Sudden silence, awkward silence. Enlil glanced about,
but not one of the others would meet his gaze. He
frowned at a god who wore the seeming of a stocky
mortal man: Adad, whose province was that of wisdom.
"Adad, I beseech you. Who should go?"

Adad sighed. "Who would dare? We all know that
by now, Anzu has mastered the Tablets. Whoever he
commands must obey—and whoever he curses is turned
instantly to clay."

"But we can't do nothing! Anzu won't be content to
merely keep the Tablets. We don't know what he might
try—he could very well destroy the worlds below and
above!"

"Patience, Enlil. Patience and reason conquer all."

Enlil threw up his hands. "We have no time for
platitudes!"

No, Ninurta agreed from his hiding place, *we have not.*

In all that godly chaos, no one knew he was watching.
Ninurta was young as the gods reckoned such things, the

youngest son of the Mother Goddess, and as yet unproved.

That, he thought with a touch of wry humor, *is because no one will give me the chance to prove anything!*

Granted, his powers were only now beginning to come to him; he could master fog and the first edge of storm-calling. But he wasn't helpless! He was strong and lithe, and no mere seeming about it, dark of hair and storm-gray of eyes. Ninurta was a splendid archer as well, drawn to the arrow as he would someday be drawn to the lightning.

But the others say I am too young to be part of their councils. And yet, look! They're afraid, all of them! Don't they realize what will happen if Anzu keeps the Tablets? He's a creature of chaos—Enlil's right. He will destroy the world!

Let the others talk. If no one else would act, Ninurta decided, then he would. Taking up his bow and quiver of arrows, refusing to let himself think of the peril, Ninurta set out alone into the mountains where Anzu was said to have his lair.

As he went, Ninurta roused his as-yet unfocused powers. And slowly, slowly, the air swirled and condensed about him, slowly he cast a fog about himself. Let it be enough! Let Anzu not sense him till he was within bowshot!

But then a savage gust of wind tore the fog from about Ninurta. With a suddenness that made him gasp, he was staring straight at the monster. Anzu's wide wings were spread, each feather sharp-edged as a blade. His fierce talons were raised, glinting like so many knives. And his fierce yellow eyes were blazing with rage.

And madness, Ninurta thought, a chill racing through him. *That is surely madness. Aie, yes, the Tablets of Destiny have destroyed his mind.*

That made Anzu all the more terrible. "I have swept aside all rites, all rituals!" he shouted at Ninurta. "There is nothing left to worship, only Me! I control the very gods! Who are you, small thing, to dare challenge Me?"

I dare not give my true name, not to a mad thing wielding Power. "I am the avenger come to trample you!"

Anzu's laugh became a roar so loud and long that Ninurta clapped his hands over his ears in pain. All about them, the mountains shook, and great dark clouds came rushing in, turning the sunlit sky black. "Do you see what powers I command?" Anzu shrieked. "And do you *dare* to challenge Me?"

Ninurta's heart was racing. But he thought, *Shriek away, monster. You're giving me just enough time!*

In one swift motion, he put arrow to bow, drew and fired—

But Anzu held up the Tablets, blazing in the darkness. "Turn back!" he shouted.

And the arrow turned back in its flight. Ninurta twisted aside as it whizzed past him, and Anzu gave a mocking laugh.

"You see, oh, would-be hero? You cannot harm Me!"

Ninurta dropped to one knee, notched an arrow and fired again—

"Turn back!" Anzu commanded.

The arrow whizzed back at Ninurta, grazing his arm. He looked down at the thin line of blood, barely believing, then turned and fled for the safety of the rocks, Anzu's laughter roaring in his ears.

But Anzu didn't follow.

Of course not. He's so contemptuous of me that he doesn't even see me as a threat! And why should he? So far, I'm not!

Hidden there among the rocks, the young god caught his breath and tried to plan. As long as Anzu held full Power, arrows were useless; he would just bat away any rocks thrown at him, and even a storm's fury wouldn't touch him.

Ninurta groaned.

Did I say Anzu was mad? Here's the madness, to think that I could win. He can simply keep tossing my arrows back at me till I run out of strength, or he . . .

Ninurta straightened with a sudden sharp jolt of an idea. *Or he runs out of strength! Yes! No matter how much Power he wields, Anzu is still a solid, tangible being. He* must *tire!*

Patience and reason, Adad had counseled. Adad might just be right.

He'd better be right: I'm risking my life on it!

Ninurta raced back up the mountain to where Anzu stood poised, waiting.

"Ah, the little avenger wants to play with Me!"

"I do, indeed," Ninurta said, and loosed an arrow.

"Turn back!" Anzu commanded.

Ninurta ducked the arrow's return, dodged behind a rock, and loosed another arrow. Another. Another.

"Turn back!" Anzu shrieked. "Turn back!"

Another arrow, another and another.

"Turn back! Turn back! Turn back!"

Ninurta's quiver was nearly empty, but he couldn't stop now, he must keep the monster busy—yes, here was a fallen arrow, and another, loose and fire, loose and fire—

"Turn back!"

Was Anzu's voice beginning to falter? Oh, let it be so!

"Turn . . . back!"

Yes! Anzu wasn't made to wield so much Power, mind or body; he *was* growing weary! The Power was feeding on him, tearing the life-force from him, and a storm of sharp-edged feathers all at once molted from his great wings. Anzu staggered, exhausted, his mad eyes raging.

"Now, little one, you shall die!"

I'm out of arrows!

No. One was left, but to Ninurta's horror, he saw that it was damaged, its fletching torn: It would not fly true.

I don't have a choice.

"Here I am!" Ninurta cried, springing up from behind his rock. "Here! Come to me, Anzu! And the Light be with me!"

With a wordless roar, Anzu leaped, wings spread wide, and Ninurta fired the last arrow straight up at him—

And he pierced Anzu to the heart.

In the next instant, the creature came crashing down on Ninruta, and for a terrible, breathless moment, he thought that he was dead as well—

No. Anzu lay lifeless, and Ninurta wriggled his way free, scratched and bleeding from the edges of those feathers, and staggered to his feet. Overhead, the great dark clouds still loomed, their power unfulfilled, and Ninurta, not even thinking about what he did, raised a weary hand to them and said, "Rain."

As simply as that, the clouds tore open, and rain stormed down about him. For a moment, Ninurta stood in wonder, realizing the Powers that now were his.

Ah, but the Tablets must not be left here! Ninurta quickly gathered them up, wrapping them safely in cloth torn from his tunic, feeling the wild forces surging in them even so. And for a moment more, he was fiercely tempted.

I am not Anzu. I could use them . . . only for good . . .
Use them? Or, in time, be used?

"No," Ninurta said to them. "I am not that foolish. Or that vain! You belong back where you were, safely locked away."

Snatching up his bow, Ninurta left. And behind him, only the rain mourned Anzu.

A man of robust body and deep mind is already standing when the Walker of Two Worlds returns his attention to the Seekers, signifying his acceptance of the last part of his journey. Beams of silver and gold entwine, rushing from the Guardian's fingers to touch his chest. Beyond the mist of his door stands a campaign tent. He ducks through its flap, finding ancient weapons of war lining its walls. He stops to look at the antiques, but only for a few moments: his interest in knowledge is a much greater desire than curiosities from the past. The man bends almost double beneath the tent's second flap to enter the:

FINAL CONQUEST

by Dennis L. McKiernan

*Of all the kingdoms of all the worlds,
none is greater than that of the heart*

THIRTY thousand strong we came, riding o'er the plain, the great Khan in the lead, his warrior son Batu at his side.

I was in the next rank back, for the Khan would always have his chief scribe at hand.

"That which I do shall be recorded," he had proclaimed long past. "So I have said; so shall it be."

And so it was.

And on this day over the wide plain we rode, fearful peasants fleeing before us, crying, "They come, they come," as they had always fled and cried.

Once we would have ridden them down and taken their heads for prize, yet not on this day, for the land was strange and unknown to any, even the soothsayers, for the entrails were silent.

Rich with trees and flowers it was, the soil dark and fertile, yet the trees were unlike any we had seen on our journeys of conquest afar, and the blossoms fragrant and vibrant with color, yet foreign in form.

35

It was not what we had expected, this land we had entered, for it was not anywhere we had been before: neither Junggar Pendi, nor Tarim Pendi, nor Qaidam Pendi, nor any other plain we had ridden, from the salty waters of the Dong Hai in the east to the green valleys of Persia in the west, or from the deadly sands of the Great Gobi in the north to the towering peaks of the Gangdise Shan in the south. And surely we should have been somewhere within that vast grasp, but we were not.

And even the stars were strange, for none of the outlines of the gods could be discerned: neither the Great Dragon, nor the Red Tiger, nor even the Bamboo Bear.

And the moon was unlike any we had ever seen.

We were lost in a strange land under strange skies and strangers fled before us.

Yet the great Khan rode forward rather than sit and ponder, and of course did not retreat.

"Those mountains," he said to Batu, pointing ahead, "there where they seem to reach out to embrace, that is where we shall go."

So he had said; so then it was; and so did we ride toward a valley enfolded by the snow- capped peaks.

As the sun of this land stood overhead, golden, more golden than I could ever recall it as having been, two of the outriding scouts came racing back.

"A city, a city, my great Khan, the most wondrous city of all, for it floats above a great lake."

They pointed toward the valley.

My Khan, as usual, had been right to ride this way.

He set his plan, the usual plan, one which had ever proved successful. And the following morn we laid in wait for the skirmishers to come racing back, the foe in hot pursuit.

Yet they did not come racing back.

Nor did any foe.

My Khan was wroth—and three hundred slaves paid with their lives—yet their entrails revealed naught.

And so the great Khan sent out more skirmishers the next day.

These, too, did not return.

"I shall go, Father," said Batu.

Yet the great Khan shook his head, *No*. "You are a mighty warrior, my son, yet the magic we face is great. I will use cunning and guile to achieve our ends. I and my chief scribe will go alone."

As usual I wrote all this down, though my hand did tremble, the brush strokes not deft and sure, for so he had said, and so it was, and so we rode out at dawn.

Across the bountiful plain we fared, just the two of us, and into the embracing mountain vale, and as we approached we could see a marvelous city of towers and spires and wondrous domes and great colonnades and edifices rising up.

And closer we came until we could see that indeed the city did float in the air.

It was all I could do to keep from crying out in fear.

And now we rode within the embrace of the mountains, and below the city was a lake so pellucid, so clear, that it seemed made of crystal faintly blue.

And a heady fragrance filled the air, and a vision of my sweet Sujin came to mind and my heart raced afire.

We found the skirmishers sitting along the lakeshore, their ponies cropping the rich grasses.

"She said you would come, my Khan," reported the senior of the two commanders.

Perhaps it was the wonder of the city afloat, or the crystalline lake below, or mayhap the fragrance filling the air and heart, but that my Khan did not strike the head from this languid commander was a wonder in itself, for not only had he failed to draw the enemy into our trap, he had failed to return at all.

Yet my Khan forbore to strike him dead, but instead asked, "Who? Who said I would come?"

But ere the commander could answer, a soul-piercing lyrical voice replied, " 'Twas I said thou wouldst come."

And behold! There before us stood a celestial creature, a lady so fair my heart clenched, and I could not withstand the blaze of her regard, and so I looked away.

But as stunned as was I, my Khan seemed thunderstruck.

And for the first time ever he seemed at a loss for words, stammering, "I-I-my na—"

She laughed, the sound of silver had it a voice. "I knowest thy name, Temujin, son of Yesukai; or wouldst thou prefer the name thou hast taken unto thyself?— Genghis Khan: 'supreme conquerer.' "

Collecting himself, the great Khan dismounted, as hastily did I.

"You know of me, then?" said my Khan.

She nodded. "Indeed, it is why I brought thee here."

"Lady?"

"You may call me . . . Princess, for in this place I am the Aeon Princess."

"And this is your city?"

"It was built for me."

"And you brought me here?"

"Indeed."

The great Khan took a deep breath and stepped closer, yet he did not reach out and touch her as I had seen him do to many a woman of the conquered. It was as if he were afraid she would vanish were he to lay on hands.

"Then here I stand, Princess. What would you have me do?"

The Aeon Princess turned and pointed at the wondrous towers and spires and domes floating above. "I would have thee bring the city crashing down."

"You would have me—?"

"Destroy it, Temujin. That is what I would have thee do."

I do not know all the powers she commanded, yet with a wave of her hand she summoned two creatures of light, each a spirit, a demon, a—a something for which I have no name, though the Aeon Princess called them "Starstorm" and "Sungale," and these entities "released" the two commanders with their companies of skirmishers and bade them to go. And so they did.

And the spirits then vanished with the great Khan and the Aeon Princess, and left me alone on the shore, with nought but two ponies—the Khan's and mine.

I waited there by the crystal waters as the too-golden sun swept across the cerulean sky and down.

Days passed, it seems, or mayhap none, for I neither

hungered nor thirsted, but I seem to recall golden dawns and silver twilights, or perhaps I merely dreamed of them, I cannot say for certain.

Yet whether it was one hour, one day, one week, or more, my Khan did return, borne hence by three creatures named Lotus Orchid and Moon Blossom and Night Flower, and the Aeon Princess was not among them.

And I was thunderstruck, for he struggled and wept, did my Khan, and reached out toward the city in despair, and never before had I seen him weep, not even when his favorite wife had died in childbirth, taking the babe with her.

Yet now he wept, though he did not say why.

The three spirits vanished, leaving us together alone.

We rode back to the army yet waiting there on the plain, and a great shout greeted the supreme conquerer as he rode in among the men.

But he did neither smile nor acknowledge the greeting in any way, saying only unto his son Batu to make ready to ride.

Away from the city we turned, back across the plain, and when the next dawn came we found we were back in Ningxia, not far from Yinchuan, a day's ride south of the Great Gobi. And all the men cried out in gladness for we were home again, where the sun was not too golden, and the moon and stars were right, and the soothsayers could read the entrails once more. Where we had been and how we had returned neither I nor any other knew, yet we were back and glad of it . . . all that is but the Khan.

Our great leader seemed desolate, bereft of all interest, as if nothing whatsoever mattered in the least.

Nevertheless, we rode on a mission we well understood, a campaign in the northwest of the land some call China, though we knew it by a different name. This was the campaign upon which we had originally set forth, when we had suddenly found ourselves in that strange land.

And though the Khan rode to that northwestern province, it was Batu who commanded in truth, for the great Khan seemed not to care at all.

Not even when captured women were brought before

the Khan did he care, women of great beauty of face and form; he would merely look at them in their nakedness and despondently wave them away.

My Khan, he never spoke of what had happened there in the floating city, and within three moons of his unwilling deliverance from that wondrous place he died in his yurt in the night, some say in silence, but not I, his chief scribe, ever at hand.

When he died he was weeping . . . when he died . . . . . . when he died . . . . . . I think of a broken heart.

The Master of the Archives points and sends a different thread of light to the next human ready to fulfill her quest. This woman is the youngest of the Seekers at the table, but has proved mental capacity and understanding beyond her years during her time on the material plane of existence. The light touching her is different because she is one of the few the Guardian has judged worthy to live the memory of another's life. Her experience must expand wisdom.

She follows the footsteps of the previous Seeker through the same doorway, but their routes differ beyond the threshold. This hallway is made of plain wood paved with stones cut to rest against one another. The door at the end of the corridor is old and weathered, set with sturdy leather hinges. She presses her palms against it. For a long moment the door does not move, as if to deny her passage. Finally it shifts, opening into the time of:

THE WISDOM OF SOLOMON

by Kristine Kathryn Rusch

At Gibeon the Lord appeared to Solomon in a dream by night; and God said, "Ask what I shall give you."

—1 Kings 3:5

THE story as you know it goes like this:

Two harlots and a baby were brought before King Solomon. The women lived in the same house. On the first day, one of the women gave birth to a baby. On the third day, the other woman gave birth. The second child died, and the second woman took the first woman's child and claimed it as her own. When the first woman woke in the morning, she was clutching a dead infant that she knew was not hers. The women brought the dilemma to the king who was known for his wisdom.

The king asked for a sword. When the sword arrived,

41

he said: "Cut the living child in two, and give one half to one woman, and one half to the other."

At this point, the women cried out simultaneously. The first woman said, "Oh, sir, let her have the baby. Do not kill it."

The second woman cried out, "Let neither of us have it. Cut it in two."

The king, in his wisdom, gave the child to the first woman, as her response proved that she was its mother. And when Israel heard the judgment which the king had given, they all stood in awe of him for they saw that he had the wisdom of God within him to administer justice.

> *And Solomon said, ". . . And now, O Lord my God, thou hast made thy servant king in place of David my father, although I am but a little child; I do not know how to go out or come in. And thy servant is in the midst of thy people whom thou hast chosen, a great people that cannot be numbered or counted for multitude. Give thy servant therefore an understanding mind to govern thy people, that I may discern between good and evil; for who is able to govern this thy great people?"*
>
> —1 Kings 3:7–9

The story I know is this:

My mother was a midwife, gifted with second sight. In those days, she was still young and beautiful—her skin the color of olives, her hair dark and flowing. When she described herself as she was in those days, she would laugh and say that her neck was an ivory tower, her eyes pools in Heshbon, and her cheeks like halves of a pomegranate. People would frown when she would say that, and a courageous few would correct her, saying that her hair was her most glorious feature. *Yes,* she would say. *Kings were held captive in its tresses.*

In my old age, I have heard the poetry of the king who was held captive, poetry immortalized as his Song. In it, he quotes those lines, and a hundred others. I realized then, if I hadn't known it before, that I am his daughter and throughout his life, he never acknowledged me.

His son did. Shortly after Rehoboam took the throne, he saw me in the palace attending an ill concubine. He recognized my fine gold skin, my wavy dark locks, and my eyes "like doves beside springs of water, bathed in milk, fitly set." My skin, my hair, my eyes, so like his. So like his father. The image was stamped on my face, just as it was stamped upon Rehoboam's. It was as if the mothers did not matter; they were only the receptacles for children born in the image of their father.

When Rehoboam saw me, he banished me from the city forever. I live in a small village, a small village that will gain importance centuries from now when the Messiah prophecies come true. You see, I may have my father's eyes, but I have my mother's sight. And the things I see do not always please me.

It pleased the Lord that Solomon had asked this. And God said to him, "Because you have asked for this, and have not asked for yourself long life or riches or the life of your enemies, but have asked for yourself understanding to discern what is right, behold. I now do according to your word. Behold, I give you a wise and discerning mind, so that none like you has been before you and none like you shall arise after you. . . ."

—1 Kings 3:10–12

I was eight and had not yet come into my sight when I accompanied my mother to that ill-fated house. In the middle of the night, she woke me, tears streaming down her face.

"Rebekah," she said, "we must go now. You must do as I tell you and nothing else."

I nodded, frightened. My mother never cried. She never asked for my help, and she never woke me in the middle of the night. Sometimes she disappeared to help with difficult births, but she always warned me ahead, and when I would awaken, in our small hut on my soft pallet, I would visit the women we saw during the day, until I found my mother tending one of them, assisting in the births, easing the pain, bringing the children forth.

It was glorious work, the work of miracles, although

I didn't realize it then. My mother never lost a child. The babies she brought into the world were born alive and not a one sickened and died within its first year.

I didn't realize what a miracle that was until I took up her work. I did not have her gifts, her healing touch, and when I lost my first babe, born with the cord wrapped so tightly around its neck that the tiny flesh had indentations, I sobbed for weeks. If I had to make a choice of my mother's gifts, I would have chosen her ability to heal, not her ability to see.

But we are not allowed to make those choices.

That night, she bundled me in my cloak, grabbed my hand, and pulled me behind her. I remember it as if it had happened moments ago. The sky was dark and clear, the stars bright points against the inky background. The air was chill, made even more so by being rudely dragged from my warm bed. I clutched my mother's hand and ran behind her, afraid that she would leave me behind in her fear.

For that was what she felt: fear. I felt it, too, the way a child always feels what its parents do. She was afraid she was not up to the task, and she was afraid she would be too late.

Of course, she was.

She was.

"I give you also what you have not asked, both riches and honor, so that no other king shall compare with you, all your days. And if you will walk in my ways, keeping my statutes and my commandments, as your father David walked, then I will lengthen your days."

—1 Kings 3:13–14

We entered a section of the city I had never seen before. People slept in doorways and on the streets, their robes filthy and tattered, their bodies disease-ridden. The stench was nearly unbearable. I felt my stomach churn, and I cried out to my mother, begging her to let me go, but she only held tighter. My cries awakened some of the sleepers, and they held out their thin hands, imploring us for help.

I had known such poverty existed, but I had never seen it. My mother said it had grown worse in the years of my life. Wealth, she used to say, had to come from somewhere—what one man had, another man lost—and then she would look at the palace on the hill.

She had never brought me to this section of the city, but she used to come and minister to the dying. On this night, though, she ignored them and continued hurrying. I was so weary now that I stumbled more than I ran. My mother finally stopped, gathered me in her arms, and carried me. I tried to push away—she had not carried me since I was a little girl—but she would not let me go. Her breath was coming hard now, her hair falling loose over her face, her robes drenched in sweat despite the chill. She carried me past dilapidated huts and tents that should have been disassembled long ago.

The neighborhood changed, but only a little. Drunken men shouted the beggars away. Well-dressed men passed out on the road. Others staggered out of well-lighted houses, women on their arms. The women were thin, their eyes harsh. When they saw my mother, they turned away.

There was money here, but it was money taken in the most painful of ways, the sale of the only commodity some of these women had: themselves. I had been here once before, with my mother, helping one of the thin, harsh women give birth. She had sobbed when the child came from her, not from joy, but from sorrow.

Take her, she had whispered to my mother. *Let her see something else of life.*

My mother, who told me in later years how often she had heard this request, had said, *She is yours. You must give her the best life you can.*

My mother had compassion and understanding, but she also had strength they did not. We could have ended up in that horrible place after I was born, but my mother refused. She chose a marginal life that used her skills, and somehow she made us happy. But she never lost sight of the fact that she could have been one of those sobbing women on a filthy bloody pallet, giving birth to a child whose future was as sad as their own.

My mother went past the lit houses to one that was

dark. Setting me down, she took my hand and pulled me through the front door.

Unfamiliar scents made me shake. I know them now: the musk of sex, the sharp odor of spilled semen. Overlaying it, the stench of blood and urine. Harsh breathing came from a room to the side, and beneath the curtained door, I saw a thin light.

My mother let go of my hand, told me to stay, and pushed the curtain aside. She gasped once, said, "Stop!" in the most hideous voice I had ever heard, and then let the curtain fall back into place. I heard another woman's voice rise in response, and then break as if something had caused her pain.

"Remain still. There's another." My mother's harsh voice remained. It frightened me almost more than this place had.

The area I was in, too small to be called a hall, was a waiting area. The walls were made of brick so old it was crumbling. The chairs were broken. This place had an abandoned feel, except for that small room with its fragile light.

Outside, laughter rose and fell. Women called to men in ways that I knew were not proper. I moved closer to the curtain.

My mother was speaking, softly, her voice still hideous. The other woman was sobbing, begging her to leave her alone.

My mother would not.

My own mouth was dry. I did not know what was happening, only that it frightened me. It had to be horrible for my mother to be so harsh, to be so frightened, to be willing to leave me alone in this waiting room that stank of things I did not understand.

The woman cried out—a sound I recognized, the anguish of childbirth. I had heard it my whole life, usually at my mother's side. I reached for the curtain, my hand shaking. I was going to disobey my mother again, only this time, I told myself, it was because she needed my help. Because she had to have my help.

I see it even now as if it were painted in a tableau: my pudgy hand pulling the curtain aside; the strange woman crouching, her hands braced on both walls; my mother's hands below her to catch the child; and a new-born baby, tossed on the floor like a forgotten doll, its head spun all the way around its neck, skin blue, eyes open, the tiny bubble at its mouth showing that, for a brief instant, it had lived.

I saw that image for no more than a heartbeat, but it is burned into my mind forever. I can close my eyes and see it, conjure it at will. My mother turned and said something to me—now lost—and I let go of the curtain. The dead child's face held me—I had never seen death before, but I knew it for what it was and I did not want to look at it. I did not want to know that it could happen in such an awful, careless way. Before I even had a chance to think, I ran, screaming, into the street.

It was nearly dawn. The king's guards were making their rounds, waking the drunken sated men and sending them home, warning the women to get off the streets. The guards must have heard me before they saw me for they came running. One stopped before me, a young man with golden eyes and the thinnest stubble on his smooth skin. He caught my shoulders and said, "It's all right, child. It's all right. Tell us what happened."

I waited and pointed to the house. The other guards went inside, but the young one stayed with me. His compassion astonishes me, even now. For he must have thought I was a daughter of a harlot, beneath anyone's notice, and yet he had treated me as if I were a child of his own.

Within moments, a guard came outside, his hand on my mother's elbow. In her arms, she held a bloody new-born. She cooed at it, wiping the blood and mucus from its eyes, nose, and mouth as if nothing had happened. Another guard half dragged, half carried the other woman out. She left a small trail of blood behind her that my mother, surprisingly, did not comment upon. And a third guard carried the broken baby out as if it were still alive, cradled gently in his huge arms.

I do not know who decided to take us to the king. I think there was no question. These young men, most of whom did not yet have wives, misunderstood what they saw, and thought the women were fighting over the children.

I was no help; I saw the shattered life in the guard's arms, and began crying anew.

And God gave Solomon wisdom and understanding beyond measure, and largeness of mind like sand on the seashore, so that Solomon's wisdom surpassed the wisdom of all the people of the east, and all the wisdom of Egypt.

—1 Kings 4:29–30

The kind guard took me to a small room through the back of the palace courtyard. There he perched me on a table, gave me dates, a flat cake, and water, wiped away my tears, and then let me rest on a small pillow he placed near the door. I did not see where they took my mother. I asked for her, and he said I would see her soon enough.

I slept, even though I didn't want to. When I woke, it was midday. The heat seeped in through the crack beneath the door. I drank some of the warm water, and waited. Eventually my guard came for me. He brushed me off as if I were his own child, then led me through wide corridors. When we reached the king's audience chamber, he had me stand against the wall beside him.

Here, in this wide square room, my kind guard looked like a man who would protect the king. He wore his uniform, a sword at his side, and he stared straight ahead as if he could see and hear nothing. He was not the only guard; there were a dozen or more, and they all stood like that. I squirmed, and he gripped my shoulder, holding me in place.

Eventually, other guards led my mother into the room. She was still carrying the babe, although it had been washed and wrapped in soft blankets. She looked tired and dusty, my mother, a streak of blood drying on her face. The other woman followed, walking better than she had before. She wore different clothing—the other apparently too foul for her to wear before the king—but it hung on her, making her seem gaunt. Her skin was ashen, her eyes dark and glittering.

One of the guards took the babe from my mother over her protests. He cradled the infant as if he had done so before, and he looked at my mother with a gentleness that implied he would take good care of the child. My mother turned, saw me, and her eyes filled with tears. She nodded once. My guard nudged me. I nodded in return.

Heralds announced the arrival of the king. My mother and the woman fell prostrate to the tiled floor, their hands outstretched. The guard helped me down, and I extended my arms against the cool smoothness of the tile. I was glad for the food, water, and sleep; otherwise I might have slept there, in that quiet place, waiting for the king.

After what seemed a long time, a male voice with no warmth bade us to rise. We did. I brushed the dust from my cheek, and my guard caught my hand, bringing it down to my side.

The king was in his throne. I had never seen so magnificent a man. He was slender and younger than I expected, not a wizened old man, but someone of an age with my mother. He had eyes so black they seemed to hold the entire night sky. His skin was golden, like mine, and his hair matched the color of his eyes. His robes were made of many colors, most of them setting off the beauty of his face. He was looking at my mother with a sadness so profound it shook me although I did not understand it.

She raised her chin defiantly. One of the guards moved to make her submissive; the king stopped him with a curt cut of the hand.

"What has happened here?" he asked.

"This woman has stolen my child!" the woman cried before anyone else could speak. She moved toward my mother, lost her balance, and had to be caught by the guards.

The king looked at my mother. She did not respond.

"If this is so," he said to the main guard, "why did you not return the child and let the issue rest?"

"My lord," the guard said, bowing slightly as he spoke. "It is more complex than that."

"Proceed," the king said.

"There were twins. This woman," the guard said,

looking at my mother, "killed the first babe, and was about to steal the second when we entered the room."

I felt my heart stop. My mother had done no such thing. She had been afraid she would be too late. I knew then what she would later tell me. She saw the childrens' death in a dream, and woke, grabbing me and running to the ill-fated house to see if she could prevent her own vision.

"You are sure of this?" the king asked. "Tell me what happened, and how you came upon it."

The guard then told the story. When the guard spoke of my screams, the king's dark eyes found mine. He started and his face paled as if he had seen a ghost. Then he looked to my mother, mouth in a line.

"It seems you have stolen a child before, madam," he said.

My mother looked over her shoulder at me. "She is my daughter by birth," my mother said.

"Does her father know?" the king asked.

I felt my cheeks grow warm. In all the years of my life, we had never spoken of my father.

"Her father," my mother said, "made an unacceptable offer to me after she was conceived but before I knew of her. I refused the offer, and he told me I should never contact him again. I have listened to his wishes."

"Perhaps he would have wished otherwise had he known of the child," the king said softly.

"Perhaps," my mother said. "But would he have changed his offer?'

"Concubines—"

"Are not wives, and their children are as illegitimate as my own." My mother clasped her hands behind her back. Her fingers shook.

"But they are honored," the king said.

"All three hundred of them?" my mother asked.

The king's eyes narrowed.

"And seven hundred wives?" my mother said. "One wonders how many of them love the poet I knew. How many of them have met him?"

"Sire." The main guard had his hand on his sword. His face was flushed. He looked as if he would rather be anywhere else. "I shall remove her if you wish."

"No," the king said. "She has made her choice." He looked again at me, his dark gaze like a live thing upon my skin. "Child, come forward."

My guard put his hand behind my back and pushed me toward the king, whispering that I should prostrate myself when I drew close. I stopped beside my mother and started to bow, when the king left his throne and caught my arms. His hands were warm, his touch gentle.

"No," he said. "Do not humble yourself before me."

He crouched so that our faces were only inches apart. "Your mother," he said. "What do you think of her?"

I wanted to look over my shoulder. I wanted to see her eyes. But I could feel her fear again as if it were my own, and I knew that everything that would come after was based upon my answer.

"I love my mother," I whispered.

He tilted his head slightly. "If you were told you could live in finery, have all the riches in the world, wear beautiful clothes, and eat all you wanted, but to do so, you would have to leave your mother forever, would you do so?"

This time I did look at her. Her eyes were wide, but dry, and they stared at the man before me with something like hatred. I did not know my mother could have such emotions.

He put his finger beneath my chin and turned my head back toward him. "It is your decision."

"It is a real decision, then?" I asked. "You want me to choose?"

"Yes," he said. "You would stay here under my protection, or stay with your mother."

"I am but a little child," I said, my voice shaking.

His eyebrows came together and formed a slight crease in his forehead. It was as if he recognized the words. "Even children must choose," he said.

My heart was pounding. I no longer wanted to be close to this man, no matter how beautiful his face. "Then I would like to remain with my mother."

The crease grew deeper, and I sensed, behind his perplexity, a pride. "Why?"

"Because my mother has taught me there is more to life than riches and comfort," I said. "Because—"

"Rebekah!" My mother sounded shocked and frightened.

"No," the king said. "Let her finish."

"Because she is the kindest person I know."

"Did she kill the babe, as has been accused?" the king asked.

"No," I said, raising my chin as my mother had. "She has never killed anything in her life."

He nodded, as if I had said what he expected, then he touched my cheek and said softly, "You may change your mind at any time, child. You know that?"

"I will not change my mind," I said, with more sureness than I felt. My guard came for me then, and took me back to our wall. His hand remained on my shoulder, not to restrain me, but to comfort me.

The king rose from his crouch and walked toward my mother. She began to bow, but he caught her arm. She looked at him. They were of equal height, and together they had a strength, a beauty, I have not seen between two people before or since.

"You midwife now," he said to her.

"Yes."

"You were called to help this woman."

"No." She continued to gaze at him. He looked away. I wondered—later, not then—if he knew of her visions. What had she told him, in the days when they spent their afternoons in his garden? Had she told him what she had seen for him, in the years ahead?

"No?" he said.

"No."

"She came unbidden." The other woman's voice was harsh, raspy. "I sent the others away, and then *she* came."

"You sent the others away?" the king asked.

The woman nodded "I cut at them, made them leave. None would stay with me, in the end. They thought I would die."

"You thought you would die," my mother said.

"Better that I had. You don't know how I live. How my children would live. My mother—" she spat the word as if it were an obscenity, "—died in that house. She left me there to be just like her."

"But your babe," the king said, "is a son."

"You think such a life is not possible for a boy?" the woman asked. She swung, moving with such swiftness that her guard could not hold her. She lunged for the guard's sword, grabbed it and raised it above her head, turning, turning, until she saw the child.

My guard left me as she grabbed the sword. He hurried across the room. The king stepped before my mother, protecting her, and I huddled against the wall alone.

The woman moved toward the child. She stood before it, and brought the sword down with a strength I did not know she possessed. The guard holding the boy turned away, and my guard grabbed the woman by her waist, wrestling her to the ground.

They took the sword from her and led her away.

The guard holding the child cradled it against himself as if it had already died. The babe squawked in protest.

My mother walked to the infant and touched it with her healing hands. The boy grew quiet. His small hand reached up, and got tangled in her hair.

"I did not think a woman in the process of birthing twins could kill one," the king said.

"Babies are fragile things," my mother said. "A twist of the neck, a sharp throw, and they do not survive."

"You were heroic," the king said. "You saved this lad."

My mother bent her head to the small babe, touching her nose to his. "I failed," she said softly. "If I had gotten there moments earlier, there would be two babies here, not one."

"I shall proclaim tomorrow a day in your honor," the king said. "We shall celebrate your courage—"

"No." My mother rubbed her nose against the babe's. He cooed. "A child is lost and should be mourned."

"Good lady," said the guard who held the surviving child, "babies are lost all the time."

"And perhaps," my mother said, keeping her head bowed, "if so much were not spent on palaces and fine clothes, on three hundred concubines and seven hundred wives, then women would not believe their children would be better dead than alive."

"You don't think we should punish her, then?" the king asked.

"Do what you must," my mother said. "She took an innocent life, and there is no excuse for that. But if you saw her life, as I had, perhaps you would understand what drove her to this."

"She was mad," the king said.

"If only she were," my mother whispered. "If only she were."

> *Thus King Solomon excelled all the kings of the earth in riches and in wisdom. And the whole earth sought the presence of Solomon to hear his wisdom, which God had put into his mind.*
> —1 Kings 10:23–24

My mother took the boy. The king wanted her to keep the child in trade for me, but my mother would not hear of it. When I heard their argument, I cried out that I had made my choice, and the king had looked at me.

"You are but a little child," he said.

"But I know what I want," I said. He had stared at me for a long time, then he looked at my mother.

" 'Many waters cannot quench love,' " he said softly.

Her smile was sad. " 'Neither can floods drown it.' "

He touched her face. I thought then they were speaking of my love for her. It was not until years later, when I first heard his poems, that I realized they were speaking of something else altogether.

We never saw him again. My mother continued her practice and when she was dying, she told me of the dream she had had, the dream of two boys who would grow tall and strong in the sun. She still had the dream, but of one boy, and until she drew her last breath, she mourned for the child she could not save.

When my brother grew tall enough to become one of the king's guards, my mother sent him to another village to apprentice with a carpenter. "Better to learn a trade," she said, "and to take one wife. To live in harmony with the world, and to make your own way in it, than to be led astray by others."

My brother did not understand that. He was a gorgeous child, but unremarkable except for his beginning; he went on to live an unremarkable life. His children and his children's children are with us yet. They are the strength of my old age. Their lives and the lives of those who come after them, will continue in obscure happiness as far as my inner eye can see. That gives me joy, as it gave my mother. Some good did come of that night.

I have lived long enough to see everything come full circle. The king ruled our people for forty years, and toward the end of his reign, it is said, that he turned his back on God. God objected, it is said, to Solomon's foreign wives and his many concubines. My mother had known it would be so. Vision does not work backward; I cannot tell you if her loss to him was the beginning of his decline. I can only suspect that it is so.

And yet, Solomon, for all his sins, is known for being wise. As I draw closer to my end, I hear the stories. The story of the Queen of Sheba who came to prove Solomon's wisdom a lie, and who left singing his praises. The story of the two houses, the fleets of ships, the greatness to which he had taken our state. And then I heard the story of the two harlots.

It took me time to realize that story was the story of my brother's first day upon this earth. It took even longer to realize that one of the harlots was supposed to have been my mother. The story, if one looks at it, makes no sense. What woman would call for the death of a child that she had fought so hard to take for her own? And what wise man would propose chopping an innocent in half to determine who its mother was?

Solomon was not a wise man. The Lord appeared to him in a dream, he said. Who could dispute it? Solomon was a great politician, and great politicians make others see as they do.

That, I believe, is why he could not remain beside my mother. For her vision was clear, and always would be. She knew he would turn from her. She knew he would bring other women into his world, and that through them would come his downfall. She had probably even told him of that. But he, thinking she was a jealous lover, did not listen. At the end of his poem, he wrote, "Love is as strong as death, jealousy as cruel as the grave."

She refused him, thus becoming dead to him. And it was his lack of faith in her, not his offer, that made her turn away.

But she did not see all clearly. None of us do when it comes to our own lives. It is our curse, those of us who are given the gift of sight.

She did not see how he trusted her, even then, that day I met my father for the first and only time. He could have taken me from her. He could have left her with nothing, no daughter and no adopted son. Instead, he trusted her to raise a boy with no parents, and a daughter of his own.

Was that wisdom? Some would say it was. But I do not believe it. I believe it was what his poems reveal:

Love is as strong as death.

And as eternal.

The Guardian again considers those waiting about the table. The heartbeats of the Seekers measure his thoughtful perusal. His permission goes to a small woman possessed of an indomitable spirit. She smiles as she rises, the expression suffusing her entire being with the joy she feels. Warm gold light braided with silver touches her lips and flows downward across her chest to her arms and hands.

She enters a door to a corridor where symbols associated with Egypt's Middle Kingdom line the walls with vibrant colors. Two massive stone pillars mark the hallway's end, leading to a desert of sand. A ribbon of brown water shimmers in the near distance. Sitting patiently beside the pillars is this Seeker's special guide. The sand-hued cat leaps into the woman's arms. Delighted with her companion, she steps beyond the columns to experience:

BAST'S TALON

by Janet Pack

BAST is angry. Do not go out today. Anything you do on this day will turn to dust.

Katiri-Maat sighed in frustration as she read the beautiful papyrus calendar near the altar in the small temple. She should follow that warning, but circumstances dictated otherwise. There was yet another meeting at the palace regarding what figure the huge outcropping of limestone close to Pharaoh Khafre's new pyramid should take.

The first extended debate had been about whether or not to move the stone from its substantial bed. The Son of the Sun finally agreed with the priests that the great rock should rest where it lay in the desert and not be dragged to another site. A group of artisans working on the pyramid were directed by their overseer to camp at the toes of the limestone, ready to begin carving as soon as His Majesty's decision was made.

That was two weeks ago, twenty days by the Egyptian calendar. Pharaoh Khafre still hadn't made up his mind. Instead of working, the artisans argued and diced and sharpened their tools while the pharaoh listened to incessant wrangling from priests, advisors, and other factions here in Memphis. It was, Katiri-Maat thought, as if the arguments had made the great man's mind seize up. He seemed no longer passionate about the monument's form, only that it was enormous, could be completed in his lifetime, and immortalized his name in the eternity of stone.

Yes, Bast was very angry. That limestone belonged to her—she herself had claimed it for a monument. Almost every other god in Egypt had an obelisk or huge statue dedicated to their glory, but not the cat goddess. Katiri-Maat's small voice had been ignored or shouted down every time she'd tried to argue Bast's cause during the meetings. Now the oppressive heat of the goddess' displeasure rippled in from the desert. Sekhmet appeared in league with Bast because the Nile inundation, which happened twice a year and was now supposed to be at its apex, was sparse this season. Very little black dirt was being deposited on both sides of the river for planting. Red dirt, the not-so-fertile soil where people lived sandwiched between the black dirt and the desert, was far more abundant. The harvests would be small.

Her goddess required appeasement, but what would serve? The high priestess of the temple of Bast in Memphis could feel the unusual heat creeping even within the thick stone walls to this inner sanctum. Katiri-Maat, in purified state after ritual prayers and bathing at the temple's pool, served the statue of the goddess by dressing her and offering food. This small edifice was normally filled with peace and coolness. Even when the kittens disturbed the hangings in their play, or tumbled, claws shrieking against stone, across the altar itself, the goddess proved indulgent of her servants.

But not now. Katiri-Maat licked sweat from her upper lip. Nervousness as well as heat caused that dew. This morning she must again insist in her goddess' name before Pharaoh Khafre that the outcropping should be made feline. And she finally had the means to influence the ruler's mind. Last night Bast had given her a dream.

Katiri-Maat bent her knee to the statue of the goddess behind the altar and stepped forward to twitch a wrinkle from the beautifully embroidered cape that fell from the gold-and-jeweled collar about Bast's neck. The Eye of Horus forming that collar's fastener, made from lapis lazuli inlay and a cabochon of dark carnelian, glowed like a living organ of sight as it caught the light from tiny lamps spaced about the temple's interior.

"What you demand of me is difficult," the priestess prayed in a whisper. "The other priests won't like my dream because it thwarts their own plans. I am both young and new here, and hence have little influence. May I gain enough strength in my heart to carry out your wishes."

"Rheeeowwwrrrr."

The familiar touch against her ankle brought a smile to Katiri-Maat's troubled face. Reaching down, she scratched the soft fur behind the ears of Syrannidis, matriarch of the temple guard cats. The golden-eyed, sand-hued feline always seemed to know when the priestess needed reassurance, and somehow managed to find her anywhere within the temple's confines.

"My good friend Syri," acknowledged the priestess, kneeling to rub the always itchy spot between the cat's shoulders. The feline arched her back against Katiri-Maat's hand and purred. "How did you get in with the door closed? Did you come to bring me luck?"

Syrannidis stretched upward to place a forepaw, claws well sheathed, against the priestess cheek.

Katiri-Maat smiled with pleasure at the cat's rare gesture. "Thank you, Syri. Today I need all the support I can find."

The guard cat turned abruptly to stare at the door to the sanctum. The priestess sighed and straightened. "That's probably Neseriti, announcing the arrival of my chair." She bent her knee and her head to Bast's statue before turning and exciting the peaceful room.

"High Priestess," whispered a voice as soon as she stepped beyond the threshold, "your— "

"—conveyance to the Pharaoh's meeting is here, I

know." Katiri-Maat heard the novice's intake of breath. Let another bit of "clairvoyance" add to her reputation as High Priestess of Bast, she thought. It couldn't hurt. Mentally she thanked Syrannidis for the warning.

"Thank you, Neseriti," she said aloud, hoping her roiling emotions didn't show in her voice. "Come help me dress." She dreaded putting on the heavy black ceremonial wig surmounted by the small statue of Bast. The wig was hot even on the coolest days, and the statue, though hollow-core gilded bronze, made the headdress difficult to balance on her shaven head. Headaches always resulted when she wore it.

Katiri-Maat sighed as they entered her apartment. Neseriti helped her into her finest linen robe, then set the wig carefully on her head and slipped her best sandals on her feet. The high priestess stood and stepped to a table. There she lifted the lid of her magic box and withdrew her wand from its silk-lined interior, a gold-covered rod that ended in a gilded carving of Bast's head. Taking a final glance into her metal mirror to make certain all was as it should be, she lifted her chin, willed strength to her heart, and strode into the corridor as the novice opened the door.

Heat assailed her as she stepped from the temple's shadows to the sedan chair. The uneven motion of its four burly bearers made Katiri-Mat slightly nauseous as she was carried through the crowded streets of Memphis toward the palace. Even with a linen shade and two ornate feather fans held above her by servants, the sun's strength made her body feel listless, her heart numb.

I serve the pharaoh, true, she told herself. *But my first allegiance is to Bast. By so naming the goddess, let her presence partner me today.* Climbing from the sedan chair and entering the palace, Katiri-Maat vowed to do her utmost.

The guards bowed her through the outer doors, recognizing the high priestess from previous gatherings. Katiri-Maat could hear the arguments already started in the Meeting Room of Great Decisions as soon as she turned into its long stone hallway.

"But you notice, mighty Pharaoh, the shape of the

limestone is already that of a great snake," Zanzerif, high priest of Aten-Ra, pronounced in his powerful baritone. "The gods have already determined its shape, and so it should remain."

"It could be a huge obelisk," argued the Pharaoh's adviser Hephepiset. "The Pharaoh's remarkable history could be written on the four sides of its surface, then the whole thing cut from its base and raised toward Nut of the sky. That would take less time than other figures, and would still be a fitting monument to His Majesty."

"No, Hephepiset, your suggestion is completely wrong and should not be considered," declared Kharisesti, ancient High Priestess of the temple of Isis, in a voice that always reminded Katiri-Maat of an off-pitch wooden flute. "The stone should have the form of our brilliant Mother Goddess in her bird form, wings outstretched protectively over Osiris' reconstructed body."

Shepri-Atun-Tenys, High Priestess of Hathor, a woman in her prime, glowered at her rival. "That would certainly take the rest of the lifetime of our esteemed Pharaoh, and both his brothers as well, to complete," she said, rustling her starched linen skirt as she eased her position in the wooden chair.

"Begging pardon, High Priests and Priestesses, Exalted Highness," burly Remtaniteff rumbled. "As head of the artisans, I've drawn up plans for a beautiful temple with many columns, cut into the living stone itself. It will be a grand monument, and a fitting companion to the pyramid. Now allow me to show you the new changes I'm suggesting . . ." He unrolled a parchment across a table. Few looked at the drawings as he rattled on, pointing out each highlight.

The Pharaoh Khafre sat at the far end of the room on a small gilded throne, body unmoving but his brown eyes restless. Katiri-Maat's entrance arrested his attention.

"And what says the High Priestess of Bast?" the Son of the Sun asked, interrupting Remtaniteff. "She has not yet spoken this morning."

No matter that she'd just gotten here, that she'd had no time to draw breath and prepare herself. Katiri-Maat straightened, her short stature not impressive among others inches tall than she. Looking directly into the eyes of her ruler, she spoke after making obeisance.

"Bast is angry," she said softly, causing the others to lean forward to hear. "That outcropping is hers, claimed long ago for her monument. It is not right that every other god in Egypt is represented in great artworks, but she is left out. You have ignored her, and she is past patience." The high priestess stopped speaking and moved forward several paces, resettling her wand of office in the crook of her arm to call attention to her station.

"It is Bast that causes the heat we suffer now. It is Bast, in association with Sekhmet, that caused the Nile to narrow its flood during this season of inundation. And Bast is ready to do more if you do not listen to her words. You should not incur her wrath. Even the other residents of heaven fear the cat goddess when she is displeased because she assigns harsh punishments and possesses a long memory."

The meeting hall was silent as Djoser's tomb. Raising her wand, Katiri-Maat continued despite the words sticking in her dry throat. The harsh gazes of the head artisans, advisers, and high priests seemed like stone chisels and drills, boring holes in her hastily-built mental armor. But she couldn't stop now. There was too much at stake.

"Bast gave me a dream last night, and it is a true one. Hear you now the dream of Bast. I stood beside the Pharaoh, our exalted ruler, as he faced the limestone outcropping where it sits on the plain. Stretching forth his hands, he turned it into a huge scarab in an instant. The sky shuddered, became black with Bast's displeasure, and rained hard, cold balls that chipped away the artisan's good work. Soon it looked like mere limestone again, but pale and unweathered, as if the wounds made by the ice had sucked the spirit from the living stone. This is not the right design for the new monument.

"I stood beside the Pharaoh as he stretched forth his hands a second time. The limestone turned into an obelisk, filled with hieroglyphics of the glorious history of our ruler incised by the best stone cutters in Egypt. Despite being well done and beautiful, the ground shook with palsy when it was complete. The obelisk toppled, broke into three parts and fell into a crack in the earth which opened up beside it, never to be seen again." Katiri-Maat shook her head. "This, too, is not the right design for the great limestone which should honor Bast.

"A third time I stood beside the Pharaoh as he stretched forth his hands. They trembled with true magic, for the right intention this time was within our ruler. The stone appeared to shape itself, pieces falling from it and making piles at the outcropping's feet until its form was revealed." The High Priestess paused to draw breath.

"Well," Shepri-Atun-Tenys prompted, her tone sharp enough to etch stone. "What was it?"

"The sculpture became a cat, a huge cat lying in the desert, with its long tail wrapped about its body," Katiri-Maat stated. "Its head is raised to see all that goes on about it, and its front paws are stretched out in an attitude of alert repose. Its ears are straight up, its eyes wide. A carved collar lies about its neck. There is a stone tablet against its chest revealing his history and the honor the Son of the Sun gives to Bast."

The thoughtful brown eyes of Egypt's ruler sought hers. "And this is your true dream."

"Yes, Great One." The high Priestess bowed her head. "Except there's more."

"What else does your goddess demand?" Hephepiset asked waspishly.

"That the interior be at least partially hollowed for a temple, also a storehouse for knowledge. Imagine the fame coming to our ruler and our country should that happen. Imagine people traveling from great distances to learn medicine and arcane knowledge given us by our gods. Imagine those people walking between the paws of the stone feline, in awe and full of respect for Egypt and Pharaoh Khafre as they make their way to the temple and the library." Her background as a merchant surfaced. "Imagine the revenue the students would bring in. Foreign visitors would return to their countries full of esteem for Egyptian knowledge and for our excellent preservation of it. Those from Egypt who passed two years in attentive study would return to their districts as certified scholars, and teach others what they learned between the paws of Bast." She bent both her head and her knee to the Pharaoh. "That is my true dream, Son of the Sun. If you do this, your name will be remembered forever."

She expected instant argument. The silence in the Meeting Hall of Great Decisions surprised and worried Katiri-Maat. She continued standing where she was, stared at by a dozen advisers, high priests, and the ruler himself, until she thought she'd wither beneath their regard like a papyrus shoot deprived of water.

The Pharaoh finally spoke, still looking thoughtful. "I don't see how I can go against the goddess' wishes since she did send you a true dream. However, the suggestions of these others also have merit. Ra should have another monument."

Now protests filled the chamber, as loud as the silence had been profound. Katiri-Maat wanted to run back to her peaceful temple, but forced herself to stand still as the comments, swarming like angry bees, stung her mind.

What was wrong with these people? Could they not tell a true dream from a false? Did they not feel the depth of the magic given her by the goddess? She was young, true, and new to the duties left to her by her mother, but why could these others not accept her as Bast's servant and representative?

When she finally escaped the meeting a long time later, the High Priestess of Bast thought she'd heard every argument that a human mind could invent against her dream and her goddess's desire. Quaking with repressed anger, Katiri-Maat felt sullied by the insults delivered against herself and Bast. She couldn't wait to divest herself of her ceremonial clothing, rush to the purification pool within the temple, and wash most of those feelings away.

Once there, her mind refused to repeat the ritual words of purification. A niggling thought stopped them. It would not wash away as she poured water from a gilded dipper repeatedly over her head and shoulders. She'd failed her goddess. Dully she finished her ablutions and completed her duties about the temple, including serving Bast in the inner sanctum. After that she fed the guard cats and the kittens. Tonight she found no enjoyment in the task even though the small ones were frolicsome. With thoughts as gray as the silt-filled Nile, she went to bed.

Darkness did not soothe her. Nor did night offer rest. Katiri-Maat stared at the invisible ceiling with eyes open, listening to the soft noises of cats hunting mice. The night seemed interminable until Syrannidis leaped onto her hard bench-bed, kneaded her stomach with soft paws, and settled down to sing the high priestess to sleep with her purring.

"High Priestess! High Priestess, please, we need you!"

Katiri-Maat groaned awake and rolled over. She'd fallen asleep sometime after Syri had begun purring, but her dreams had given her only visions of Bast's displeasure. She sat up, realizing suddenly that the temple was darker than normal for the hour of rising.

"High Priestess!"

"I'm awake, Neseriti," she replied, recognizing the novice's voice. "What's wrong?"

The wail was replaced by the voice of one of the priestesses, an older woman with a distinctive dark alto named Hennet. "High Priestess, something's amiss in the temple. We thought you ought to know."

"What is wrong?" Katiri-Maat rose and reached for clothing. Drawing back the curtained doorway of her room, she confronted the women in the corridor. Light wavered from their lamp, throwing spectral shadows against the walls and ceiling. "Tell me!"

"The cats are gone," Hennet stated. "All of them. The kittens, too."

"Even Syrannidis," quavered Neseriti. "High Priestess, has this ever happened before?"

"I don't know." Katiri-Maat pushed past the duo as she spoke, her need to get to Bast's inner sanctum urgent.

"What shall we do?" Hennet asked, trying to remain calm.

"Follow me. Make certain I'm not disturbed while I pray to the goddess."

Katiri-Maat's footsteps were sure in the dim hallways of the temple. This was a route she could walk night or day because she'd done it so many times. She halted just long enough to open the door of the inner sanctum and close it firmly after her.

"Forgive me, Bast, my goddess, for disturbing you at this hour." The high priestess genuflected lower than usual to the statue behind the altar. "I am in need of enlightenment. Your mortal scions, the cats of this temple, have disappeared. No one knows when or where. I await your advice as to where they went and when they will return."

She stood alone in the room, the silence broken only by an occasional sniffle from Neseriti beyond the wooden portal. The Eye of Horus on the goddess' breast caught light from somewhere. For an instant, the carnelian winked fire. Katiri-Maat swore forever afterward that the statue's eyes flared golden-green for an instant.

The answer formed in her heart, a gift from the goddess. The high priestess laughed and bowed before Bast. Eyes shining with mirth and satisfaction, she whirled to open the door.

And nearly knocked the kneeling Neseriti into the far wall. Closing the sanctum's portal, Katiri-Maat helped the young woman to her feet while giving orders to her and Hennet.

"Quickly, quickly, get everyone in the temple up. No, everyone, without exception. Have them put on their best clothes and meet me at the outer door as soon as they can. I know where the cats are, and everyone from the temple is needed to help them! Hurry!" Neseriti sped away as the high priestess grabbed the older woman's elbow. "Hennet, help me into my ceremonial robes. And the wig."

She shuddered at wearing the thing again, but it was necessary. She needed to appear in her full regalia as High Priestess of Bast during the ensuing events.

The women dashed back to Katiri-Maat's apartment. She put on the same robe of fine linen she'd worn to the palace yesterday. It was a little wrinkled, but she couldn't help that. There was no time to refresh it. She could hardly make herself sit down long enough for Hennet to set the cumbersome wig on her head and fix it in place with a circlet of gold.

"Get the ceremonial platform ready," the high priestess ordered the older woman. "And form women into relays to carry it. Have the first two teams meet me at the Inner Sanctum, and bring some lamps. We're taking Bast with us."

She gave no heed to Hennet's amazed gasp. The statue was removed from behind the altar only for state funerals and a few High Holy Day processions each year. Katiri-Maat was already opening her magic box and taking out the golden Wand of Bast that completed her religious ensemble. Turning, she shouldered aside her door curtain and headed back to the Holy of Holies, followed by Hennet.

The group of women beginning to congregate there were too curious to be sleepy. The temple membership was seldom roused at night, a very superstitious time. Katiri-Maat allowed the two dozen to assemble before she addressed the group.

"Servants of Bast, we're taking the goddess in procession through the streets tonight," the high priestess announced. "It is a needful thing we do in the darkness, and we must arrive at the pharaoh's palace before daybreak."

"Won't we be eaten by crocodiles?"

"Or magicked by a wicked necromancer?"

"I have read the calendar. The portents for today are very favorable." She smiled at them, her face lighted by the small lamps held by several women. "Do not fear. Bast is giving her full protection and support to this endeavor. Her magic is with us. Our only problem will be getting the statue of the goddess to the palace courtyard while it's still dark. Pass the word among the others about what we do. Now let me dress and feed Bast. After I'm finished, be careful with the goddess, but hurry!"

The statue required fifteen strong women to lift it, but even so the stone representation was bulky, difficult to maneuver through the temple's corridors. Those not carrying directed those who did. Chewing her lip, Katiri-Maat silently supervised the goddess' uneasy passage through the temple, to the portico, and onto the platform. Neseriti and several other girls tossed hastily-made green garlands against the feline's paws. The first team of sixteen divided themselves into fours, and lifted the platform by long poles protruding on either side. Led by Katiri-Maat, the procession started into the night.

Lighted by torchbearers on either hand, the high priestess began having second thoughts even before she turned the corner where the temple's street poured into the main avenue of Memphis. What if she was wrong? Her reputation and that of her temple would never regain their status. Bast's name might be stricken from stone inscriptions and papyri all over Egypt. No, she corrected herself. It would be Katiri-Maat's name that would be erased from human memory by inking over or chipping out all references to the High Priestess of Bast during the Nile Inundation in the midst of the reign of Khafre. If she was wrong, the indignities would fall on her shoulders alone.

So be it. The high priestess straightened her slump and lengthened her step. Startled, the servants of Bast hurried to keep pace.

The procession paused to set down their burden and change teams of bearers several times, supervised by Hennet. Everything went smoothly until they were stopped at the gates of the royal palace by the guards.

"Open for Katiri-Maat and the servants of the temple of Bast," the high priestess announced. "We have business within."

"And what is your business?" snarled the guard captain.

Hearing the cacophony of hundreds of cats singing behind him, Katiri-Maat smiled. "We're here to assist with your cat problem. You *do* have a cat problem, do you not?"

"Just listen to 'em," the captain grumbled. "Started coming in from all sides earlier tonight, gathered in the main garden. No one can get any sleep with them all over the place. Katiri-Maat. You were in the meetings that have been going on, I recognize your name. Bestris, give me that torch." The man studied her face in its light for several moments. "Yes, I recognize you. If you think you can do something about all these cats, I'll let you in. No one, not even the pharaoh, can get any sleep."

"I guarantee we can help," assured the high priestess.

"Who better than we who serve the feline goddess herself?"

"Very well." The man gave orders and the stone gate creaked open. The procession of women with the statue passed within.

Hennet caught her shoulder. "What now?"

"Hear the chorus?" Katiri-Maat asked. "We're going to join our friends. But we must hurry. Nut is almost ready to give birth to the sun."

They did their best, setting down the carrier with Bast facing the Balcony of Appearances overlooking the lush garden just as the sky gained the first grays of a new day. The place swarmed with cats—old and young, sassy and scared, toms, queens, and kittens of every size and coloration. They all had two things in common: all were felines, and all were meowing, hissing, or purring at full volume.

Katiri-Maat heard a distinctive wavering yowl as a sand-colored ball of fur launched itself into the air and landed on the goddess' platform beside her. "Syrannidis!" the high priestess greeted her friend. "I thought you might have your paws in this endeavor."

The cat smiled, hiding secrets and looking immensely pleased about something. She demanded a scratch under her chin.

Katiri-Maat turned to her followers after complying. "We will join this song with the chant 'Welcome the Day when Nut gives Birth to the Sun.'" She lifted her soprano into the lightening sky. The servants of the temple of Bast followed her lead, gaining confidence as their high priestess continued the familiar words. The wailing of the cats increased.

"What's the meaning of this?" An irritated adviser to the pharaoh, wig and clothing askew, emerged on the Balcony of Appearances. Katiri-Maat recognized him from the meetings.

"I am the High Priestess of the Temple of Bast in Memphis, o wise Sekkis-Atun-Sotar, known as He Who Has the Pharaoh's Ear," she announced. "I am here with the Servants of Bast and our feline friends to make certain the goddess' wishes are carried out."

"What wishes are those?" growled the advisor. He knew them as well as she, but was stalling.

"That the Pharaoh should honor Bast in giving the limestone outcropping close to his pyramid feline form, and that it should be a temple to knowledge and the greatness of Egypt," Katiri-Maat intoned. "That the true dream which Bast gave me to bring to the Pharaoh is given the credence it deserves and not ignored. And that the goddess I serve does not disappear from the mind of the Son of the Sun, the other high priests and priestesses, and his advisors again during his lifetime."

"There is a threat implied in your words," Sekkis-Atun-Sotar spat. "How dare you bring it to the Pharaoh himself!"

"I do not bring it," Katiri-Maat flung back. "I do as the goddess orders. We—" she gestured at the crowd of felines and women about her, "—are here at her behest. And I am to tell Pharaoh Khafre himself that if he does not recognize Bast with that monument, the goddess will send more cats to disturb his sleep for the rest of his days." She smiled slightly. "Every cat in Egypt serves the goddess Bast."

He Who Has the Pharaoh's Ear opened his mouth to speak, then paused. "Wait here," he spat, and disappeared. Katiri-Maat began another chant, both to keep the temple servants soothed and to give her own heart encouragement.

The man who appeared on the balcony was not Sekkis-Atun-Sotar, but the Pharaoh Khafre himself. Katiri-Maat broke off the chant and bent her knee. The women from the temple did the same. Even the cats quieted.

"Katiri-Maat, High Priestess of Bast's Temple in Memphis, I recognize you," the pharaoh said. "You claim you are here by the order of your goddess, and brought the cats?"

"No, Revered Majesty. The cats came on their own, following the order of Bast. We servants of the temple followed later."

"Sekkis-Atun-Sotar said you carry a threat."

Katiri-Maat sucked in a deep breath. "I bring words from my goddess that only threaten if you ignore her desire. If you resist ordering the artisans to give that limestone outcropping close to your pyramid the form of a feline, Bast will cause every cat in Egypt to disturb your rest for as long as you live in this world. She did not mention what might happen in the next. The unusual heat will continue, and the floods will be slight."

The high priestess expected to hear anything but her ruler's soft laughter. "By all the gods in heaven, Katiri-Maat of the Temple of Bast in Memphis, you and your goddess have won. I will give the order to Remtaniteff for the artisans to begin at once making a feline form from that limestone. It will stand for ages to the glory of Ra and Bast." He turned away, then hesitated. The ruler of Egypt faced her again. "When you go, please take the cats with you. Except for Kiris-Tennidasifire and his family, who are my personal guardians."

"It will be as you wish, Son of the Everlasting Sun."

"Ah, no, young High Priestess." The pharaoh laughed again. "It will be as Bast wishes. She has won the battle with cunning, as usual."

To Katiri-Maat's joy and Bast's everlasting satisfaction, Khafre did as he promised that very day. The imposing figure still stands guard in the desert.

The Guardian of Light considers his charges again, carefully weighing who is most ready for knowledge. His nod goes to a man of wiry physique who has been tireless in his search. Both curiosity and the unquenchable flame of intelligence burn in his eyes as he rises from the table. The Guardian points at the man, sending the touch of golden light to his forehead. It creates a starburst pattern that glows against his skin for a few moments. The man reaches up, touches it, and smiles. Turning, he walks around the table to the other side of the room and exits through a plain doorway. Past the mist barrier he finds a portal made of white marble pillars capped with stylized pomegranates. Ivy drips down their length, and lush young laurel trees grow beside them. Stepping between the pillars, the Seeker enters the Eternal Archives to learn:

WISDOM

by Richard Lee Byers

ON the eve of his son's second birthday, Odysseus saw the brilliant blue waters off Ithaca run black for the space of an hour, and the next tide wash a multitude of dead, stinking fish up onto the shore. The following morning, a number of the trees in the olive groves slowly twisted like prisoners in the grip of some corkscrew torture until, creaking and groaning, they tore themselves apart. Thus the king knew that the foul miracles that travelers had warned him of, the upheavals in the natural order itself, had found his island realm at last.

Once again, and with a new sense of urgency, the diviners cast lots, studied the flight of the squawking gulls and the entrails of sacrificial oxen and lambs, but still to no avail. The gods remained as silent as they had been for the past year.

At twilight, Odysseus escorted his queen Penelope to the Fountain of Arethusa, where, on the first anniversary of their wedding, after they had had a year to discover just how profoundly they adored one another, they had exchanged private vows of love. When they'd watched the gurgling water for a time, he said, "When Telemachus was born, I decided that my wandering days were over. War and perilous undertakings I would leave to others. But now . . ."

"Now a plague has come to Ithaca," Penelope said, taking his hands in hers, "and the king must strive to put an end to it, lest the crops fail and the herds fall dead in the fields, as has happened in other places. My dearest lord, I understand. But how can one mortal man cure a sickness which afflicts the entire world, even when that man is my clever husband?"

Odysseus sighed. " I have no idea, save that the first step must be to identify the cause."

"Clearly. But how will you even accomplish that, if the gods refuse to speak?"

"They refuse in Ithaca, but perhaps they'll be more forthcoming at Delphi. After all, the Pythia *is* the greatest oracle in the world. Tomorrow morning I'll sail east to consult her."

"Then let us make the most of tonight," Penelope said. Her eyes shining, she drew him down onto the soft grass.

As his galley beat its way up the Gulf of Corinth, Odysseus encountered one unsettling wonder after another. Rocky crags that pulsed like beating hearts. A rain of sparks, which nearly set the ship on fire. An instant when the world itself seemed to flip upside down. The king fell away from the deck, then dropped back onto the planks when the universe righted itself once more.

By the time they were halfway to their destination, the crew was near panic, and when a large brown owl swooped from the amber sky to perch on the yardarm, a stooped, swarthy deckhand named Euphiletos snatched for a javelin.

Odysseus seized his arm and kept him from casting the weapon. "Leave the bird alone," said the king.

"But, Sire," replied the sailor, "it's flying over the sea.

In the sunlight. It's unnatural, too, just like all the other dreadful things we've seen."

"That may be," Odysseus said, "but it's not doing any harm. For all we know, it's come to help us. So for the time being, at least, we'll make it welcome."

"Yes, Sire," Euphiletos grumbled. The owl inclined its head as if acknowledging the service that Odysseus had done it, and as it did so, he noticed that its enormous eyes were not yellow but silver. Although the least of the oddities he'd encountered that day, for some reason, the discovery made him shiver.

The galley put in to the south of Mount Parnassus. Impatient to consult the oracle, and knowing that when he ran at full speed, none of his men could keep pace with him, Odysseus left his human companions behind to secure the vessel. The owl, however, elected to accompany him, soaring high above the road.

When the king reached the foot of the mountain, his eyes widened in dismay. Where were the priests and other temple functionaries, to say nothing of the crowds of pilgrims come to seek enlightenment? Although the white marble columns and statues were as imposing as ever, the site appeared abandoned. Evidently the voice of prophecy was no longer heard in Delphi either.

But no. Odysseus refused to accept such a disheartening conclusion, at least until he'd investigated the situation thoroughly. As ritual demanded, he bathed in the cool waters of the Castalia Spring. He should have offered a goat as well, but no one remained to sell him one or sacrifice it. So he contented himself with leaving seven drachmas and two obols— the customary fee when one wished to inquire after the fate of an entire kingdom—on an altar, then hiked up the paved path called the Sacred Way.

At the top he found the round Omphalos stone, said to be the navel of the world, and behind it, the Temple of Apollo. Here, too, all seemed deserted. His footsteps echoing, he walked through the spacious building, kindled an oil lamp, and then, shrugging off the feeling that one should not enter such a holy place unbidden, descended into the cramped subterranean passage that ought to lead to the Pythia herself. The owl flapped along behind him.

A soft whimpering sounded from the gloom ahead. Frowning, he quickened his stride. In another moment the passage opened out into a cavern, where gray, faintly phosphorescent fumes rose from a narrow chasm. A thin woman wearing a golden pectoral and white linen tunic sat on a stool beside the cleft, her shoulders shaking as she wept. The king was surprised at her appearance, for she was quite young, probably several years younger than Penelope, who was not yet twenty-one. Evidently the previous prophetess, whom he remembered as a waspish crone, had died.

"Sacred Pythia," Odysseus said. Startled, the priestess looked up, and he dropped to one knee before her. "What's wrong?"

"Don't you know?" the oracle replied bitterly. "Apollo has forsaken me. And when they learned of my shame, everyone else abandoned me as well."

"You have no cause to feel ashamed, " Odysseus replied. "The gods have fallen silent all across the world. It's all part of an even greater calamity. Did no one tell you?"

"Of course they told me!" spat the girl. "Because even after all the other oracles failed them, they trusted the Sibyl of Delphi to advise them. But I couldn't!" She sobbed,

The king put his hand on the Pythia's shoulder. "I am Odysseus of Ithaca," he said. "I, too, have come to you for help, and I promise you, this time, you won't fail. Together we'll find a way to rekindle your power."

She snuffled. "How?"

"I don't know yet," he admitted. "First you must tell me exactly how the prophecies came to you."

The Phythia gestured to the crack in the floor. "I breathed those fumes," she said. "Sometimes Apollo would appear and speak to me. Sometimes I would only hear his voice. On other occasions I saw visions, or suddenly simply knew the answers to the petitioners' queries."

"What happens when you inhale the vapors now?"

"Are you a fool? Nothing! That's the problem!"

"Nothing at all?" he persisted.

"Well . . . sometimes I feel them plucking at my inner eye. But without Apollo's grace, they lack the strength to open it."

"Then we must find a way to strengthen them," said Odysseus, and at that instant, the owl swooped at them.

Evidently noticing the bird for the first time, the Pythia jumped and squealed. Ignoring her, the owl seized the leather-wrapped hilt of Odysseus' knife in its talons and jerked the weapon from its sheath.

The king tried to snatch the knife back. His hand was an instant too slow, but it didn't matter. The silver-eyed owl lit on the floor in front of him, set the weapon down, and gazed steadily up at him. At which point he realized what it wanted.

"It's inviting me to sacrifice it," he said in amazement. The owl inclined its head. "It believes its blood will strengthen the smoke."

"I . . . I suppose it might," the Pythia said dubiously. "Plainly, it's no common creature, and there *is* power in blood. But—"

"Don't undermine my resolve with 'but,' " Odysseus said. "We're going to try it." He picked up the knife and the owl, which bore his touch without struggling. "Thank you for this, my winged friend, who—or what—ever you truly are."

Odysseus was no priest, but kings too were obliged to offer sacrifices on certain occasions, and he managed the prayers and the cutting ably enough. Holding the owl's body in both hands, he let its blood drain into the lightless depths of the crevasse. No matter how hard he listened, he never heard the crimson drops hit bottom.

For a moment, nothing happened, and he feared that the owl had given its life for naught. Then a thick mass of vapor, red now and bearing the coppery scent of blood, billowed up from the depths. When he inhaled the fumes, his head swam, and then, to his surprise, he found himself sharing the Pythia's vision, and comprehending it in all its aspects.

The young shepherd Paris, slender, curly-haired, and fair of face, peered about the green slopes of Mount Ida, making sure that none of his flock had wandered too far away. All the sheep were within a comfortable distance, so, seated with his back against a rock, he lifted his syrinx to his lips to resume his piping.

Then the golden sunlight brightened, dazzling him, and an instant later, three goddesses and a god stood before him in all their majesty. Aphrodite, wearing a girdle that shimmered like sea foam wrapped about her hips. Hera in a cloak of peacock feathers. Gray-eyed Athene, a crested helm on her head and a shield on her arm. And Hermes in his winged sandals, a staff entwined with serpents in one hand and a golden apple in the other. Paris hastily knelt before them.

"Rise, mortal," Hermes said, a hint of laughter in his musical baritone voice. "The gods have a task for you. Some mischief maker inscribed the message 'For the Fairest' on this apple, then hurled it into one of our gatherings. It is the will of Zeus—who knows how to sidestep trouble—that *you,* who are accounted both sagacious and a connoisseur of beautiful women, decide to which of these ladies it belongs."

"I?" asked Paris in consternation. "How can any mortal make such a choice?"

"I know not," said the god, "but you must obey Zeus and do your best." He pressed the golden apple into Paris' hand, then vanished.

"Don't be afraid," said Hera gently. "We three pledge that whomever you choose, the losers will not chastise you. And it is the nature of the gods that, unlike mortals, we are truly constrained by our promises."

"Very well," said the shepherd, finally rising to his feet. "If Zeus commands it, I will try." His dismay was giving way to excitement, for he was bold by nature, and after all, how many mortal men are given the chance to closely inspect the charms of even one goddess, let alone three?

"Put aside your magic girdle," said Athene to Aphrodite. "Otherwise, he will not be able to judge fairly."

Aphrodite smiled impudently. "Indeed, let us remove all our garments, so he can truly judge."

The chaste goddess of wisdom stiffened, but she said, "So be it."

"My ladies," said Paris, a little fearfully, "if you truly mean to do this, perhaps you should appear to me one at a time. If I were to behold all three of you, in all your divine glory, at once, I might be too overwhelmed to determine anything, or even come to harm." He'd heard tales of men blinded or even slain by a glimpse of the unveiled radiance of a goddess.

"That might be wise," said Hera. "I will go first." Abruptly, the other deities were gone, and she was naked, her ivory form so beautiful that Paris trembled.

Hera turned for his further inspection. "Should you choose me," she murmured, "I will make you the king of the richest realm in the world."

It hadn't occurred to Paris that an Olympian might stoop to bribery. "Uh, thank you," he stammered, not knowing what else to say. "I've seen enough, I think."

Aphrodite appeared in Hera's place. Her voluptuous body was even lovelier than that of Zeus' queen, so much so that Paris cried out as if someone had pierced him with a blade.

Yet even so, she, too, sought to subvert the judgment. "Choose me," she whispered, smiling seductively, "and I will give you the most beautiful woman on Earth to be your wife."

Less surprised and consequently less flustered this time, the shepherd said, "Thank you, Divine Aphrodite, I will remember that. Now, I believe, I'm ready for Athene."

The slender goddess appeared, standing rigidly and glowering. She was the least beautiful of the three, though still more perfect than any mortal maid. "I'm certain those bitches tried to bribe you," she gritted, "so I will not scruple to do the same. Award me the apple and I will share my wisdom with you."

"You are very generous, my lady," Paris said suavely. "You may cover yourself." An instant later, she was clothed, and the other goddesses, clad also, stood beside her.

"What is your decision?" asked Hera, smiling confidently.

Paris hesitated, considering. Had no bribes been offered, he would unquestionably have chosen Aphrodite. But now, his cupidity aroused, he meant to have the best of the treasures, whether that meant judging fairly or no.

The throne of a wealthy kingdom would be fine thing, provided he could defend it against would-be usurpers. So would a gorgeous wife, at least until age leeched away her looks. But couldn't a man who shared the wisdom of the Olympians conquer all the dominions and beautiful women he wanted? Indeed, wouldn't he be a veritable god himself?

Paris handed the apple to Athene. " 'For the fairest,' " he said.

The gray-eyed goddess beamed. Hera and Aphrodite glared so fiercely that Paris feared they meant to strike him dead despite their promise. But then they simply disappeared.

"Friend Paris," Athene said, "you have made me very happy. Now take your reward."

She touched her forefinger to his brow, and he swayed at his mind opened to a torrent of knowledge and ideas. But when the flood subsided, he said, "Is that all?"

Athene lifted an eyebrow. "All?"

"You taught me how a man lives in peace with his family and his neighbors," Paris replied. "How a merchant prospers, a warrior prevails on the battlefield, and a king makes just laws. How the wretched maintain their courage in the face of calamity. It's all well enough, I suppose, but we mortals already know much of this, even if we often fail to put the knowledge into practice. Surely this is not the arcane wisdom of the gods."

"Ah," Athene said, "I perceive you aspire to bind the occult forces of nature to your will. I warn you, such lore does not rest easy in the mortal mind."

"I don't care. Instruct me." She touched his forehead again, and this time he moaned and crumpled to the ground. Yet when he gazed up at her, he said, "There is still more."

She eyed him quizzically. "I assure you, there is not."

"I now know how to raise a storm, or quell one," Paris said, dragging himself unsteadily to his feet. "How to dowse for water or buried treasure, or make a maiden love me. How to bless a friend, or curse an enemy. But these are the common tricks of witches and sorcerers. I know the gods possess greater secrets."

Athene frowned. "Beware, my friend, lest you overstep. Those secrets are forbidden to mortals."

"Not to me," said Paris, "not anymore. You promised me your wisdom, and I will have it." Prompted by an instinct as unerring as it was impious, he flung his arms around her and pressed his lips to hers. She struggled feebly but, bound by her vow, could not resist him. And thus he learned more than even he had ever aspired to know.

For there existed a knowledge so terrible that even Zeus the Thunderer did not wish to possess it, for fear he would misuse it in a moment of anger and so unmake the world. It was for that very reason that Athene had sprung full-grown from his brow. Unbeknownst even to herself, the forbidden lore slumbered inside her for her father to invoke at need, and now it flooded into Paris' mind. Alas, no merely human intellect could safely contain such secrets, and when he screamed and pushed the goddess away, his dark eyes seethed with madness.

"Very well," Athene said, scowling, not understanding the magnitude of what had just transpired, "you have had your reward and now you shall have this." She dropped the golden apple, and a long spear appeared in her hand.

Paris tied a knot in the corner of his chiton, and Athene instantly became large, silver-eyed owl, which wheeled and fled in terror. The shepherd's demented laughter pursued the bird across the sky.

Odysseus cried out in horror as he comprehended what creature he'd just sacrificed. For a second, he was back in the Pythia's cave, and then the vision abstracted him once more.

When Paris climbed above the clouds that eternally veiled the summit of Mount Olympus from the gaze of humankind, a company of the gods stood waiting in front of their alabaster palaces. Lame Hephaestus clutched his hammer, and fierce Ares, his spear. Armored in the hide of the Nemean lion, brawny Heracles brandished his club. Golden Apollo had an arrow nocked to his bowstring.

"Good morning," said Paris, smirking and undaunted. "I have come to claim a place among you, that place which formerly was Athene's."

"You have come to die," said Heracles, striding forward.

"I think not," the shepherd, deftly tying a knot in the length of rawhide he carried. In the blink of an eye, Heracles became a chattering monkey. His fellow gods cried out in dismay.

"Do you see now?" Paris asked. "I know the secrets of Chaos, Erebus, and Nox, the primordial powers who presided at creation before any of you were born. I am greater than you. Proclaim me a god, or I will punish you for your insolence."

Apollo loosed his arrow, and Ares, his spear, but somehow, neither missile struck its mark. Smiling scornfully, Paris tied three more knots. The god of music and prophecy became a crow, the lord of war, a hog, and Hephaestus, a lump of iron.

The shepherd strode on through the city of the gods, transforming all who dared to confront him, until at last he invaded the hall of Zeus himself. The curly-bearded lord of Olympus glared from his golden throne, a sparkling, crackling thunderbolt in his hand. "Abase yourself, mortal," he said. "Beg for mercy."

Paris laughed. "Why would I do that? You sent your children out to fight me while you cowered here. You fear me, Zeus, as well you should. Had I been welcomed as I deserved, I might have contented myself with Athene's station, but now I see no reason not to claim *your* throne. Yield it at once, and perhaps I will grant *you* mercy."

Zeus roared and hurled the thunderbolt, but like the weapons of the lesser gods, it passed harmlessly by its target. Paris tied a fresh knot in the rawhide, whereupon the deity became a ram, which ran bleating down the mountainside.

Paris strode across the chamber and flung himself down on the throne, from which, it was said, a god could observe all that transpired in the world. At the same time, Ganymede, Zeus' cup-bearer, ashen and trembling, emerged from his hiding place behind a pillar and attempted to steal away.

Alas, Paris noticed him. "Stop, slave!" he shouted. "Serve me wine!"

The terrified youth broke into a run.

"One way or another, you *will* serve my pleasure," the usurper said. "Everyone will." He knotted the cord, and Ganymede became a kneeling statue, perpetually weeping tears of wine into the basin which had materialized in his hands.

In the months that followed, Paris hunted down and transformed some of the surviving gods. Others hid in the far corners of the world, too afraid to take up arms against him.

And meanwhile, the cosmos sickened. Sometimes the former shepherd's insane whimsy was to blame, as he tampered with nature for his amusement. More often, the droughts, blights, floods, earthquakes, plagues, and stranger calamities occurred simply because the old deities were no longer performing their offices. For no one personage, no matter how powerful, could properly govern all the myriad aspects of creation. It was for that very reason that Zeus had given Poseidon dominion over the sea, Helius, authority over the sun, and every other deity his special sphere of influence, and without their guidance, the universe was gradually breaking down. With his plundered wisdom, Paris should have been aware of this, but if so, his madness was such that he didn't care.

The final vision melted away. "Oh, no," the Pythia moaned. "Oh, no. Curse you, O King, and your divine owl, too! We were better off not fathoming the truth. At least then we might have dared to hope that the world would somehow be mended."

Her despair nettled Odysseus, and so freed him from his own trance of dismay. "It will be mended," he said.

The oracle laughed harshly. "How? How will you, a mere mortal, cast down a power mighty enough to humble the gods?" She hesitated. "Or did you find an answer in some final vision that was denied to me?"

"No," he admitted. "But now that I understand the problem, I will endeavor to think of one. Farewell, and thank you for your help." He opened his leather wallet, pressed a loaf of bread, some figs, and a hunk of cheese into her hands, then strode back toward the surface.

The tunnel was wider than the passage that had led to the Pythia's lair, and ran on endlessly into the bowels of the Earth. The cold draft blowing from the depths made Odysseus' torch waver, and set vague shadows dancing along the rocky walls.

The goat didn't care for the journey, and after the groaning, seemingly compounded of the misery of a thousand feeble voices, began to murmur through the darkness, it liked it even less. It balked so persistently that, despite his other encumbrances—the torch, his spear, and his round shield—the king ultimately found it easier to pick up the animal and carry it than to drag it along by its leash.

At last a gray illumination like twilight bloomed in the darkness ahead. A moment later, the terminus of the passage swam into view. When he reached it, Odysseus peered out into the subterranean realm that was the Underworld.

Just a few feet away flowed the broad, murky, rippling expanse of the Styx. If certain tales held true, a traveler who crept down to the land of the dead via the back entrance at the Laconian Taenarus, as Odysseus just had, would find a ford immediately before him. He could cross the poisonous river without the aid of Charon the Ferryman, who was forbidden to transport the living. On the far shore lay the bleak, gray meadows of the Asphodel Fields, where those souls who were neither good nor evil languished, and beyond those, the Pools of Lethe and Memory, and the ebon-pillared palace of Hades. On the other side of that, supposedly, were Elysium and Tartarus, the haven of the blessed and the torture chamber of the damned, but even Odysseus' eyes weren't keen enough to discern them in the gloom.

"I'm sorry, my friend," said the king to the goat. "You

were wise to try to escape me, for now it's time to put you to use." Setting his other burdens aside for a moment, he cut the animal's throat and caught its gushing blood in a wineskin.

That accomplished, he discarded the carcass, extinguished his torch, and advanced into the Styx, discovering to his relief that at this particular spot, the water was indeed shallow enough to cross. As soon as he waded ashore, pale, mewling shadows surrounded him, plucking feebly at the wineskin. The ghosts scented the blood, and were frantic for a taste of the one elixir that could make them feel vigorous and alive. But they lacked the strength to hinder him, and, scattering them periodically with a casual sweep of his spear, he marched toward the palace in the distance.

Suddenly, a hideous howling echoed across the fields. Squeaking in terror, the ghosts scattered, and a black, three-headed dog, big as a farmhouse, bounded from the darkness. Its six enormous eyes shone like moons, while foam dripped from its terrible jaws.

"Easy, Cerberus!" cried Odysseus, dropping his spear. "I mean no harm. To the contrary. I've come to aid your master and his kin."

Undeterred, trained to devour any living intruder it discovered in this place, the monstrous watchdog crouched to spring. Odysseus hastily grasped the wineskin and sprayed the contents in the hound's eyes.

As he'd hoped, the liquid blinded it, and it craved fresh blood as avidly as any other denizen of this murky place. Startled, disoriented, intoxicated, the three heads began to rip at one another. In another moment, the beast would no doubt realize that it was only savaging itself, but Odysseus didn't permit it that moment. Snatching up his spear once more, he drove it deep into the monster's breast.

Cerberus bellowed, fell, struggled unsuccessfully to rise, and then sprawled motionless. If not slain, the hound was at least incapacitated, and so, sprinting now, the king proceeded on his way.

Passing between Lethe, which erased the recollections of anyone who drank from it, and Memory, from which a shade might imbibe and yet recall his time on Earth, the king trotted into the precincts of the black palace. No retainers appeared to greet him, but, hoping to discover someone still in residence he found his own way to a spacious hall.

On the dais at the opposite end, beneath a pair of obsidian thrones, sat a jackal and a woman grooming it with a tortoiseshell brush. From the visions he'd shared with the Pythia, Odysseus recognized the animal as Hades, transformed by Paris' malice. Judging from the woman's unearthly beauty, which even the anguish in her expression couldn't tarnish, she must be Persephone, the death god's wife. Odysseus thought fleetingly how strange is was that she, who had been taken by force, who spent only three months out of every year with her spouse and those supposedly under duress, should grieve so at his degradation. But perhaps she was lamenting the fate of all the Olympians.

"Divine Persephone," Odysseus said. "I've come to help you if I can."

"I know of your errand," the goddess replied glumly. "Alas, your courage far exceeds your wisdom. You may be a mighty warrior, but you would be helpless against a foe mighty enough to vanquish the gods."

"No doubt," said the king, "if I challenged Paris as others have, face-to-face in open combat. But I propose to take him by surprise."

Persephone shook her head. "Impossible, especially now that he sits on the throne of Zeus. I wouldn't be surprised if he's watching us this very minute."

The thought of that made Odysseus' skin crawl, but he said only, "I never heard it said that even Zeus could look in all directions at once. At any rate, I mean to try, and I need your help. I wish to borrow Lord Hades' chariot and horses, to carry me to the summit of Olympus swiftly, and his helmet, that I may become invisible."

"The casque won't veil you from Paris."

"We can't know that for certain until we try."

Persephone hesitated. "If I help you and you fail, he might choose to punish me."

The king grimaced. "He's likely to harm you eventually in any case, simply on a whim. Even if he doesn't, do you believe you can survive the dissolution of the cosmos itself? *Please,* Divine Lady. We *must* attempt to set matters right for everyone's sake, your husband's not least."

Though the jackal seemed to have little more intelligence than any common beast, it nonetheless sensed that Odysseus had made reference to it. It gazed up at Persephone's face and whined.

"Very well," the goddess said, rising, "come with me." The jackal slinking along at her heels, she led Odysseus deeper into the palace.

The gleaming black armor and arms of Hades reposed on a stand in an alcove. Odysseus briefly considered borrowing all of it, but decided that his own gear, whose heft and balance he knew so well, would likely serve him better than unfamiliar equipment, enchanted though it likely was. So he only took the ebon helm with its towering horsehair crest, leaving his own bronze casque in its place.

Persephone then conducted him on to the stable, where a matched team of four sleek stallions, dark as night from head to tail, waited in their stalls. "These are no common horses," the goddess said. "They can run and even fly faster than the wind, and no one but Lord Hades has ever driven them. I hope you can master them."

"We shall see," Odysseus said. One by one, murmuring to the horses, gentling them, he harnessed them to the death god's shining golden chariot, then climbed aboard. "Farewell, Divine Lady. Wish me luck." He flicked the reins.

Despite Persephone's warning, he hadn't comprehended just how fast the team would move. When they plunged forward, the lurch almost tumbled him out.

The stallions careered wildly back and forth across the rolling gray slopes of the Asphodel Fields, while, using all he'd ever learned of the charioteer's art, Odysseus labored to bend them to his will. Gradually his skill began to tell. The horses galloped through the Pool of Lethe, splashing up water, soaking his tunic and cloak, and then he finally managed to bring them to a halt. When he set them in motion again, he was in complete control.

After a bit of experimentation, he discovered how to prompt the team to take flight, and how to direct them back to earth. He urged them into the air, then headed for the primary passage connecting the Underworld to the surface. In all likelihood, that tunnel was the widest, and thus the easiest for the chariot to negotiate.

Skeletal Charon in his barque stared at him as he soared above the Styx. At instant later, he was hurtling up the cavern, the dank stone walls streaking past with unsettling speed. The newly dead, trekking to their new abode, squealed and scrambled frantically out of the way.

The chariot burst into daylight in a grove of black poplars by the ocean on the western edge of the world. After Odysseus' sojourn underground, the radiance was dazzling, and it was only after a minute of blinking and squinting that he discerned that *two* suns now shone in the azure sky, and at the same time realized just how hot it was.

He wondered grimly if an overheated Earth would eventually catch fire, or merely bake hard and dry like a pot in a kiln. With luck, no one would ever have to find out. Shouting to his team, he urged them into the sky and turned them east.

Green-and-brown lands and blue water passed beneath him in a blur. Soon the mountainous coast of Thessaly appeared on the horizon, and moments after that, hurtling inland, he sighted Olympus itself.

Paris would surely notice his arrival if he flew the chariot into the city of the gods itself. Instead, he set down just beneath it, in the ring of clouds, then donned Hades' helmet and climbed upward through the pearly mist.

Emerging, he beheld the alabaster metropolis of his vision, which, now silent and empty, possessed an air of desolation, its splendor notwithstanding. Prowling on, he soon came to the palace of Zeus, grandest of all, seated on the very apex of the mountain.

His mouth dry and his heart pounding, Odysseus crept inside. As he'd expected, Paris sat enthroned in the great hall, seemingly lost in thought. A knotted red cord lay in his lap, a silver goblet sat on the arm of his chair, and an oaken chest with brass fittings reposed at his feet.

Holding his breath, Odysseus edged toward the madman. His path took him close to the petrified Ganymede. The cup-bearer's red, vinous tears plopped into the bowl in his grasp.

After what seemed an eternity, the would-be assassin was close enough to strike. He hefted his spear, and at that instant, Paris turned his head, grinned, and snapped his fingers. Odysseus discovered that he could no longer move.

"I've always heard that the king of Ithaca was cunning," Paris said, "but I see now that the storytellers lied. Did you truly think you could catch me unaware? Me, the possessor of all wisdom and the only true god? Persephone even warned you that I likely had my eye on you. It seems only fitting that you wear the form of the ass you are." He tied another knot in the red cord, and Odysseus became a donkey.

The king could feel that the transformation had somehow rid him of his paralysis, and he spun, hoping to kick Paris in the head. But a small iron cage materialized around him, and his hooves merely clanged against the bars.

"You still seek to kill me?" the lunatic cried. "In my mercy, I might have permitted you to go free, but now you can rot in that enclosure. It will be my pleasure to watch you perish of hunger and thirst."

In the hours that followed, Odysseus' throat did indeed grow parched as desert sand, just as, unable to move about in the cramped confines of his prison, his body ached cruelly. Worst of all, he felt his human reason and memories begin to slip away. In time, he would be a beast in mind as well as body.

Meanwhile, Paris played with his cords, either the red one which had transformed Odysseus or some other that he removed from the chest on the dais. Sometimes he laughed crazily, no doubt at some magical prank he'd played on the world beyond Olympus.

Eventually the shepherd exclaimed, "Amending the universe dries a fellow out. Come, slave. Bring your master wine."

Though still made of marble, Ganymede nonetheless took on a semblance of life. He rose slowly, advanced stiffly, and refilled Paris' goblet from his basin, then returned to his place.

The madman gave Odysseus a cruel smile. "Would you like a drink?" he asked. "If so, you have only to ask politely, with that notoriously honeyed tongue of yours." The king had no doubt that, even had he cared to beg, his ass's throat could only bray. "No? Well, suit yourself then." Paris saluted his prisoner, then drank deeply.

Odysseus tensed in anticipation.

After a moment, a look of confusion and terror crept over Paris' face. "What's happening to me?" he cried.

The king heehawed to remind his captor that he couldn't speak.

Paris frantically untied the last knot in the red cord. Odysseus became a human being again, crouched on his hands and knees. "What have you done to me?" the shepherd wailed.

"I *did* understand that you might be watching every move I made," Odysseus said, "and that if so, I wouldn't be able to creep up on you and spear you. Therefore I devised a second means of attack, which I could attempt simultaneously. Did you see Hades' chariot splash through the Pool of Lethe?"

Paris nodded.

"I drove through it deliberately, " said the king, "so the water would wet my garments, and when I crept past Ganymedes, I surreptitiously squeezed a few drops from my cloak to fall into his bowl. Now that you've drunk them down, they're washing away your memories, including the secrets you wrested from Athene." He smiled. "It's one thing to see, another to observe and understand, and sometimes all the wisdom in the world is no match for guile."

Paris shrieked and fumbled with the scarlet cord, but before he could tie another knot, appeared to forget why he was even attempting to do so. Dropping the rope, he gawked about in utter bewilderment, and then, evidently possessed of a vague sense that he'd intruded somewhere he didn't belong, blundered from the hall.

Extending his spear through the bars of the cage, Odysseus managed to draw both the red cord and the wooden chest within reach of his hands. He commenced untying Paris' bindings, and the gods, restored to their proper shapes, soon began to appear in the hall. The first to arrive was swift Hermes, who dissolved the mortal's prison with a wave of his hand. In a matter of minutes, all the Olympians were present. All, that was, except Athene, and Odysseus suspected that even she might return in time, once Zeus ransomed her shade from Hades. In any event, the king wasted no time returning the black helm to the gaunt, pallid death god, and in thanking him for its loan.

Hermes laughed. "I think that this once, noble Odysseus, even my cold and haughty uncle would agree that your humility is out of place. It is the gods who must thank you, not the other way around."

"Indeed," rumbled Zeus, ensconced once more on his throne. "How may we repay you, mortal? Shall I make you a god?"

Odysseus held in a shudder. "I have just seen a mortal who aspired to be divine, and the spectacle was less than inspiring. Thank you, mighty Zeus, but I am content as I am."

"Then how shall I reward you?" asked the king of the gods.

"I would like to ask for three boons," the mortal said. "First, restore the proper order of nature."

"Of course," said Zeus. "That we would have done in any case."

"Second, refrain from punishing Paris."

Zeus scowled, his brow darkening like a storm cloud, and some of the lesser deities cried out in protest. "You ask much," the Thunderer said. "No other mortal has ever affronted us so egregiously, or done such injury to the world, either."

"I know," Odysseus said, "but he could never have committed his outrages, had one of your own not tempted him with a bribe she should never have offered. Surely he will suffer enough as it is, wandering alone in a strange land, bereft of any notion of who he is."

"Perhaps," said Zeus. "In any case, we will spare him for your sake. What is your third request?"

Odysseus smiled. "A very modest one, Divine Zeus. Merely send me home."

"So be it," said the king of the gods. Hermes put his hand on the mortal's shoulder.

The world dissolved into a chaotic blur, and Odysseus had the vertiginous feeling that he was hurtling through space even faster than Hades' chariot had borne him. But the sensation only lasted an instant, and then he found himself standing near the Fountain of Arethusa. Her back to him, Penelope stood gazing out at the azure sea, which reflected the radiance of a single sun.

Grinning, Odysseus tiptoed up behind her and kissed her on the nape of the neck. When she gasped and spun around, he took her in his arms.

Much history is lost to time. The Guardian makes his decision, pointing to another woman. She rises slowly, almost reluctant to take the first step, but is impelled by her need for understanding. This woman is quiet and seems to have a hard-edged personality. Her personality's foundation, however, is a thoughtful mind and a considerate heart. Light from the Master of the Archives' fingers swirls about her and enters the back of her hand. She steps away from the table, guided to a dark-hued door in a far corner of the hall. Her path beyond it leads through ancient wooden enclosures threatening collapse. A finely-wrought gate of iron stops her; it is sealed with the mark of Hades. Golden light arcs to touch the closure as she raises her hand to toward it. Hinges creaking, the gate opens to:

THE LAST SUITOR

by Kristin Schwengel

FOOTSTEPS broke the quiet that surrounded the slave enclosures. A lone nightingale, startled from her perch, gave a low, warbling cry as she flapped off into the night. The footsteps grew louder as a guard passed, his sandals raising puffs of dust in the fine sand, then receded. Silence, however, did not long remain.

Inside, the faintest of rustlings marking their movement, the men gathered. They eyed the trail the guard had taken, not daring to breathe until it was sure that they had not been heard. The oldest among them, their leader by default, stood in the center of their group. He listened to the guard's tread with his head cocked, until even his ears, with the acuity often found in the blind, heard only silence.

"Tomorrow night, there will be an opportunity for one man, and one man only, to escape," Denios whispered, waiting while his words were passed from one ear to another. When the barely audible murmurs had died, he continued. "A girl of the Black Land of Egypt will aid him to avenge both our homeland and hers. Tonight, we draw lots for this chance. I have broken straws from the roofs of our huts. One among them is longer, and it will fall to the man chosen by the gods for our purpose."

Akheas stepped forward on his turn, selecting his straw from the bunch held by Denios. As each man drew forth his twig, Denios murmured, "Zeus grant that justice be served."

When all the slaves had drawn, Denios had each one file past him again, measuring the lengths of their straws each to the next, searching for the difference that would indicate the chosen one. Akheas held out his stalk to the blind man, who ran his sensitive fingers over it and compared it to the one held by the man next to Akheas. He stopped, took Akheas' straw in his hand again, and murmured, "Zeus be praised, the choice is made." Stunned, Akheas could only stare at the dim moonlit outline of the old man's face. "Come," Denios whispered. "The guard will return soon, and I have much to tell you." The other slaves melted away in the darkness, returning to the tiny huts that served as their meager shelter. Akheas followed Denios, who was led by a young boy, to his hut. Though slaves were not allowed to have their own huts, by an unspoken agreement, the other men had kept this hut reserved for the one who would have been a seer.

When the three were settled within the hut, Denios spoke in the same low voice he had used for the drawing of the lots. "You know your chosen purpose. What I shall tell you is the means by which it shall be accomplished. The girl I spoke of, once a slave taken from the lands of Egypt, works for the man that owns us now. She has been given her freedom in payment for her obedient service. It is she who will help you escape tomorrow, and hide you for the day in a warehouse. She knows a woman in the palace and will take you there. This woman will let you in, and the final outcome is in your hands and those of the gods. May Apollo and Ares bless our cause."

Akheas touched his fingers to his lips at the names of the gods. For ten years they had been the rock and support of his people, though at the last they had abandoned those who had faithfully served them. "But how will this girl find me?"

"We are to be taken to the slave market tomorrow. They do not know how many we are, for so many have died from among our number. You will stay here when they take us in the morning. The boy and I have dug a pit here in the corner for you to hide in, if the guards even enter this hut. They know that I sleep here alone. The gods saw fit to take my eyes and not replace them with the gift of othersight, but even that curse now proves a blessing. Always have our people treated me as a seer, and the guards may believe that I truly have that gift. Would that I did, for perhaps then I could have warned my lord and king." Denios' voice trailed off, and he was lost in thought for long moments. Even in the darkness, Akheas thought he saw a tear sliding down from Denios' sightless eyes.

"Do not blame yourself for the gods' rejection of you and our people," Akheas reassured him. "Other seers knew the truth, and yet our king ignored them. Kalkas fled, and Kassandra has ever been disbelieved. There is nothing that could have been done."

Denios nodded in the darkness. "It is difficult, though," he murmured, "to accept that one's own part is so insignificant." A long silence again filled the tiny hut, until Denios turned back to Akheas. "As I said, you will hide here while the rest of us are taken to the slave market. The servant-girl will come to you when all is clear, and take you to the warehouse. At nightfall, she and her friend will help you inside the palace. From there, the path is yours to tread." With a soft rustle of fabric, Denios turned his back on the young man, arranging his robe on the matted dirt floor. Soon, his breath deepened in sleep.

Rest did not come as quickly to Akheas. Long into the night, he pondered his fate in the darkness. Would he achieve his goal? Or would he be stopped, captured and slain before he had even begun? In either case, he knew, the end result for him would be the same—death. Hades would come for him as he had for so many others in the last ten years. The tread of the passing guards rang a death knell in Akheas' ears, and he prayed to gods that had abandoned him and his people.

Rosy fingers of light slanted across the ground with the coming of the dawn, waking Akheas to a momentary early peace, soon disturbed with the din of change in the slave pens. With shouts and threats, the men were gathered and bound into the great oxen-drawn wagons that would take them to the slave market. Huddled in the muddy pit in the darkest corner of Denios' hut, Akheas listened to the sounds of his companions being herded together. More than once, he winced at the crack of a whip lashing against bare flesh, as someone did not move with enough speed to please the guards.

Denios rose with quiet dignity and stood outside the hut with his young guide beside him, waiting in silence for the soldiers to approach. By neither look nor word did he betray Akheas as the men led him away. At long last, the whips were turned to the hides of the oxen, and with groans and creaks the loaded wagons pulled away from the holding area.

The morning crept on, and still Akheas kept himself curled in the pit, wondering at every moment if the servant-girl would arrive, or if she had forgotten, or if she had betrayed them all and was even now bringing the house guards to capture him.

A soft tread in the sand, lighter by far than that of the night guards, pulled Akheas from his fearful thoughts. The faint scuffing paused near the hut in which he hid, then, with a quick flurry of movement, a small figure threw itself through the door and into the shadows beside him. Akheas watched in silence as the slight newcomer pulled back a hood, revealing a girl younger than he had expected.

"I am called Iris," she said in a whisper, her voice thickly accented. Her eyes were as black as obsidian, deep-set in her dark face. "I have agreed to aid you in a revenge for both our peoples." Her eyes went hard with hatred, but she did not elaborate her thoughts and turned away from him. "Come," she continued, having caught her breath. "We have only moments." She stood and moved to the doorway, keeping to the shadows as long as possible. Only once did she turn and look back at Akheas, who followed her closely.

The gates to the slave pens stood open, ready for the master's next shipment or capture to arrive, and the girl hastened through them to a grove of trees that stood near to the guardhouse. Once within the sheltering branches, she stopped and knelt, reaching underneath the raised root of one of the trees for a small bundle.

"Here, put these on," she murmured, handing the bundle to him and turning her back. "They are the clothes of a servant of the master. If you are discovered, it is best that you do not wear the garb of a slave. It is fortunate that they did not collar you and your companions until the guards put them on the wagons, for we could never have removed or disguised that."

"We must hurry," she said when he had changed, taking his other clothing from him. "The mistress will be requiring my services soon. One of the warehouses at the edge of the street is not frequented. I shall show you to a hiding place there, and will return for you when night has fallen." After a furtive glance around the area, she led him out of the grove of trees.

The storehouses were at the edge of the master's property, built into and against the enclosing wall. From the sounds outside the wall, Akheas guessed that the street was a marketplace. A question to the servant girl confirmed his thought.

"The master is a trader in many things," she said quietly, "and slaves are least among them. This street is the market of jewels and fine goods, and it is here that he does most of his business. Come." Walking swiftly, she followed the line of warehouses to the very last one, an older building that sagged against the high stone wall.

Guiding him inside the dark building, Iris led Akheas to a room on the upper story. Great crates stacked higher than his head filled the room, with only narrow aisles around the outer perimeter of the chamber. Iris nodded as Akheas squeezed himself inside.

"You will be safe from discovery here. These crates contain simple pottery, stored here in case the master runs out of merchandise of greater value. No one comes here save the master and his scribes once a month when he must take his inventory. There is a small window to the front, which you may look out of if necessary." She moved to the door, then looked back at him one more time. "I will return after nightfall and guide you."

Akheas listened as the door closed, then heard the thud of the bolt dropping into place. He was alone.

After a long moment of listening to the sounds of the street drifting into the room, Akheas began to edge his way around the crates to the window. A small area was clear here, large enough for him to sit. Leaning his head to the side so that he was all but invisible, he looked out onto the street.

At first, he let his eyes rove over the jubilant activity before him, darting from a flash of bright color to a swirl of movement. It had been a long time since he had seen such a thing—over ten years, for although markets go on in a war, a pall is cast over them along with everything else.

He watched a dealer in lamps for a few minutes, the little old man's exaggerated expressions easy to read even from a distance. Akheas almost laughed, for the man must have been a fool to think that anyone, even a young man barely past boyhood, would fall for his overdone haggling. As he watched, Akheas could see that the lamp seller was getting the worst of the deal, for he became subdued and genuine dismay crept into his face. After a few moments more, there was a quick exchange of coin and the young man walked away with his tiny oil lamp, lightness in his step and a smug smile on his face.

Intrigued, Akheas observed the progress of the lad down the street.

He paused for only a brief moment before a display of fine new silks, raising a single finger to touch the delicate fabric with reverence. As if disbelieving what he felt, he brushed his hand along the coarser weave of his tunic, then raised it again to the imported cloth. The silk merchant, knowing that no one so awestruck would have the means to purchase, waved him off with angry gestures.

The boy stood a long time at a silversmith's booth, for here were knives and daggers to catch a man's eye.

Akheas eyed them appraisingly from his distant vantage point. No true weapons, he was sure, for would not arms be found near the horses and slaves, rather than by the silks and perfumes? No doubt these were more table utensil than weapon, decorative—and dull.

The next stall, where the young man who had held his attention waved off the dealer's offers and moved on, made Akheas' heart stop. A jeweler.

He closed his eyes, rolling his fingers together as if he could still feel the smoothness of pearls slipping between them, the hardness of sapphires, the roughness of agate, and the sharp bite of the diamond. For a long time he stood there, resting his head against the wall, the pain of what he had lost coursing through him.

Once, that had been his life. He stared down at the stall with glazed, unseeing eyes. He, too, had been a merchant of gems, and even on occasion a goldsmith. Certain gems had demanded a particular setting, which he had fashioned himself. Not every stone had spoken to him in that way, and so he had resisted the encouragement of others to become a goldsmith exclusively. But those works he had done had been well-received, noticed and worn by some of the greatest names of the city.

His crowning glory, though, his greatest work, had been the great tiger's eye pendant, studded around the central stone with amber, that the king himself had bought for his wife. It had suited Her Majesty well, for she bore in her soul the strength of the tiger. He closed his eyes and could see her at her husband's side, the sunlight glinting off the shining gold and catching in the fire of her eyes. But that was all long before . . . and now long gone.

He opened his eyes again, his mood somber as he watched the bustle of the market. What could he do, after all? If the gods had abandoned his people, how could he hope for the success of his mission? He was no soldier. He was a merchant, a man of words, not of action. He knew nothing of the arts of war.

And it was that, a tiny voice inside reminded him, that had kept him alive. The fighters, the warriors, had all been put to the sword. Only those deemed harmless— an ungifted seer, merchants and tradesmen, those who were already servants or slaves—had been spared. Captured as slaves, they had been packed like animals into the holds of the invaders' ships and made to endure a miserable ocean crossing where many sickened and many died. But he, Akheas, had survived. Did that not mean something?

The sudden quiet that fell over the marketplace startled Akheas from his reverie, and he returned his attention to the scene before him. It seemed that all below had turned their eyes in one direction. He looked up the street, and a cold wave of fury washed over him.

She dared! She *dared* to appear in public! Her lord and husband was surely besotted to allow such a thing, Akheas thought. Ladies did not appear in the common market without particular, grave reason. Even then, they traveled surrounded by slaves and waiting women. Yet she traveled with only a single slave carrying a basket and walking two steps behind her. Did not those in the market care that for ten years their lives had been disrupted because of her?

Looking down, he could see that they did not. The servant women cast their eyes to the ground and stepped aside from her path in respect, while the men, well, the men fell over their feet to do whatever they could for her.

She was Helen. All the dreams of all the men who had ever lived could not have matched her. Even from his vantage point, Akheas could see that. She was tall, and slim, but the long tunic she wore could not hide the curves beneath. She wore her hair loose and unbound, like an innocent girl—or a whore. It was long and black, and brushed against her legs as she walked, swirling around her in a silken cloud. Her skin was a smooth dusky color, neither dark nor light. All that he could tell of her eyes was that they were large and dark. Her lips were curved in a constant smile, which she bestowed on every man she passed.

She was to blame for the deaths of many, for the ruin not of one, but two nations. And yet she moved through the street as if unaware of what she had done, smiling at the men who worshiped her with their eyes. She paused at the silk dealer's table, skimming her finger over the same fabric that had caught the eye of the young man earlier. Before she had taken two steps away from the display, a bolt of the cloth was placed in the basket her slave carried. The lamp seller offered his finest, most ornate gold lamp, a fatuous smile on his lips and another offer in his eyes. She fingered a few of the gems and jeweled pieces at the goldsmith's, then made her selection and moved on.

As she passed beneath the window and out of his sight, a flash of light nearly blinded him, reflected from something at her throat. He turned as far as he could to keep watching her, nagged by the feeling that there was something odd in that sparkling glint. Her back was to him now, however, and he could see nothing but the trail of worshiping men she left behind her.

The sight of her had soured his enjoyment of the market, and he sat down in the small space between the crates and the wall, leaning against the wooden slats in despair. Seeing her had reminded him of the task that had fallen to him when the lots had been drawn, unqualified though he was. He could only hope that his resolve would hold when the opportunity came.

Why else would Menelaus have brought her back as his queen if not for her beauty and allure? She had betrayed first Menelaus, then Paris, and then again Menelaus. Who could know how many others had been caught in the traps she laid? She had lied with no regard for others, telling whatever she thought would be best for her own interests. Her lies and webs of deception had brought death and destruction to everyone around her, and yet she herself remained curiously untouched.

He would be numbered one more of the dead. He knew that. But he would be named hero when the history of Troy was sung. He thought of the other men, driven off to the slave markets like so many cattle this morning. How did they fare? And how would they fare if he was successful? Denios, he was sure, would be slain. Though Denios had never shown any true gift of prophecy, a blind man was always under suspicion when strange things occurred. As for the others, he could not say how his actions might affect them and their lives. These thoughts sobered him. Though he cared not for himself, he would not like to be the one to cause, how-ever indirectly, the death of the last of his people.

The scrape of the heavy wooden bar sliding out of its position across the door woke Akheas, and he stared into the darkness in confusion before remembering where he was. He stood and edged his way past the crates to the door, scraping his skin on the rough wood. Iris stood waiting for him, carrying a tiny oil lamp much like the one he had seen so many hours ago. Taking his hand, she led him out of the warehouse to a small gate in the wall, hidden by overgrown olive bushes.

"I shall take you to my friend who works in the pal-ace," she whispered in his ear. "You will need to climb the wall in order to get inside. The signal that all is clear is the call of the nightingale, given twice. I will not be able to wait with you." As earlier that day, she stooped and drew a small package from beneath the shrubs, handing it to him to open. Akheas unfolded the black fabric to reveal a knife as long as his forearm, with a blade that gleamed in the lamplight.

"The cloak is to hide you in the darkness. The moon is dark tonight, but we dare take no chances," Iris said, gesturing at his light-colored tunic. His eyes, however, were only for the dagger. "It is a knife of Egypt, brought to my master from Troy. It is fitting to use such a weapon, that bears the anger of two lands."

Akheas turned the dagger over in his hands. It was an exquisite piece of workmanship, well-balanced. The blade had a wicked curve to it, and the hilt was set with dark gemstones. Both hilt and blade were finely engraved, but in the dim light even his goldsmith's eye could determine no more of the work than that. The knife, it seemed, was Helen herself—beautiful, yet cold, dangerous, and cruel. "It is fitting, indeed," he mur-mured, more to himself than to the servant girl beside him. He secured the dagger beneath the belt of his tunic and turned back to her.

"Come," she said, extinguishing the lamp and placing it where the cloak had been hidden. She opened the door and slipped out ahead of him, pulling it not quite closed behind them. He followed her through the dark passages and back streets, where they met no one but the rats that plagued the city. At last, they came upon another wall and stood for a moment beneath a sheltering tree.

"The wall is not too difficult to climb," Iris murmured. "Remember the call of the nightingale, and may the gods watch over you." She reached out and brushed her fingers reverently over the bare blade that hung at the outside of his thigh, then disappeared into the night.

In the stillness, Akheas could hear the music of the king's banquet in the distant hall, the faint sounds of harp and lyre, the cheering of drunken voices. He had waited just long enough to start to grow worried and fearful when a low, warbling cry from the other side of the wall broke the silence. After a pause of two heartbeats, the cry was repeated. Akheas moved from the shelter of the tree and began to scale the wall.

As Iris had promised, the wall presented no great difficulty, and soon he crouched atop it. After a few moments to gauge the distance, he half-climbed, half-jumped to the ground on the opposite side. A young woman stepped from behind a nearby bush and took his hand. In silence, she led him across the palace grounds to the servant's entrance, drawing him down an empty passage. Looking up at him, she spoke.

"We are only safe here for a few moments. I, too, am of Egypt, and this is also my revenge." She paused for a moment, staring at him as though she would see into his soul. After a few moments, she nodded as if what she had seen pleased her. "Iris and I are of the same family. Although Egypt still stands, our family and our neighbors were destroyed and captured when these Greeks tried to control the land of the Nile. Our revenge is of a more personal nature, but no less important to us." She glanced away and would have spoken more, but a noise at the end of the hall startled her, and she continued, speaking quickly. "Helen is at the banquet, but will leave soon. The fool king is bold enough to allow her there, but not enough to let her stay to the end. She is there because he wishes to have all of his companions and followers see the prize for which they lost their sons and friends. I will hide you in her room, and you must wait until all her servants are gone. I will make the call of the nightingale outside her window when all is safe." She reached out, as Iris had, and touched the blade of the knife as though in blessing and worship. Turning, she continued down the hall, and Akheas followed her through the corridor to Helen's room. The young woman opened a large basket and he climbed inside it, draping some sheets of fabric over his head. Once again, he settled himself to wait.

He was not alone for long. Soon, he heard the voices of women approaching, the murmurs and giggles growing louder as they came down the hall. As they entered the room, he held himself as still as he could, and waited.

Akheas dared not move, hardly dared to breathe. The time passed with agonizing slowness, seeming longer than the entire day until that moment. It sounded like Helen was determined to keep her maids with her for the rest of the night. Just when he thought he could no longer bear it, she dismissed them. After a few minutes more, he heard the soft warble that came twice from the ground below.

Akheas lifted the lid of the basket the width of his hand, looking around the room. Helen lay sprawled on her bed, gauzy sheets tangled beneath her, gazing out her window at the blackness beyond. She was not aware of him until he had stepped out of the basket and stood beside it, letting the fabric slip to a rumpled pile at his feet.

She turned and gazed at him, unaware of the blade hidden beneath his cloak.

"So, you are not content to see me from afar in the streets, but must invade my very chambers?" Her voice was light and musical. He could only watch her in wonder as she sat up and turned the seductive power of her alluring eyes upon him. He had seen her beauty in the market, had recognized it, but this, this was beyond imagining. Her eyes were wide and dark, a rich brown lightened with flecks of gold that caught the lamplight and flamed on their own. Her lashes were long and thick, and she half-closed them in a sultry smile. She was confident in her security, for who could ever harm her in her own husband's palace? Not a mere servant, she was certain. His master would no doubt whip him well for his absence tonight, if it was discovered. She tilted her head to the side and gave him the same appraising glance she used on every man she met, noting his every feature.

Akheas stared at her and felt her eyes travel over him. He could feel his purpose slipping away as surely as he felt desire surging within him, throbbing in his veins. He was not sure if the trail of sweat beading on his brow was from the room or from the heat of his blood.

She leaned toward him, smiling in gentle reassurance. He could see in her eyes that she liked what she saw of him, that she enjoyed the effect she had on him, as on all men. She would have him, if she wanted to. Her self-confidence was evident in her face, in the easy way she moved. But he could see in her eyes a cold calculation, as if she was wondering if he was worth any effort. She ran her finger along his chin, lifting it so that she could see him clearly.

"So, my young bull, why are you here?" Her voice, along with a pointed glance down his body, made the question into an invitation rather than a demand.

"I am here . . . for something . . . important." Akheas forced the words out over the pounding in his ears. His thoughts themselves were no longer coherent, and his chest tightened unbearably.

"Of course," she said, her voice coaxing, as though she were playing a child's game, "but not so important that it can't wait, hmm?"

"Lady . . ." He fought with himself, furious beneath the lust. He was falling under her spell, bewitched by her beauty.

She leaned toward him a little farther, allowing her sleeping robe to fall open at the neckline. When she did so, the pendant around her neck fell forward, hanging between them. Akheas stared at the piece, stunned, for he knew every turn and loop of the setting as well as he knew the paths of the veins of his own hands.

Noticing the object of his fascination, she laughed. "A pretty little bauble, is it not? But it is in the way." She raised her hands to remove the chain from her neck.

Looking over at him, her eyes smoky with suggestion, she froze, stunned by the fury in his face.

"You are not fit to touch Queen Hecuba's pendant," Akheas snarled, tearing it from her hands. "You profane it, whore."

Helen's eyes widened with surprise and, now, a hint of fear, and she backed away from him, sitting on the bed.

The sight of the tiger's eye, which he had set with such care, that had once hung at the throat of the greatest queen his people had ever known, brought back to him with shattering force all the things that his momentary lust had blinded him to. Priam and Hecuba, Hector and Andromache, Paris, Skamandrios, and his own wife and beloved young son, who had burned when Troy itself had burned. The thought of his lost wife and child, who waited for him on the River Styx' far side, strengthened his resolve, doubled it. Reaching to his belt, he gripped the hilt of the Egyptian knife, drew a deep breath, and spoke.

"I am here for one thing, lady. The revenge of my people and the people of the Black Land of the Nile. And it will be accomplished in one way, and one way only." He drew out the knife and stepped towards her, his face dark with anger.

Helen stared at him in horror, realizing for the first time his intent. A choked scream escaped her lips before the blade found its way into her heart. Akheas stared at the blood flowing over the white covers of the bed, listening to the steps of guards pounding down the hall and bringing his own death with them.

"So, lady," he whispered to the room, holding the bloody knife in one hand and Hecuba's pendant in the other, "there is one suitor alone whom you could not seduce to do your bidding. Hades comes to woo us all, and his kiss is death."

Occasionally Seekers come to court the angel of Mirth, who is said to stand near the throne of the Eternal. The next human is such a one, seeing the knowledge gained in the Archives in a different way. The Master of the Archives' red beam reaches toward a young man with pale hair and humor-filled eyes who has a permanent smile lifting the corners of his mouth. The light dances about the Seeker, cajoling him to enter a plain, serviceable door. Beyond its threshold, the rich scents of baking mix with the pungent scent of perspiration. He enters a well-loved house filled with laughter to learn about:

TWO-FISTED TALES OF ST. NICK

by Kevin T. Stein and Robert Weinberg

YOU want to hear this story again? What is it with you kids? Every year, the same celebration, the same story. Fine, fine, just throw another log on the fire and help me off with my boots. These winters are getting harder and harder. It's not like when I was a kid, I tell you. Something unnatural's in the air. What? I don't know what. I suppose the gods are fighting their wars, and we little people down here just have to take what they dish out. There's something strange you can smell in the wind, with all the new religions around and cults and whatevers. No, I'm not talking about those perfumes from the East. Don't play so smart. You know exactly what I mean. A wise man can always tell when things are changing by the smell. Good smells, good changes, bad smells, well, you get the picture.

Ooh, thanks. These boots may be old, but they're still my favorites. I replace the soles every summer and they're still worth the gold coins I paid for them, and twice that again. Here, smell them. Go on, smell them. Good, no? And the best part? They'll always be in style, not like those sandal-things you kids are wearing these days. Always with the changes, you youngsters. Learn a lesson from me. Black will always be in fashion. It don't matter if you're a king or a slave, you'll always look smart and sharp in black.

Meanwhile, do me a favor? Show a little class. Get those rings out of your noses and knock it off with the tattoos. What will they think in a hundred years when they see paintings of you sprouting metal from your heads like demons? Think about it. You'll see your Uncle Hammer is right.

Listen? Smell that? No secret your aunt's cooking something special tonight. Something good. You kids, you don't pay attention enough with your nose, with your eyes and your ears. You're always standing around like those Egyptian statues with the long, long faces and the downcast eyes, moping and always thinking—thinking instead of just doing and being and acting and playing.

What've you got to complain about? You live at the heart of a modern empire, and let me tell you things have been much worse. So stop complaining how adults don't understand you. Think the world's so different from when I was a kid, or when my dad was a kid? It's not. Go out sometime, have some fun. Live life. Get in trouble, but not too much. There's only so much gold around this house for me to keep you all from being sold into slavery.

Of course, I'm kidding. Hey, I'm a kidder, you know me. Lighten up.

Seriously, though, I've seen you all standing around with nothing to do and all kinds of wonders going right past before your eyes. Camels stumbling under the weight of exotic oils from Persia. Caravans loaded with strangers from places the sun only knows. Beautiful slave girls, and boys, yes, dancing along with plundered jewels on their fingers and cymbals in their hands announcing the arrival of the latest war hero. What more could you ask from life?

And the smells! All these things are good, they smell right. Trust me, you can always depend on your nose. There is nothing in this world that smells bad and tastes good, and the opposite is true, too. Oh, sure, I know these new priests are saying ignore the body, concentrate on the soul or whatever. You ever seen a soul? How about you? Me neither. You ever smell a soul? Can't trust something you can't smell, is what I say. Sweat and hard work, those you can smell, those you can trust.

You all should try some hard work sometime. Do you good. Come down to my gym and I'll show you hard work. Learn you how to box like the greats, how to fight! You get done with that, a day in the pit, and you smell things you never knew were there. It really opens up your eyes.

Why the gym? Well, I guess that's a good question. Now, don't play wise with me, you kids. I know your game. You'll get your gifts soon enough, but not before and no extra money this time! Last year you started me talking about the gym and you walked away with my entire purse, I was so happy thinking you might be interested and needing some fighting togs and bandages and things. You really know how to hurt an old-timer. Ah, but what am I gonna do? I love you all and am glad to give what I can—maybe even a little extra if you sneak into the kitchen and get me some of your aunt's sugared pastry. Go on, while she's drawing water!

Hey, you didn't have to bring the whole lot! Go on now, take the tray back quick, before she notices and threatens me with all the circles of hell. Wait, leave me one! You'd think your little brother thought I was going to buy them, he brought so many. She didn't see you? Good, good, here's a half silver for being such a good boy. You others could learn something from him. Loyalty goes a long way, even if it's a little too enthusiastic, eh?

So, talking about the gym, I suppose really leads to the War. It was a terrible thing, terrible, probably the worst there ever will be. That's where I got this scar here across my chest, from one of those wide bronze blades sharper than a bird's claw. Still itches sometimes, reminds me of how bad things used to be. It's good to be reminded of how bad things were, just so you appreciate how good they are now. Maybe that's what you kids need, a little suffering to show you how easy you got it. Come on down to the gym, and you'll experience a little suffering, but not too much. Learned a hard lesson when first I opened it. Don't drive away your customers by being too harsh with the boxing and the training, and don't be too light on the instruction and the compliments, but don't give too much. Even a fly can die on a sugar mound.

Nick and I met during that war, though we weren't in the same unit. We just happened to keep running into each other at the mess halls and the streets and the . . . well, you don't need to know about that, right now, not till you're older at least, then you'll find out soon enough, I'm sure. Though I knew nothing much about him, Nick grated on my nerves. Why? Because he didn't come from poor family, like I did, not like you kids having it so easy. All right, all right, I'll stop bringing that up, but it's true you know. So anyway, Nick, he always wore this family ring, see, a big old thing with a ruby the size of your fist, well, maybe your fist, a little smaller than mine. But he wouldn't be wearing nothing else so you'd know he was rich. And he didn't flash the ring, you understand, he just wore it like it wasn't important. Still, it was important to me.

Actually, he and I didn't talk much during those early days. We both started learning boxing from a Greek named Lefkes, a big man taller than even me and wider, too, with long curling black hair and black eyes that were hot like coals, but cold, too, you know? The Greek was smart. Somehow he realized the way I felt about Nick. He paired us up often. Because whenever I saw that ruby, something in me snapped.

To me that ring said Nick, he had it all and I had nothing, and went into the army so that I could just live day to day and maybe save something on the side, so one day I could have kids, and they could have kids, and we wouldn't have to fight no more. Learn a craft, become respectable tradesmen, whatever, long as me and my family didn't have to fight and didn't have to struggle, that's all I ever asked.

So I'd see this ruby of Nick's, this ruby bigger than your fist, and like a bull I'd be, in the ring. I would jab and cut and sweep, bob and weave, and bam bam! I'd let Nick have it right in the jaw, and every time he'd bring his hands up, I'd hit him somewhere else, in the ribs, in the stomach, then back to the jaw, but I never punched below the belt. I might have been angry, but I had my pride and I ain't no cheat. Then, afterward, I'd walk away from the ring thinking I'd accomplished something. Like I'd done something good for myself, and something good for all the ones before me who'd always been poor and worked for the rich. Like, every time I punched Nick, I was hitting back for all the beatings to every man in the street and every slave, and just everyone.

Why didn't Lefkes stop me? For what would he stop me? It's not like I was some kind of animal, just bucking and goring and hitting. I was learning how to box and putting everything I had into the arena and from Nick I got the reason to stay on my feet where I might have grown tired against someone else. And in fact, that's exactly what happened. When that Greek would send in another of his students to fight me, I'd hold my own for a while, then get just as tired as the next guy. I wasn't anything special anymore. He was smart, that Greek. Wonder where he is now. Hope he didn't follow those new priests and lose his boxing edge.

So every time I'd fight Nick, I became not an animal but a monster, a tool of the gods themselves, if they don't mind my saying, and I couldn't be stopped. And let me tell you, Nick was good, even then. And don't tell anyone this because I might lose business, but he was better than me. The only thing I had was my anger, and that eventually ran out.

One day I was laying into his stomach, real hardlike, jab jab jab, left right right. I could use both hands real good then, before I eventually broke all my fingers. I remember I had my eyes closed, and when you come down to see me you'll learn that's something you never do. Still, I had my eyes closed and I was punching and punching and Nick was just standing there and taking it, his stomach hard as a rock. Harder, even, because behind his stomach there was heart, and it was heart that made me finally look up and open my eyes to see him there, with sweat on his face and his eyes closed against the pain.

I stopped then and there and took a step back, feeling

suddenly ashamed for everything I had done to this man. To this man, who for no reason other than he wanted to learn to fight had the misfortune to run into me. He never commanded me to stop, as he could have, being from one of the city's better families. He never had me beaten afterward, or sold into slavery, or just killed. All he wanted to do was learn, like all of Lefkes' students wanted. I looked at Lefkes and asked him why he had never said anything about the way I acted, and you know what that big Greek did? He laughed. He just stood there and laughed at me in his big Greek voice and I felt like the smallest, littlest man in the world. It was then that I understood that while I had beat on Nick— to get back at everything and everyone who had ever done me wrong—he was taking it for the same reason, giving me my chance to do just that.

But what was really great about that, what was really smart and noble and wise and all the other things Nick is, is that while Nick was learning how I felt, he was also teaching me about how he felt. That he didn't consider himself to be above or better than anyone else. He was going to let me beat on him till my anger was gone or he was dead. And it was there and then that I looked up at him, into those dark friendly eyes of his, called him brother, and embraced him. That's how we became friends.

Yeah, back in those days, I remember when St. Nick was just plan old Nick. He didn't become a bonafide for-the-people saint until after he had gone up against that monster, that real monster from the gods called the Mangler. What weird name, what're you talking about? What's wrong with the Mangler? It was apt I can tell you. How the hell you think I became Uncle Hammer, pardon my Gaulic? Tickling boxers to the sand? Using harsh language?

Anyway, the Mangler, he was bad news defined. His reputation preceded him from the farthest reaches of the empire, and the empire reached pretty far. He was as tall as Lefkes, only wider, and his arms were the size of tree trunks, and he had a chest like a barrel from an infantry barracks. That's big, let me tell you. The first time I saw him, I had just earned the name Hammer after winning ten consecutive fights in a row. Staring at him, I felt fear. Real fear. That's a smell not to be forgotten.

He was in the city for a three fight match. Pretty decent award for winning each round. First two matches you fought no-names trying to earn a reputation for themselves. Beat them, and you ended up facing the Mangler for the grand purse. That was the killer. I would have challenged him for that prize money, if it wasn't for your dear aunt not letting me. We were just new sweethearts, then, and she didn't want me fighting professionally no more. Of course, I kept fighting, what do you think? I'm a boxer, that's what we do, box, but I never did go up against the Mangler, which in the long run I suppose was a good thing.

By that time, Nick and I had become great friends. We were out every night, drinking and carousing and carrying on, though I did most of the drinking and carousing and it was Nick who would carry me on home. Came one night, while passing through a poorer section of town, we passed by this window and heard this old man crying in the night.

Now, I don't take well to men crying. That's something for the women. Men, they should not cry, and those that do, well, they got something wrong with them. Still, the old geezer sounded pretty unhappy. Being taller than me, Nick, he stops and looks right into the window of this old man's house and sees something that makes him stop. I ask him what it is, but he won't say anything, he's just standing there like he's been turned into a statue or something.

Then I hear the old man's talking and realize why he's crying. He hasn't got the money for his three daughters so they can get married, you know, have a dowry. He's going to have to sell the oldest into slavery so the other two can get married. And I hear this and I see this look in Nick's eye like he's got something in his head, and I'm thinking, he's rich, he can just give them the money. The old guy keeps on crying, and I finally get wise to the fact he's talking to his daughters, and to the gods, and to whoever else will listen. Tear must have blinded him so not as to see Nick's head poking through the window.

Nick ducks back out of the window and looks at me, and shakes his head, like he knew what I was thinking. He points to a poster stuck to the wall—there were a lot of posters back then announcing all kinds of things—and this one announces the competition with the two nobodies and the Mangler. I remember I gave him this look like he'd just said he had wings and could fly. Nick shrugs and to me he says, it's not enough to just hand them the money, but the money must be earned with honest, hard work.

Now that was something to say and I'll never forget it. I understood his point right away. Charity that robbed a man of his dignity was worthless. It was hard work and honest sweat that made a gift truly valuable. I don't know why I said it at the time, but I just held out my hand and offered to help train him for his fight. Naturally, he accepted on the spot. Only before we left, he looked back into the window and put his hand over his heart like there was an ache there. I didn't understand that for a long time, not until I saw the crying man's oldest daughter.

So the training began in my new gym, and let me tell you, it was something to have Nick there, punching the bag, hands wrapped in new leather, sweat pouring over him like precious rainfall. Oh, the smell of the place, it was so fine! The walls were pretty much like they are today, with good clean rocks and solid planking, a high ceiling that let just enough of the sun in, a common room in back with a bath, and lots and lots of room for sparring. Some other places what teach boxing, they rely too much on all that fancy equipment, bags of grain that look like people or whatever they're using now, but there's no substitute for simply wrapping your hands and getting dirty with another man. Not much in this world feels as honest.

The first night came around, and I have to say, there's not much to tell. Sorry, sorry, but there isn't! Nick walked into the ring which was inside a public forum. People had to pay to get in or the promoter couldn't award those big prizes, you see. Oh, sure, there were others who fought before Nick, but they didn't last long. I think I recognized some of them, and they wouldn't have lasted against me on my worst day with my arms tied behind my back and all my fingers broken. But there were plenty of them and they helped keep the routine of the challenge going, and the money pouring in to the promoter's hands.

The fight itself went one two three, Nick lands three solid punches into the guy's jaw and the stiff drops like a sack. The crowd didn't like this much as Nick didn't even break a sweat. Nick dressed like a nobody, wearing poor clothes, even removing his ruby ring. I kept it on me, just in case there was trouble and we needed to scare someone who took unkindly to Nick's victory.

The prize wasn't much, but it was a good amount for a fighter, who didn't really get paid all that much, especially in those days when you could throw a half-copper on the floor and see who'd kill to get it. For my troubles, Nick gave me a half-gold, which I naturally refused, since we were working for a good cause. Instead, we went out for a meal and a drink, which was mostly drink, and before I knew it, we were standing again in front of the old man's house, and I know I was wondering what we were going to do.

Before I knew it, Nick pulls himself up and jumps through the window. The old man and his daughters must have been asleep because all the lamps were out, and I turned around and kept an eye out for the city guard. Wouldn't they be surprised if they saw we weren't stealing, but putting money into a home. Fortunately, nobody came, and Nick dropped out the window as easily as he had pulled himself in. At the time I thought he must be leading a charmed life, everything went off so easily. I remember I looked back up into the windows on the top floor and thought I saw a light, but assumed it was just a trick of my eyes. We didn't wait around long, and both got good a night's sleep.

The next evening, the arena was really full, even more than the night before. Nick's success pulled out the usual band of dogs that liked to watch men fight, but didn't do it themselves. There's a lesson in that somewhere, about men liking to watch other men fight, but are too weak or afraid to do it themselves.

Anyway, this time Nick fights a Turk, a really huge guy with dark skin and dark eyes done up with kohl to make them look darker, and they did. This Turk had arms like a statue, rock hard and perfect, and when he crossed them over his chest, I was surprised he could do it at all, his arms were so big. He had a big mustache, too, and kept his face screwed up in an evil smile. When Nick entered the ring, and don't forget Nick was bigger than me by a half foot and wider, this Turk made even him look small.

Nick, though, wasn't afraid, and I think I understood why. When I had spent all that time punching him in the stomach with him not stopping me, he let me because he wanted to. Because he had a reason, and the reason wasn't something as regular as money. Nick's will was iron.

It was the same for Nick that night. He was a man with a purpose, and a man with a purpose could stand up to a hundred Turks like that one, and Nick only had to stand up to one.

When the fight started, the Turk just flexed his arms, strode out, and started swinging. The first hook took Nick by surprise. It wasn't fast, it was just assured. Sometimes a punch with assurance behind it can get you just as bad as something that's fast. That hook actually knocked Nick off balance and against a rope barrier. And there was blood coming out of the side of his mouth, which is bad to show when you're hit for the first time. Gives the other guy confidence to see he can hurt you so easily.

The Turk had plenty of confidence. Too much so. He flexed his arms again, and his hand actually whistled in the air as it swung for Nick's head. Only this time, Nick was ready. He ducked, like this, held up his hands like I showed him, then bam bam, landing two quick ones under the Turk's jaw.

Now the Turk, mind you, wasn't a bad fighter. But he wasn't used to someone giving him what-for so handily. I'm sure nobody saw it but me, but the light dimmed in his eyes a moment, though he never dropped that big evil smile. The Turk immediately clenched with Nick, and the two struggled mightily, the Turk's dark skin against Nick's tanned, both sweating but neither moving very much. Their muscles stood out from their bodies and veins popped in their necks.

Finally, with a great heave, Nick forced the Turk back against the same ropes he himself had fallen on, and when the Turk came back up, Nick let him have it full in the face with a hit so solid you could feel it from the noise it made. I admit I gave him a good talking to when the fight was done because a boxer should never use a punch like that. It's just a way to get yourself in trouble—of course he won the fight, but that's not the point! You gotta fight right or you'll make a mistake when you can't afford to, see? Please, please! Don't argue, believe your Uncle Hammer when he tells you this.

So there's this huge crack like thunder, which we all feel, and everyone watching the fight sort of staggers back a step. Even I wondered how bad the punch had been. Only when the Turk fell straight backward, smile still on his face, I knew. The fool didn't even have time to close his eyes before he hit the floor! What a punch that was, and this time, this time the audience whoops and shouts and claps and slaps each other on the back, wondering who this newcomer is, this big man with the dark eyes and the calm look. I found myself caught up in their excitement, and it was like I saw Nick for the first time, as if he were something truly special, more special than just my friend.

Then, as I'm looking around, I catch in the background the monster himself looking to the ring, standing at the back of the crowd just silent as one of those Egyptian statues I mentioned earlier. There was the Mangler, the man Nick had to fight in the next and final round of the challenge. I was so knocked off balance that I forgot everything but the smell of this man, noticeable even across the arena. He smelled of power. Sheer physical power. Power like the sun has power, like the ocean has power, like the earth and weather and all the other things you can't explain and can't stop. I shiver even now thinking about him.

Fortunately, Nick didn't notice. He just took his prize money and walked out like nothing had happening. He ignored all the backslappers and offers to pay him to fight for private ventures in whatever private wars were going on at the time. Of course, I followed after him to see what was on his mind. Not that it was hard to guess.

He walked straight to the old man's house, crept inside, and came out with nothing but a little smile. When I tried to tell him I thought I saw the light on again in the window upstairs, he just shook his head and pushed me in the direction of home. I remember I felt like I had been fighting, too, I was so tired. Without even anything to drink, I dropped off the moment my head touched the pillow.

All right, I'll get to it now. We don't have much more time anyway, if I know the smells of your aunt's cooking. The food's almost done.

The next night is when Nick finally must fight the Mangler, and let me tell you, the sound of the arena the evening before was nothing compared to what it was that night. You couldn't even hear your own voice with the shouting and the whooping and the carrying on. Even the city guards were there, and the coin that passed from hand to hand to hand made the air taste like gold, which I assure you is not an altogether wholesome taste.

I tried to tell Nick, we were waiting already in the arena, I tried to tell him to be extra careful of this Mangler. I spoke about what I had felt the night before. Of the Mangler's sheer physical power. But Nick was a hundred leagues away in his thoughts. I looked at him close. I think I may have even waved a hand in front of his face, and I saw something there that I never thought I would see in any fighting man. Peace. Yeah, really, peace. He was calm as a lake in the morning, calm like a city sleeps after a festival, calm, like moon in sky, I tell you. For a moment he reminded me of those new priests preaching about their souls and whatever. After that, I swear on all the gods, I just stopped talking, which I know none of you believe, you're all so smart.

Now, when the Mangler entered the arena, everyone suddenly hushed up, like it was them what was going to be in the arena and not our Nick. And the monster was just as I remembered, powerful like the forces of nature, and seeming like he could just call on them whenever he needed to beat his opponent down. I suddenly felt as if all this brawling was a great mistake and Nick was being foolish wanting to help the old man and his daughters. I wanted to call the fight off and I leaned over to Nick to ask him, beg him, plead with him to stop the fight, because I realized it was insanity, I tell you, for any man to go up against the Mangler.

Nick, though, Nick, he just stood up and bowed in the fighting style, held up his hands like this, no, right hand higher, somebody rang a bell, and the fight began.

Now normally, two men facing each other would duck and weave a bit to see what the other one has, try to learn if he can be faked out or not. Normal, I assure you, was not the case that night. Nick and the Mangler just walked up to one another and stared, their hands up but neither of them moving. They just stood there. And stared. And stood. And stared. After a minute, I realized I hadn't let out a breath, which I slowly did and I think everyone else in the place did, too. And still they stood there staring, Nick looking up into the Mangler's face, whose actual features for some reason I can't remember, even to this day.

After a while, the crowd grew a little restless. They shuffled their feet, looked at one another, but always came back to stare at the two men, locked in a type of mortal combat the likes of which none had ever seen before. In fact, now that I think about it, I'm pretty sure the Mangler was trying to scare Nick to death. But whatever was in Nick's heart and in his eye that day would not be slapped down by mere stares. Finally, I think the Mangler understood that, because after a long while, like, forever it seemed, he raised up one of his fists, the size of a melon, and laid it straight into Nick's face.

Nick, to his credit, did not cry out when the Mangler broke his nose, which is the mark of a true warrior. Never, never, show your enemy your weakness, not even if it's merely in a practice arena. You need to wipe off some sweat? Do it later, when nobody can see you. Never let them see you sweat, I say. So Nick falls flat on his back, like the sun struck him down, blood pouring down his face. I was ready to throw in the towel right then and there, I tell you, but Nick just pushes himself up on his elbows and forces himself to stand. All the time staring at the Mangler. The crowd never made a sound.

The two men, if they could be called that, the two men stared each other down for a while more. They just stood and stared, neither breathing very hard, I don't think, while blood just poured from Nick's nose. Then the Mangler reached back with his other fist and let Nick have it again, this time in the jaw.

Nick, bigger than me, spun around like the ocean had him in a whirlpool and he dropped flat on his face. Blood everywhere. I could see his jaw starting to blacken with bruises and again I was going to throw in the towel. Yet, before I could, Nick just turned himself over, stood up, and looked into the Mangler's eyes.

This time, there was no staring contest. The Mangler let him have it. Punch after punch, blow after blow, to the face, to the body, to the face again, hit after hit after hit—and the audience, the audience started clapping with the punches, like they were keeping time or something. Clap punch clap punch. I thought the sound was going to drive me crazy. And Nick just took it all, being beaten and bruised, battered, as if the earth itself were striking him with rocks and earthquakes and everything else it had to throw at him. He ducked and dodged, blocked every hit he could, but the Mangler wouldn't stop. Until finally Nick fell to the ground in a heap of blood and sweat.

Obviously sensing it was all over, the Mangler just stood there, looking down at Nick like Nick was a piece of work that was just completed. I don't know, I remember thinking how strange everything had become. Nick had never lost, and here he was, utterly defeated. I was afraid he might never be the same again, what with broken bones and the like.

And then, yes, and then, the part you've all been waiting for, the part where Nick, our Nick, my Nick, Nick, he rises up from the ground and there was a sound of silence like has never been heard amongst the dead in any man's hell. He slowly pushes himself to his elbows, then raises himself on his knees, then gradually straightens his body until he is again standing face-to-face with the Mangler, who looks down at him again, ah-hah, the work not yet complete. And the Mangler raises his fists again for what's going to be the death of Nick, I'm sure, and suddenly lowers his fists, and his shoulders, they sag. And I suddenly smelled the smell of his loss!

I am defeated, he says. I cannot break this man.

And with that, he turns and leaves the arena, never to be seen again.

So, now, there you are, the story of Nick. Why is he called St. Nick? Why, because of the great deed he did, the sacrifice he made for the old man and his daughters. He gave them all the money they needed so they could be married and all be happy. That look Nick had in his eye, like he was a hundred leagues away, that's the same look those new priests have in their eyes, too, and it was they who first called him saint, which I guess is a word that means holy or strong or something. Everyone seemed to like it, so it just stuck.

What of the old man's last daughter? Well, let's just say she was almost as beautiful as your aunt, and you might know her as Nick's wife, if you were clever enough. You see, when Nick last crept into the old man's house, he didn't really do a very good job, and he was caught when he went in, so he had to explain what he was doing. He told me later that he felt very foolish confessing to a good deed, but, there you are.

What? Why do I give you all gifts every year this time? Hm, that's a question I ask myself, since none of you have been good enough to deserve them, not coming down to see me in my gym. But since I love you, I give them to you nonetheless. I think I do it to remind me of the good St. Nick did for others, and hope I can do the same in my little way for my family, and maybe my friends. And maybe, the lesson I learned from St. Nick will be carried on by you and your friends, too. For a few years at least, until his name's forgotten, like those of all good men.

Okay, that's enough. Your aunt's done cooking, and St. Nick will be here soon. Hey, don't eat all the pastries! You now how Nick likes his cakes. And leave some milk for him, too. Helps settle his stomach.

The golden glow surrounding the Walker of Two Worlds dims as he studies those Seekers still with unanswered questions. Not all challenges can be met during an individual's lifetime: sometimes battles must be fought in the places between time. The light that streaks from the Guardian's fingers is surprising silver-white as it touches a tall, stately female. She stands with a graceful movement and bows her head in respect to the Master of the Archives. This woman has done well in more than one career; now she anticipates the answer to a question which has troubled her for years.

Her door is white. Beyond it, a corridor forms for her through a blizzard. Ice paves her way. An ancient tree appears through the storm at the end of the tunnel. Icy runes limned with snow show against the trunk, which she translates:

KINGS' QUEST

by Mickey Zucker Reichert

DEATH'S darkness faded from King Harald Sigurdhson's blue eyes in a dizzying array of flashing, white pinpoints. His hands flew to his neck, where once an English arrow had lodged, leaking a warm and sticky trail of blood. His touch felt distant, disconnected, the shaft gone and the tattered flesh tucked neatly into the hole. His breath no longer rasped; in fact, it hardly seemed to stir at all. A strange silence surrounded him, devoid of the familiar war howls, the chime of steel, and the rhythmical thump of weapons against shields. Even the whisper of wind through the dry grasses and curling leaves of Stamford seemed to have wholly disappeared. Desperate for vision, he blinked away the last of the swirling spots.

Harald crouched on featureless earth, surrounded by a mist that seemed more black than gray—and endless. To his left, jagged, knifelike cliffs rose into a mountain without passes. Toward the base, a shadow darker than the general murk defined a cave. He studied it, blinking against the unnatural darkness, and believed he saw movement at the opening. A line of dirt led to it, slightly bleaker than the plain on which he poised; perhaps a road.

The king rose, unfolding a frame taller than seven feet, and glanced in the opposite direction. The mist boiled outward, a shifting chaos that made his eyes water and obscured his vision. He could make out only one detail, a large figure moving toward him through the gloom.

Harald adjusted his kyrtle and breeches, shook long golden hair from his face. His hand fell naturally to his sword hilt, cleansed of its battle blood. Memories assailed him, of the army thousands strong that had met his forces at the Stamford Bridge, instead of the promised hostages. He cursed falling to such a simple trap, yet he had met his fate bravely. And his men had done so as well.

Only then, Harald Sigurdhson thought to wonder for his whereabouts. He was dead, he felt certain; yet this place seemed nothing like the glorious Valhalla that his death in battle should have earned him. He saw nothing of the towering gates, no golden sunlight flickering from the swords of heroes crossing weapons, no image of the great house where they shared nightly feasts and the talents of honey-voiced skjalds. None of his courageous followers attended him. Apparently, the stories of a resplendent haven for the world's bravest, where dead warriors honed their skill by day and those reslain rose each night to party together, was the myth his devoutly Christian half-brother, Olaf, had claimed it. Yet this desolation did not meet the description of heaven either.

The other drew nearer, now clearly a single man dressed in armor that looked clunky and ancient compared with Harald's own. Nevertheless, he moved like a warrior and with the confidence of one accustomed to others' obedience. He stopped suddenly, apparently noticing Harald for the first time. Then, he shuffled forward again, his gaze clearly locked on the newcomer. He still appeared large, with a corpse's pallor, but shorter than the king, as all men he had met in life. The stranger wore a wide, crude sword thrust through the belt of a bulky byrnie. As he moved, the mist seemed to part to reveal more of him: white hair and braided beard, skin like hoarfrost, and fierce features little humbled by death.

The stranger spoke first, in a rumbling voice with just a hint of fatigue. "Who are you that roams the outskirts of hel . . . as I do?"

The outskirts of hel? Anger flared at the bare thought. "I am King Harald Sigurdhson. And if this were the outskirts of hel, I would not be here."

"And yet," the other said, "you are." His pale eyes narrowed then. "King of where?"

The words seemed as much raw profanity to Harald as those that had come before. "Of Denmark and Norway. Rightfully of England, too."

The warrior's eyes nearly became slits, and his fingers glided toward his hilt. "You speak impossibility, man. These kingdoms you name as one were separately ruled. I, myself, was king of Denmark; and no stranger could have succeeded me."

The ridiculousness of the man's claim transformed Harald's anger to amusement. "My nephew, Magnus, preceded me—as king of Norway *and* Denmark. Before him, Svein Alfifasson ruled as viceroy for Knut the Great. Before him, Olaf—"

"Bah! I've heard of none of these." A glimmer of confusion, bordering on fear, tinged the other's tone. "My name is Ragnar. I was called Lodbrok . . ."

Harald gasped. The name practically defined the term Viking; and thousands, including himself, had modeled their courage, their very style of battle, on this long-ago king. "But Ragnar 'Hairy-breeks' died centuries ago!"

"Centuries?" The last vestiges of color drained from Ragnar's face. "I've wandered this nothing-land for centuries?"

"If you are who you claim to be."

Ragnar jerked his head toward Harald. "Do you doubt my word?" His great fist clenched around his hilt. "I could prove it."

Harald Sigurdhson's fingers curled, and his chest tingled where his heart would once have pounded an eager cadence. He had long anticipated a chance to pit his war skill against a man many considered the first real Viking. *In Valhalla,* he reminded himself. If one or both of them died here, they might find themselves no longer on the outskirts, but in the icy heart of hel. "No need to prove yourself," Harald said graciously. "I believe you, Ragnar Lodbrok." He gave the ancient king a probing look, meeting eyes still savagely green despite their death-glaze.

Ragnar accepted the truce. "I have little choice but to believe you, too." For the first time since noticing Harald, he took his eyes off the towering man to glance around the mist. "There's much I would like to know. Once we've fought our way to Valhalla, perhaps we could discuss the fates of my sons?"

Harald stroked his yellow beard thoughtfully, savoring the idea of a great battle at the side of his hero. "Valhalla? There's a way there from here?"

"Not a direct way," Ragnar admitted. "There's nothing out there but infinite plains and fog." He made a sweeping gesture in the direction from which he had come. "Apparently, I traveled for hundreds of years seeking. I found nothing." He inclined his head toward the crags Harald had earlier noticed. "There's only one way off hel's periphery."

Harald went utterly still. "You can't mean . . ."

"Hel," Ragnar finished. "Yes. As I was returning here, a plan came to me so suddenly, I believe a god inspired it. Enter hel. Kill the goddess who bears the name of her realm."

Harald managed only a blink.

"From that moment on, no man could die of illness or age; she would not exist to claim them."

Harald struggled for words. "Are you . . . sure?"

"I'm certain of it. All brave warriors would find Valhalla, no quibbling over whether he died of war wounds or the festering of those wounds."

Harald shook his head. "People argue over that?"

"Not while I lived." Ragnar wiped his mouth on a grimy, tattered sleeve. "But that's why we're here."

"It is?" Few words could have shocked Harald more. "But I was shot through the throat." He traced the hole with a finger. "Surely I didn't live long enough for it to fester."

Ragnar considered. "All right, that's why *I'm* here. The cause of your death was also equivocal, or you wouldn't be here."

Ragnar's claim still confused Harald. "But you died when King Aella of Northumbria threw you into a pit of vipers."

"Vipers?" Ragnar laughed. "There hadn't been a viper in Ireland since St. Patrick."

Harald swallowed hard. "If your sons had known that, they might not have conquered York and Northumbria. They might not have tortured King Aella to death." He shook his head at the realization. "Although, come to think about it, they did the same to King Edmund of East Anglia." Suddenly remembering that Ragnar had asked about his sons, Harald finished, "Great warriors, all three of your boys."

"Good for a father to hear."

"Yes." Returning to grimmer matters, Harald Sigurdhson shook his head. "Kill a goddess? Wouldn't that be—?"

"A challenge?" Ragnar's voice gained the same booming, excited character as Harald's did just before a victory.

"I was thinking, a sacrilege."

"Well, that, too," Ragnar conceded. "But we are, after all, speaking of Hel."

Harald glanced nervously through the fog. It was one thing to face hordes of enemies, quite another to talk openly of slaughtering a goddess in her own hall. "Afterward, brave warriors will go to Valhalla."

"As always." Ragnar nodded. "And people like us will no longer get trapped on the fringes. We'll go to Valhalla, too."

Harald crinkled his brows.

"I'm absolutely sure." Ragnar's certainty proved uncompromisingly contageous.

"What about the cowards? The infirm? Women?"

"That's part of the beauty." Ragnar grinned broadly. "Those who fear death can *live forever.*"

Harald Sigurdhson would not have believed Ragnar could render him speechless again. "But how—"

A man appeared suddenly amidst them. Blond and handsome, he seemed to come from nowhere: one moment he did not exist and the next he surveyed both warriors with sneering impudence. Though slender and of average size, he demonstrated not the slightest hint of concern to have interrupted two of history's most fear-some. Unlike them, his skin held the rosy glow of the living, all the more reason why he should have worried for their wrath. "How does Ragnar know this?" the man fin-ished Harald's thought, then answered it without awaiting confirmation. "Because I let him know the truth."

"And you are?" Harald demanded.

"Loki."

Though short, the name held more significance than all of their titles together. Had he still had breath, Har-ald would have lost it. "Loki Laufeyjarson? The gods' very trickster? The future betrayer of Asgard?"

"None other," Loki said, mouth twisted in an evil par-ody of a smile. "And to answer your other questions:" He looked upward, as if reading them from the misty darkness, "The uncertainty of your death's worthiness is that you suffocated beneath the bodies of your own men before the wound claimed you. This is, indeed, Ragnar Lodbrok. And killing Hel *will* bring both of you to Valhalla. Once she's dead, no future man will find himself here."

"Perhaps," snarled Harald, "killing you will accom-plish the same."

Loki's smile remained, as if plastered to his face. "It won't."

Since infancy, Harald had heard stories about the evil deity who would deliberately set the *Ragnarok,* the de-struction of the gods, into motion. The opportunity to slaughter the Father of Thieves and Monsters became throbbing need.

Apparently driven by the same desire, Ragnar drew his sword with a swiftness that sent silver highlights spin-ning through the mist. "If nothing else, killing you will satisfy me." The blade sliced toward Loki.

Harald leaped beyond range of an errant stroke, pull-ing his own sword free. The god did not move. Ragnar's blade skipped through Loki's torso, drawing no blood. Unexpended momentum staggered Ragnar, and he held his next attack.

Loki shrugged. "The dead have no power to harm the living."

Harald slammed his sword back into its sheath, disappointed but unsurprised. He had instinctively doubted that Loki would place himself at such risk.

Ragnar sheathed his weapon also, grumbling unintelligibly. Red-faced, he lurched back into position. "Killing Hel will get us to Valhalla?"

Loki rubbed lean hands together, without retribution. "Yes."

"So you say." Harald continued to study Loki, seeing agility in the shape, origins, and insertions of his sinews. "But you are known as the First Father of *Lies*."

Loki shook his head, still grinning. "Very well." He made a forswearing gesture. "I promise, from this moment until I take leave of you, to tell nothing but truth by the lives of my sons and my bond with Odin." He looked askance at Harald. "Will that do?"

Harald scowled. "Now explain how we get to Valhalla, again."

Loki's brows rose. "Killing the goddess Hel will get you, Ragnar Lodbrok, and you, Harald Hardráda—"

"Sigurdhson," Harald said.

"Pardon?"

"Harald Sigurdhson."

Loki corrected, ". . . Harald *Sigurdhson*, to . . ."

"Start over," Harald demanded, concerned Loki might find a sneaky way around his vow by chopping up his phrases.

Dutifully, Loki obeyed, "Killing the goddess Hel will get you, Ragnar Lodbrok, and you, Harald *Sigurdhson*, to Valhalla." Once he had spoken the necessary, Loki defended, "By the way, Hardráda is what the living call you now."

Harald chuckled. "They call me 'Ruthless'?"

"I can't lie, remember?"

Ragnar finally added his piece, "Better than 'Hairybreeks.' "

Harald still found the solution difficult to believe. "But why, Loki? Why would you want us to kill your own daughter?"

"I have my reasons." Loki refused to elaborate. "I have my reasons." Then, he was gone, as quickly as he had come.

Harald traced a finger along the bulbous end of his pommel. "So?"

"So." Ragnar turned his attention toward the cave. "Convinced?"

"Yes," Harald said, then added, "Forgive me for doubting you. You mentioned the idea for killing Hel seemed divinely inspired, and Loki had centuries to influence you."

"I wasn't offended." Ragnar did not bother to look at Harald as he spoke. He headed toward the entrance.

Harald caught up with a single long-legged stride. Side by side, they walked to the mouth of the bleak entrance to the land of the dead. The everpresent fog seemed to crush more deeply around them with every stride, and the world grew ever darker.

The dead kings peered through the opening, and Harald's gaze could not penetrate the blackness. "I'll go first." Without awaiting a reply, he started into the cave mouth. A growl echoed abruptly through the confines, followed by a torrent of harsh barks punctuated by snarling. A massive figure rushed toward Harald.

Startled, Harald retreated clumsily, a hand's breadth ahead of a huge, shaggy hound, its chest hair matted with crimson. Throwing one hand up to guard his neck, he drew and slashed. The sword cleaved harmlessly through the beast. Its shoulder crashed against Harald, sprawling him. He toppled backward, rolling, anticipating the sting of teeth through flesh. It never came. The baying and growling continued, accompanied by breathless barks. Harald raised his head.

The helhound, Garmr, reared at the end of a chain. Ragnar examined Harald mildly, beyond reach of the bound monster. "Are you well?"

Harald scrambled to his feet. "As well as a dead man can be."

Ragnar smiled. "A bit ironic that you chose to protect your throat." He flicked his gaze toward the gaping wound the arrow had made.

"Habit." Harald watched Garmr writhe and snarl, hoping the collar bit uncomfortably into its neck. "We can't fight it. Remember, it's living. Loki said the dead can't harm the living."

"That's right." Ragnar had clearly forgotten until that moment. He frowned suddenly. "Harald, isn't Hel living, too?"

The realization stung like a slap, and Harald knew the overwhelming events since his death had stolen logic. He considered. "Actually, she's only half alive."

"That's right." Ragnar quoted a line from a famous story: "Like a normal woman above; livid below."

"So, all we have to do is strike a fatal blow to her lower half."

"Right."

It didn't seem right to Harald. "But can the dead be killed at all?"

Ragnar showed a tight-lipped grin. "That's not wine on Garmr's chest."

Harald sheathed his sword; it could not help him here. "Perhaps that's the blood of a living person who tried to enter hel."

Ragnar shook his head. "Not in the last couple of centuries, at least. Only dead went in." His brow furrowed. "And the dog never challenged any of them."

"Did you talk to any other of the dead? Besides me?"

"Several, at first. They never answered. Just blundered through the cave." He added thoughtfully, "Unchallenged."

Harald took a few more backward steps, and the hound returned quietly to its cave. "What made you decide to talk to me?"

"You were different than the others. You didn't head straight for the entrance, and you carried weapons. You clearly didn't belong."

Harald looked at the cave. "So Garmr's job . . . ?"

"To keep in those who belong. And out those who don't."

An idea struck Harald Hardráda. "Take off your armor."

Ragnar stiffened as if affronted. "What?" Then, apparently, he deciphered Harald's plan. "Got it." Moving a safe distance from the crags, he started to undress.

Garbed as commoners, swords secreted beneath their rags, the dead kings slipped past the hound of hel with little more than a few suspicious sniffs. The darkness further intensified, the fog becoming more like a solid entity than a cold and swirling background.

As Harald's eyes adjusted to this new measure of gloom, he found himself surrounded by aimlessly wandering figures. Some appeared pale and glaze-eyed, the newly dead. Brittle, yellowed skeletons mingled with others of stronger bone. The ones between bothered Harald most: green with mold or slick with gore, rotted flesh dangling from emaciated frames. Those who still sported eyes and mouths bore expressions that ranged from despair to agony. One brushed against him, its touch like ice chilling him to his marrow.

Ragnar howled. His sword licked from its sheath and swept down three with a single stroke. They collapsed and shattered into a still pile of bones. The others crushed in then, their frigid presences sending Harald into spasms of shivering. He freed his weapon, too. Together, the warriors cleaved a path through the walking dead. Though neutral in temperature, Ragnar's presence seemed warm compared to the chill around Harald. Soon, the bodies parted, opening a path toward the River Gjöll.

"The bridge is there." Ragnar's voice rang like thunder among the silent corpses.

Harald followed the course of Ragnar's finger to a brilliant, yellow glow in the distance. "This is just like Valhalla."

"Huh?" Ragnar turned Harald the same stern look he might one of the daft. "Exactly opposite, you mean."

"No." Harald chopped at a moldering head that drew too near, and it exploded into shards. "I mean at the *Ragnarok*. The heroes of Valhalla side-by-side, fighting the hordes of hel, preventing them from overtaking the gods." He grinned at a long-held image. "I always dreamed of battling these creatures beside Ragnar Lodbrok, but I never fancied it occurring inside hel itself."

"You honor me." Ragnar paused long enough to bow. "I regret I never imagined myself warring with you as an ally, but . . ."

Harald laughed. "I wasn't born yet."

The dead became more sparse as they gave the Vikings a wider berth, and the kings rehid their weapons before arriving at the Gjöll Bridge. Gold burned on the rooftop, yet the sturdy wooden braces did not ignite. The river roared beneath the planking, too wild to attempt to cross directly.

Harald swept an arm toward the bridge. "You first this time."

Ragnar neither questioned Harald's courage nor hesitated but stepped boldly onto the planking. Harald followed, surprised to find his footfalls making no sound against the wood. A large man, frequently armored, he had grown accustomed to the clomp of his boots against timbers. Above, metallic gold reflected the writhing, red glimmers of the fire, though it neither liquefied nor became consumed.

As the bridge began its upward curve, Harald spotted a figure on the pinnacle. He nudged Ragnar. "Módgudr?" He named the mythological guardian of the bridge, a mysterious woman about whom the skjalds had written little.

"I would suppose," Ragnar returned calmly.

"Look like we belong," Harald whispered, "and she may not bother us." He patted the hilt of the sword that ran up his breeches to his waist. "I believe she's living, so there's no need for steel."

"We don't, you know."

Harald glanced at his companion. "Don't what?"

"Don't belong," Ragnar hissed.

"Of course not. We belong in Valhalla."

Ragnar gave his white locks a frustrated toss. "I mean there's nothing equivocal. Whatever we believe we deserve as an afterlife, we clearly weren't meant to be here. Even those who entered after I arrived can't speak. And they're rotting. I'm n—" He broke off suddenly, eyes widening, to paw at his cheeks.

"You're not rotting," Harald reassured. "We'll just have to hope Módgudr mistakes you for newly dead."

The two men fell silent as they drew within hearing range of the creature on the bridge. The flickering firelight drew dancing swirls of amber and scarlet across a curvaceous feminine figure. Long, black hair curled softly around an oval face. She studied the approaching men with the same intensity they did her. She did not move aside; and, since she blocked the way, Harald and Ragnar stopped.

"Who are you?" Módgudr said at last. "You have the tread and coloring of the dead, yet you are different than the others. Why do you come down the helway?"

Harald refused to lie. Whether or not they could harm Módgudr, she could not stop them from crossing. "We are King Harald Sigurdhson Hardráda and King Ragnar Lodbrok. We have come to find Valhalla."

Módgudr's dark eyes flashed. "This road will not take you there, only to Sleet Cold, the palace of my lady, Hel."

"Please step aside," Ragnar said. "We must find Valhalla by killing your lady."

The woman glanced from king to king. "I appreciate your honesty but do not understand your path. How do you suppose such murder will get you to Valhalla?"

"She can no longer hold us where we do not belong," Harald explained.

Ragnar interpreted the question differently. "Loki informed us that doing so would bring us to Valhalla."

"Hel's father," Módgudr said carefully, "is also the Father of Lies."

"Indeed." Though impatient, Harald would remain polite as long as Mógudr did so. "But he was under an oath of truth when he spoke of this."

"Please," Ragnar repeated. "Step aside."

Módgudr pursed her lips. "I will do as you ask, with this one warning: Oath or not, beware of the Trickster's promises." She shuffled to the left and made a broad gesture for them to pass her.

"Thank you." Surprised at how easily they had gotten past one of the guardians of hel, Harald walked around Módgudr. Ragnar followed.

Harald scanned the mist for their next obstacle, refusing to let Módgudr's cooperation make him careless. The darkness became even more oppressive. Had he not come upon it gradually, Harald guessed he could not have seen anything. As it was, he made out the shifting movement of corpses and, beyond them, a towering gate.

"Look there!" Ragnar called as they walked. "Hel Gate Bars."

"I see." Harald dismissed his companion with those

few words. Inside, worry gnawed at him. He wondered if the circumstances of his death made him more suspicious, and tested the thought aloud. "Has this whole mission seemed too simple to you?"

"Simple?"

Harald amended. "Well, not simply exactly. Just simpler than expected."

"Simple isn't always a bad thing." The fog tightened around Ragnar as he stepped from the bridge onto hel's plain again. He freed his sword in time to sweep it broadly, shattering a decaying man. "You were a warrior leader. You should know things rarely turn out as we expect. Each battle is what it is."

Harald nodded, though he doubted Ragnar could see him through the gloom. "Perhaps finding a Saxon and English army instead of promised hostages has made me cynical; but if entering hel were really as easy as this, why haven't men come to retrieve their dead?" As the corpses shifted toward him, he pulled his sword from his breeches.

Ragnar hacked down three more bodies before replying. "We got here, past the helhound and over the bridge unchallenged, because we're . . . um . . . dead, remember? Besides, would you risk yourself to bring back that woman behind you, even if she was once your sister?"

Harald whirled to face a woman at least months dead. Worms crawled from an eye socket and the strip of flesh that still composed her nose. Though he had seen far more than his share of death and destruction, Harald suffered a pang of nausea that nearly doubled him. He managed enough control to hammer his blade against her face, knocking her sprawling. "I . . ." He gagged. "I see your point."

Ragnar laughed. "Facing Hel likely won't prove as simple as all that. Now stop grumbling about how peaceful and fun hel seems and start figuring out how to get over this gate."

Harald stared at iron bars that rose to twice his height, the space between barely wide enough to admit the skeletal figures of hel's oldest occupants. At the top, a rust-colored rooster paced, glancing at them through first one golden eye, then the other. "A watch cock?"

Ragnar seized a bar in each hand and attempted to climb by bracing a knee against each one. "Ignore him. He's supposed to crow when the *Ragnarok* happens, to rally the wraiths to their boat, *Naglfar*, so they can sail to Asgard and fight the heroes of Valhalla."

"Including us." Harald grabbed a different set of bars and also tried to climb.

For longer than an hour, the two men worked to scale the Hel Gate Bars, neither managing more than half the distance. At length, they stopped to rest.

"So . . . much for . . . simple . . ." Ragnar panted. "Are you . . . happy . . . now?"

Harald smiled weakly.

Several more moments passed. The dead continued to shift around them, pausing to stare but no longer daring to come within sword range.

Attentive to the wraiths, it took Harald unusually long to notice his companion studied him also. "What?"

"You're awfully tall, aren't you?"

It was a common question for Harald Sigurdhson. "Seven foot, more or less."

"That should get me almost halfway. And it should be easier at the top since it curves in some." Ragnar handed Harald his sword.

Harald needed no further explanation. Rising, he rested Ragnar's sword against the bars, then held out a hand for his companion to climb.

Ragnar clambered to Harald's shoulders as quickly as a cat, his weight noticeable but not intolerable. Bracing himself once more against the bars, he scurried to the top. Once there, he called down. "I see the palace."

Concerned for his rear guard, Harald hefted Ragnar's sword, surprised by its bulkiness. He whirled to face corpses that had not come any closer during the process. "Now how do *I* get up there?"

Ragnar crouched on the bars. "I don't know."

"Some great strategist you turned out to be."

Ragnar took no offense. "I was a great Viking, not a great strategist. I rushed in and killed. If I thought about things too long, I'd probably have lost my nerve."

Though a competent strategist himself, Harald had to secretly admit that most of his ability to lead came of his own impulsiveness in battle. "Rip your tunic into strips, then tie them together. I'll do the same."

"Armor gone. Clothes gone," Ragnar grumbled. "Am I supposed to face a goddess naked?"

You're going to kill her, not marry her. Harald set to work. "Have you noticed anyone around here besides us and the bridge guardian wearing clothes? Besides, you've still got your breeches."

"I doubt they'll be naked in Valhalla." Nevertheless, Ragnar stripped off his tunic and set to work. Shortly, they had fashioned a rope. Using it, along with his grips on the bars, Harald managed to work his way to the top. From there, they used rope and iron to descend, retrieving their swords through the bars.

Now the darkness became as heavy as a mantle. Harald forced himself to focus on the outline of the castle, all towers and crenellations, a slightly darker shadow against near-blackness. He kept track of Ragnar more by feel than sight, much as he knew the positions of his own limbs. Because of the intensity of his gaze, he nearly missed the creature shuffling toward them.

"Ragnar." Harald spoke in soft warning.

"I see it," the Viking whispered back. "I think it's . . ."

Then the thing came one step nearer and into focus. Harald looked upon a woman with features so twisted and coarse they scarcely seemed human. She stood in front of them, naked above and below. Brown hair hung in spikes of random length, as if cut by a young child in the dark. Her shoulders, arms, and breasts bore a healthy hue. Below the waist, her thighs and legs appeared pale and rotted. Harald measured the split, for an instant imagining himself burying his blade into a thigh or, perhaps, cleaving her just below the division.

In that instant, Ragnar drew first and rushed the queen of the under-realm with the same brash fervor that had won Harald many battles . . . and lost him his last. *Too simple.* Even as Harald raised his own sword, memory assailed him in Loki's voice: "I have my reasons" and in Módgudr's: "Oath or not, beware of the Trickster's promises."

Loki's role is to lead the dead against the gods at the

Ragnarok. Understanding struck like Thor's lightning. *Equivocal death.* "Ragnar, no!" Harald hurled himself at the other man.

Harald crashed into Ragnar hard enough to slam pain through every part and to bite his tongue. Both men tumbled, Ragnar twisting to face this new threat. A knee slammed Harald's groin. Agony shot through his gut, and he barely writhed far enough to rescue his head from Ragnar's blade. "Rag . . . nar!" he gasped.

Ragnar sprang to his feet. "What in—" The curse seemed inappropriate. "Have you gone mad? What are you doing?"

Harald clutched his gut. "Not . . . mad. Killing Hel . . . *will* . . . get us . . . to Valhalla . . ."

Hel finished, "But it will also begin the *Ragnarok.*"

Ragnar spun back to face the goddess, sword hovering.

Harald continued, "Without her . . . the dead . . . go free to attack Asgard."

"But the helhound—"

Hel explained, "Garmr keeps them from escaping back through the entrance. Only I keep them docile and from the boat."

Harald finally caught his breath and rose. "Ragnar, I want Valhalla as much as you do. But not at the cost of all mankind."

Apparently convinced, Ragnar lowered his sword. "How did you know?"

Many things had come together in that moment, but Ragnar would understand the latter best. "Loki called our deaths equivocal, but that just didn't make sense. War wounds rarely kill a man immediately. And, yet, we were the only ones to wind up on hel's outskirts in longer than two hundred years? He shook his head. "We didn't see any warriors in hel, so I had to assume they all found Valhalla. If *we* didn't, it was because someone tricked us there on purpose."

"Loki."

"Right. Which means he planned Hel's death centuries ago."

Hel stood still and silent, making no threatening motion.

Ragnar ran a hand through sweat-plastered, blond
hair. "But why wait so long? I knew many brave men
in my time who could have served as well as you."

Finally, Hel spoke again, understanding dawning.
"Ragnar Lodbrok and Harald Hardráda. The first real
Viking and the last."

Harald pointed at Hel to indicate she had the answer
he did not.

The goddess gave both men a hard look. "Loki cannot
master another convergence like this for centuries. In
the meantime, the *Ragnarok* cannot occur."

Harald lowered his head as the truth of his sacrifice
became painfully apparent. *No Valhalla for us.* He would
not have done anything differently, yet he would lament
surrendering hundreds of years of the gods' greatest reward. He looked at Ragnar, wondering if his hero would
agree to fight him to the death. At least then, he would
have one last great battle. And one of them would not
have to slowly rot.

Before Harald could suggest the solution, Hel raised
another. "You two do not belong here, and I will not
have you. Head deeper and farther north to Náströnd,
the Corpse Strand, and take the boat, *Naglfar.* It's set
to sail to Asgard, where you'll find Valhalla."

The kings stared. Harald could not believe Hel's cooperation. The legends called her a monster, though none
of them showed her doing anything particularly
monstrous.

Hel's creased face pulled into something akin to a
smile. "My father will have centuries to build another
ship. And, this time, I won't help him."

"Thank you, my lady." Harald executed a bow appropriate for goddesses and queens. "How can we repay
you?"

"You spared my life and rescued my job." Hel continued grinning, lips stretched in a tight rictus. "That cour-
tesy, Sire, was more than enough."

Uncertain whether Hel meant the sparing or the bow,
the last Viking headed for the Corpse Strand. And the
first joined him.

The Walker of Two Worlds nods toward a tall man with medium-dark hair and the pale complexion of a scholar. This person is dressed in patched robes, obviously one of the Seekers who spent his life in the rigorous pursuit of knowledge, not caring for the social or political implications of what he found. The Guardian of the Light points, and the golden beam lances from his fingers.

The energy whirls around the man's head and strikes him in the back of the throat. The scholar rises, a little stunned, and glances about. He finally discovers what he's looking for in a shadowed part of the room: a plain doorway which appears just a trifle shabby despite good care. It is obviously old, and has been carefully tended. With a sigh of anticipation, the man disappears through the doorway and into the mist. There he discovers a cave. The short path is illuminated at first by the Guardian's golden light, which changes into a fine silver thread suspended by nothing. Following it, the scholar arrives at the mountains beyond, and discovers the secrets within:

SILVER THREAD, HAMMER RING

by Gary A. Braunbeck

"I wish to offer a glorious crown for labors done, by singing the praises of him who descended into the darkness of the earth's realm of shades . . . For the renown of noble deeds is a joy to those who have died."

—Euripides, *Heracles* (352–356)

ON the evening before the great contest John Henry dreamed again of the strange and beautiful bird-man who had been haunting him for so long. It was a wondrous sight to his weary soul, Good Lord knew that to be the truth, yessir, but despite its beauty—or maybe *because* of it, for he felt somehow unworthy to gaze upon such splendor—it sparked a frightful suspicion in his heart.

Surrounded by the eerie blue radiance that always came with him, the bird-man whispered something.

John Henry gulped a deep breath and coughed.

The bird-man unfurled his magnificent wings, transforming their variegated plumage into a feathery rainbow, and John Henry's own chest suddenly felt as tight as if it had been wrapped in steel cables.

He saw that the bird-man felt this pressure as well, and an odd thought, unbidden and unexpected, came to him: *Was I once this, or is it what I* will become?

This seemed to make the bird-man happy. It came closer, and John Henry saw that the layers of each wing held pictures and designs, faces of people he had never seen, small dramas played out in the wingspan, all parts of the same story, the same puzzle, all joined together by a thin silver thread that extended from the bird-man's body like a puppet's string, leading into the deeper darkness where John Henry knew a terrible thing, a thing so awful it might damn well frighten God his own self, was coming, maybe even for him.

The bird-man whispered to him again, and this time John Henry heard it speak what might have been its name.

And it frightened him more than any master's whip.

His fisted hands gripped the sheets of the bed, and he began to sing in his dream, softly, with a hoarse, broken voice, his Hammer Song, imagining himself striking stone and rocky hillside with each verse:

> *Oh, my hammer,* (WHAM!)
> *Hammer ring,* (WHAM!)
> *While I sing, Lawd,* (WHAM!)
> *Hear me sing!* (WHAM!)

"Perdix," whispered the strange and beautiful bird-man.

John Henry came awake and sat up choking.

Across from the bed, on the other side of the room, the picture-box . . . what did they call it here? . . . the *television* screen displayed snowy static. To John Henry's frightened eyes, it looked like the mouth of Eternity.

Polly Ann, his wife, sat up and took hold of him. "John Henry, what is it? You have that dream about Martin again?"

Martin. John Henry almost laughed. Considering the way the bird-man dream made him feel, a nightmare about his brother would almost be welcomed. Poor, ignorant Martin, whipped to bloody ribbons by a group of Klansman the night before Master was to grant him his freedom. And it wasn't enough for them Klan-boys to just whip every emancipated nigger they could lay hands on, no; they had to go and kill the ones that were still too frightened of their new freedom to know they had the right to fight back.

"No, honey, it wasn't 'bout Martin."

Polly Ann rubbed her silken hands over his massive arms. "Wanna tell me 'bout it?"

"It was a bird-man. And it was showin' me its story."

After a long moment of silence, Polly Ann kissed John Henry's cheek. "That all?"

John Henry shrugged. "I don't quite remember. I know there was something about his killing or . . . or maybe *bein'* killed by someone in his family and . . ." Then he realized that if he went on, he'd have to tell her things he promised he'd keep to himself. ". . . and the rest of it's kind of blurry."

"Here, you just lay your head down here on my shoulder and—shhh, there you go—just lay your head down and go back to sleep. Gonna need all your strength for tomorrow."

"Yes, I am . . ." Lord, how he hated having to keep anything from his dear Polly Ann. Maybe that's why he'd been having such awful dreams.

". . . ain't no one can make a hammer sing the way you can, John Henry . . ."

". . . no one . . ."

". . . and you know you're the only man alive who can take down their machine . . ."

". . . no machine can do better work than a man . . ."

". . . gonna show 'em all, John Henry . . ."

". . . gonna show 'em all . . ."

And as John Henry fell back into a dreamless sleep, he recalled everything that had led him and Polly Ann to this moment, and prayed a good Christian man's prayer that he'd grown stronger of body, character, and will for the remembering . . .

"You sure sound happy, John Henry," said Polly Ann. "And I hope for both our sakes that it's like they sing in that song, that we've found our home. I don't know about you, John Henry, but I, for one, am powerful tired of all this roaming."

"I've got a feeling this is it for us, honey," he replied. "And I can't help but think that we've had plenty of signs, as well."

"Signs? Like what?"

John Henry smiled at her. "Look what year it is—1872. Add one and eight and you get nine. Add seven and two and you get nine. My lucky number is nine, Polly Ann. There's nine letters in my natural-born name, I weighed thirty-three pounds on the nose when I was born—and you multiply three times three and you get nine— this is bound to be our lucky year! Hey—listen!"

What they heard was the sound of hammers ringing on steel in the distance, and the songs of the workers working.

"That's the finest music I ever heard," said John Henry, putting his arm around Polly Ann as they continued on down the road. "It reminds me of those times when Martin and I would play with Daddy's hammers when we were kids."

When they got to the place where the hammers were ringing, it was a mountain. And the men who were hammering and singing were at work building a tunnel.

It wasn't much of a railroad, so far as size went. John Henry had worked all of the big ones, too—the Union Pacific, the Sante Fe, the Southern Pacific and the Northern Pacific, even the Great Northern, and this here railroad, the Cassiepea, well, maybe it wasn't so big right now, but John Henry had a feeling about it. Yessir, something in his gut told him that this railroad was going to become one of the biggest and most important ever to cut a path through the Confederate States of Mexico.

God bless the States and President John Brown and all they'd done.

Besides, its name had nine letters, as well.

A man named Captain Tommy was the boss of the men working the tunnel. John Henry watched him for a few minutes to make sure he was a man who knew how to run a railroad team.

Captain Tommy oversaw every aspect of the work. He made sure that the first line of men drove the long rods of steel deep into the rock, then stayed on the tails of the second line, whose job it was to put nitroglycerin and mica powder and dualin into the holes and blow away the rock, huge chunks at a time. And this Captain Tommy, he didn't flinch at any of it, even went so far as to apply the dualin himself. Man seemed to John Henry a born rail-boss.

"You look big and strong enough," Captain Tommy said to John Henry when he braced him for a job. "We might be able to make a steel-driving man out of you, sure enough."

John Henry laughed. "You don't *need* to make a steel-driving man out of me, nosir—*I am one already!*" He reached into his bag and pulled out his Daddy's twelve-pound hammer. "You bring me a shaker and stand out of my way, 'cause I can drive more steel than any nine men."

Captain Tommy laughed. "You're either as good as you say you are, or you are one crazy sumbitch. Either way, I think you're gonna provide us with lots to talk about over our supper tonight. Li'l Bill, you get yourself over here and shake for this big-mouthed black man. The rest of you, stand back, smoke 'em if you got 'em, and be ready to laugh until you bust, 'cause what we got here is a man what talks mighty big, and if his say-so is bigger than his do-so, we'll laugh him right out of the camp!"

The shaker held the steel, and John Henry kissed his Polly Ann and raised his Daddy's hammer, readying himself to swing. He took a deep breath to get a feel of the rhythm in his arms and chest, his legs, his stomach and shoulders and arms and, most important of all, in his head. He and Martin used to joke that you couldn't do nothing with a hammer if you couldn't get the beat going in your head.

Martin.

Poor, dead Martin.

And John Henry, he tapped into the most important part of the rhythm in his head, his anger over his brother's senseless death, and just like every time he drove steel, he focused his eyes between the shaker's hands, right there at the center of the steel, and he imagined the white hoods of the Klansman who'd whipped his brother to pieces, then afflicted every form of degradation on his ruined body as he lay dying, and—*wham!*—there it was, the rhythm, the power, the focus, and the song:

> "Ain't no hammer"—*WHAM!*
> "Rings like mine"—*WHAM!*
> "Rings line gold, Lawd"—*WHAM!*
> "Ain't it fine?"—*WHAM!*

Captain Tommy and the steel drivers laughed at his song, slapped their knees and pointed at him." Ain't never heard such bragful singing in all our born days!" they cried. But that didn't deter John Henry, not one little bit.

> "Ring like silver"—*WHAM!*
> "Peal on peal"—*WHAM!*
> "Into the rock, Lawd"—*WHAM!*
> "I drives the steel."—*WHAM!*

The laughter of the steel-drivers and Captain Tommy grew softer, then died altogether as they watched his hammer swing round his shoulder in a rainbow arc faster and more precise than any man's they'd ever seen. Li'l Bill, the shaker, had to work mighty hard to loosen the steel after each mighty ring of John Henry's hammer.

Everyone's eyes grew big and round as dinner plates.

"If'n I dies, Lawd"—*WHAM!*
"I command"—*WHAM!*
"Bury me with my hammer"—*WHAM!*
"Hammer in my hand!"—*WHAM–WHAM–WHAM!*

*   *   *

Captain Tommy rose and ordered John Henry to stop so he could examine the work.

Captain Tommy's eyes grew even bigger, and he let fly with a long, low, loud, impressed whistle. "Well, John Henry, looks like your do-so is as good as your say-so and then some. You aren't just bragful and uppity like I thought, and I hope you'll accept my apology for the way I behaved earlier. Yessir, you drove the steel as good as you promised, better than any nine men could into this here mountain."

"Of course he did," said Polly Ann, smiling her pearly-whites and taking hold of her man's hand. "He's a natural-born steel-driving man, and what my man says, he means."

Captain Tommy took off his hat to John Henry—something he'd never done for another steel-driver—and offered his hand. "You work for me, if you care to."

John Henry shook the man's hand. "Praise the Lord, we got ourselves a home now."

"That you do," said Captain Tommy. "The boss himself is going to want to meet you someday, mark my words."

"Can I ask a favor?"

"You name it, John Henry."

"Can I have me a little advance? Enough to go into town and buy me a couple of twenty-pound hammers? This hammer here, it belonged to my daddy, and I don't want to be bustin' it on no mountain-work."

Captain Tommy handed John Henry a small roll of bills. "You got it. And this company, it don't charge its workers for their housing either. Mr. Daedalus—he's the boss—is a damned decent fellow about the way he treats his workers."

John Henry turned around and picked up his Polly Ann in one arm and lifted her off the ground. "I told you there was signs!" he said, then kissed her. "Praise the Lord, honey, we have come home!"

He kissed her again.

The steel-drivers cheered him.

So John Henry came to work for Captain Tommy's

team, and Polly Ann set about taking care of their cozy little house.

It was hard work in the tunnel. The smoke from the blackstrap lamps and the dust from the red shale were so thick that a tall man like John Henry couldn't see his own two feet without stooping almost double. The thick air was hot, and the men stripped to their waists before working.

But John Henry was the best steel-driving man in the world; he could sink a hole down or he could sink it sideways, in soft rock or in hard—it made no difference. With his twenty-pound hammers in each hand, it sounded as if the mountain was caving in, the ring of the steel was so loud.

Everything was going fine until a man calling himself Mr. Minos came along trying to peddle his steam dream to Captain Tommy.

"No, sir, don't need it; I got me the best steel-driving team in the world."

"We'll see about that," said the man.

The next day, when the men came to work, they found that a full one-fifth of the tunnel had been filled back in overnight, and at the mouth of the tunnel stood a man with a bull's head, his massive arms looking even bigger than John Henry's. One of the shakers tried to make the Bull-man step aside, but it just grabbed him up in one hand and snapped his neck like a twig.

Captain Tommy pulled out his carbine and shot the thing many times, but it didn't so much as make a scratch.

Around noon, with no work done and the Bull-man still standing guard at the mouth of the tunnel, Mr. Minos came back with his steam drill and asked Captain Tommy, "Change your mind about my machine yet?"

"You get that goddamn filthy beast away from my mountain!"

"*Your* mountain?" said the man, laughing. "Hell, that mountain don't belong to nobody—no *man,* at least."

"You take your monster and you take your machine and you go to hell, sir!" yelled Captain Tommy.

Mr. Minos laughed even louder at that one. "I never visit the same place twice, buster. Now, you go to your boss and tell him that if you don't buy my machine and use it to make your tunnel, there's gonna be worse than that—" He pointed at the Bull–man. "—coming here to stop your working."

Captain Tommy stared hard at the man, then spit a wad of chewing tobacco at his feet. "I'll be sure to pass along your message."

"You do that," said Mr. Minos, then handed Captain Tommy a letter. "Give that to your boss, while you're at it."

"What's in here?"

"It's personal business. Just make sure you give it to him. You don't, and I'll have my stepson over there kill an even dozen of your men in their beds tonight."

John Henry—who'd been standing over to the side listening to the exchange—stepped forward and said, "You got enough faith in your hell-fire machine to accept a challenge?"

Mr. Minos looked John Henry up and down, then sneered. "What you got in mind, boy?"

Every man there saw John Henry stiffen at the word "boy," and knew just what was going through his mind: He was thinking back to his slave days, and, more to the point, he was thinking about what the Klan had done to his brother, Martin, how they'd finished with him, then hung him by his ankles from a tree and split him down the center like some hog and tied a sign saying THE ONLY GOOD BOY IS A DEAD ONE! around one-half of his head. John Henry had been the one to cut his brother's body down, and to weep over it, and to bury it.

You did not call John Henry or any man he called friend "boy" and expect to walk away in one piece.

The steel-drivers held their breath, waiting for John Henry to snap Mr. Minos in half just like the bull-man had done the shaker, but John Henry held his temper. When he spoke again, his voice was tight and quiet: "What I got in mind is that I go up against that machine of yours, and the two of us, we keep going until one of us beats the other through the mountain or one of us gives out."

Captain Tommy said, "John Henry, there's no need for you—"

"Yessir, there is! I don't mean no disrespect, Cap'n, but this man, he comes here with his fine suit and his murdering bastard monster of a stepson and his hell-fire machine, and he looks down his nose at us like we were something you scrape off the bottom of your shoe, and then he makes sport of Li'l Bill's being killed—well, you all are my friends, you all are the men I work with and respect, and ain't no uppity man with his damned machine gonna take away no part of the home me and Polly Ann have come to love so much." He stepped right up to Mr. Minos and glared down; and John Henry's glare was a fiercesome thing to behold. "You just name the day."

"Dawn, day after tomorrow."

"I'll be here."

"I bet you will," said John Henry. "I'll just bet you will."

Then he did something no one expected.

John Henry walked right up to the bull-headed man and pulled back a fist and socked the monster so hard in the jaw that he cracked some bone in the thing's face. The beast staggered back a bit but did not drop down—which surprised everyone because John Henry's punch had enough fury in it to kill any ten men—then it righted itself, wiped the blood away from its snout, and snorted foul-smelling sulfur into John Henry's face.

"That was for Li'l Bill," said John Henry. "And it ain't half of what I'd've liked to've done to your sorry ass."

The Bull-man only stared at him, hate burning in its eyes.

John Henry spit tobacco juice onto the Bull-man's boots, then picked up his hammers and walked away.

No other man there would have had the nerve to turn his back on that thing, but, as any of them could tell you, John Henry weren't just any man.

It was getting near bedtime when someone came knocking on the door to John Henry's home. Polly Ann answered.

"Evenin', Mrs. Henry," said Captain Tommy. "Is John busy?"

"No, sir. Come right on in."

Captain Tommy did, removing his hat as he stepped through the door. "My, my, you have certainly done a fine job of turning this place into a right lovely home, Mrs. Henry."

"Thank you, Captain. Would you like something to drink?"

"No, ma'am, afraid I'm here on—" John Henry stepped into the room.

"John Henry," said Captain Tommy, "Mr. Daedalus has requested that you come up to his house to speak with him. He has sent his private car for you. It's right outside."

"He ain't angry about my challenge, is he?" asked John Henry. "I'd hate for the boss to be upset with me. Polly Ann and me, we really like this place and—"

Captain Tommy held up his hand. "Mr. Daedalus is far from upset with you, John. In fact, I think he's right pleased 'bout what you did. I asked why he wanted to see you and he told me—as politely as possible—that it was a matter between himself and you, and it needed 'immediate attention.' His very words."

John Henry took his best shirt and tie from the closet and readied himself for the visit.

"Real nice seein' you again, Mrs. Henry."

"It's Polly Ann to you, Captain. And you are welcome in our home any time."

"Thank you, ma'am. Maybe sometime John Henry will bring me for supper. He talks all the time about your rhubarb pie."

Captain Tommy escorted John Henry out to the long, black, shiny car that idled near the bottom of the hill. "Don't you worry none, now, John Henry. But if you and the boss don't mind, I'd appreciate bein' let in on anything that might affect the crew."

"I will be sure to mention that to Mr. Daedalus. Ain't right, keeping folks in the dark."

"Much appreciated, John."

The two men shook hands, then John Henry climbed in the back seat of the limousine and was off.

Now, John Henry knew from the other steel-drivers that all the fantastic machines that abounded within the camp were designed and built by Mr. Daedalus—who, before going into the railroad business, had been an inventor of some renown. If the television that came with the house hadn't been enough, nor the voice- and music-box that Captain Tommy called "a radio," nor the electric ice-box with its three different compartments that all could be set to different temperatures so's to keep the beer cold, the eggs chilled, and the meat frozen—if all that weren't enough to prove that Mr. Daedalus was a man of great mind (and even, some said, of supernatural power), then what John Henry was about to encounter would leave no doubt, for when the limousine pulled up in front of Mr. Daedalus' resplendent home, the driver opened the door and John Henry climbed out—

—to find himself looking into the face of a man who was made of metal—at least, his hands and face were, and John Henry assumed that the rest of him was, too. Bright, shiny metal, with only two red lights where on a regular man there would be eyes. The metal-man said nothing, only gestured for John Henry to go on up the steps and through the door.

He did, and was greeted there by another metal-man, this one dressed up as a butler, who escorted John Henry down the long marble hallway and through a set of oak doors into a study where a fire burned and music played from the radio and huge, ancient paintings hung on the walls.

To the left of the magnificent fireplace was a large desk. Behind it sat a small, gray-haired, very distinguished-looking gentlemen who was examining a set of blueprints with great intensity.

"John Henry," said Mr. Daedalus. "Forgive me for not rising to shake your hand." He looked up from the blueprints as his hands disappeared behind the desk. There was a *click,* then a *whirr*ing sound, and Mr. Daedalus rolled out from behind the desk in a motor-powered wheelchair.

"A little something I've been working on since the arthritis rendered my legs all but useless," he said, then rolled right up to John Henry and shook his hand. "A great pleasure to meet a man of singular nerve such as yourself. Please, have a seat. Would you care for a drink?"

"No, sir, nothin' for me. Just had me a fine supper."

"Ah, yes. I've heard it rumored that your Polly Ann is an artist in the kitchen."

John Henry smiled. "That she be, sir."

Mr. Daedalus regarded John Henry for a moment, but not in an unfriendly or judgmental way; he looked at his guest as if he were seeing a fine work of art. "I hope my servants didn't unnerve you too much."

"I have to say, sir, that I ain't never seen nothing like them in all my born days."

"President Brown commissioned me to build them as personal security guards for himself and Vice-President Castilla. They will be present at the signing of the Russo-Japanese Pact next month. There have been threats against not only Nicholas II and Emperor Meiji, but any world leaders who attend. A pity that there were factions out there bent on destruction. Don't you think it sad? I mean, not only will that agreement ensure peace between those two warring nations, but it will stop the budding revolution in Russia, as well. Do you follow politics, John? May I call you John?"

"Yessir, please do. Afraid I don't much follow what goes on in the world these days."

Mr. Daedalus smiled. "Probably a very wise thing to do. It can get awfully depressing."

John Henry liked Mr. Daedalus. The man spoke to him as an equal. When John Henry had said he didn't follow politics, Mr. Daedalus hadn't given him a look of disgust like a lot of folks would have—*That's what I get for talking to you like you have a brain*—but instead listened and smiled and made him feel as if he were just as smart for *not* following the goings-on of world leaders.

A nice man. Yessir.

"I'll come right to the point, John. Mr. Minos—charming fellow, isn't he?"

"Right cordial, if you like rattlesnakes."

Mr. Daedalus laughed. "That's a good one, John. May I use it sometime?"

"Be my guest."

Mr. Daedalus rolled back behind his desk and wrote it down on a sheet of paper, laughed again, then gestured for John Henry to move his chair closer to the desk.

"Mr. Minos and I used to be partners in a design company that we started some years ago. We are both inventors—well, *I* did the designing and building, Minos sold the ideas to customers.

"Mr. Minos became greedy, John. He took several of my prototypes—inventions that weren't quite ready yet—and stole all my files, most of our profits, and disappeared. He reemerged a few years ago with his own company—one that, might I add, had been built with my designs and money.

"That steam drill he's trying to force us to use? I designed it. I wish to God now that I'd burned the plans . . . but no use crying over that. Isn't that always the way? One is more concerned with the immediate result, with *succeeding,* than with any long-term consequences.

"Both Minos and I have sons—*had,* in his case. Perdix was a ne'er-do-well to top them all—a gambler, heavy drinker, loud-mouth, ladies' man. One night about a year ago, he ran into my own son, Icarus, in a tavern. Kept going on about how his father was going to beat the pants off me, break my company, you know the sort of boasting. I'll not sugar-coat it; Icarus can be an unruly handful himself, and he was a bit toasty on whiskey that night. To his credit, my boy didn't start the fight, but he has a nasty temper problem, and when Perdix hit him in the jaw and accused *me* of being the thief, Icarus tore into him with all he had.

"I'll skip the sordid details. Suffice to say that it was an extremely violent fight, and Icarus wound up killing Perdix. Then my son did a most foolish thing, John; he ran off. I never knew to where. I received only one phone call, and that was far too brief to give me much to go on. I posted a reward for any information leading to the discovery of my son's whereabouts. I would gladly give half my fortune for his safe return. Icarus may have his faults, but he is still my son and I love him with all my heart." He rolled around until he sat directly next to John Henry, who turned to face the man.

"Minos has my son, John. And I need for you to get him."

"I don't understand, sir. How can I—?"

Daedalus held up a hand to silence John. "What have you heard about me? And please spare me the nice things folks say about the wages I pay and how I treat the workers and the rest of it. There have to be rumors about me, and I'd like to know if you've heard them. *One,* specifically."

John Henry thought on it for a moment, then recalled a tall tale one of the shakers had told round the campfire one night. "There's some folks that think you might have . . . Well, divine blood in you. Like Jesus."

Daedalus grinned. "Not quite, John. But I have, in my time, broken bread with such supernatural beings."

His thumb hit a switch on the arm of his chair, and he rolled even closer. "I have supped with martyrs, saints, and angels, John. I have been commissioned to build for the Divine."

Looking into his eyes and hearing the awe and conviction in the man's voice, John Henry didn't doubt it one little bit. "I certainly believe you have, sir."

Daedalus smiled, squeezing John Henry's hand. "Good. That saves me the time of having to prove it to you." He reached over and pulled several sets of blueprints across the desk, keeping some for himself, handing some to John Henry. "You much for reading surveyor's charts, John?"

"I am. I can also understand most blueprints."

"Geological maps?"

"Some."

Daedalus nodded. "That's not going to be a problem, I can answer any questions you might have.

"Now, one very important thing, John: Until the contest is finished the day after tomorrow—and allow me to say that I have no doubt you'll rule the day over Minos' contraption—until that time, I want your word as a good Christian man that what we're discussing will stay between us. Not even your wife can know. I know that's asking a lot for a man so honest as yourself, but ask it I must. Have I your word?"

"Yessir."

"Good man." He smoothed the largest of the maps on his lap, then turned it to face John Henry. "Recognize it?"

"That's—why, that there is the very mountain that we're tunneling through!"

"Yes." Daedalus pulled back the top portion of the map to reveal an equally large blueprint beneath, one that looked to be part blueprint, part archeology chart, part geological map. "Can you make out what this is?"

John Henry studied it carefully. "Can't say for certain, sir, but it looks to me like that's . . . that's a sketch of what the inside of that mountain looks like."

"You're right there. Do you see how it's all solid for three-quarters of the way through, then there is this small chamber—antechamber, actually? That's where you'll enter to find my son. Minos has him trapped beyond that antechamber. That's where you'll find it."

"Find what, sir?"

"The entrance to the Gates of Hell, John. I designed and built it."

"The entrance?"

Daedalus shook his head. "More than just that. *Hell*, John. I conceived, designed, and oversaw the construction of Hell."

The morning of the contest arrived, and when John Henry turned the bend in the road to walk toward the mountain, he was stunned to see that both sides of the road, for as far as his eyes could see, were lined with people come to witness the great event. There were banners and a band playing songs and cotton-candy vendors and barbecues and even folks laying money on who was going to emerge victorious.

The people cheered John Henry as he made his way to the mountain, his loyal and loving Polly Ann by his side.

"They come to cheer you on, John Henry."

"Looks like it," he whispered in reply.

She took hold of his hand. "Don't you fret none, honey. I know you'll win." She nudged him, then pointed to the set of cases he was carrying. "Are you gonna tell me what it is that Mr. Daedalus gave to you?"

"A special set of hammers. Thirty-pounders. Said they

was a gift from a foreign fellow of his acquaintance, a man named Thor. Told me these was the finest, most powerful hammers on Earth."

"That why you didn't bring along your twenty-pounders or your daddy's?"

"Mr. Daedalus said these two would be all I'd need."

"I sure do hope he's right."

"Makes two of us."

They arrived at the work site. Sure enough, there was Mr. Minos, looking arrogant as ever, leaning against his steam-drill and saying something to the Bull-man—who was checking the controls.

John Henry grinned. He liked the idea of going up not only against Minos' machine, but being able to beat it *and* that monster of a stepson driving it . . . that was almost too sweet.

Don't get uppity now, he cautioned himself. *Ain't no guarantee you're gonna beat nothing, even with these hammers Mr. Daedalus gave to you. Pride cometh before a fall, John. Don't forget that.*

There were a lot of people depending on him today. He would not disappoint them.

"John!" cried Captain Tommy, pushing his way through the throng of steel-drivers and shakers who'd mobbed John Henry as soon as they caught sight of him. "How you feeling this morning, John?"

"Ready to do me some work, sir. Been a few days and I get impatient."

Captain Tommy smiled and smacked John Henry on the arms. "That's my man! You're the best, John Henry, no man nor machine can best you!"

The steel-drivers and shakers cheered, each slapping John Henry on the back or shoulders as he pushed through to the face of the mountain.

He looked around for Polly Ann—he'd lost track of her when the workers rushed him—and saw her over to the side, sitting next to Mr. Daedalus and his metal-man attendant. Mr. Daedalus was whispering something to her. Polly Ann watched John Henry as she listened, then nodded her head, took something that Mr. Daedalus placed in her hand, and started over toward her husband.

John Henry set down the cases, then opened them, removing the two magnificent golden hammers that Mr. Daedalus had given to him the previous evening. They shone bright as sunlight in his grip, and he swung both of them—one at a time first, then together, giving his body the chance to get the feel of their power—and powerful they were, for with each swing John Henry could feel his muscles grow tighter and stronger, and the rhythm in his chest and arms and legs and shoulders and head came together quicker than they ever had before.

"I want you to think only of your brother Martin," Mr. Daedalus had told him. *"I want you very angry when you first strike those hammers against the mountainside. Spare no thought for anything else until you reach the antechamber, John Henry. You'll not need any shaker, nor sharpened steel, nor dualin—only these hammers. And don't ask me any questions—you'll know why I ask this of you soon enough. There will be rewards for you, John; on that you have my word."*

Polly Ann embraced him as everyone else moved away. The Bull-man powered up the steam drill, poisoning the air with an awful racket.

Under the noise, Polly Ann leaned up and shouted in John Henry's ear: "Mr. Daedalus asked me to do this, so don't you be gettin' mad with me." And she tied something to the back of John Henry's belt, but when he looked down to see what it was, there was nothing there.

Polly Ann was holding a spindle in her hands but there was no thread.

"He said you can't see it in the light," she shouted over the roar of the steam-drill. "But once you get into the deep dark, it'll shine silver so's you can find your way back if you get lost." There were tears in her eyes as she finished speaking.

John Henry's heart welled with tenderness for her. He reached out and touched her cheek, trying to find the words, but he saw from her face that everything he wished to convey was in his touch.

She moved back into the spectators.

The sheriff stood at the mouth of the tunnel, one hand holding a pistol in the air, the other holding a stopwatch that he was watching intently.

John Henry glanced at the Bull-man in the steam-drill's seat.

The Bull-man made an obscene gesture at him.

John Henry raised his hammers, then swung them down once, cracking their heads together and producing not only a ringing that was louder than the steam-drill's engine, but causing the air between the heads to spark.

He looked at Mr. Daedalus, who nodded.

The crowd fell silent.

John Henry took a deep breath and held it, thinking: *This is for you, Martin.*

The sheriff shouted very loudly, so as to be heard over the roar of the engine: "On your mark, gentlemen: Four . . . three . . . two . . . one—" He fired the pistol. "—Go!"

—and the drill was screaming and chugging and chewing through rock, and John Henry was swinging the hammers and singing "Oh, My Hammer," "Water Boy," "Where Is You Hidin'," "If I Die A Railroad Man," and every hammer song he could remember, all the time thinking only of his brother, of poor Martin and all the wonders of this here world he never lived to see, dying at the hands of ignorant, mean-spirited men who couldn't see beyond the color of a man's skin, and while he was thinking these thoughts the hammers swung and blasted through the rock like it was glass, sparking fire and lightning that illuminated the way, and John Henry began to realize, somewhere in the back of his mind, that the hammers were as much using him as he was them, for his arms were no longer making steady rainbow-arc swings, nosir, they were pinwheeling, hard and constant, and his muscles screamed, but he didn't care, this was a sweet pain, Lord, it was so sweet, because he glanced over his shoulder only once and saw that the light from the steam-drill's lantern was several feet behind him, nearly swallowed by darkness and smoke, and he was far ahead and that was fine, yes it was, swing that hammer, make it ring, raise my hammer, hear it sing, and the rock blasted away in the wake of the hammers' lightning, and John Henry felt tears in his eyes because he could swear he felt Martin right behind him, shouting, "You show 'em, Big Brother, you show 'em good!" and he was doing just that, he was showing them all, moving ahead, going faster, rock disintegrating under the hammers' will, and he stopped only once to take a breath, having no idea how long he'd been at it—

—and that's when he saw a small sliver of reddish-orange light glowing from behind the wall of stone before him.

John Henry wiped the sweat from his brow, lifted the hammers, made sure he was still in the lead, then struck at the rock in four successive blows—

—and stood at the top of a stone staircase.

Sulphuric fumes, made fiery and frightening from the reddish-orange light below, wafted up the stairs and around his head, trying to choke him, but the light from the hammers kept it at bay.

He looked behind him and saw that Polly Ann had been right—there was a long, shiny silver thread trailing from the back of his belt, leading back to the tunnel's entrance.

He flexed his arms and shoulders, took a deep breath, and started down the chaotic staircase of massive, wedge-shaped boulders. At last, his feet touched ground in some vast, silent, ancient chamber. Ahead, through the fiery, sulphur-choked gloom, he saw a bluish radiance, haloing some kind of vaguely familiar rock formation. He hung the hammers from his belt and climbed an enormous slab of limestone, scraping his shins and cutting his arms, then scrabbled onto a ledge.

On a small plateau, under an overhang of surprisingly white calcite that curved gracefully upward like a snowdrift hollowed by the wind, stood a cluster of meticulously-carved stones, each roughly the size and shape of a man, arms outstretched, holding something whose shape he couldn't quite discern. Their bodies were complete, but all of them lacked faces. Beyond these figures he saw the retreating blue radiance and beyond that the entrance to another passageway.

All around John Henry there echoed the sounds of tortured souls crying out for mercy and forgiveness, but too late, too late.

He said a short prayer. It seemed the Christian thing to do.

The odd radiance guiding him, he maneuvered toward the entrance, which looked more and more like the gaping mouth of some mythic titan, frozen into a perpetual scream at the moment of its death. He moved slowly, his back pressed against the wall, feet sliding slowly to the side, the ledge becoming tight and close, less than seven inches in depth. He slipped only once but did not let it shake his resolve, and as he safely reached the far and much wider side of the ledge he saw that the faceless stone figures on the plateau had changed position, then realized it was only an illusion; he was now seeing them from a different angle.

Instead of being a random cluster, they formed an eerily straight line that stretched toward the center of the chamber; not six, but several dozen bluish-gray faceless figures, about his height, standing silently by under their white canopy, cowled voyagers waiting with no hope on the frozen deck of an icebound ship, each holding a raggedy whip—

—and that's when he realized who they were.

These were the Klansmen who had killed his brother, who had so brutally cut short Martin's life. It wasn't that they were faceless, no; they had been sent here still in their robes and hoods.

Even from where he stood, John Henry could see the recognition in their eyes, could see them remember his face when he'd come to cut down his brother's body and weep over his mangled remains.

In their eyes was fear and pain and regret.

John Henry listened, listened real good, and heard that from beneath their robes and hoods came the sounds of whips cracking and men screaming for mercy.

Even though he was a Christian man, John Henry couldn't find in himself to pity them.

"He was a fine man," he snarled at those frozen figures. "He wanted to be an artist. Martin, he could paint a picture like nobody's business. But you didn't care about that, did you?"

Don't be like this, he thought.

And found some touch of pity in his heart for these men.

So John Henry said a little prayer for them.

But only a little one.

And moved on.

He stepped into the opening and saw the wispy tail of the blue radiance disappear around a bend. Following it, John Henry found himself stumbling downward once again. The humming grew louder, becoming a keening that filled both the air and his chest with a dull, despairing throbbing.

The ground evened out, trembling. Down here, deep in the mystery, the walls and roof, glistening with a ghostly iridescence, dripped with moisture—salty and heated. John Henry took a drop on his finger and tasted it.

Tears.

The walls of Hell wept with the tears of the damned.

The keening increased its volume, growing steadily more intense, becoming a full-throttle roar of anguish. He saw a bit of the radiance, churning slowly, moving forward, a worm wriggling its way into the dirt as it vanished into the mouth of a tunnel. Whatever it was that was in such pain was at the end of that tunnel. John Henry had no doubt it was Mr. Daedalus' son.

I'm coming, he thought, then dropped onto hands and knees and crawled into the opening. For a while there was enough room for him to use his hammers to clear the way, but suddenly and without warning, the passageway narrowed to a few feet in width and the roof soon dropped down so low he could touch it with his fingers. When John Henry moved—which he could do now only in bursts of mere inches—his shoulders scraped the sides of the crawlway, and the roof above pressed mercilessly onto his back. He didn't even have enough room to raise one of the hammers—not that he would want to, not in something this tight; the hammers might have special powers, but they didn't mean nothing to the rock, nosir: One good hammer-blow might bring the whole thing crashing down on his head.

The air grew thin. He stopped after every movement to gulp in great lungfuls of stale, mephitic, sulphur-tinged air, trying to control the rabid panic he felt snarling to the surface. All his life John Henry had never been afraid of enclosed spaces, but now he tried desperately not to imagine himself becoming wedged in or being crushed or buried alive. He thought only once of trying to go back, but the keening drew him toward it, begging for help, have mercy, don't leave me here, please, oh, please, God, don't leave me here, it's so lonely—

—he managed to get on his side and in a burst of near-panic scrabbled forward, catching sight of an opening ahead and hoping it would be big enough for him to get through, pushing and clawing with all he had, wriggling forward, closer, he could see the blue, could almost grasp the keening in his hands, and then the roof began to crumble down around his ankles, collapsing with every move he made, and John Henry thought he might have started screaming, but he couldn't be sure because it was happening too fast. He had to stay ahead of the collapsing ceiling that was catching up with him too fast, too fast, and he lunged forward as his mouth filled with dirt dropping down in clumps from above—

—and he emerged into a grotto, shoving himself out of the tunnel just as the last few feet of it filled with something organic; part placenta, part earth, part anguish.

John Henry could see that the silver thread still shone brightly, only it didn't lead into the collapsed tunnel as he'd expected; it led in the other direction, as if he'd come from *over there instead of*—

—he turned around—

—and saw the Gates of Hell.

John Henry whistled long and low, for the gates were an impressive sight, extending to either side of him for as far as he could see, and rising above him so high that he could not hope to see the top.

But he could see the young man who was chained to them, one arm outstretched on either side and his feet manacled one atop the other, looking for all the world like Christ on His cross.

Except Christ didn't have a set of wings that were bound together with barbed wire.

The young man looked down at John Henry and said, "I . . . I made these so I could . . . could fly and it . . . it caught me . . . please . . ."

Icarus had evidently inherited his father's talent for invention.

"Your daddy sent me, son," replied John Henry, and started marching toward the terrible gates—

—and stopped dead in his tracks, less than three yards away, when he heard a growl from the surrounding shadows, and remembered . . .

. . . *a terrible thing, a thing so awful it might damn well frighten God his own self, was coming, maybe even for him* . . .

. . . the unseen terror from his dreams.

"Ahgod," croaked Icarus, tears streaming down his cheeks. "It heard you."

"Shh!" snapped John Henry, peering into the darkness.

At first he thought it was some kind of great and terrible horse, its head was so far above the ground, so far above his own, but then he saw the red, glowing eyes—all six of them—and heard the mad-dog snarl, and smelled the sickening mixture of sulphur, fur, and waste, then it emerged from the blackness and John Henry nearly cried out, for what stood before him, towering over his own massive body by a good eighteen, twenty inches, was a giant three-headed dog with glistening foam dabbling from all its jaws.

"Save yourself, sir," cried Icarus.

"Shut your fool mouth, boy!" John Henry would not break eye contact with the creature. It might be a good hundred feet away from him, but one good jump and it would be right on top of him, chewing him to pulp.

He dared not look down at its haunches to see if it was readying to spring.

John Henry had no idea what he was going to do.

His weight suddenly shifted, and without looking away from the beast's faces John Henry became aware that the hammers were moving, shaking themselves in his belt as if to say, *Let us swing free, John Henry, let us swing free!*

"Good boy," he whispered, easing his hands down to his sides, "good little doggie."

He gripped the hammers and began easing them out.

The beast moved forward, slowly, rippling the muscles in its back.

"Damn if you ain't one ugly sumbitch," John Henry said in the same sing-song voice he'd used before.

The beast bared teeth. A whole lot of teeth. John Henry wasn't sure, but he thought he could see little bits of flesh flapping in there.

"Good little ugly-sumbitch-doggie," he said, the hammers firmly gripped in his hands.

The beast reared back, tensing its haunches, then barked a Hell-hound's bark.

And John Henry swung the hammers up, then brought them down in a crescent-arc, slapping the heads together just below his belly, and the thunder rolled and lightning burst from their heads.

The beast yelped as if in pain but did not stop coming toward him.

John Henry swung the hammers up, bringing them together over his head. This time the thunder was a small earthquake and the lightning was Nature's wrath.

The beast howled.

He brought the hammers down—*WHAM!*—and the Earth cracked around him and the lightning was the center of a twister, snarling outward in jagged streaks, blasting against the walls.

"Oh, my hammer," he sang—

—*WHAM!*—thunder from the beginning of the universe, lightning from its end—

—"Hammer ring"—

—*WHAM!*—the walls began to crumble from the vibrations of the peal—

—"Hear them ring, Lawd"—

—*WHAM!*—jagged, whipcurling bolts of lightning shot nearer the beast, blowing holes in the ground—

—"Hammer sing!"

And John Henry kept slapping the heads together, filling the bowels of Hell with the peal of a steel-driving man's might and brightening the place up a bit with the dancing bolts of lightning.

The beast fell on its belly, crippled by the noise and power, but John Henry kept slamming his hammers together, feeling the power shake his guts loose from his bones yet, he would not stop until he was certain that the beast was too stunned to come after him.

WHAM!

The beast jerked and snarled and whined.

WHAM!

It rolled onto its side, legs licking in the air.

WHAM!

Finally, its eyes rolled back into its heads and its tongues lolled from the sides of its mouths and its legs stopped kicking.

John Henry stopped.

He watched very carefully to see if the beast was still breathing.

He heard the raggedy sound of a steam-engine train idling in a station, and knew that he'd not killed the beast. That was good—not just because John Henry was not a killing man, but also because something about this beast's awful magnificence told him that it could not—and possibly *should not*—be destroyed.

He whirled around and ran up to the Gates, grabbed onto one of the bars as if it were a rope, and shimmied up until he was level with the manacles that held Icarus' wrists and arms in place.

He drew back one hammer, then froze.

"What is it?" said Icarus, great panic in his voice.

"Seems to me I ought to do your feet first," said John Henry. "Less you feel like flopping face-first down to the ground." He slid down a ways and struck his hammer against the manacle trapping Icarus' ankles, then slammed it against the other, freeing the boy—

—who did not fall to the ground as John Henry had expected, but instead unfurled his wings and flew upward, laughing.

John Henry dropped to the ground, picked up the other hammer, and watched the boy enjoying his freedom.

"We got to get out of here," he called.

"Try and stop me!" yelled Icarus, swooping down to piggyback John Henry and lifting him off the ground.

"Which way?" he shouted in John Henry's ear.

"You see the silver thread behind me?"

"Yes?"

"Follow it."

Straight up, they went, following the path of the thread as it wound through Hell, somehow ending up back at the foot of the same staircase John Henry had descended before. Icarus flew up the narrow passageway, setting John Henry down where he'd stopped his hammering.

"Looks like the machine's got a bit ahead of me," said John Henry, gently pushing Icarus to the side to resume his labors.

Before he got back into the race, John Henry did something he swore to Mr. Daedalus he'd do—seal up the antechamber.

Three good strikes did the job.

"Time to show that machine who's boss." This time, the hammers roared, and the rock didn't so much fall away from his blows as it did *run* away, and soon, bellowing his hammer songs for all he was worth, John Henry regained the lead.

The steam-drill kept chugging and snarling, but it was no match for a man who'd been to the bowels of Hell and lived to tell the tale.

When John Henry at last hammered his way out the other side of the mountain and into daylight, the crowds cheered, and the band struck up with a rousing rendition of "Oh, My Hammer," and John Henry dropped to his knees, weeping, then threw back his head and let fly with a whoop of victory they heard three counties away. He held up his magic hammers—

—and saw that they weren't gold at all.

They were his own, regular old twenty-pounders.

He brought them down, dropped them to the ground, and stared.

Polly Ann ran to him, threw herself on her knees next to him, and held onto him as if she never planned to let go again. "I knew you could do it, John Henry, I just knew you could!"

". . . the hammers . . ." he muttered to himself.

He looked up as Mr. Daedalus wheeled over, Icarus by his side. "Thank you for my son, John Henry. Thank you." Then: "How does it feel to be something of a god?"

"Beg your pardon?"

Mr. Daedalus pointed at the hammers. "You know, don't you, that you were using them all the time?"

"But . . . how? I done things that no natural man ought to be able to do with them."

"Some men grow into their divinity, John Henry; other have to be tricked into it."

"Then you lied to me?"

"No—I *fooled* you. There's a difference."

Icarus placed a hand on John Henry's shoulder. "Thank you for freeing me, John."

John Henry could only nod his head.

"Well, then," said Mr. Daedalus, looking into the mountain. "Seems my ex-partner's contraption's nowhere near making it out here."

John Henry nodded. ". . . not even close . . ."

Mr. Daedalus grinned as Captain Tommy brought John Henry a tall, cold glass of water.

"You know what I'd like to do, John?"

"No, sir."

"I think I'd like to devote more time to my inventions—and to getting to know my son again. I need someone to take over this railroad for me. Any suggestions?"

"Captain Tommy's a damn fine man."

"That he is, but he doesn't want my job. Do *you* want my job, John Henry?"

"You foolin' with me again?"

"Absolutely not. As far as I'm concerned, this railroad belongs to you, John Henry. Treat her well, and she'll take good care of you and yours." Mr. Daedalus turned and began wheeling away.

John Henry called out, "You was plannin' on giving it to me the whole time, weren't you? This here railroad's my reward."

Mr. Daedalus, not looking back, wagged a finger in the air. "Never jump to conclusions, John Henry. It drains all the surprise out of life."

Mr. Daedalus and his son disappeared into the limousine and drove away before John Henry could ask why he'd been told to think only of his brother on the way in.

"Well," said Captain Tommy. "Looks like I'm working for you now."

John Henry looked at him and grinned. "I don't know. Uppity fellow like you—is your do-so as good as your say-so?"

"And then some."

"Okay, you're hired."

And they laughed loudly, as did the other steel-drivers, and the crowds.

When the steam-drill finally emerged, some two hours later, Minos and his monster stepson were laughed out of the county.

The steam-drill? The crew decided to keep it.

Never could tell when a working man might need a good laugh.

Later that night, after all the singing and dancing and celebrating had died down, John Henry and Polly Ann walked back to their home, hand in hand.

"What a day this has been!" declared Polly Ann.

"That it be," replied John Henry.

Polly Ann poked him in the ribs with her elbow. "Where is your mind at? You been looking at the ground and mumbling to yourself for the last half-hour."

"I was just . . . wondering about something Mr. Daedalus told me to do. Something he told me to think about while I was hammering my way—"

He stopped speaking as he looked up and saw the figure standing on the front porch.

". . . can't be."

"John Henry, what you looking at?"

"That fellah on our porch. In the moonlight it almost looks like Martin, but that can't be."

"Why not? We got his letter two days ago tellin' us he was coming."

John Henry whirled on her. "A *letter?* That can't be, Polly Ann. Martin's been dead goin' on six years."

She laughed. "Oh, my poor John." She placed a gentle hand against his cheek. "I do believe that all that hammering must've shook loose some of your brains."

"You two comin'?" shouted Martin from the porch. "I been waiting here a while and I don't mind saying that I'm . . . well . . . kinda *hungry*!"

"Oh, my Lord," whispered John Henry under his breath.

Then remembered Mr. Daedalus's words: *There will be rewards for you, John; on that you have my word . . . . . . How does it feel to be something of a god?*

"Some men have to be tricked into it," he whispered.

"What are you going on about?" asked Polly Ann.

"Nothing," said John Henry, wiping the tears from his eyes so she wouldn't see them and promising the universe that he would be a worthy god. "Nothing at all. Now, come on, let's go feed that brother of mine."

The Guardian stretches his hand toward a young man with the look of a dreamer. He seeks what all dreamers seek, to know he is not alone in his quest. To do this, he desires knowledge regarding his champion, a hunter of ancient secrets. Rose-shaded velvety light shimmers from the Walker's fingers and caresses the man. He smiles, rising, and turns toward a door opening in the wall behind him. Within, tall columns of pale golden and red sandstone, inscribed with stories of successful dreamers who have preceded him, mark his way. He steps beyond them into a vista of rolling desert, journeying past the forgotten city of Abydos to discover:

MEMNON REVIVED

by Peter Schweighofer

THE lateen sail billowed, pulling the barge up the Nile, the flags of France and Tuscany snapping on the mast. The third flag did not belong to any nation; beneath a sewn pyramid read the words "Champollion Expedition, 1828–1829." Several figures in Arab garb lounged on the aft deckhouse roof. The breeze carried their voices— some bickering, most laughing—over the mountains of traveling chests, baskets, and supply crates piled on the foredeck.

Jean Champollion sat between a leather trunk and the bow, a sultan on his throne. His eyes gazed up the Nile from beneath the turban. He breathed deeply, savoring the air and the dry desert smell it carried: warm and comforting, but tinged with thirst. The soft breeze rippled the water, whispering from thousands of years before.

It seemed at least that long since he had confronted the puzzle of Egyptian hieroglyphs. Others had competed against him, vying for the distinction of bringing one of the greatest cultural and scientific discoveries to the world: a window into the most ancient period of history. But his determination and years of classical training finally paid off, making him the first to translate the writing on the Rosetta stone.

He had consumed Vivant Denon's *Description de l'Egypt*. The report on Napoleon's Egyptian campaign and the scientific survey of the Nile valley monuments was the most comprehensive one in history, providing both written and pictorial evidence of ancient civilization and the people who lived there now. But soon engravings and words could no longer satisfy Champollion's curiosity. He had translated hieroglyphs from books long enough. Now he was going to read them firsthand, touch the stone they were chiseled in, and breathe new life into a long-dead language.

Of all the pictures Denon's expedition had published, one stood out in his mind: the Colossi of Memnon.

"Jean, hello." Rosellini's voice seemed to float in from the Nile, Champollion was so absorbed. His chief artist peeked around the crate, his head swathed in a turban and his Arabian robes fluttering in the wind. "Jean, come back and sit with us. Omar's daughter has prepared some lunch for us. And when we're finished, Omar wants to hear about your fascination with Memnon. L'Hote thinks it might keep him from telling any more mother-in-law stories."

Champollion pulled himself from his seat, then followed Rosellini over the mountain of crates. The other expedition members were sprawled over the flat deckhouse roof, a living area used often when the cabins became too hot. Most wore Arab dress, but one, Nestor L'Hote, hadn't yet shed his European clothes for the cooler caftan robes. Everyone was scribbling in sketch tablets, putting the final touches on their pictures of Cairo. Some detailed the hieroglyphs found on the monuments there.

Their Arab guide motioned for Champollion to sit near him. Omar leaned against the tiller, swaying lazily with the beam and keeping his boat, or dahabeeyah, as the Arabs called it, on course. Omar's musket sat beside him; he never used the gun, but it made L'Hote feel safer.

"Come, sit," Omar said, nodding to Champollion and

showing a broken, yellow-toothed smile. His daughter handed out flat bread smeared with red bean paste. Most of the expedition members, Frenchmen and Tuscans, took it and munched on it, but L'Hote only nibbled and finally set it aside.

While they ate, Omar began to relate another story. "Once mother-in-law went to the camel dealer to purchase a fine camel . . ."

"Don't you ever stop chattering?" L'Hote asked, not even looking up from his sketch.

"Mother-in-law always says he who does not speak keeps silence."

"How profound," the Frenchman noted.

"Maybe you should take his advice," Rosellini suggested.

"I'll shut my mouth when you change out of those ridiculous infidel clothes," L'Hote sneered. "You look like a desert bandit."

"Mother-in-law tells the camel dealer she needs a camel, a very big one, to help her loyal son-in-law move carpets to market."

"These clothes are much cooler than the stuffy European rags you wear," Rosellini said, straightening the turban on his head. "We've only been here a few weeks. After roasting a month or two, you'll be wearing this Oriental dress, too."

"At least I'm not going about in someone's bed sheets," L'Hote spat.

Champollion ignored his colleagues. They would soon tire of their petty arguments. He peered at the shore instead. Miles of desert stretched beyond the thin edge of vegetation, and sandstone cliffs crept past on the horizon.

"How long until we reach Thebes?" L'Hote pestered their guide. "We've been on this miserable boat all afternoon. And this sun is so unbearable . . ."

"We shall reach Thebes by nightfall," Omar said. "We shall dock on the eastern bank, at Luxor. Mother-in-law says Thebes, in the west, is home to bandits and jinni."

"Sounds like your kind of place, L'Hote." The other expedition members laughed with Rosellini:

"You're so pathetic," L'Hote growled. "I'd rather be

trapped in the pyramids than on this barge with you and your band of rowdy Tuscans." He conveniently ignored the other Frenchmen chortling at him.

"Will we have time enough to see the Colossi of Memnon?" Champollion asked.

"You know we can only stop overnight," Rosellini said. "The monuments upriver await us. Belzoni reported that Abu Simbel was filled with vast painted scenes from Ramses' conquests. The hieroglyphs there are in excellent condition. We'll be back this way soon enough. Then we can visit the tombs and ruins. And you can see your beloved Memnon."

"Who is this Memnon you speak of?" Omar pestered. He scratched his stubbly chin. "I cannot remember anyone named Memnon in Luxor."

"Memnon isn't a person," Champollion explained. "Well, at least nobody still living. The Colossi of Memnon are two massive statues of pharaohs seated on the plains of Thebes. Legends say one of them sings at dawn."

"You don't really believe that rubbish, do you?" L'Hote glared skeptically at Champollion.

"Mother-in-law doesn't know that story," Omar said. "Perhaps you shall tell it to me."

"Jean, don't do it," L'Hote groaned. "He'll never stop repeating that boring tale."

"Omar wishes to hear the tale," their guide insisted, a mock expression of anger on his face. His face lightened a moment and he nodded to Champollion. "Please, *effendi,* continue."

"Memnon is the Greek name for the pharaoh Amenophis the Magnificent," Champollion explained, appealing to everyone and only finding a rapt audience in Omar. "According to Homer's *Iliad* and Ovid's *Metamorphoses,* he was a king of Ethiopia who was a nephew of King Priam of Troy. The myths claim his mother was the dawn goddess Aurora. When Troy was besieged, Memnon brought ten thousand soldiers to his uncle's aid. Nestor, a wise and just Greek warrior, challenged him to single combat."

L'Hote scowled at his name being discussed in such a dubious story.

Champollion gently raised his hand and turned to Omar. "But, being an honorable pharaoh, Memnon refused because of Nestor's distinguished age and his great wisdom. Achilles took Nestor's place in the challenge, and slew Memnon on the battlefield."

"Poor King Memnon," L'Hote teased.

"Quiet," Rosellini whispered.

Champollion ignored his comrades. He leaned closer to Omar, trying to convince him the legends were true. "The myth says when Aurora found her dead son, she commanded the four winds to carry him to Thebes, his home. There his people mourned; to remember their king, they constructed two enormous statues bearing his likeness. These colossi face the east. Legends say that when the morning sun strikes the northernmost figure, it sings."

"Goodness, singing rocks."

"Keep silence! It is a fine story." Omar scowled at L'Hote, then turned a peaceful face to Champollion. "Why does Memnon sing only at dawn?"

"He cries to his mother, Aurora, praising her for the warmth and light she provides. Memnon weeps for his mother like a child taken from his parents."

"Oh, please, Champollion, don't make the story worse than it already is."

"Stop interrupting," Rosellini barked.

"Well, it's only a legend," Champollion reluctantly admitted. "Denon's expedition found historical evidence that the colossi were dedicated to the pharaoh Amenophis the Magnificent. They might have guarded the entrance to a long-gone temple. Many ruins cover the plains of Thebes, and statues of seated pharaohs guard the temple entrances in Luxor."

"Do you think Amenophis figures historically into the Troy myth?" Rosellini asked.

"I don't know. If Amenophis was powerful enough to construct the colossi and some of the Luxor temple, he might have warred against other nations during his time. Whether or not he was contemporary with the Troy legends I do not know."

"I like the story of Memnon. I shall tell it to my mother-in-law. Her stories are never about dead kings.

But once mother-in-law went to the Sultan's palace in Cairo. . . ."

"Not another mother-in-law story."

"She went to sell a carpet to the Sultan."

"Do you think the statues really sing?" Rosellini asked.

"Oh, rubbish," L'Hote sneered. "You've seen Denon's engravings of the statues. They're just two very large, faceless pharaohs sitting in the middle of the desert."

"But do they sing?"

"Everybody knows that rocks only make noise when somebody bangs them together."

"The Romans heard it," Champollion said. "Some hear a sound like a harp string snapping. Hadrian said Memnon wept like a man."

"But nobody in our lifetime has ever heard the statues sing," L'Hote said. "Denon's expedition didn't hear anything, and neither did Belzoni."

"I will camp at Memnon's feet tonight," Champollion declared, smiling at Rosellini. "I want to hear for myself whether or not the colossi sing."

"The sheik says nobody shall camp in Thebes tonight."

Champollion turned toward Omar, a bewildered expression on his face. His hand reached to touch the Arab's robe, but he hesitated and allowed it to fall at his side. The others stood by the Bedouin camp pitched along the Nile's eastern shore at Luxor, Omar's dahabeeyah rocking gently against the nearby sand bank.

"Why not?" Rosellini demanded. Several Arabs scuffed by with muskets cradled in her arms.

"The sheik says bandits lie waiting in the hills. They shall cut your throats and steal your money."

"But if we can see the colossi from here, it must be safe," Champollion said. He had already discovered the two specks on the western horizon. The megaliths sat across the river on a plain of scrub and grass. They looked like two faint giants guarding the edge of the world.

"We must camp here in Luxor, then, eh?" Rosellini looked to his colleague, expecting a response. Champollion only stared at the Colossi of Memnon, silhouetted in the sunset.

"You must," Omar said, gripping his own musket for emphasis. "We shall go to the colossi tomorrow after the sun rises."

"But we will miss Memnon sing," Champollion said, appealing to Omar with open hands.

"Let it rest," L'Hote said. "When can we get some dinner?"

"The sheik's camp is near the temple." Omar pointed to the ruins with his musket. "We have been invited to dine with him tonight. It is a great honor."

The expedition members traipsed up the beach and over a dune, sketch tablets under their arms. The sheik's camp was nestled next to the pylons and lotus columns of an ancient temple. Champollion stopped a moment to stare at an obelisk; his eyes scanned the needle, reading the hieroglyphics. The monument glowed gold in the last rays of the sun, but the spire's point was smeared white with pigeon droppings.

They ate in the sheik's spacious tent. L'Hote would not eat the Arab's food and Champollion picked at it. When Omar started another anecdote about his mother-in-law, L'Hote returned to the boat with a headache.

After dinner Champollion wanted to explore the temple ruin by torchlight. Omar refused to let him go alone, grabbed his musket, and scurried after him.

"What do the pictures tell you?" he asked. Champollion brought a torch closer to a wall of hieroglyphs which danced in the firelight.

"This is the cartouche for Amenophis the Magnificent. And beneath it are pictures telling why he built this temple."

"Please explain: what is a cartouche?"

"It's a symbol in which a pharaoh's name is depicted. They are usually formed by squares or ovals. Like this. . . ." Champollion pointed to the oblong sign carved into a lotus column.

"Ah, I see. Cartouche." Omar showed a crooked, yellow-toothed smile. Champollion continued down the colonnade, reading the hieroglyphs. Omar followed, pointing out every cartouche he found.

When they reached the last lotus column, Champollion spoke. "Omar, I must hear Memnon sing. Will you row me across the Nile? You can use our dahabeeyah's skiff."

"The sheik says bandits will attack. We shall not go at night."

"But if we are not at the colossi when the sun rises, we won't hear the song."

Omar leaned against a lotus column and scratched the fuzz on his chin. "I do not know," he mused.

"Why don't we go just before dawn," Champollion suggested, placing a gentle hand on Omar's shoulder. "You'll be armed. And I could get a gun from the supplies."

The Arab stared off into the temple. He pushed away from the column and scratched beneath his turban. He straightened up and slung the musket over his shoulder. "We shall go before dawn. And I shall take you, protecting you from any bandits we might meet."

A smile dawned on Champollion's face. He patted Omar on the back. "You are a fine man, Omar, and a good friend. I am glad we have you along as our guide."

Omar grinned and wagged his head. "Thank you, *effendi*. And you tell very good stories. I, too, wish to hear Memnon sing. We shall go. We shall hear his song." The two walked back through the temple to the Bedouin camp, Omar pointing to every cartouche along the way.

Omar pulled the skiff onto shore. Champollion hopped out and handed the Arab his trusty musket. They trudged up the sand bank until they came to the plains of Thebes. The gray glow of the eastern horizon cast a film of light over the desert.

"We go quickly," the guide said. "The bandits shall not see us if we hide behind the statues." Omar gripped his gun, prepared to shoot any attackers who might present themselves. Champollion slung his musket over his shoulder, and the two crept through the scrub toward the Colossi of Memnon.

As they drew closer, Champollion could see the monuments took the form of two pharaohs seated on thrones. The faces had been worn away, but the Frenchman

could still trace outlines of the Egyptian headdresses.
With back erect, hands on knees, the twin guardians
stared into the east.

Champollion stood at the northern colossus' base. He
craned his neck to see the statue's head.

"It is very big," Omar noticed. "Never have I seen
such large pharaohs."

"They are more than sixty feet high," Champollion
whispered. He had to squint to see the features: the
head, squared shoulders, stiff back, legs which melted
into the throne.

The morning air smelled of dry grass and dust. The
sun had not risen above the eastern desert, but it was
warm enough already that Champollion could wipe the
sweat from his brow. He paced around the base of the
northern statue and kneaded his hands behind his back.
A breeze crackled through the grass and tingled Champollion's sideburns. "She is almost here, Memnon," he
whispered. "Almost time to sing." He spoke more to
reassure himself of his own belief, but Omar heard him
and helped vanquish the last shred of skepticism.

"Dawn comes," Omar said. "Then the statue will
sing." He leaned against the base of the colossus and
scratched the stubble on his chin. His eyes scanned the
western horizon for bandits.

Now there was only eagerness, with no room for
doubt. Champollion circled the monument's base, inspecting it in the gray predawn light. The lower portions
were defaced with carved graffiti. He moved closer to
examine the Latin words etched over the hieroglyphs.

"I, Vitalinus of Thebaid, with my wife Publia Sosis,
have heard Memnon twice at the dawn." Champollion
spoke to himself, his lips quivering with every syllable.
He read further.

"Sabina Augusta, the consort of the Emperor Caesar
Augustus, has twice heard the voice of Memnon during
the first hour."

"I found a cartouche," Omar whispered, pulling
Champollion back to the present. He led Champollion
to the statue's side and pointed to the inscription on
the throne.

"This is the sign for Amenophis."

"What does this writing mean?" Omar poked his musket at the hieroglyphs beneath the cartouche.

"They say, 'Amenophis made this as a monument to his father Amen, making for him a huge statue of costly red stone.'"

Champollion ran his trembling fingers through the stone grooves of Amenophis cartouche, reading the hieroglyphs again as the diffused light slowly increased. He peered at the horizon, then up at the monument's blank face. Any moment now the sun would rise over the eastern desert. "Let's move away from the statue a bit," Champollion suggested. "Then we can see the first rays of the sun bathe Memnon." They walked in front of the colossus until the Frenchman could see the Egyptian headdress without straining his neck.

Instead of looking up at the statue, Omar grasped his musket and peered out among the far bushes. Champollion saw several shadows moving closer, each swathed in Arab clothes and carrying a musket or scimitar. Bandits.

The rocks at the edge of the Theban plains caught fire. The golden glow passed slowly down the cliff face, consuming it in morning flames. Air rushed in and out of Champollion's lungs. His muscles contracted and his eyes bulged as he turned to watch the monument shimmer in the dawn. The thieves could take what they pleased, but they would not steal his dawn moment with Memnon.

The statues' heads burst in white light, illuminating the plains and almost blinding the two men. The sun seemed to fill in the statues' ruined sections, adding detail to the headdress, eyes, nose and mouth to the face, and a golden sheen to the skin. The monuments glistened with the sun's fire, as if Aurora herself had brought her beloved Memnon back to life.

Light and flames burned in Champollion's eyes, too, for there, bathed in the dawn's full glory, sat fiery Memnon, Pharaoh of Egypt. The air stopped flowing through his lungs. He stood gaping at the sunlit colossi, searching the atmosphere for sound. He felt Omar freeze and the bandits halt their advance.

The statue's glowing eyes burned brighter, and Champollion saw the golden lips move. The pharaoh's chest swelled as if breathing air and sunlight into its stone lungs. Memnon exhaled, lips moving, eyes blazing.

The sound which burst forth was so deafening within Champollion's head that he stumbled away from the statue. He knew Omar, too, had been thrown to the ground, and felt the thieves fleeing in terror from Memnon's cry.

Champollion could discern no familiar words from the cacophony blasting from Memnon's lips. He wasn't even sure it was ancient Egyptian. The noise rose and fell, with pitches deep and high running in an unearthly harmonic syncopation. Champollion heard all at once a majestic bass voice and a sweet soprano, accompanied by more instruments than man could create.

His eyes grew wider as lights danced before the pharaoh's face, forming into what seemed to be pictures. Pinpoints formed into bright stars, blurred clouds of swirling gases, and fleets of angular, almost pyramid-like shapes with blue-glowing bases. Lines of color superimposed themselves over the scene, forming vectors and angles with small scribbles of light adding notes at important intersections.

The images faded, and Memnon was left glowing gold in the sun's light. The sounds still burst from its lips when one of the pharaoh's arms lifted from the throne and pointed calmly to the heavens.

Silence.

Champollion woke to someone shaking him vigorously.

"Jean, get up. Are you all right?" Rosellini dragged him to his feet. Two other expedition members armed with muskets stood guard nearby, their robes fluttering in a faint wind. "What happened?"

Champollion straightened his turban. He tried blinking the sun's glare from his eyes. "I'm not sure. I thought I heard a wondrous sound, but . . . How long have I been here on the ground?"

"When you weren't at the boat, we went looking for you. It's a good hike from the shore, so I'd suppose you were here for at least twenty minutes. We heard reports of bandits."

Champollion stared at the sun, no longer close to the

eastern horizon. He shook his head, wondering if it all were just some dream.

Omar sat on the ground some ways off, hugging his musket for comfort, his eyes shut tight. L'Hote was poking at him with his shoe. "Get up, Omar," he demanded.

"What did you see, Omar?" Champollion asked while Rosellini led him forward by the arm.

"Nothing!" Omar cried, shaking his head. "I did not hear Memnon sing his frightening song. There were no terrible sounds. Please tell Omar that the sun is up."

"Of course the sun's up," L'Hote sneered. "You obviously can't feel it baking your brain into delirium." Omar opened one eye, peered around, and rose from the ground. He dusted himself off, shaking the fear from his head, too. "The bandits are gone," he proclaimed, standing a bit straighter and holding his gun more like a soldier.

Champollion scanned the area. The plains of Thebes were engulfed in sunlight, showing no signs of the thieves. The colossi had lost their golden features: no more moving lips, glowing eyes, or rising chest. All that was left were two faceless stone idols, their bodies worn away by time.

"Come, Jean," Rosellini said. "We must get you out of this sun. Once we're back on the boat, we'll get you some water and you can rest."

Champollion stood there a moment, looking at the empty face of Memnon. The Egyptian headdress and the face were smeared with bird droppings.

A firm hand touched his shoulder. Omar smiled his yellow grin. "We must continue up the Nile," he whispered. "But we shall return when you have finished drawing the temple writings, and you can listen to Memnon's song again. Perhaps by then Omar shall have his courage back." Champollion returned the smile.

He peered back at the colossi as the expedition turned toward the Nile. If he could unlock the secrets of the Rosetta Stone, he could discover the lost power of the ancients . . . a force somehow locked within the Colossi of Memnon.

The Guardian's light swirls into another Seeker's heart. This strong-minded woman came to the Eternal Archives understanding that histories written by humankind are seldom accurate. Her search is for facts. She rises to meet the light and strides to a door of plain wood, with metal hinges set to swing both ways. She enters it, finding beyond the humid lushness of early Arkansas summer and the rhythmic thud of horse's hooves on a dusty road as she experiences a new verse of:

THE BALLAD OF JESSE JAMES

by Margaret Weis

WE—by which I mean Jesse, his brother Frank, Cole Younger and myself—was riding through the south of Missouri that day, somewhere down around the Arkansas border. I don't say where, for folks was good to us down there and I don't want to get no one in trouble with the law, who would surely come down hard on 'em if they knew they had been offering help to the James gang, which is what the newspapers were calling us by then.

My, but it was a fine summer day, the best sort of summer day in Missouri. The sun was shining and the mockingbirds were out on the fence posts, trying to see which of them could jump higher and sing louder. I have always took to mockingbirds, and I thought to myself that day that we was like the mockingbirds who never work a stitch, but live off sunshine and whatever the good Lord provides. And since only a day or two earlier the good Lord had provided us with a train full of Yankee money, I could have sung a tune myself for the pure beauty of the day. We were in friendly country, where folks knew us and liked us and knew the Pinkertons and hated them, so there wasn't much to worry about, though we kept our eyes skinned and stayed on the back roads.

Jesse was riding in front. He most always rode up ahead of everyone else. We none of us rode fast enough for Jesse, not even at a tearing gallop. He was always eager to ride round the next bend, always itching to get where he was going and never satisfied once he got there. He had blond hair or would have if he didn't keep dyeing it with walnut juice, which was a disguise he used, and pale blue eyes that never changed expression. They never looked happy, never looked sad, never looked sorrowful nor angry. They just looked. And they looked until they'd looked clear through one side of a man and out the other. Not one of us looked Jesse in the eye for too long, though we liked him fine otherwise.

Cole Younger said it was because of the blinking. Jesse had some sort of something wrong with his eyes. Frank called it "granulated eyelids" which Frank says is like having grains of sand stuck beneath your eyelids and it was right painful. Well, now, if you've ever had a clump of dirt in your eye, I guess you know how Jesse must've felt and he felt like that every time he blinked his eyes, which a fellow has to do a lot. You just can't help it, except when you're sleeping.

Frank rode in the rear, reading a book aloud to us. Frank was older'n Jesse by about four years, and Frank was smart, smarter than any school master. I recalled the time when we was waiting for the St. Charles train to come along in order to relieve the Yankee passengers of their valuables and make them pay back some of what they stole from us during the war. The rest of us was sweating and pacing and checking for the umpteenth time to make sure our guns was loaded proper, or maybe taking a crap in the bushes, for the bowels grip when you are coming up on some fun. But not Frank James. He just sat there with his back against a rock, cool as a cowcumber, reading a book by some fellow called Shakespeare.

There never was such a person for reading books. Why Frank even got the notion of holding up the train at a place called Gads Hill 'cause some fellows who rode with this here Shakespeare fellow had once done a robbery at a place called Gads Hill. I was sort of worried about this, for it's not right to horn in on some other man's territory, but Frank said that this Gads Hill place wasn't here, it was somewhere in England. Anyhow Frank thought it was the funniest kind of joke and he chuckled about it to himself for days after. The rest of us just laughed polite-like.

Frank was reading a book to us that day. He most always carried a book or two in his saddlebags. I didn't understand much of the story, which was about some politician who was cut down for robbing honest people of their rights. It put me in mind of old Abe Lincoln, but Frank said no, it was a different tyrant. I didn't much understand the story, but I enjoyed listening to Frank roll the words like thunder rolling over the Kansas prairie, shaking the ground and flatting the wheat as the storm passes.

And when Frank got tired of reading, Jesse dropped back to ride with us and he got to telling us a funny story about a man he had shot point blank in the center of the forehead during a bank robbery. Jesse figured he'd killed the man, but the man lived, though he had a dent in his forehead as big as a goose egg. And from that day on, the man was known for miles around as "Bullet-head" and he was proud as punch of that bullet wound, and every time anyone strange came to town, Bullet-head would whip off his hat and point to the dent and say, "Know who did that? Jesse James did that! I was shot by the famous Jesse James!"

Well, we all laughed, and Jesse said that one day he'd go back to that town and shake that man's hand, and we all agreed that would be a fine thing for him to do and probably set the man up for life. And we talked about this and that, about the good old days riding with Bloody Bill Anderson and how it was a shame Bloody Bill had met such a terrible end and how the Yankees had been so scared of him that even after he was dead they cut off his head and his hands and buried them in separate graves to make good and sure he stayed dead.

By then it was getting to be about midday. Frank went back to reading his book and Cole Younger, who was riding alongside me and rolling his eyes some whenever Frank paused to draw breath, Cole says that he's starting to feel a mite hungry. The rest of us says that we could eat, and so we start looking for a likely farmhouse.

Now that was in the days when a person could stop at any farm in Missouri and ask for food and shelter for the night, and you would be as welcome as if you were their kin they hadn't seen for a month of Sundays. So we stopped at the very next house we come to on the road.

It was a little house, with some flowers in the yard and that meant there was a woman living there, and a barn that was sort of rickety like and tumble-down and that meant that the man of house was likely shiftless, for no man lets his barn go to seed. And there was a stack of wood that needed chopping and some chickens running around, so we knew that there would be chores we could do to pay for the meal and we also knew what the main course was likely to be. Nothing better than fried chicken and biscuits and honey. Nothing.

There was some fields in back of the house with corn standing about up to your knee and a crick cutting across one corner with some cottonwood trees shading the bank, and all in all it was a right pretty parcel of land. But there was something wrong here. Jesse said so right off, and I'll tell you how he knew.

There was two children, a little boy and a little girl, maybe about eight and nine between them. But they were not acting like children are supposed to act. They were not doing chores or pinching each other or pulling one another's hair. They sat on the porch, huddled real close together like they was cold, though the sun couldn't have been shining much brighter if it had been paid to do it. They just sat and they just looked at us and they did not say nothing, and I don't mind telling you, as Cole said, that it gave us the creeps.

We climbed off our horses and tied them to the hitching rack and Frank put his book away in his saddlebags. And about that time the boy jumps to his feet and runs into the house, banging the door, and yelling for his ma to come because there's "genlmen outside."

A woman come to the porch. We all took off our hats and Jesse was always the one to speak for us, "Afternoon, ma'am. My friends and I have ridden long and hard this day and we could do with some dinner. I see

you've got some wood that needs choppin'. We'd be glad
to—"

Well, that was as far as he got. The woman was a
young thing, and might have been good looking if her
eyes hadn't been all red and her nose swole up from
crying. She'd been holding it in when she come out on
the porch, but the minute Jesse says that about chopping
the wood, her well sprung a leak and she starts to bawl
like a new-born calf.

Now I have faced my share of Yankees in battle. I've
heard Yankee bullets hum like bees around my ears,
and I've seen their cannonballs pitch down around us
thicker'n a Missouri hailstorm. But I'm here to tell
you there's nothing shrivels a man's guts like seeing a woman
cry. Well, we was so uncomfortable that I think we
would have rid away right then and there but that, as
Jesse said later, the woman put him in mind of his
mother.

Now I've met Jesse's mother, and I'm here to state
that the two couldn't have been any more different if
one had been a rabbit and the other a catamount, which
is what Jesse's ma was, no disrespect intended. Jesse said
the same thing. He was proud of her for being so fiery
and strong-minded. He tells the story of how once the
Yankee militia rode into his house looking for him and
Frank, who were known to be riding with Quantrill's
Irregulars. And the Yankees took old Doctor Samuel—
that was Jesse's step pa—and strung him up to a tree,
trying to make him tell where his stepboys was hid.

The militia hauled Doc up and down four or five times
and he was turning real blue in the face, and it seemed
likely that he wouldn't be telling anybody anything for
much longer, when Jesse's ma come raging out the
house. She lays into those soldiers, screaming and
scratching and whacking them with whatever farm im-
plement come to hand. She was over six feet tall, was
Zerelda Samuel, and she must've looked taller'n that to
the Yankees, 'cause it took more'n a few soldiers to hold
her off. The soldiers eventually cut down Dr. Samuel,
seeing that he wasn't likely to tell, even if he'd knowed,
and he probably didn't. He was alive, but he was never
quite right in the head afterward. I guess hanging does

that to a fellow. You can see the rope burns on his neck to this day.

So anyway we were all standing there watching this young woman cry and now, of course, her young'uns, seeing their ma cry, they start into bellering. And we're all feeling about as low as a whipped pup, when Jesse takes charge. He tells me to go round up a couple of chickens and chop off the heads and bring 'em to the kitchen and he tells Cole to go chop some firewood and he tells Frank to water the horses. We're all pretty well used to doing what Jesse says, even Frank, and besides chasing chickens was a hell of a lot better than hearing a woman bawl. So we went and did what we was told.

I can state here and now that I never ate a more dismal meal. Cole said later we didn't need to salt the chicken 'cause it had salt enough with all that woman's tears dripping into it. She cried while she plucked and she cried while she fried and cried while she rolled out the biscuits. The children eventually give up crying— ran out of steam, I guess—and they just sat at the table and hiccuped.

Her tears was starting to affect my appetite and the same with the rest of the boys and finally Jesse just flung down his spoon and asked her, real gentle like, what was matter and where was her man, for we'd been there some time now and no man had come in from the fields yelling for his dinner.

"My man's dead, sir," she said, crying afresh. "He died during the war. He was at Pea Ridge, fightin' for General Price."

I suppose you could say we'd fought for "Old Pap" Price ourselves, though mostly unofficial, around in Jackson County, Missouri, and cross the border into Kansas. I wasn't at the Battle of Pea Ridge, which took place just across the border in Arkansas. The widow's man must've joined up when our boys were running for their lives down Telegraph Road into Arkansas with the blue bellies hot on their heels.

"I never knew what happened to him," the widow sobbed. "He didn't came back, and I asked around and it was then one of the men who'd gone with him said he heard he'd died at Pea Ridge, but he didn't know any more than that."

"I'm sorry to hear that, ma'am," Jesse said. He had been shot twice himself during the war, once when he was trying to surrender. "But you must take comfort in knowing your husband died for the good cause and that he's gone to a better place."

"It's sinful to keep grieving for him," added Frank sternly, and he started quoting a Bible verse which I forget.

The widow said she knowed all that, and it wasn't for her husband she was crying but for her young'uns. It seems that there was a mortgage on her house and farm and that the man who owned it had come and told her that the house was too good for seccesish trash to squat in and that she and her whelps were going to have to either pay off the mortgage or he was turning them out into the world with nothing but the clothes on their backs. He was coming today to foreclose.

I could see that Jesse was taking this to heart. "How much do you owe, ma'am?" he asked.

"Eight hundred dollars," she cried, burying her face in her hands, "and it might as well be eight hundred thousand, for I can never in all my life raise enough money to pay him."

Jesse never said another word. We ate our fill and Cole started telling stories to make the young'uns laugh and after that even the widow cheered up and quit crying and ate a morsel or two. After dinner, we hauled water and saw to it that the widow's wood box was filled and the stock fed and tended to, and then it was time to ride on.

While we was working, Jesse had been rooting around in his saddlebags. When he found what he wanted, he wrapped it in a spotted kerchief and took it to the widow and handed it to her on the porch. The widow opened the kerchief and danged if she didn't start to cry all over again.

"No, no, sir!" she said to Jesse. "I thank you kindly, but I can't take charity from strangers! My man wouldn't like it."

"We're soldiers like your husband, ma'am," said

Jesse. "We're not strangers. Frank, draw up a receipt. Now, ma'am," Jesse said, after Frank's had it all writ out legal, "when this Yankee comes to foreclose, you had him this money and you make him sign this receipt. And if he gives you any trouble, which I misdoubt he will, you get the law after him."

"There's an unusual number of lawmen in the area about now," Frank added and the corner of his mouth twitched. "Pinkerton men. They'll help you. Just don't tell anyone how you came by the money."

The widow fell to her knees and called down the Lord's blessing on Jesse. He looked real embarrassed and made a sign to us. We all jumped on our horses and we started to go, when a thought seemed to strike Jesse.

" 'Scuse me, ma'am, but when did you say this Yankee was coming?"

"This evening, sir," she said.

Jesse nodded. "And which direction will he be riding when he leaves?"

"He'll be goin' back to town, sir. Up this road, headin' north."

"And what kind of horse will he be riding, ma'am?" Jesse asked.

"He doesn't ride a horse. He drives a buggy with yellow wheels," said the widow.

"Thank you kindly, ma'am," says Jesse. He tipped his hat and we rode off down the road.

That night, we was hiding in the brush, thinking back to the fine chicken dinner, when Cole Younger said, real sudden like and unexpected, "I was at the Battle of Pea Ridge."

We all stared at him, none of us knowing this before.

"I heard it was bad," said Frank.

"It was early March," said Cole, like he hadn't heard Frank at all, "and it was colder'n frozen hell. The kind of cold that settles in your bones. The night after the first fighting, some of the wounded climbed into a hay rick to try to keep warm. The hay rick caught on fire. The hay was tinder dry from having been stored all through winter and it went up with a whoosh and a roar. It might have been gunpowder, but it wasn't. It was just hay. You couldn've read one of your books by the light."

"What happened to the wounded?" Frank asked.

"They burned alive," said Cole. "We tried to help, but no one could get close on account of the heat. You could hear them screamin' for a long time. A real long time. Sometimes I think I still hear 'em."

He was quiet for a spell. So were the rest of us.

"I was thinking that it might have been that woman's husband in that hay rick." Cole said.

"Was the wounded all our boys?"

"Dunno. Don't 'spose it matters. There wasn't much left when the fire died down and what there was the hogs et."

We all agreed it might have been the widow's man.

"They whupped us bad at Pea Ridge," said Jesse.

"So I heard," said Cole. "You couldn't prove it by me. It was then I decided for myself the war was over."

"What'd you do?"

"Picked up my gun and started walking."

"Where to?"

"Didn't matter." Cole shrugged. "Just so I got far away."

"Where'd you end up?"

"California."

We all of us sat there and said nothing. The stars were scattered across the sky like white hot cinders and the moon was up and so bright that maybe Frank could've read a book by it. The night air was soft to the touch like it sometimes is in a Missouri summer. I thought I heard a mockingbird, but likely they'd all gone to sleep, so probably it was only an old hoot owl.

We cleaned our guns and made sure they was loaded proper, and I took a squat in the brush and we waited to hear the sound of yellow buggy wheels coming down road.

The Master of the Archives points again, this time at an older man. His hair is powdered with the white of age, but that has not dimmed his enthusiasm, his humor, nor his energy. He stands to receive the golden light, knowing suddenly that not all that is black belongs to darkness, neither is all that is white owned by light. People change with the pressures of living, and are consistently remolded by the decisions they make.

When the mist beyond his door clears, the man finds heat and harsh sunlight, the scent of sagebrush, and a hard life where the dedicated must do their best to be remembered. He enters:

LEGENDS

by Ed Gorman

THEY were mocking the eastern reporter again, speaking in lisps, having him say all sorts of nancy boy things.

Pat Garrett, the lawman, was getting tired of it. They'd been two days traveling and the two deputies wouldn't give it up. True, the reporter, Giles Staley, hadn't been a prime example of masculinity, but he'd hadn't been the prancing flower they made him out to be. They didn't really believe he was a flower either.

What they did believe was that he was an educated man and all educated men were to be mocked, at least behind their backs. They probably did the same to the rugged six-two Garrett himself. He'd come from a moneyed family in the South—moneyed at least until the war—and was reasonably well-educated.

These two, Logan and Kerry, were prairie scum, gunnies down from Kansas who'd ended up as lawmen despite lengthy criminal records of their own. Garrett had taken them along because he couldn't find anybody and was in a hurry.

This was the night of July 12, 1881, around a campfire on the Pecos River. Garrett, the sheriff of Lincoln

County, had received a tip 48 hours ago that Billy The Kid was hiding at Pete Maxwell's ranch near Fort Sumner. Billy had been sentenced to hang for murder—one of several he'd been eligible to stand trial for—but he'd escaped and was now on the run again. Hunting Billy was awkward for Garrett. For a three-month period between lawman jobs, Garrett had been a bartender at a saloon where Billy hung out. They two became friends. Billy was bright, amusing, and difficult to rile unless you really worked at it.

Now Garrett was hunting him down.

Logan, wearing the yellow mask the campfire painted on his features, finished sipping coffee from a battered tin cup and said, "You know what, Sheriff?"

"What?" Garrett said wearily. He just wanted to be shut of these two. They were always picking at him in the guise of asking him questions. They despised anybody they suspected was superior to them. They despised a lot of people.

"We've been wonderin' if you could actually kill him if you had to."

"Yeah" Kerry said, "You bein' friends with him and all."

"I can handle it."

"Maybe when we find him, you should let us go in and take him," Logan said.

Garrett sighed. "If you're worried about the reward, we split it three ways, no matter who actually brings him in."

Logan and Kerry looked at each other with their stupid prairie faces and grinned like birthday kids. "You mean you're cuttin' both of us in?"

"That's what I said, isn't it?"

"Sumbitch," Logan said gleefully. "Sumbitch!"

"There's two things I'm gonna be buyin' myself," Kerry said, "a bottle full of good whiskey and a dress full of bad woman."

Garrett pulled his hat down over his eyes and lay flat on his bedroll, pretending to sleep. He was thinking about what that reporter, Staley, had said, the advice he'd given Garrett. Garrett had been angry. "I'm just tellin' you how things are back in New York, Mr. Garrett. That's all. The rest is up to you. Entirely your decision."

Garrett didn't want to think about the advice, but he couldn't help it.

Logan and Kerry finally went to sleep. Garrett lay there enjoying the moonshadow night and the Pecos symphony, frog and hoot owl and rolling star-glistening river.

I'm just tellin' you how things are back in New York, Mr. Garrett.

The rest is up to you.

"That the best you could do for deputies?" the town marshal of Fort Sumner asked Garrett the next morning. Logan and Kerry had put on their usual show of smirking and winking at each other and trying to bring everybody around them down to their level.

Garrett snorted. "Hell, I was gonna ask you if you needed a couple of new deputies. I'd sell 'em to you real cheap."

O'Gar was the town marshal's name. Like Garrett, and despite the heat, he wore a suit. Also like Garrett, he carried a Single Action Army six-shooter.

"I went to a sheriff's convention up in Denver last year," O'Gar said, putting his well-polished boots up on his desk. "They say that the days are coming to an end when men like those two can wear a badge. Personally, I won't hire nobody who hasn't been through the fourth grade, and have nothing worse than drunk and disorderly on their law record."

Garrett had liked the man at first. Now his self-importance was getting wearisome.

Apparently, O'Gar sensed this because he changed the subject. "You and Billy were friends."

"Yes."

"Hell of a thing, have to go after a friend this way."

"It's my job."

O'Gar's eyes narrowed. "You figurin' on takin' him alive?"

I'm just tellin' you how things are back in New York, Mr. Garrett.

The rest is up to you.

"If I can."

O'Gar nodded. "Good. I had to hunt down a cousin of mine. Sonofabitch forced me to draw down on him. I meant to wound him, but he moved at the last minute, and I got him in the chest. He was dead by the time we got a doc there. Now half my family won't speak to me. Every time I go to a family reunion some uncle or cousin of mine gets drunk and wants to fight me. It just ain't worth killin' anybody you like, believe me."

"Thanks for the advice." O'Gar didn't seem to get the irony.

O'Gar took his feet down. "You want any help? I'd be glad to ride along."

"No, I just wanted to let you know what was going on."

"I take it you'll wait till night."

"Sure. Though I'll probably ride out there this afternoon. Take a look at the place. See how it's all laid out."

"You know how to get there?"

Garrett smiled. "I will as soon as you draw me a map."

"Billy The Kid," O'Gar said, marveling. "Now there'll be somethin' to tell your grandkids."

He took a piece of white paper and began to draw Garrett a map.

The Texas sun was never kind. Today it was sadistic. Thunderheads rode the sky to the west, but too often the rains were as bitter and humid as the heat. By the time he reached the grassy hills above the Pete Maxwell ranch, Garrett had laid his suit jacket across the pommel of his saddle and unbuttoned his shirt until the slight hairy pot of his belly could be seen. Wasn't likely he'd meet any womenfolk out here.

After ground-tying his horse, Garrett took his field glasses and canteen from his saddlebag and walked over to a corpse of scrub pines. This was a good vantage point, he could see the ranch house as well as the outbuildings.

Pete Maxwell was an old friend of Garrett's. He was also an old friend of Billy's. He was in the same situation as Garrett. He probably felt he owed it to Billy to hide him out.

The ranch was prosperous, the outbuildings newly painted, the ranch house neat and trim with flowers planted along the front walls and fresh white curtains hung in the windows. Maxwell's wife had obviously been busy. Men talked about the hard work they did. Women did the same amount or more, but kept their mouths shut. One more reason that Garrett had always preferred the company of women. Men were too full of themselves.

He spent an hour in the shade, watching. Through his field glasses, he watched as Pete and his hands worked in the barn and then led a couple of mustangs down to a rope corral. Not exactly what you'd call thrilling. There was no sign of Billy. Garrett was beginning to wonder if his tip had been wrong. He knew a U.S. Marshal who'd traveled all the way to Illinois to pick up a long-sought fugitive only to learn that his information had been wrong. The fugitive was in Ohio. The informant had gotten his states confused. Such were the vagaries of tips.

As the shadows grew longer and darker, and the wind began to carry a hint of thunderstorm coolness, Garrett saw Billy peek his head out the front door and yell something at Pete. Garrett stared at Billy. The Kid looked tired and pale. He slouched against the door. He wore no shirt and looked frail, with noticeably stooped shoulders and prominent ribs. Garrett wondered if he'd been sick or wounded somehow. But, no, it was being on the run. Even for somebody like Billy, who'd never seemed to run out of energy, hiding out had to take its toll. Being trapped could sap a man as surely as a bullet.

Garrett thought of what the reporter had said. He had to smile about the way Staley would write this up. Instead of a pale and worn Billy appearing in the door, it'd be a snarling Billy with guns in both fists, beating up on the ranch hands because he didn't have anything better to do. All those eastern reporters wrote that sort of thing. Truth didn't seem to inhibit them.

I'm just tellin' you how things are back in New York, Mr. Garrett.

The rest is up to you.
Garrett mounted up and headed back to town.

Garrett had just hitched his horse to a post when Marshal O'Gar spotted him and walked quickly across the street.

"Those deputies of yours?" he said. "None of my business, Sheriff, but they're in the Silver Saddle over there gettin' good and drunk with one of Pete Maxwell's boys."

Garrett didn't want to give O'Gar the pleasure of feeling any more superior, so instead of cursing or groaning, he simply said, "Obliged." Then he headed across the dusty street to the saloon.

Logan and Kerry were at a poker table in the back. He saw them through a literal fog of smoke. The place was crowded as the day drew to an end. It was the usual Texas saloon mix of drovers, town laborers, gamblers, and men who tried to convince you they were gunslicks. They mostly paraded around with low-slung holsters and high-slung sneers, trying to impress each other like ladies with new dresses on Easter morning. There were a few hurdy-gurdy girls, too. There'd be many more tonight, charging clumsy men 20 cents a dance to the songs the player piano put out. Other favors bestowed by the hurdy-gurdy girls cost even more.

Garrett went over and sat down.

"Hey, Sheriff," Logan said, his voice wobbly with liquor. "Want you to meet a good friend of ours, Burt Wylie."

Wylie was dressed dusty, a callow cowpoke who might not have reached his majority yet. "I've heard a lot about you, Sheriff Garrett."

"I'll bet you have," Garrett said. He glared at Logan and Kerry. Oh, they were fine ones, they were.

Wylie said, "I guess I'd better be headin' out. I told Pete I'd only be gone a couple hours and it's been four already." He smiled drunkenly. "He talks a lot about you, Sheriff Garrett. How you're friends and all."

"He's a good man."

"Yes; yes, he is," Wylie said. He looked as if he might cry. He was suddenly stricken with that beery sadness only drunks know, when you can get sentimental about virtually anything, from another person to a rock you found on the railroad tracks. "I'll tell you, you couldn't ask for a better boss." He still gave the impression he was about to burst into tears.

He stood up. Or tried to. He was weaving pretty badly. "You gents take it easy."

"You take it easy, too, Burt," Logan said.

"You're a good man, Burt," Kerry said.

They were just as drunk and ridiculously sentimental as young Wylie. They sounded as if they'd start bawling, too. What a fine trio they were.

Garrett watched Wylie until he made it outside.

"You boys happy?" Garrett said, scowling at them.

"You pissed or something?" Logan said.

"Am I pissed or something? Do you know who he works for?"

"Sure. He told us," Kerry said. "He works for Pete Maxwell."

"Exactly. And he's going to ride back to Maxwell's ranch and tell him all about meeting you two and then me."

"We didn't say nothin' about Billy to him," Logan said. "Honest. We're not exactly stupid."

"Damned right we're not," Kerry said.

"But you said something about me."

Logan and Kerry glanced at each other then looked back to Garrett.

"We said we was your deputies, was all," Logan said.

"We didn't say nothin' about huntin' Billy or nothin'," Kerry said.

"You didn't have to. You think Pete won't be able to figure that out for himself when he hears I'm this far up the Pecos with two deputies? What the hell else would I be doing up here?"

Garrett stood up.

"Hey, where you goin'?" Kerry said. "Sit down here and have a drink with us."

"I've got business," Garrett said. "You two haul your asses down the street to the restaurant and put some food in your belly. And start pourin' coffee down your throats. That's an order."

Garrett left.

He stood under the overhang of the saloon looking up and down the street. The day's activity on main street had slowed considerably. A water wagon went by, hosing down the dusty street. A pretty young woman passed on the boardwalk across the street, a bright blue parasol shading her face and giving her an air of fetching impertinence.

No sign of young Wylie anywhere. Hard to believe that he'd been able to mount up and ride already. Not in his condition. But apparently he had because there was no sign of him.

The sound came from around back. It was a comic sound, a drunk imploring his horse to stand still. Wylie.

Garrett went around back. It was a pathetic sight. Wylie had ground-tied his piebald in the narrow alley that contained loading docks for the various businesses.

"Just hold still, Rimrock," Wylie was saying to the horse. The horse was standing perfectly still, of course. It was Wylie who was having the trouble. He couldn't get his foot in the stirrup. He came close a couple of times. Close.

"Aw, Rimrock, why you doin' this to me? Ain't I always been nice to you?"

Garrett went over and picked up Wylie and pitched him up on the saddle.

Then he went around and picked up Rimrock's reins and started leading the animal out of the alley.

"Hey," young Wylie said. "Hey."

"Hey yourself."

"Hey, what the hell you think you're doin', anyway?"

"Just shut up and enjoy the ride."

Where he led Rimrock was the Sheriff's office. He yanked Wylie off Rimrock and dragged him inside. "Hey," Wylie kept saying. "Hey."

When he reached O'Gar's own office, he pushed Wylie inside.

"Drunk and disorderly, Marshal," Garrett said.

"Hey," Wylie said, petulantly drunk now. "I wasn't no drunk'n disorderly."

"I'd appreciate it if you lock him up for the night," Garrett said.

O'Gar saw what Garrett wanted. Or didn't want. No way Wylie could tip off Billy if Wylie was sleeping it off in a cell.

"My pleasure," O'Gar said. He looked at Wylie and smiled. "He looks like a pretty dangerous sonofabitch to me."

"He is," Garrett said. "He killed twenty-four men at the Silver Saddle this afternoon."

"Hey," Wylie said, glaring at Garrett. "Hey."

"I'll bring his horse around back and tie him up there." Garrett said.

By the time he walked back to the Silver Saddle, night had started to stain the sky with gray and starry dusk.

He did his best to disregard Logan and Kerry on the ride out to the Maxwell ranch. They were sober now, but that didn't make them any smarter or more tolerable. He didn't say much to them, and after a time they took the hint and didn't say much to him either.

He spent his time mostly thinking about his life. He'd had big ambitions twenty years ago. None of them had come true. He thought his family background would help him, but it hadn't. Not even Rebs cared much for the fallen Southern aristocracy. Rich folks hadn't treated poor whites much better than they'd treated poor blacks.

As Staley the reporter had reminded him, Garrett's life as a lawman would have to be "sweetened up some" to make a book. Sweetened up being the treatment that the heroes of dime novels got. And then the only way the book would interest the New York folks was the Billy The Kid story.

Riding out to capture the Kid, he felt more alone than he ever had in his life. His marriage hadn't given him comfort in years; and his prospects for reelection to sheriff (after next year, the job would no longer be an appointive one) were grim.

They came to the ranch. It was night now. Lamplight glazed the windows.

Ranch folks went to bed early. Garrett and his deputies had to wait until the windows went dark. No way they'd go in now.

"You scared, Garrett?" Kerry said, climbing on Garrett's ass again. They stood behind some pines, about three hundred feet from the ranch house.

Garrett said nothing.

Kerry winked at Logan. "I think he's scared."

Garrett turned and put a fist deep into Kerry's stomach. Kerry puked up all his booze and dinner. Logan started to draw, but Garrett was fast enough to put his gun in Logan's face before Logan could even find his holster.

Kerry kept whimpering like a sick animal in the swimming mosquito-thick gloom.

The lamps didn't go out for another hour and a half.

"I guess we can go in now," Logan said.

"Another half hour," Garrett said.

Logan frowned at Kerry, but said nothing.

Garrett consulted his railroad watch three times, during which Kerry took a noisy pee against a birch tree, and Logan twice asked Garrett why he couldn't light up a smoke. He sounded like a peevish child. Finally, the last time he consulted his watch, Garrett said, "Let's go."

They'd already discussed the method of attack. Garrett would go in the front door, the other two in the back.

They fanned out, crouched low, guns drawn, angling toward the house from different directions. They were half-running. The horses in the corral made some noise. So did the chickens in the small red shack. It was good noise, noise that covered the movement of the three men.

Garrett was freezing with sweat. He should be hot.

When he reached the front door, he hesitated only long enough to put his ear briefly to the slab of wood that filled the frame. He heard nothing. He opened the door and stepped in.

Moonlight was sufficient to show him the front room and the dining area to the right and the kitchen beyond. There was a hall straight down the center. This would be where the bedrooms were. He was still freezing.

He tiptoed to the hallway. There were two doors. Both were slightly ajar. He tiptoed down the hallway. He didn't worry about Logan and Kerry now. He heard snoring, wet loud middle-aged snoring. He eased open the door and peered inside. Pete Maxwell and his wife lay in a double bed. It was Mrs. Maxwell who was the snorer.

Suddenly, Pete sat up, wide awake. He started to go for the holstered pistol hanging on the bedpost above him. But Garrett pointed his own six-shooter directly at Pete's face and started walking silently forward.

When he was half a foot from Maxwell, he whispered. "I want Billy, Pete. This doesn't have anything to do with you."

Maxwell, a tall, gaunt man, grabbed Garrett's arm. "He's our friend," he whispered. "Yours and mine. You want to take him, take him alive."

"I plan to," Garrett whispered back.

Mrs. Maxwell went on snoring.

Garrett reached over and yanked Maxwell's six-shooter from its holster. "Wait here."

Just before he was to turn, he saw Pete Maxwell's face tighten in recognition of something behind Garrett.

Garrett turned. Billy The Kid stood in the doorway. Holding his own six-shooter on Garrett. The Kid wore a white cotton shirt and Levis.

"I'm not goin' back with you, Pat," Billy said. "They'll hang me for sure."

At this point, Mrs. Maxwell woke up. She sat up and drew the covers modestly around her neck and shoulders. She made wet smacking sounds with her lips. She looked profoundly confused. Her husband putting a steadying hand on her arm.

"Then I guess you'll have to kill me," Garrett said quietly.

"Then I guess I will, Pat."

Billy raised the gun. "I thought we were friends, Pat."

"I'm just doing my job, Billy. You know that."

"Some other lawman could've come after me. It didn't have to be you."

"It's my jurisdiction, Billy. I didn't have any choice."

"I'm sure sorry you came here, Pat. I surely am."

Billy raised the gun even higher.

Garrett waited for the feel of the bullets tearing into

him. He could raise his own guns and fire. But he'd be dead by the time he squeezed off a shot.

"I really am sorry, Pat."

Billy pulled the hammer back.

Garrett could hear Mrs. Maxwell gasp. She knew that Billy was about to fire.

Billy lowered the gun and set it on a chair just inside the door.

He smiled. "Isn't that the damnedest thing, Pat? I can't do it. I can't shoot you." He put his hands out, as if waiting for handcuffs. "I guess I'll just have to escape all over again. And this time, you won't be able to find me. I promise you that."

I can't tell you what to do, Mr. Garrett. But I will say this. Put yourself in the reader's place. Which would be a more satisfactory ending for you. Pat Garrett brings Billy in peacefully—or Pat Garrett is forced to kill his old friend? Put yourself in the reader's place, Mr. Garrett. And put yourself in the publisher's place. Which ending do you think the publisher would like best?

"Out in the hall, Billy."

"What?"

"You heard me, Billy. Out in the hall. We're going straight out to the horses."

"You're the boss, Pat," The Kid smiled. "At least you think you are."

With no resistance whatsoever, the Kid turned around and started to walk out to the hall. "Appreciate your hospitality, Pete and Dora. Hope I can repay you someday."

Garrett followed Billy out into the hall.

Mrs. Maxwell said, half in tears, "I'm going to make Billy some fried chicken and take it to him in jail."

She'd lost two sons in her time. Billy had quickly become her new son. She was so attached to him that it scared Pete sometimes. Could a woman lose three sons and survive?

Pete saw two figures passing down the hallway now. Pat's deputies. Even in the shadows, they looked scruffy.

The shots came then. Two of them. Two quick shots. Booming and echoing in the house.

Mrs. Maxwell screamed.
She knew full well who'd been shot.

They threw Billy's body across of one of Maxwell's horses and started back. Even when they were a good distance away, they could hear Mrs. Maxwell sobbing and cursing Garrett.

They rode slowly down the dusty moonlit road. The horse carrying Billy lagged behind. The night smelled of the Pecos and the dusty bamma grasses and the dead heat of the day.

Kerry said, "You know, it's a funny thing, Sheriff Garrett. You know how you told Maxwell that Billy spun around and tried to jump you. From where I stood, it looked more like you turned him around and shot him."

"That's kinda what it looked like to me, too," Logan said. Winking at Kerry.

Garrett said nothing. He'd brought a couple of saddlebums along because he'd known that whatever happened, nobody would take their word over his. Nobody.

I'm in the legend business, Mr. Garrett. Yessir. Some people say I'm in the writing business. But that's not true at all. I'm in the legend business. And you bring Billy The Kid in dead—well, you'll not only make a lot of money, Mr. Garrett. You'll be as big a legend as The Kid himself. You've got my word on that.

All those years of drifting from his home in the South, all those years of one quiet defeat after another. But there were all behind him now.

As the lights of Fort Sumner began appearing in the prairie to the west, Garrett wondered what kind of cover they'd put on his book.

Throughout history, there are individuals who achieve great honor. Some are forgotten from the annals of mankind. For those who become the embodiment of that virtue, a special place is reserved in the Archives. The Walker of Two Worlds turns his attention to a woman of strong heart and clear mind. She rises as black-and-rose light cascades from the being's fingers and surrounds her like a cloak. Pacing across the hall with her back erect and head held high, she finds her door. Beyond it, she makes her way through dry windswept terrain to the shelter of jagged cliffs. She will now experience:

THE WIND AT TRES CASTILLOS

by Robyn Fielder

OCTOBER 15, 1880

Jagged rocks bit into Lozen's fingers she scrambled into the stone cleft where her brother lay. She squatted next to him. His gray-streaked dark hair danced under her heaving breath, and the sandstone beneath him was dark with his life's blood.

Two years at San Carlos had brought solemn age to his features.

She touched his face once, briefly. "Ah, Victorio . . ." she murmured. "Stay with me, Victorio, for just a little while. . . ."

His chest rose and fell, but no light came to his eyes. The rifles had gone quiet.

She crept to the ledge and peered over. The fall sun hung high in the south, and glinted dull silver from the barrels of Mexican rifles aimed at her people. She wiped stringy spittle from her lips; her hand tasted of dust. Against the east mesa, soldiers piled the bodies of the fallen warriors, her neighbors and friends, with less care than an Apache would take in stacking fire wood.

Moving back to her brother's side, she lowered her eyes; he might suddenly wake, and he must not see her desperation.

Her practiced touch poked life back into the smoldering medicine fire she'd built beside him. She twirled a leaf of nopal into the flames, burning the thorns from it. As each thorn blackened, a drop of nectar sizzled and effervesced sweetly. When the last thorn had hissed away into the fire, Lozen lay the leaf on a flat rock and split it precisely in two with the oak-handled bayonet she'd once pulled from her own shoulder in battle. With fingers as light as butterflies on trembling petals, she redressed the wound in Victorio's chest.

Too soon she would be the last of her clan.

Many of the women and children had been captured and herded together like cattle at the back of the ravine under Mexican guard. Out of the nearly two hundred Apache who had been here yesterday, less than thirty held out with her in the rocks of the mesa—and ten of those had just arrived with her from the horse raid.

All the horses and the mules had been taken, even the burros; she'd seen the Mexican soldiers feeding the gaunt, desperate animals, had seen their starvation-defined ribs heaving as they bit and kicked at each other, vying for the best feeding spots. Yet, back in the ravine, watched by high-capped soldiers, the captured women and their belly-swollen children had suffered, forced to sit without shade or water in the hot noonday sun. And then, under guard, they'd been marched out toward Mexico City.

Those who would survive the long march without food or water would be sold. The Mexicans found no profit in caring for them: everyone knew the Apache made poor slaves, anyway.

This disaster, it was her fault. She could have saved them.

She should have been here.

Victorio's blood-black bandage came way with the original nopal leaf; fresh blood leaked from the wound. His stomach was distended and hard. She quickly placed the freshly prepared leaf on the wound, and began the binding ritual.

As her mouth stumbled over the words of healing, her rough bloodshot eyes tracked the slow arc of a fly that lazily circled the open wound in Victorio's chest. The fly lowered, preparing to settle and suck at the sweet clotting blood of the dying chief. Lozen snatched it out of the air; in the same motion she threw it into the wind.

Her dreams had been full of flies.

The dark dream had come upon her for the fourth time early last night, just after she and her small cadre of warriors had reached the United States Army outpost just across the border. They'd made a cold camp and had tried to sleep under the stars before raiding the horses.

The dream had seized her immediately: an owl called and flew through a hollow ring-cloud of swarming insects, flies that filled the night; the owl swallowed the morning star, and landed on the top of a pole flying a Mexican flag, and beneath the flag hung the scalped, dismembered, naked corpse of her brother. Black death-blood pushed out his eyes, his stomach swelled and burst. His entrails tumbled to earth in slick ropy loops, while all around him the white man laughed.

She'd woken in a sweat, ready to abandon the horse raid. But Victorio's plans—the survival of the tribe—hinged on fresh horses.

In the mad race into the desert that followed the escape from San Carlos, many of the mounts had been ridden to foaming death. They'd been eating those horses that had come up lame, or had exhausted themselves.

They needed speed to stay ahead of the white man's armies. She'd waited half the night for the best opportunity to steal the fresh horses for Victorio, and it had cost him his life.

She had to get her brother out of here, dead or alive.

His wound was the same as in the vision.

The ends of the fresh bandage pulled tight in her hands. At her touch, his eyes opened and dragged themselves into feeble focus. She pursed her chapped lips. The gentle tending of his wound had been painful enough to rouse him.

His eyes smiled up at her, their crow's feet crinkling the same as they always had. "Lozen," he said in quiet greeting. "Welcome back, sister. I am sorry that I slept through your return."

By way of answer, she put the sweet meat of the nopal fruit in his mouth; he sucked on it gratefully, smiling still wider as the medicine she'd put in the nopal eased his thirst and fever.

With all of her power, she could do no more than prolong his life a few hours. She'd done this more for her sake than for his; she could not let him go. She couldn't save his life, but she would never surrender to that dark vision.

A twirling tendril of smoke climbed between them and stung her eyes, drawing tears that muddied her dust-caked face. She turned to tend the small medicine fire; it shouldn't be smoking.

It wasn't.

Curious, she sniffed the air. An unmistakable reek of fresh fire rode the soft breeze. For a moment her eyes refused to focus. She teetered to her feet. Strong magic tossed her like a current in an invisible river. She stumbled and caught herself against the rocks, hugging the warm stone until the dizziness passed.

"Scayocarne," she called, low. The young warrior turned from his cover in a rocky cleft. "Tend the chief," she said, "and give me your rifle."

He nodded silently; he handed her his rifle as he passed by to Victorio's side. The weathered stock was warm and dark with his sweat.

She pulled herself up onto the sharp ledge, balancing painfully on her belly. Pinpoints of red-and-orange fire winked dimly at her, dotting the base of the mesa as far as she could see to either side: small kindling fires with black-shirted men to tend them. The men signaled each other with shouts in a foreign tongue.

A squat, fat black-shirted man near the largest fire threw back his head and pummeled the mesa with a shrill cowbird song, singing a spell that pulled at her like quicksand. The kindling fires burst into flame in unison. Soldiers stationed at each fire leaped back startled, and jerkily turned and unrolled long heavy blankets, revealing bodies of fallen warriors.

Sun-kissed metal drew her attention back to the fat screeching shaman. He'd pulled a knife, then fell upon the corpse at his feet, slicing with long-armed arcs. His knife came away glowing red and with something skewered that could be a liver or perhaps a heart. He turned to the fire, still singing, and threw the scavenged organ into the flames.

Instantly, cascading rainbows haloed each fire, then each rainbow darkened as though scorched and charred, and melted into the crackling flames.

Lozen thumbed the range gauge on the rifle's rear sight into position, centered the front sight on the fat black-shirted chest, and fired.

A harsh wind howled across the open mesa, buffeting tumbleweeds high into the air. Lozen's hair whipped violently around her head, stinging her face and eyes. She was nearly sucked from her precarious perch. Pain stabbed deep inside her ears as though she'd climbed a high mountain. She opened and closed her jaw, her ears clicking until the pain subsided.

The wind died; the shaman stood unhurt. She fired again, and again, kicking dust up from the desert floor far from him.

There must be a wind between them that she could not feel.

A dead calm settled the dust, and she watched a tall warrior approach the shaman as though to strike him. Without fear this warrior walked past the Mexican soldiers.

She knew this man, she felt sure: his gait was familiar to her, agile and powerful at once.

The warrior faced the short singing shaman, and every sinew in his lean body tensed. The shaman spoke to him; he turned to the fire and reached into its yellow center, pulling the seared organ from the flames. As though fire could not burn him, he did not flinch from the heat.

This was not man, but spirit.

He held the smoking organ in his hand and turned to face the mesa; he blew his breath across it. Smoke poured from his hand and he began to lope with a wolf's easy pace around the mesa's base. Each fire that he passed erupted with the same thick smoke, forming a bridge linking them one by one.

His path led him below Lozen's position. As he neared, she gasped.

She did know him. She had known him more than half her life.

It was the Wind himself: the Gray Ghost Chief.

As he passed below her, his head snapped up and his spirit eyes looked into hers.

She swallowed hard, but no use: her heart was caught in her throat.

A blanket of churning smoke boiled up the base of the low mesa. The smoke roiled and tumbled; first thick, then thin, climbing the steep walls like a sea of lizards. It rose and arched up severely, wiping away the horizon.

The boundaries of her world were shrinking.

The nightmare vision unfolded.

"Lozen . . ."

The deep breathy voice caressed her ear, drawing out her name with a long soft sigh. He had come to her.

Something stroked her inner thigh. She dared not look behind her.

Jumping down, Lozen ran for a new vantage, heading across the mesa. As she dashed past Scayocarne and Victorio, she snapped. "We must get him out of here now!"

Nana, the tribe's eldest councillor, had also crawled close. Scayocarne snapped Victorio's salt-stained horse blanket in the air. Before it had settled flat, Nana was tossing Victorio's belongings onto it.

"No. Stop," Victorio whispered. The frail words stilled both warriors. Lozen had no time to stop and argue; she ran on.

Her strong legs quickly gained her a view of the circumference of their mesa camp. Leather-clad bodies hugged the cover of the sandstone. Straight black rifle barrels pointed off in all directions, their metal glinting in the sun like gem fire. The smoke clung tightly to the rocks and swarmed up the sides of the mesa, dwarfing her people in its scale; they were as ants in a mudslide.

The sweetness of roasting flesh filled the air. They were using the bodies of their own dead to smoke them out.

The Wind whispered in her ear. *"Lozen. You met my eyes once. Look at me."* His words clung to her like cobwebs. He was following her.

He was spirit and bound to her enemies: she must not look at him.

He carried with him the smell of coming rain, the scent of dark magic. As the leading edge of the smoke approached, wisps broke away from the cloud and seemed to fight for freedom, but were sucked back with violent force.

Her mouth went dry.

The smoke would settle on them, crawling inside their gasping noses and mouths; it would suffocate them. For those whose wills would break, rifles waited. Blind and helpless from the poisoned cloud, her people would emerge as targets.

She lifted her chin and set her lips in an uncompromising line. Standing in the open upon the rocky ledge, a black silhouette against the midday sky, she announced flatly, "They try to smoke us out."

Rifles barked below; she had attracted the attention of the Mexican soldiers.

Ignoring the sizzle of passing bullets, she leaped off the high rock with an easy grace. Her long, loose hair sprayed out against the pale blue sky like the outstretched wings of a raven. As she fell, she lifted her arm, twisting it in an obscene gesture at the soldiers below.

Tired laughter rumbled from the rocks around her; some of the bitterly exhausted warriors managed to smile. Their applause was the scraping clicks of levering fresh rounds into their rifles. Quietly she added, "Fire into the smoke at the foot of the mesa."

Their answer was a fresh volley of rifle fire. The taste of burned gunpowder peppered her mouth.

Soft laughter also followed at her heels.

"You are still the girl I knew." His words smiled with their sound. *"Unbind me, Lozen."*

He smelled of the tall trees and yucca flowers of home. She felt at this moment as though she could sleep with the peace of a child.

Quietly alarmed by the range of his power over her, she said, "I know you. For the first time, I know you for what you are, Gray Ghost." She gathered her will and forced herself to name him, "You are Wind."

She stared out over the vast empty desert, beyond the ring of soldiers. "You teased me before with your promises. You are Wind. If I free you, your rage will sweep us all away, friend and foe, to a pounding death." Bitterness painted her words.

"And if I kill you all, no white man will defile your

brother's body, nor the bodies of any of the rest of you. This I promise." His voice was warm and kind on the surface—but she heard the echo of his buried fury.

Scrambling nimbly over the rocks, she made her way back to her brother's side.

Victorio drowsily watched her spring from boulder to rugged boulder like a mountain lion. His grinning face was pale, like the moon riding low over the red horizon of the sandstone at his back. Night was closing in around his life. If he could see the spirit at her shoulder, he made no sign.

Lozen tucked the rifle into the crook of her elbow. She fished a rag out of the water bowl at his side, squeezing the dripping water from it with a shake, and wiped Victorio's flushed brow. His hand met hers and pulled the cloth from her fingers. He dragged it across her face, pulling it back dark with the dust of three days' hard riding. Suddenly aware of her sweat-stiffened clothes and sour reek, she took the rag back from him and silently cleaned her own face.

From behind her, a cool gentle breeze rubbed under her arm and along her breast, hardening her nipples. The Wind was at her back. She remembered meeting him so many years ago, when he'd come as a guest to their homes in the Black Mountains.

She had been so young, and he had been so beautiful. . . .

His cool breeze blew past her, moving across them all, drying the fever-sweat on Victorio's face.

"Victorio, can you move?" she asked. Her voice trembled; the spirit was becoming ever harder to ignore. "We must fight our way out *now*—it is almost too late."

"Surrender, sister. As soon as I die . . . surrender. They believe that I am already dead. When the time comes, do this. Surrender . . . for me. Do not fight Geronimo's endless war . . . Choose *life*."

Her veins frosted with the cold of a desert night. The hair prickled on her arms. Had he gone mad with fever?

Her voice failed her; a muffled moan escaped her throat. He was throwing himself off the dark cliff of her dream.

Cocking her head to the left and lowering her forehead like a bull, she stared down at her cracked and dusty boots, avoiding Victorio's eyes. "Victorio, do you *remember* San Carlos?" Her voice faltered.

He said nothing.

He reached up and gently took the rifle from her arm. She gave a sigh that was almost a sob; he caught her hand, and pulled her against him; though his lean arm had no strength, he tried to comfort her just as he had when they'd been children.

Between them hung all the days of San Carlos, each day rotting in memory, flightless and still; the unrelenting heat and the tiny brick ovens that the soldiers called houses, the idleness and the pointless pacing within the stagnant cage. She thought of little Eliza: a two-year-old girl who'd been born in San Carlos. For the child, the world stretched only as far as the high stockade wall. During the escape, she had wailed in terror at the sight of the setting sun.

An Apache daughter afraid of the open earth and sky.

How many had died at San Carlos, of sickness and broken spirits?

Lozen could never forget—and she could see the memory in Victorio's eyes.

After their escape, they had not run toward Geronimo; they had not tried to join his war. They had run for home. Their mad dash east had come to this ugly end, here in this foreign desert.

They'd raced blindly from one white army into the sights of another.

Smoke poked at her eyes.

"There was no wind at San Carlos, Lozen." Each whispered word tapped the artery on her neck. *"But here I can help you, if you free me."*

He was a liar. He served the black-shirted shaman.

Blood pounded in her ears.

She broke from Victorio's embrace. Gaining her feet, she left the rifle behind and moved low along the rocks. Ahead, she saw a pair of blackened barrels pointing down at the soldiers below; one of the barrels bore a bright scrape that she recognized. "Gouyen?" she called, hoping.

A pair of eyes came up over the ridge: it *was* Gouyen, her short black hair stringy with sweet and dust. A smile flickered briefly across Lozen's hard mouth; her first bit of luck this day was in finding her friend alive.

The second rifle barrel weaved unsteadily. Gouyen reached back to steady it, and out from behind the boulder stepped her four-year-old son, Kaywaykla.

"Make a travois for Victorio," Lozen told her. "We will fight our way to the fresh horses."

Gouyen gave a quick nod. Taking both rifles, Gouyen surged through the rocks, her tiny son close at her heels.

Lozen came back silently to Victorio. She furrowed her brow and chewed her lip, absently batting at the swirling smoke that the Gray Ghost threw at her. Coughing broke out in the lower rocks.

A strand of her long hair flicked across her face; it already reeked with the sweet-sour smoke.

She moved her face against her brother's cheek and softly stroked his hair as she whispered, "We must try to run to the fresh horses now, Victorio."

His breath rattled deep in his chest. He clenched his teeth, his eyes flinched, and then weakly he slurred, "No . . . sur . . . surrender now . . ." He fought for air and continued with stoic determination. "Live—don't die the same day I die . . . our clan dies with you . . . as if we never were."

His hand edged up his dark, heavily muscled chest; his fingers touched her lips, begging her not to speak. Satisfied that she understood, he let his hand drop limply to his side. After a long pause of labored breathing, he continued, "They promised no harm . . . surrender, let no more die. The war is over. Live now, sister."

She didn't know whether to lie down in the dirt next to him sobbing, or shout at him and shake sense into him.

No matter how many times he'd been betrayed, he gave faith to a man's word until he was proven wrong. Lozen didn't know if Victorio truly believed the Mexicans' promises. On a different day, she would have sharply reminded him of the betrayals they'd suffered. It was Victorio's way: he had always sought peace, had always counseled against Geronimo's hopeless desert war to the death.

She had seen the end to which surrender would bring them; she had dreamed it.

She swallowed her bitter words, and mopped his hot forehead with a clean bit of cloth.

She'd never been more alone.

"There is another way." The soft voice behind her froze her in her tracks.

A faint breeze tickled the nape of her damp neck. She could almost feel his lips against her ear. *"You are more powerful than they are, Lozen. . . . You alone have the power to break the magic that binds me to the smoke and to this mesa. . . ."*

The Gray Ghost reached an arm around her. His perfectly formed hand waved before her eyes, and he showed her that the wisps of smoke writhing around her were the convulsions of tiny spirits-of-the-air. She gasped and unconsciously rolled back away from the tortured spirits, and into the surprising firmness of the Gray Ghost behind her. His other arm slipped around her waist. Holding her gently, he revealed to her the agony of a thousand twisted shrieking faces.

It was to her spirit eyes as though Slayer of Monsters had never existed.

The Gray Ghost's desert breath tousled her hair playfully against her neck and cheek, *"Unbind us, and I promise that Victorio's body will not be defiled."*

She felt ancient and feeble.

Choosing between two deaths did not come easily to her.

Silently she pulled herself free of him and reached out to Victorio again.

Behind her she felt the mounting power; her skin tingled as though lighting had struck nearby.

His voice spit venom into her ear: *"Or you can choose to die here like a whipped dog, and let them parade your contrary corpse on a stake in front of the Apache that you left behind in the stockades of San Carlos. Or perhaps they will send the head and scalp of the great Lozen, Shaman, Horse thief, Spirit Woman, Warrior, as a message to Geronimo himself that the white magic is greater and their council wiser."*

She turned on her heels, snarling like a bobcat, and

raised her hand to strike him. The smoke was thick. She gasped once, reduced to a fit of coughing. The smoke squirmed through his body; every bit of him was alive and twisting in silent agony. His desperate eyes clawed at her like a bear, holding her tight, tighter . . .

"Lo-zen . . . are you here?" Victorio sputtered weakly, ". . . can't see you . . ."

Tears ran down her cheeks, blurring the Gray Ghost's power; she pulled free with a gasp of effort.

Victorio's eyes were wide open, death-blind. "I'm here," she said. Her fingers feebly twined themselves into her brother's.

Chin trembling, his face contorted as he gathered strength to speak, "Surrender. San Carlos wasn't as bad as dying here."

He coughed shallowly, and blood trickled down his pale lip. He quieted and braced himself to go on. "Wherever they send you can't be worse . . . we escaped—can escape again . . . Lozen, please—fight later. You are all . . . my family . . . dead—wife, children—they wash us away like so much sand in a river. . . . Marry, make children, find a way home. . . ."

Victorio's head fell back against the filthy horse blanket. His fingers quivered in her hand. ". . . gave your life as council—my guide . . . do this last thing—*live.*"

His body jerked once as his muscles gave out with the effort. His wild eyes closed, and she listened as his short breaths rasped in his throat.

What could she say? He had always treated her with respect, as though she were White Painted Woman herself. How could she dare to refuse his dying wish?

She pulled herself up just short of revealing her vision to him.

She fought to swallow around the lump in her throat. That his body would be used as a weapon against them all—she would *not* let that be his dying thought.

The coughing rose from all around the mesa camp.

Someone sputtered within the smoke at Lozen's back. It was Gouyen, with the travois.

Victorio continued, "Nana. You—chief . . . surrender . . . now . . . I . . ." Victorio's fingers went suddenly limp in Lozen's grip. His mouth hung slack, and his wild eyes quieted and fixed on a point far above and to his left. She followed his eyes to the sky to share his final vision.

The morning star shone near the afternoon sun. And then the sky was swallowed by the smoke.

Now it was too late: her silence had betrayed her.

Nana was older, and weary, and loyal to the bone. Without fail, he would solemnly fulfill his chief's last request.

Lozen's face contorted with anguish; it was as if she were tumbling out of control down a black pit, her body buffeted from wall to wall.

On the other side of Victorio's body, Nana turned away from her. Holding a dampened cloth to his nose, he muddled his way through the rocks and was swallowed by the venomous veil of smoke.

Gouyen stood still holding the travois, on her face a silent question.

"Help her," Lozen snapped at Scayocarne who kneeled across from her at Victorio's side. He paused. And then, deciding that there was no conflict in placing Victorio's body on the travois, he slowly complied.

Nana's ragged voice cut through the smoke, "We will come down now. We put down our rifles, and we will come down."

"They'll kill you all and flaunt your corpses," the Wind howled in her ear.

Lozen frantically tied Victorio's body into the travois. "Up. Now *up!* To the horses. *Go!*"

At the head of the travois, Gouyen lurched forward and was nearly thrown off of the rock with a jolt. Scayocarne, who held the travois' foot, hadn't budged. Victorio's body pitched and rolled, falling half out of the travois.

Scayocarne turned on Lozen, and met her gaze, defying her. Just as she dared defy the new chief's surrender.

In heavily accented words, a Mexican soldier called up from below, "Send down Victorio's body. Then each of you can follow—one by one. With no weapons in your hand. No guns . . . no knives . . . no—"

Lozen's head snapped around. A roar of curses ripped from her throat like a barrage of thunder rolling across a blackened sky. As though from a great distance, she heard her own husky voice.

"I would first *eat* Victorio, before any white man should even *see* his body!"

The faint echo of her words bounced back and forth between the high dry mesas of Tres Castillos.

The wind whispered at her back, *"For love of your brother, unbind me. End this."*

She could see no other path.

Slowly she turned, daring not to breathe.

The tall, proud form coalesced out of the smoke—the Gray Ghost Chief stooped before her. She looked into his face. Her hair blew back away from her face, and she found it hard to breathe, as if she stood at the edge of the world.

Seventeen years had left no mark of age upon him. He was more handsome than even her generous memory recalled. She'd been sixteen when he had ridden into her village; he had spoken their language with ease, and had befriended Victorio. He'd stayed for weeks, and had weakened the knees of all the women in the village. Even her milky-eyed grandmother had giggled and blushed in his presence. In those days, they'd only *suspected* that he was not a man.

Lozen had measured all other men by the standard of beauty and power set in her adolescent mind by the Gray Ghost.

None had been able to compete. At thirty-three, she'd never married.

On a beautiful spring day seventeen years ago, he'd mounted his horse and rode out of Lozen's life without a word.

She faced him, knowing him, without fear. He stepped toward her, a head taller than Victorio, and though his features were similar to hers, his skin had gone darker. His eyes shone with lunacy, or malice. He held his hands clenched in white-knuckled fists at his side. He needed her.

His beauty pulled at her, singing of honorable death.

Gouyen touched her shoulder. "Lozen—what do you see?"

Lozen could not take her eyes from the Ghost Chief. "The wind," she said. "Death."

Gouyen was a warrior; somehow, she understood. Her touch became a squeeze of friendship, of trust. "But you are unarmed."

A ray of sunlight glinted on metal; Gouyen held out her knife, offering it to Lozen's hand—the very knife with which Gouyen had scalped the Comanche who'd murdered Kaywaykla's father.

Lozen could choose death for herself—but not for her whole people. She took the knife and broke away from the Ghost Chief's gaze. "We must run." She could feel his rage at her escape, and knew that he would punish her for this.

She stuck the knife behind her belt, and turned her gaze upon Scayocarne. "And you?"

The young warrior met her eyes, choosing between her fierce determination and Nana's surrender. He nodded once, and lifted the poles of the travois.

The smoke burned their eyes.

Blind, they stumbled through the rocks. Lozen led Gouyen forward by a fistful of her shirt. Little Kaywaykla clung with both hands to Lozen's belt. Lozen crept low, sending out her right hand as scout. Her extended fingertips jammed and split against the rocks in her search for solid ground. Lozen's foot skidded on loose gravel, rocks clattering down to either side of the narrow mesa ridge. She clutched Gouyen's shirt tighter, scrambling to get to her feet. Gouyen fell to her knees with a cry. Scayocarne's foot caught the edge of a boulder, anchoring both women with the lifeline of Victorio's travois.

Lozen's knees burned from the scraping, and her head throbbed with the poisoned air. She and Gouyen staggered to their feet. Kaywaykla still clung to Lozen's belt.

She brushed the gravel from her knees. Her hand came away sticky with blood.

And without warning they stepped into open air.

They stopped, stunned. Over the edge of the charcoal smoke lay the western horizon; thunderheads gathered in an azure sky.

A path had opened, like a cave with walls of black

smoke that led down to the deep reds and oranges of the desert floor. At the smoke-cave's mouth waited a cadre of rifle men, planted and ready. The Gray Ghost stood behind them, his arms extended, clearing the smoke from their line of sight.

They opened fire.

The first report split Lozen's sky in two. Wrenching her shirt out of Lozen's grip, Gouyen dropped the travois and covered Kaywaykla with her own body.

Victorio's head bounced ridiculously on the jagged rocks. Young Scayocarne numbly held on to the foot of the sliding travois. Mouth agape, he turned for cover, pulling Victorio behind him. Cloth ripped; the travois tore in half.

Lozen lunged to catch hold of Victorio's body. Her stone-split fingers caught his legging. She braced herself, and with all her might she stood straining; a profile of bloody soot. Her back arched against the weight of her brother's corpse as she used every fiber of muscle, every ounce of strength to stop him from falling away from her.

The broken pole of the travois had wedged between two boulders. Growling with determination, she heaved. With a lurch the travois came loose, clacking harmlessly against the rocks. As she stepped sideways and pulled his body to her, her own leg was knocked out from under her.

Searing heat radiated up her thigh as though the muscle had been packed with white hot coals. She fell sideways, scraping her ribs and shoulder against the unforgiving stone. Clenching her teeth against the pain, her contorted face squeezed fresh tears from under knotted lids.

Her bloody fingers locked on Victorio's lifeless leg.

"You can end this. . . ." The Gray Ghost's breath flirted with her ear. *"Break their binding spell."*

She twisted her head toward his voice. The shredded flesh over her ribs screamed with the movement. The Gray Ghost hovered over her; his face fluid with monstrous contortions. The unnatural magic ate away his beauty.

"You did this. You tricked me again."

"Not by my *will. Break the binding, you stubborn witch!"* The blast of his words scalded her face.

He'd gone mad. "Make a promise to me, Gray Ghost."

His response was a wordless howl of rage.

She dragged Victorio's body up behind the rocks. Blood pumped from her leg. Bullets splintered the rock all around her. The shards rained a thousand tiny cuts on her back and head, each one spitting blood onto the stone around her.

An occasional grunt followed a wet pop as enemy bullets found their targets. She could hear the soldiers below whooping with delight, cheering the marksmanship of their comrades.

Once she had Victorio's body securely hidden, she bound up the wound in her leg with cloth from the wrecked travois.

She could not carry him now.

She could not run.

The soft earthy smell of death surrounded her.

With extreme caution she raised her head inch by inch, checking all directions, to take in the situation of her warriors.

Her dead friends stared back with sightless eyes.

The smoke dipped and dodged at the edge of her vision.

The Gray Ghost would kill her people, one by one, before her eyes, until he had pushed her into complying with his demands—until he pushed her into releasing him to kill them all.

"Promise me," she cried. *"Promise me anything I ask, and I will break the binding!"*

His response was a bitter howl, and she understood that he could not violate the power that bound him.

The Gray Ghost whipped the spirits-of-the-air into a frenzy. The air around the mesa buzzed with the building fury of the host of tormented air-spirits.

They picked up sand and splintered rock, whirled it like daggers, scraping and pelting the entire mesa. Warriors dropped their rifles and batted at the smoke around them. The blinding sand in their eyes and mouths and throats was all they knew.

In her mind, the massacre before her slowed. She watched as her friends, men and women she'd known all her life, fearless warriors, stumbled blindly out from behind the rocks, rubbing at their sand-scored eyes. They jerked awkwardly to escape the biting fury of the flying stones. The Mexican army below shot them mercilessly.

Dimly she heard a baby shriek.

There would be no returning home to the gentle green of the Black Mountains, the healing warm springs, and the cold thrill of fresh mountain streams full of fish.

The baby went silent in mid-wail.

Lozen found herself on her feet out of cover, as though suspended by invisible hands. She held in her mind the lush hills of home. She watched herself walk east along a gently winding white path. A double of herself approached to meet her, just as had happened to White Painted Woman.

The bullets whizzed around her. She calmly faced the Wind.

It was too much. This would end now.

Low words tumbled loosely from her calm face. "Gray Ghost."

He stopped his torment, and rushed her as a hunting hawk swoops down on its prey. His teeth were jagged and dark, his face ugly and pointed, the flesh stretched tight, his beautiful eyes gone to pinpoints of pure malice.

"Just as White Painted Woman spent her life alone, so have I." Her words set a cadence, their magic surged up her spine, nearly lifting her toes off the ground.

In the world of spirit she greeted her double. They merged together and turned sunwise west, the direction from which she had just come. They walked as one into a spectral sunset of golds, reds, and star-speckled deep azure, just as White Painted Woman had done.

The Gray Ghost flashed in circles around her, concealing Lozen in a vortex of smoke, that she might finish the unbinding without threat from the Mexican army's bullets.

"I cannot refuse White Painted Woman," he murmured. *"Her, I promise anything."*

In the world of flesh her voice continued, slowly, deliberately cutting through the death rattles of dying warriors all around her.

"For want of children and power White Painted Woman first slept with the Sun and gave birth to Slayer-of-Monsters, and four days later she became pregnant by the Water, and gave birth to Born-of-Water. Together Slayer-of-Monsters and Born-of-Water left home. Following their mother's counsel, they rid the earth of most of its monsters . . ."

Gray Ghost slowed his movements and stared at Lozen with blazing eyes. He coiled tightly, and subtly weaved side to side in the air before her like a mountain lion waiting to spring on prey.

The spirit-Lozen walked back down the white path wearing the face of her youth, her strength restored, just as White Painted Woman had once done.

". . . in the path of White Painted Woman, I bind myself in marriage to the Wind, the Gray Ghost Chief, who as husband must live with and serve Lozen and her clan before his own. As wife I will have no other than him, faithful unto death."

Lozen's eyes focused on the form of the Gray Ghost; he hung stunned in the air before her.

"Sweep back the enemy . . ." she whispered, ". . . my husband."

The top of the mesa howled in the chorus of the loosed wind.

The Gray Ghost turned, his hand dragging gentle warm gusts beneath her clothing, accepting the pact between them, accepting her promise to him.

He ran down the ragged mesa as easily as if it were a gentle grassy slope. His strides were long and sure, faster than any mortal man.

With an unearthly boom, as though a drum as big as the mesa itself had been struck, the smoke was released in a blinding flash up into the sky, a streaking cloud disbursing into the deepening autumn light. A succession of echoed reports kept time with the Gray Ghost's strides.

With each of the Gray Ghost's footfalls, a swirling ruddy dust leaped to life behind him. Following closely at his heels, it climbed higher and higher toward the cobalt sky. The Gray Ghost reached the gorge, and the red earth around him burst into a whirling dance.

Lozen turned. The survivors pulled the dead and wounded from the rocks and carried them toward the cache of horses hidden beyond the perimeter of Tres Castillos.

Above and to her right stood Chief Nana. She gave a quick silent prayer of thanks to USSEN, the Creator, that he'd survived. Nana took her arm to steady his descent from the rocks above.

She helped him down, then limped away, caked with dirt and smoke, her hair a matted mess and her clothing torn and bloodstained. Relentlessly she made her way toward a high point in the rocks.

The outcropping of rock upon which she clumsily climbed jutted away from the low mesa camp as a thumb to a hand. From its summit she asked USSEN for the power to locate her enemies. She turned sunwise with an odd bobbing motion; unable to trust her full weight to her injured leg. Her palms burned without respite; armies in all directions.

With her vow she'd separated herself from his world.

The bride of the Wind has no home. She would never rest again.

She'd annihilated any hope for future generations of her clan. Lifelong battle would be her only legacy.

In the gorge below, the Gray Ghost ran with the easy lope of a stag; his silhouette and movements had regained their former grace. His fury found outlet in the growing sandstorm. The coppery earth swirled and spiraled into a dry blizzard that colored the sky and reached up with slender fingers to touch the sun.

Wind-shredded remnants of shouts came from behind the sienna curtain of earth that shielded Lozen from the scattering Mexican army. In her mind's eye she could see the distant men coughing and gagging on the thick ruddy air as their magic turned against them. Unseen horses squealed, stumbled clattering over rocks as they blundered through the Gray Ghost's sandstorm.

Scayocarne and Gouyen had carried Victorio's body from the rocks with the other fallen warriors.

The horse raid had taken place less than a day ago. It seemed to her a lifetime.

From her vantage, she counted what remained of her people: 16 men, women, and children.

The Gray Ghost drove the Mexican army away from the pile of their dead, the dead that had fueled the perverse magic.

She made her way slowly back down from the outcropping and then carefully gathered her brother's few belongings. She fell in after the survivors.

She saw a beautifully painted cradle board wedged between rocks. Kneeling down next to it, as well as her leg would permit, she peered inside. A dead child . . . Eliza, the little girl afraid of the setting sun. Lozen grimaced, splitting her dry lip.

Lozen dislodged the cradle board, and hung it properly and securely in the highest branches of a scrub tree, blessing the small corpse. She clutched the bundle of her brother's possessions tightly to her chest and hobbled awkwardly away to begin the funeral ritual for all of the fallen.

They were too few to survive another battle.

They were too few to make it home.

The Gray Ghost appeared at her side, mounted on his fine gray horse, the same that he'd ridden into her life seventeen years earlier. He dismounted, all beauty and grace, and lifted her astride his beautiful stallion.

He swung up behind her, rested his hand gently on her wounded thigh and said, "Though you will bear no children of your body, I promise, wife, that you will have a thousand daughters. I will whisper your name, the seed of your spirit, to the hearts of endless generations of girls. Those who hear will be your daughters in spirit— more true than flesh."

Her proud heart soared across the desert, to the terrible storm that tumbled toward her on western horizon.

And she gathered herself up, lifted her chin, and set her split-lipped mouth in a flat uncompromising line. All she had left in this world was the Wind: a husband she would never have to bury.

She looked at what remained of her once-peaceful people, and she spoke to her husband.

"Take us to Geronimo."

One Seeker has sought the Archives to learn the truth of a secret whispered to her by the ocean tides. The Master of the Archives opens one hand; with the other he stirs blue-green light until it resembles a water spout. The small vortex vanishes suddenly, taking the Seeker with it.

She finds herself in the depths of a great ocean. Vermillion-colored coral and fish striped in vibrant hues provide a corridor which ends at the haunt of an unusual spirit. The Seeker must share time with this being if she is to learn the mystery within:

NINETY-FOUR

by Jean Rabe

THE ocean was dark this August night, a bottle of ink that had spilled to wrap around the U-boat. It was running thirty-five meters below the surface of the Atlantic, avoiding detection of the bombers that prowled overhead and running toward warmer environs—the Caribbean, where the prey was reported to be in abundance.

I found myself eagerly looking forward to the hunt.

Sonar guided her, hollow-sounding pings that cut through the water and returned to reverberate eerily through the submarine's narrow corridors. A square-jawed young Aryan who understood the nuances of the length it took each sound to echo, mechanically relayed subtle course changes.

The pings meant nothing to me, music only, discordant and uncomplicated, but not unpleasant. Interesting noise, the heartbeat of U-boat Ninety-Four. I listened for a time, then let the sound drift to the back of my mind as I picked through the darkness of the blessed water and peered far-away to the west.

Wedged at his station in the tight confines of the bridge, Oberfahnrich Rennecke monitored a coded Enigma signal sent from another U-boat many kilometers away. His hands were wrapped around an ugly box with typewriter keys and small light bulbs scattered across its surface. The lights blinked erratically as the incoming message was decrypted and spit out on curling paper. Rennecke's brow furrowed as he quickly read the note, then spun about in his chair.

"Kapitänleutnant!" Rennecke snapped. "U-boat one-twelve reports a British patrol to the north. Five ships. One-twelve requests anyone in the area to rendezvous and . . ."

The Kapitänleutnant waved a hand, stopping the rest of the Oberfahnrich's words. He drew his lips into a thin line, let out a deep breath, and closed his eyes. He was listening to another voice.

He was listening to me.

"*West,*" I told the Kapitänleutnant. "*There is another patrol far to the west. Larger, more important fish to net. American ships, bellies heavy with supplies and riding low in the water. There are other U-boats to deal with the paltry ships to the north. Ninety-Four has more significant targets. Follow me west. Follow. . . .*"

"Nein!" the Kapitänleutnant responded to Rennecke. "We are a lone wolf, Oberfahnrich. We do not join wolf-packs, not anymore. Maintain radio silence. Continue west on course. Increase speed by one-third."

He listened to me a moment more, took in my silent words that only he could understand, that were meant only for him—always only for him. I was so looking forward to spending time with him in the Caribbean, and I sensed that he shared my anticipation. The American ships were almost directly in our path and would only a minor delay and a negligible course change.

"*Bigger fish, not much farther,*" I whispered to him, my mental voice sounding hypnotic and soothing, like waves nudging a beach. "*One is especially large—a whale among ships. Prey for us, my love. More pretty ribbons for your neck.*"

The Kapitänleutnant idly reached to the collar of his uniform, to a bit of impressive decoration that hung there, a Ritterkreuz he called it—a Knight's Cross. He had other medals, too, an Eisernes Kreuz—an Iron Cross, that he wore tucked beneath his shirt. His thumb traced the silver edge in a gentle caress, then dropped to his side when he spotted Oberfahnrich Rennecke staring at him.

The Crosses were earned for his success in captaining Ninety-Four, for sinking so many enemy ships—fifty-four to date, three hundred and eight tons of metal. Given to him by the highest-ranking officers in the Kriegsmarine, I preferred instead to think that I had awarded them to him.

"Much larger fish," I repeated.

"Kapitänleutnant?" Rennecke risked after a little more than an hour. It was shortly before midnight. "Sir, the sonarman has something. He's not sure what. Readings are imprecise. Five hundred meters west, fifty meters to starboard."

I sensed Rennecke's curiosity, I did not need his words. I read his feelings with little effort, as I read the feelings of the rest of the commander's men—all forty-five of them—their thoughts more interesting than the pings of sonar.

I sensed their pleasure now, as the sonarman announced ghostly images—ships that were there but not there. They were phantoms I was creating by displacing the water, phantoms to lure Ninety-Four like chum lures a shark. I continued to bait the men with my chum-ghosts toward a seven-ship formation heading east. Finally, the U-boat's primitive equipment was in range to notice the ships—a geleitzug, was the word the commander taught me, a convoy.

"Kapitänleutnant! Seven ships, one a destroyer! Onc a carrier!" Rennecke did not bother hiding his surprise. "Apparently they have not detected us, Sir!"

"Not yet at least," muttered the sonarman.

Not ever, I thought to myself. *I would not permit this submarine to be found.*

The Kapitänleutnant's eyes twinkled as he directed his men to rise to within five meters of the surface and select targets. "Seerohr, up!" He unfolded his lanky frame and reached for the periscope. He wanted to see the enemy, the sweet prey I had found him.

I flowed over the hull of the U-boat, leaving the bridge behind, passing beyond the zentrale—the control room, and surging underneath. I let my senses drift into the metal hull of the submarine, then through it, casting aside the guttural voices that echoed off the walls, ignoring the soft slap of rubber-soled shoes against the floor, searching, searching . . . there! A man was wedged awkwardly between the torpedorohrs. He was feeding the angry metal fish into the cylinders, listening to barked commands, working faster, turning dials, pushing buttons, ducking beneath cables, rushing everywhere within the tiny room, his thoughts focused only on the task at hand. Nearby, a seaman read the vorhalterechner, a tool which provided the attack coordinates for the torpedoes.

I pulled back as suddenly the eyeless fish were racing away from Ninety-Four. The oh-so-angry fish were streaking toward the unsuspecting American convoy. One after another I watched their propeller-fins churn through the frigid Atlantic. And one after another they found their marks.

The carrier first! Carriers always must be downed first, before the bienes, as the men called them—bees—could fly from their decks. The bees were the only things I could not hide this submarine from.

Toothless mouths cut through hulls, bringing death and victory, bringing a smile to the commander's face as the carrier listed. The ocean erupted with sound and spray and the scream of more hulls sundering.

There were the screams of American men, too, but these were not as loud and dramatic, not as interesting and therefore almost beneath my notice. Their broken bodies slipped through the breached bellies and drifted with crates of supplies into the sea, spilling blood as they went—chum for the sharks.

More angry fish shot toward the convoy, the water around them displaced and energized. I absorbed everything, as I always did, the energy, movement, the rupturing of keels, the shrill metal screams of ships—sensations all more wonderful than the sea could naturally create. But Ninety-Four, with my help, was adept at creating them. I took it all in and trembled in delight.

"Kapitänleutnant! Three ships sinking, Sir. The destroyer is damaged, but she is returning fire with hedgehogs, coming closer! She seems to be firing blind, Sir, but our position is risky." Rennecke looked to his commander for evasion orders, his clammy fingers hovering above the controls, itching to relay the message to send the U-boat deep. He saw the Kapitänleutnant bring down the periscope, anticipated that they would dive to safety—where the enemy's sonar could not easily find them.

"We do nothing to hide, Oberfahnrich Rennecke." The commander's reply was even, no trace of concern. "Target torpedoes. Fire! Fire!"

Oberfahnrich Rennecke paled. A young man just turned eighteen, he was new to Ninety-Four, having joined the crew at the Germaniawerft factory in Kiel when the sub was equipped with an athos—an advanced radar-detection device and nibelung—elite sonar equipment. His fellows in the small bridge had sailed with the Kapitänleutnant for nearly a year before, since the early fall of 1941, and were used to his refusal to evade or flee. They, unlike the Oberfahnrich, were not afraid. They, like the Kapitänleutnant, somehow knew Ninety-Four would not be struck by the enemy.

Some thought the U-boat's alberich was responsible for their safety, a rubber foil designed to protect the submarine from the Allies' underwater detection devices. Others thought angels guarded Ninety-Four in an effort to help Germany win the war. A few whispered that their Kapitänleutnant had traded his soul to the devil in exchange for his ship's conquests and its preservation.

They did not know about me.

"Sir . . . Kapitänleutnant . . . the destroyer is releasing wabos. The three other ships . . ."

"Will soon be heading to the bottom of the Atlantic, Oberefahnrich Rennecke. Stop questioning me or I will relieve you. Understand?"

They did not know that I was their angel, now flowing away from Ninety-Four, drifting in the water, an invisible wave. They could not see me form hands out of my otherwise nebulous body, could not see me clap them together, forcing a strong jet of cold sea water away from me and unerringly toward an odd, cylindrical thing that seemed to lazily spiral toward the sea floor. My water jet nudged the cylinder, a wabo—a depth-charge, away from the precious U-boat. The cylinder landed on the sea floor, split-

ting like a fragile oyster and releasing booming thunder. The water roiled around it, and I soaked up the sensation. Then I turned my attention to the other depth-charges, and—one after another—I dispatched them.

"Do you understand, Oberfahnrich Rennecke?"

One final depth-charge. One final jet of water. More incredible feelings. I directed a wave of water to rush above the U-boat, just as a hedgehog shell from one of the battleships arced down. I had been concentrating on the depth-charges, forgetting about the shells the battleships could rain.

Too many ships, perhaps, for my precious Ninety-Four and myself to manage. I felt an unaccustomed sense of dread. Nervousness? Fear? We had never taken on a convoy this size before—not alone, only in a pack. But my forceful wave knocked the shell away just in time. Ninety-Four was safe, though it pitched and rolled from the force of the churning water. I relaxed and soaked up the sensations.

"Do . . . you . . . understand . . . Oberfahnrich?"

"Yes, Sir," came Rennecke's apprehensive reply. He returned to the controls, wiping the sweat off his face with his shirt sleeve. "Madness," he swore under his breath. Then he inhaled sharply as two more of Ninety-Four's torpedoes struck the great destroyer.

The U-boat trembled slightly, feeling the concussive force of the explosion because of the nearness of the target. Then the air inside the sub erupted with whoops and cheers as word carried that the destroyer was hit again. The destroyer listed and began its descent.

"Fire!" the Kapitänleutnant barked. "Fire!"

More torpedoes raced away from Ninety-Four, and heartbeats later another ship's belly was ruptured, the U-boat trembling again as the waves of sound and energy pushed through the sea. More cheering. More angry-fish released. One more ship going to the bottom.

"Only one remains, Kapitänleutnant!" Rennecke's voice was almost cheerful. "She is trying to escape."

"Nein," the commander hushed. "She will not escape, Oberfahnrich. No survivors. No prisoners."

His fingers drifted up to touch his Knight's Cross, as his men's fingers fluttered over the controls. The U-boat, like a rigid eel prowling for dinner, edged northwest, pursuing the battleship which dropped wabos that would never find their mark.

It was an hour later when Ninety-Four surfaced, taking in fresh air. The oxygen-driven diesel fuel fed the engines now, permitting the batteries that the U-boat so desperately relied on underwater to recharge. It was a danger to run too long on batteries, forcing a submarine to surface at inopportune times—perhaps within range of ships and planes that could attack.

The Kapitänleutnant had never been forced to surface when he did not want to, not in Ninety-Four, and not in the two smaller U-boats he commanded before. A wily fox more at home on and under the water than on land, he knew when to conserve the batteries and when, like now, to ride the waves.

Rennecke had sent a kurzsignal, a brief radio message to report the seven ships sunk and the position. The Kapitänleutnant did not allow long transmissions that could be detected by the Allies and used to track his sub. It didn't matter that the Allies could not read the encrypted signals, for even the genius code-breakers toiling fiercely in England could not decipher the simplest of U-boat messages. It only mattered that they could discover a signal—and by it, find a sub.

The Kapitänleutnant was on the deck, wrapped in a heavy coat and breathing deep the sweet, salt-tinged air. He stared at the stars and hummed an old tune. He had ordered even his most senior officers to remain below—so he could have some time alone, he told them.

But he was not alone. A wave surged alongside Ninety-Four in an otherwise calm sea. I was with him.

"Fraulein Faerie," the Kapitänleutnant began, "thank you for this night's victory."

"It pleased you?"

"Very much."

"It was risky."

He let out a clipped laugh. "Life is a risk. The war is a risk. I am happy."

His happiness was what I had come to live for. And if sinking ships brought him joy, together we would sink all the ships the Allies could put upon the waves. Indeed, together we had sunk more ships than any lone U-boat. I felt a giddiness course through my watery form.

"Fraulein Faerie?"

I liked the name he gave me. It sounded good rolling off his tongue. If I'd had a name before, it was lost to time. I was an ancient entity, a water sprite, and I had no family, knew no other creatures like myself. Perhaps there were others at one time. And perhaps they died, though I am unsure what could truly kill water. Perhaps there are others still and our paths have never crossed. Or, perhaps ruefully, I was always the only one. It mattered little. Since I joined company with this very special man, I am lonely no more.

He told me his name when I came upon him more than a year ago, brusque and harsh-sounding words—Otto Itesman—that seemed unimportant. I discarded them from memory, calling him instead what his men called him—Kapitänleutnant. I liked the sound of it. An important name.

"Fraulein Faerie?" he asked again.

His voice was tentative, wondering if I had moved away. I would never leave his side for long. "Yes, beloved."

"We will be in the Caribbean soon. So fortunate that orders take us there."

"I look forward to the warmth and shallow seas."

I saw him smiling. "I look forward to being with you, Fraulein."

He'd told me before he left on this patrol—his seventeenth—that we would be scouring the waters around Jamaica, Cuba, and off the coast of Colombia, hunting American ships bringing supplies and munitions to the British and French, who were starved for both. In a shallow cove he would hide Ninety-Four to recharge its batteries, as he had in coves in the Mediterranean, and we would be truly together.

"Together," I hushed.

"Together like the first time," he said. "Like all times."

*   *   *

I remembered the day in the bright blue waters off Mediera Island. The breeze was blowing warmly from the far shores of Morocco, and I was flowing with the surf and idly watching the clouds.

The submarine hid itself in the shadow of Mediera's southern rise, and men spilled from it—allowed to rest and enjoy the day.

I watched them, as I had through the centuries watched others. The centuries rarely altered the behavior of playful men—they swam, drank in the sun, and sang nonsensically—all a welcome, brief diversion for me. But one man stayed apart from the rest, swimming far to a tablerock that edged above the choppy bay. I followed this man, who was to become my beloved Kapitänleutnant.

I studied him for a time, sitting cross-legged on the rock, his body pinched together like a hermit crab drawn into its shell. He was thinking, unblinking blue eyes locked on the distant waves. He looked no better a specimen than others I had been near. And I had been near so many through the centuries—saving panicked young ones who ventured out too far from shore, foiling greedy fishermen by tearing their nets, protecting sailors by guiding their small ships around hidden reefs.

He was not handsome by human terms, I considered, judging by all the others I had watched. His ears flared away from his angular face, and his nose seemed too narrow and crooked. His lips were shadowed by a mustache that reminded me of dried seaweed, and his cheeks were covered with a stubble that looked like sand. The skin around his eyes and across his brow was wrinkled and rough—from the sea and sun. And his hands were thick with calluses, his right arm scarred.

But he seemed dissimilar, better somehow than all the others. He seemed to sense me. I was but a scintillating patch floating at the base of his rock, looking little different from the water all around that reflected bits of the setting sun. But he dropped his gaze from the horizon and stared at his reflection mirrored on my surface. He cocked his head to the side in an unspoken question. Who? he seemed to ask. Who are you?

I have no name, I answered.

"Then perhaps I should give you one."

He heard me! For the first time in all the centuries, a man had heard me!

He didn't flee, as I had expected. In my time within the seas I learned that humans were a skittish lot when confronted with something beyond their ken. Instead, he crawled down the rock and slipped into the water, his fingers touching me in curious exploration.

I willed myself to adopt a form he could more easily relate to, shaping watery arms and legs, a head that shimmered golden in the waning sunlight, tendrils of watery hair that looked like seagrass. Each time he touched me I dipped into his mind, coming away with the concepts that drove him—pride, ambition, fearlessness, loyalty, and more—all notions that refreshingly consumed me.

Were all men like this? I wondered. Had I never bothered to look so closely before? No, I quickly answered. I was always looking for a way to ease my seclusion. I had sensed something special about this one. And only this one—through all these long centuries—had sensed me. Was he the only one of his kind who had this ability? Doubtful, I finally decided, as there are so many men across the globe—the odds too great for only one of them to be so perceptive. Still, he was the only one I'd come across in my journeys who had noticed I was alive. A very special man.

Questions poured from his lips.

What manner of creature was I?

I had no good answer for this. A sprite, I told him, living water, a creature of life and of the sea.

From whence had I come?

I shrugged what passed for my shoulders, copying a gesture I had learned from men. From a time when magic was strong in the world, I replied. When pixies and faeries were in abundance. When science was not yet born.

And where was I going?

I looked long into his eyes as I pondered this. Where was I going? Where had I been going? Through the same seas over and over. Into the same coves. In my life there was no place in the seas I had not visited. Always watching, riding the waves, doing little more than existing and saving an occasional child when the mood struck. I am going with you, I answered.

He moved to me then, so more of his skin touched the watery substance that comprised my being, ran his fingers over my created arms and shoulders, cupped my created face and looked into my pupiless eyes. He brought his face in so close to mine I could smell his sweet breath.

I am going with you, I repeated.

"Please, do," he said. His words were as soft as the cry of a distant gull.

He marveled at me like a newborn dolphin wonders at the world around him, finding something new in each glance and touch. And I found something new in him. The hollowness in my heart vanished, and I let the emotions I was experiencing wash over him, practically drowning him in the myriad sensations.

He learned I was a watcher, a wanderer, a spirit who until this day had never made this kind of contact with man. I learned he was a lonely man, a commander of men whose position put him above his fellows, enforced an aloofness and a distance, compelled him to be alone. He had been alone so long.

Alone no more, I whispered.

His smile broadened and he drew me closer, lost in the magic of me as my form shimmered and enveloped him, loved him. He loved the sea, I could tell, and so loved me. He felt happier on the ocean—and now happier with me—than he could ever be on land, than he could ever be with his own kind.

I urged him to swim away with me, that I had enough magic inside for both of us, that I could carry us to the deepest part of the ocean. I would show him the creatures that lived there—creatures no man had seen, because no man could withstand the intense pressure. But he could, with me. I would take him through cities sunken long before there was a Germany and a Europe, cities ruined by the forces of magic, not war. Show him wonders he had never imagined.

A part of him wanted this—to flow like water and be part of the great sea. I could tell that his heart wanted this—desperately. But the concepts that drove him would not permit this—duty, honor, responsibility, a vow made to some powerful entity called the Kriegsmarine to captain this U-boat.

There was a war, he explained with his clever mind, and he had given himself over to it.

So I joined his war, for the first time in my existence truly meddling in the affairs of men—I had considered saving children and foolish sailors not truly meddling. I used my abilities to protect Ninety-Four, and hence to protect him. I disturbed the water for kilometers around the sub, fouling the radar and sonar of the Kapitän-leutnant's enemy. I formed a watery shield when the sky stormed and the ocean became cruel, threatening to batter the sub. I pushed away depth-charges and hedgehogs. And I created chum-ghosts for the benefit of his men—a venue to lure them to targets I had selected.

I brought him success after success, made him the most respected commander in the entire German navy. He was offered larger subs with bigger crews, but these he declined. He and I were both comfortable with Ninety-Four. He was given money and medals, promises of promotions for after the war—promises of land, which I knew he would never accept.

The Allies detested the great Otto Itesman and were always searching for him, wanting to know why this commander in his lone-wolf submarine could not be sunk and could rarely be detected.

The Kapitänleutnant's place in the records of German history was ensured.

I drank in his happiness with each enemy vessel Ninety-Four sent to the bottom, and I shared his occasional sorrow. Sometimes he slipped into dark moods, penitent for the land-bound families ruined with the sinking of each Allied ship. I did not share his compassion, for only he had sensed me, only this human was so special and so worthy of protection. Only this human had to be saved.

"It will be good to feel you around me," he said, reaching out a hand so I could caress him with a gentle splash. "Not long, now, Fraulein Faerie, to the Caribbean. We shall find a cove and swim together in the moonlight."

"Not long," I sang to him as the dawning sun edged over the horizon. *"Not long, beloved."*

I watched him reluctantly head toward the hatch. The thoughts he so readily shared with me revealed that Ninety-Four had to dive to hide from the bright morning. I clung to the hull, following the submarine down.

The sun was at its zenith by the time Ninety-Four rose to a depth of twenty-five meters and slipped into the Caribbean Sea. The Kapitänleutnant was especially alert and ordered his best men at their posts. The water was shallower here, and therefore submarines were more vulnerable to being detected visually by planes flying overhead and by the Allies's Huff Duff—their high-frequency direction finding equipment that could lock onto any signals Ninety-Four relayed.

He had sent a series of short, coded messages before entering the Caribbean, weather reports mainly for other submarines traveling this way. From encrypted missives the U-boat received earlier, the Kapitänleutnant knew a wolfpack would be prowling these waters soon, was already on its way. He responded, as orders demanded, then ordered radio silence after that.

The U-boat rose to within five meters of the surface so the Kapitänleutnant could use the periscope to look around. Ninety-Four was hugging the northern coast of South America, and was nearing the border of Colombia. The Kapitänleutnant was searching for a cove Ninety-Four could slip into and hide until sunset, surfacing then to recharge its batteries. He wanted the ship to be at its optimum before taking on any Allied vessels.

He and I were so looking forward to the hunt.

There were several vessels to be had, I knew. I was resting atop Ninety-Four, thinking of my man inside and extending my senses in all directions. Ships docked in the deep Jamaican harbors. A carrier to the north, with a single battleship escort. It must have been leaving a United States port, slipping out through the islands to head toward the Atlantic, where it would certainly pick up a larger escort. There were other ships north of Ja-

maica, close to the coast of America. These were of no consequence at the moment.

I relayed my findings, as I always did—any reason to touch his mind and share his thoughts.

"It will not be long, Fraulein Faerie, before we are together," he whispered, his eyes peering through the periscope lens.

Oberfahnrich Rennecke cast him a curious glance, but said nothing.

"Status report! The Kapitänleutnant snapped.

He was scanning toward the north, where I spotted the carrier. I knew his eyes were not strong enough to allow him to see it. I pictured it in my mind, passed the image to him.

"Canadian," he muttered, as the reports trickled in. "Odd place for a Canadian ship I would think."

Batteries were low, but they would permit a dive of perhaps two hours—all that was needed to reach the ships, destroy them, and then put some distance between the U-boat and Jamaica.

The torpedoes were at half, as many had been used in the Atlantic on the American convoy. More than enough for the Caribbean. They could be replenished in a friendly South American country.

Ninety-Four was undamaged. Her crew alert. She was ready for these Canadians.

"Enemy ships," he hushed.

I sensed his hunger and knew instantly that our planned stop in a Colombian cove would wait until the Canadian carrier was down, the battleship following, his appetite sated.

"A carrier and a battleship," I repeated. "The carrier first."

"The carrier always first," he whispered. To the crew he said, "Dive to twenty meters, change course on my mark!" He lowered the scope. "Ahead one-third. Maintain radio silence. Release pellets!"

The pellets contained a chemical that caused the water to bubble around the submarine, playing havoc with any radar and sonar searching in the area. It was a common tactic to release them in waters that were not so deep and not so cold to allow a sub to easily hide from detection.

Heartbeats later the sonarman excitedly reported the two ships. I had not needed to create chum-ghosts in this smaller sea.

"Together, soon," I told my commander. "We will finish these, and we will be together tonight." I slipped away from the bridge, flowing over the submarine's hull and to its torpedo room. My mind continued to touch his, but my senses demanded to absorb the feel of the churning water left in the wake of the oh-so-angry fish.

The torpedorohrs were loaded with the metal fish, and I found myself anticipating their release. Not much farther to the carrier now, I knew. Not much longer until the Kapitänleutnant and I would be together.

Suddenly the torpedoes were racing away from Ninety-Four, and my senses were following them, absorbing the agitated water, feeling the energy inside them, stretching ahead to the carrier, watching as the first struck its hull.

"Fire!" the Kapitänleutnant ordered. "Fire! Fire!"

Twin torpedoes shot from Ninety-Four, toward the now-listing carrier. The battleship at its side pulled ahead, as if it were trying to sacrifice itself to save its comrade ship. A futile gesture, I knew, as the torpedoes hit their mark, cutting deep into the carrier's hull, sending the sea gushing in faster and causing the once-impressive Canadian ship to head nose-first toward the bottom.

The battleship was hurling hedgehogs in our direction, and I turned my attention to forcing these away from Ninety-Four. An easy task. Much easier than when we dealt with the larger American convoy. I sent a wave at the hedgehogs, drove them away as even more angry fish were sent streaking from the U-boat and toward the remaining Canadian vessel.

Would my commander feel pity for the families of these men? I wondered. He was feeling satisfaction now, I knew. And . . . and he was feeling something else. I flowed away from the torpedo room, still watching for hedgehogs and depth charges, absorbing the scream of metal from the continually-breaching carrier hull and from the now-breaching battleship shell. The screams of

*the Canadian men were too insignificant. I thrust them to
the back of my mind.*

"What?" I asked him. "What is it that . . . ?"

*I slipped my mind inside his, heard with his ears as the
sonarman reported that he was picking up more ships—
American, Canadian, ships and planes. Headed toward
us!*

"No!" I told the Kapitänleutnant. "Only the carrier and
the battleship. That is all I sensed. Those in port are sleeping. Those on the American coast too far away. No submarines save the wolfpack nearing the Caribbean!"

"There were ships leaving the port, Sir!" It was Rennecke's voice. "They were leaving as we started our
attack. We hadn't paid close enough attention to them,
Kapitänleutnant, Sir." His nervous fingers drifted to controls that would signal a dive to the bottom of the Caribbean. "Evasive action, Sir?"

"Nein. We do not hide, Oberfahnrich."

"There are four ships, Sir. At full-speed now. Fifteen knots."

"Nein."

*He knew I would protect Ninety-Four. There was no
need to run. Never a need to run. I would not let this U-
boat come to harm. I directed my mind away from my
beloved commander and his beloved U-boat, toward the
north where the sonarman and Oberfahnrich Rennecke
had picked up more of the enemy. Indeed, there were
four, rushing toward us as fast as their engines allowed.
Only four. This would not take long, and then soon we
would be together in a Columbian cove.*

*Angry fish sped by me toward the lead enemy ship, one
passing so close to the hull it scraped it, but did no real
harm. The other, however, found its mark and chewed
deep into the Canadian metal. Two more angry fish struck
this sinking ship, sending it faster to the bottom of the
beautiful Caribbean.*

*More sped by me as I flowed toward the remaining
three ships, which were launching depth charges and
hedgehog shells. I set to work detonating them away from
Ninety-Four.*

"Soon, beloved," *my mind sent to my commander.*

"Only three ships left." And now, with this spread of torpedoes sent from Ninety-Four, only two ships.

All around my beloved erupted the cheers of his men, so pleased with their enemy's demise. So proud of their Kapitänleutnant.

In the back of my mind I heard the Kapitänleutnant mutter that we'd be heading toward a friendly country soon to replenish torpedoes, as we were using them quickly. Then I heard panicked voices swirling all around him—Oberfahnrich Rennecke's cut above the others.

"Sir!" he cried. "American planes!"

"Nein!" the Kapitänleutnant returned in disbelief.

Planes. My spirit felt a hint of trepidation. My element was the sea, and I could sense to considerable distances all the creatures and ships in it. The sky was something I could not touch. The bienes were something I had difficulty protecting against. Perhaps they had been purposely searching for this ship, picking up the brief signals sent before Ninety-Four entered the Caribbean. I knew my Kapitänleutnant was so wanted by the Allies. Or perhaps they had found us merely by accident—a dark shape beneath meters of crystal blue water.

No matter the cause of our spotting, I would protect the ship with my life.

I eased myself back toward Ninety-four. I diverted two more depth charges on my way and sent a wave above the U-boat's bow to push a trio of hedgehogs off their mark. I was so close, reaching out to touch the sub's hull, when the depth charges rained from the sky—brushing against Ninety-Four and rocking it wildly.

There was a scream of metal again, but this time not from the enemy. I felt horror for the first time in my ageless life as the cries of the German sailors reached me. The human screams were not insignificant this time.

"Beloved!" I was screaming, too.

"Report!" the Kapitänleutnant barked. Words started flying in the bridge and in the control room below. The breach was being sealed, but six men had been lost. Worse, the depth charge had destroyed one of Ninety-Four's ballast tanks, which was crucial to diving.

I formed hands and clapped them together, sent a wave surging from me to push another of the airdropped *charges away. Successful! But only for a heartbeat. Another charge followed it, too fast for me to divert. It struck Ninety-Four and shook it as a shark shakes a tuna.*

"We must surface, Kapitänleutnant!" This from Rennecke. It was quickly repeated by the sonarman and the others wedged in the cramped bridge.

"Nein! We will be all right! You will see!"

I heard more words floating in the air around the Kapitänleutnant, reports coming from deep in the wounded belly of the U-boat. Seven more casualties. Another breach, this one not sealing so easily, perhaps not at all. Water pouring in. I felt what passed for my heart racing uncontrollably.

"We're going down, Kapitänleutnant!"

"Nein, Oberefahnrich! We cannot be sunk. And we cannot be defeated." He directed all his efforts into ordering more men to work on the breach. Ordered an evasive course plotted. Ordered Rennecke to dispatch a brief message to any subs at the edge of the Atlantic—warning them, asking them for help.

I directed my efforts to warding away more depth charges. The water too shallow, the sun too bright, the planes flying overhead had spotted us again—I could tell, for they were raining death upon us once more. At the same time I formed chum-ghosts near the Canadian ships, praying that their sonar would pick these up and direct their efforts and depth charges at these new targets—leaving my precious Ninety-Four alone.

"We're going down, Kapitänleutnant!"

"Nein, Rennecke! Do not question me, or you will be relived!"

The Oberfahnrich persisted, no longer afraid of the Kapitänleutenant. The sea that was filling the sub was a greater force. "There is no angel watching us now!" Rennecke spat. "There is only death watching and waiting. You will kill us all, Kapitänleutnant!"

"Nein, Oberfahnrich!" But this time there as worry in the Kapitänleutenant's voice. He scanned the bridge, the frightened faces of his charges, imagined the frightened faces of the men he could not see, took in the words that flew around his head.

The breach could not be sealed.

There was duty and honor, his vow to the Kriegsma-rine. The war to fight. His men. His very loyal and pre-cious men.

"Surface!" he bellowed, practically choking on the word. "Surface!" Softer, he said to Rennecke, "Relay the order to abandon ship. And let us hope the Allies are merciful."

But there was no mercy in the Caribbean this day I discovered. A Canadian corvette bore down on Ninety-Four, which was struggling to surface long enough to re-lease life rafts and disgorge her surviving crew.

I released all the energy I could, jetting toward the bridge of the submarine. I spread myself and prayed to whatever forces that birthed me ages ago that I would be enough to protect this one ship. I prayed and felt, for the first time in my existence, pain.

The corvette cut into my water form, pressing through to reach Ninety-four. Despite my best efforts, I did little to soften the impact of the corvette's hull against the dam-aged hull of the sub. And also despite my best efforts, I could not reach out with my senses to find my beloved.

I felt myself slipping to the Caribbean Sea's floor. Then I felt oblivion.

The old man sat on the beach and hummed an old tune, the Sicilian town of Trapani behind him. The waves were creeping closer to him, teasing his bare feet and chilling him terribly. He had abandoned his shoes an hour ago on the docks, ignoring the protests of con-cerned fishermen that a man his age should not be so careless next to the ocean in February. He might drown or catch pneumonia.

His face was deeply cut by wrinkles, his skin all-over weathered by the sea and the sun. How he loved the sea.

After his U-boat sank forty years ago this past August in the Caribbean southeast of Jamaica, and after he and twenty-five other survivors had been pulled from the sea to spend the remainder of the war in a prison camp, he went home to Germany. He tried to build a life for him-self there, but found he was useless when not on the water. So he had worked as a fisherman for a time, then traveled throughout Europe taking odd jobs here and there to gain enough to live on.

Most of the time he fished and worked on boats—until age stooped his shoulders, slowed his step, and forced him into retirement. He settled here, in Trapani, in an old people's home so very close to the sea. And when the nurses weren't paying too much attention, he slipped away to the beach.

As he had done this cold winter day.

His eyes, still remarkably blue, peered intently at a scintillating patch of water. The late morning sun was sending a dappling of lights across the waves. But this was . . . different. The patch swirled around his toes.

Who? he seemed to ask it.

It had taken me forty years to reform from oblivion, proving to myself that water cannot die forever.

I urged him again to swim away with me, as I had that day I first saw him. I sang to him that I had enough magic inside for both of us, that I could carry us to the deepest part of the ocean.

"I will show you the creatures that live there—creatures no man has seen. But you can see them, with me. Water, we will live forever. I will take you through cities sunken long before there was a Germany and a Europe and before there was a war to end all wars, cities ruined by the forces of magic."

"Show me wonders I've only imagined," he whispered.

"Together," I hushed.

"Together like the first time," he said.

He followed me into the bay, mindless of the shouts of the fishermen and tourists behind him, focused only on the scintillating patch of seawater. I flowered over him and happily took him under.

A young man with flaxen hair stands facing the Walker, ready to begin his journey among the Archives. Light in verdant shades cascades to him from the Guardian's hand. Nodding in respect, the man stands, finding his doorway only a few steps away from the table. Opening the thick wooden portal, he passes through and finds himself on a cobblestone street, breathing misty air which carries the unmistakable scents of deep water. A well-lit building pulls at his attention. He steps through its door into a wealth of lilting accents foreign to his own, discovering the truth of:

HUNTERS HUNTED

by John Helfers

THOMAS couldn't say exactly when he fell in love with the fetching young woman sitting across from him, but he knew it hadn't happened until he had known her a good long while. About twenty minutes, more or less.

He had been sitting in Busker Brownes, a local pub, reading a book of poems by Kipling and debating whether ordering a Macallan single malt whiskey would be worth the havoc it would cause to his graduate student's budget, when he heard a woman gasp beside him.

He looked up just in time to be greeted by a torrent of earthy, dark brown lager which drenched his pullover and splattered all over the book and table. Half-blinded, Thomas took off his glasses and wiped his face down, shaking the pungent liquid off his fingers.

"Oh, my God, I'm so sorry. All you all right? Here, let's get you out of this wet thing." Thomas heard the same female voice say. Before he could protest, he felt his arms yanked straight up and his soaked sweater was pulled off over his head. It had been a relatively cool spring in Galway that year, so Thomas was wearing a reasonably clean buttondown instead of his usual T-shirt. Amazingly, except for a few spots on his collar, none of the spill had soaked through. Thomas finished drying his glasses and replaced them on his nose, then tried to salvage the now sodden book. He mopped up the worst of the wet with the available napkins at his table and the three around him, wondering all the while what the punishment for destroyed library books in Ireland was, and hoping it didn't involve wicker men. He glanced around for his assailant, but since he hadn't gotten a good look at her in the first place, he had no idea who to look for. Then came a light tap on his shoulder.

"I'm awfully sorry about the mess. Are you all right?"

"Um, that's all right, no . . . harm . . . done," Thomas managed to finish his sentence as he looked up at the slim young woman standing before him. Long, dark auburn hair fell in shoulder length ringlets that framed a classically Irish face composed of a twinkling smile, a pert nose dusted with just a smattering of freckles, and light blue eyes.

"Good, I feel bad enough as it is. Are you sure you're all right?" the young woman slid onto the stool across from him and gazed at him.

Thomas looked around, checking to see if one of his college friends, not that he had that many, might have been playing a trick on him. But no, the bar was filled with the early evening regulars and a few tourists getting a jump on the season. And if she was acting contrite, she was really good at it. "Yeah, I'm fine. Um, what did you do with my sweater?"

"Oh, I ran it back into the kitchen. It'll dry faster in the heat of the stove."

Great, now it'll smell like beer and fried fish, Thomas thought. Still, she was being helpful. "Thank you."

"Well, it was the least I could do after spilling my stout all over you. Speaking of which, what are you drinking? I insist." The woman's voice was light and musical, and Thomas realized (while wondering if he could get her to buy him a Macallan) that it was quite pleasant to listen to. *Well, she* did *drench me,* he thought.

"I was just going to order a Macallan," Thomas said.

"Ah, single malt, spoken like a true Scotsman, which would mean you're a wee bit away from home, then.

But I hear from your accent that you're definitely not a Highlander, even with your fondness for the whiskey."

Thomas nodded. "America actually. Rhinelander, Wisconsin."

"Where is that?"

"Um, it's by the Great Lakes, in the middle of the country. We make a lot of cheese and dairy products, stuff like that. *Great, why don't I just bore her to death with an economic report?* He quickly recovered. "Where are my manners? Thomas Salyer," he said, extending a hand, which she took gracefully, her handshake warm and firm.

"Noba," she replied.

Thomas frowned. "Pardon me, but that certainly doesn't sound very Irish. Is it short for something?"

"Trust me, you don't want to know," she replied.

Thomas let it go, but the somewhat familiar name settled into the back of his mind. "So, do you work here, I mean, I come in fairly regularly, and I know I would have remembered seeing someone like you here," Thomas said as a waitress set their drinks down.

"No, I just know the owners," Noba replied, coloring at the compliment.

"Ah, then you're a regular?"

Noba smiled. "Something like that, Mr. Salyer."

"Please, call me Thomas."

"Thomas," Noba tried his name out. "You don't shorten it, then?"

"No, too many bad Mark Twain references in grade school," Thomas said, sipping the amber liquor. "Once the rest of the kids got ahold of Tom Sawyer, I was marked for life. I swear, I could have been the only sixth grade fence painter in town, not to mention the Becky Thatcher remarks. Ever since then, I decided on the more mature 'Thomas,' and the rest is history."

"Is that what you were reading before I, er, drenched you?"

Thomas looked at the swollen volume on the table. "Actually, no, it's a book from the university."

"Oh, no, I've practically ruined your evening, haven't I?" Noba said.

Not from where I'm sitting, Thomas thought. "Not

really, although I don't know how the university will take it. I don't expect they still practice human sacrifice out here, do they?"

She chuckled. "Not for destroyed library books. Sacrifice was usually used to communicate with the spirits. And it helped if the sacrifice was willing. But don't worry, I'll take care of it. What were you reading?"

Thomas caught himself staring at her, and realized he had completely forgotten what the book contained. Thinking fast, he came up with, "Poem—poetry."

She leaned over to look at the author's name on the sodden spine. "Do you like Kipling?"

The ancient joke was on Thomas' lips before he could stop himself. "I don't know, I've never kippled."

Her laughter rang out into the now crowded room, clear and musical, like the ringing of a bell. *Either she has a poorly developed sense of humor or she's a really good sport,* Thomas thought. "Actually, I'm working toward my degree in Medieval Literature," he said.

Noba's eyes lit up. "Literature, eh?"

And so began a conversation the likes of which Thomas had never enjoyed before. The topics ranged from books to history to politics to music to art and back again. Noba was attentive, knowledgeable, and occasionally dissenting, a combination which Thomas found fascinating. His thoughts and opinions were challenged and debated, with him scoring some hard-won points, but often conceding the discussions to Noba. The hours flowed past like the River Corrib just outside, and before Thomas knew it, the last call was sounded.

When the bell was rung, Noba looked not at the bartender, but off at some faraway point it seemed only she could see. "Look at the time, I've got to go, I'm late," she said, scooting back from the table and rising.

"Well, wait, where do you live? Can I walk you home?" Thomas asked, rising with her.

"I don't think that would be a good idea. I'm sure we'll meet again. After all, it is a small town. Good night." With that she turned and headed for the door.

"Noba, wait." Thomas got up to follow her, but tripped and nearly fell as the stool he had been sitting on came with him. Looking down, he saw one of his shoelaces entangled in the wooden rungs. Cursing, he freed himself and took off after her.

Thomas burst through the tavern door only to find the street mostly empty. The other pubs were disgorging the last dregs of their regulars, but none of them looked like the young woman Thomas had just pleasantly spent the last few hours with. Although he ranged up and down the block from O'Briens Bridge to Flood Street, there was no trace of her.

As he was walking back to Busker Brownes, he stopped just outside the door and listened. A breeze had sprung up in the street, and brought with it the smell of the spring-swollen river and what sounded like the faint baying of a pack of hounds. Thomas turned, trying to locate the direction the barking was coming from, but had no luck. Shaking his head, he stepped back inside.

"We're closed, lad," the barkeep said as he finished wiping down the ancient wooden bar.

Thomas nodded. "I know, I just came back for my sweater."

"Ah, you'd be the one, then. The lady left it for you," the man said, lifting Thomas's neatly folded pullover out from under the bar.

Thomas walked over to the bar and took the sweater. It was fresh and clean, as if it had just been laundered. Thomas sniffed at it disbelievingly while the bartender watched him, smiling.

"This was . . . I mean, she spilled beer all over this," Thomas said. The bartender watched at him as if he heard stories like this every day. "Who was that?"

"You mean the woman you chased out of here? You were with her, don't you know?" the bartender asked with a sly grin.

"Very funny. I know her name, but I mean where is she from, does she live in town?"

The bartender inspected his spotless shot glasses. "I wouldn't know, I've never seen her before."

"What? She said she was a regular here," Thomas said.

"Well, I've been working here five years, so if she is, she must be avoiding me like the plague," the bartender said. "Lad, by now you should know women only tell the truth half the time. The problem is, men can never tell which half is the truth and which half isn't."

Thomas frowned. "I guess so. Well, thanks for holding this," he said pulling on the sweater. Then he looked at the now empty table where he and Noba had been sitting. "Say, do you know what happened to the book I came in with?"

The bartender gave Thomas a bemused look. "What, first I hold your clothes for you, making out like a bloody laundromat, and now I'm the local lost and found?" He smiled. "Sorry lad, I only serve the drinks here."

"Damn, damn, damn. Lost the woman, lost my book. Looks like my luck's running about the same as usual—bad," Thomas said.

"Ah, buck up, lad, tomorrow's a new day, and who knows what'll be waiting for you then." The bartender passed his cloth over the gleaming bar one last time.

"True, very true," Thomas said. "Maybe I'll take a walk around town tomorrow, see what I can find out."

"Maybe, but be careful what you look for," the bartender called out as Thomas headed for the door. "You just might find it!"

But as spring settled more comfortably over Galway, Thomas had no luck finding out anything more about Noba. He checked the student registry at the university and posted signs inquiring about his lost book of poems. He looked in the local phone book and ingratiated himself as best as he could with the regulars down at Busker Brownes. Although he did his fair share of pint-hoisting, none of them could give him anything to go on. Nothing was any help. She had vanished as completely as his library book.

Thomas found himself thinking about her more and more, her name contantly ringing in his head. On a hunch that it might be derived from Irish myth, he spent more than one evening combing the stacks of the university library, hoping to find some clue as to where he had seen it before. The only reference he found that was even remotely close was to Abnoba, a Celtic forest goddess. He even tried the genealogists at Venture Center, but they couldn't help either. There was no family name of Noba anywhere in Ireland.

Three weeks later, Thomas was ready to admit defeat. After a late Saturday night of cramming for his midterms, he decided to walk into town and drown his sorrows in a pint of Woodpecker.

The usual crowd was at Busker Brownes that evening, and Thomas had to battle his way through the door and into the main room. Contorting himself past knots of people to get to the bar, he found Sean, the bartender who had held his sweater, working that evening. Sean saw him coming and had a glass filled by the time he arrived.

"Thanks," Thomas said after he had polished off half the cider in one long drink.

"Perhaps your luck isn't running so bad after all," Sean yelled over the barroom din. Beside the dozen conversations running around the room, a local traditional Irish band was performing on one of the other floors of the three-story building, and the dancing was shaking the whole place to its foundation.

"Why do you say that?" Thomas asked, the noise in the room already reverberating through his head.

"Sure, isn't that your lady fair around the corner, heading for the door?"

Thomas tore his attention away from the contents of his glass to spy a familiar head of auburn hair weaving its way through the crowded room. Even though there were probably three dozen people in the room with hair colored a similar shade of red, Thomas instantly knew it was her. He looked at Sean, who smiled back at him.

"Lad, I've done my part. The rest is up to you," he said.

Thomas, having drained his cider (for nothing's worse in Ireland than leaving a glass half full), was already moving. "Noba, wait!" he shouted, trying to attract her attention. His words were lost in the crowd. Thomas struggled to get past the locals and tourists alike who packed the bar. He kept his eyes locked on that head of hair, afraid that if he lost sight of it for even a second, she would vanish just as she had the other night.

She reached the door, and with a nod to someone

nearby, opened it and slipped through. The door slowly started to swing shut. Thomas knew if he didn't get to that door before it closed, she would disappear from his life again.

"Not this time," he muttered. A large table packed with people was blocking his way. As Thomas frantically tried to figure out a way to get around it, one of the tourists got up, leaving an empty stool. Inspiration struck him, and he moved.

Leaping up onto the stool, Thomas stepped on the table, knocking over glasses and sending drinks everywhere. The tourists howled as they tried to avoid the sudden flood of lager, cider, and ale. Thomas saw an open spot by the doorway and leaped for it, getting his arm between the door and the jamb just before it closed. Tossing a quick "sorry" over his shoulder, he levered the door open and burst into the street just in time to see Noba disappearing around the corner onto Kirwan Lane.

"Noba!" Thomas ran down the block and rounded the corner, plunging straight into a thick wall of opaque fog. *What the hell—? Where did this come from?* Thomas turned around, but Cross Street and Busker Brownes were already lost in the swirling grayness. "Noba!" he called, feeling blindly for a wall, a streetlight, anything to use as a marker. He heard his steps on the cobblestones, so he knew he was still on the street. Everything was mist and darkness, with the street lights that usually lit the way strangely dark now.

Thomas stopped, listening with all his concentration. He heard a quick skitter of steps, as if someone was trying to move quickly and quietly at the same time. The noise seemed to echo off the building walls around him. Thomas spun around, trying to get a fix on where the runner was coming from.

When a hand fell upon his shoulder, Thomas gave a strangled yelp and spun around. Noba was standing there, shaking her head. She was now dressed in a flowing cloak that seemed to be woven entirely from fresh green leaves, with a matching laurel of mistletoe on her head. Thomas couldn't put a finger on it, but she seemed different, infused with a glow that he had never seen before, somehow larger than life. Her blue eyes shone in the darkness.

"Thomas, Thomas, Thomas. I did tell you we'd meet again, but not like this," Noba said.

"What's going on? Where did this fog come from?" Thomas took a breath and tried to calm down, aware he sounded a bit hysterical. Where have you been the last few weeks?"

"Oh, here and there. That's not important now. Maybe I can get you out of here before it's too late." She grabbed his arm with surprising strength and started pulling him along the street.

"What are you talking about? Get me away from what?" Thomas asked, stumbling along behind her. Just as quickly as she had started walking, Noba stopped, causing Thomas to bump into her.

"Too late," she said.

Then Thomas heard the sound. A lone hound's mournful baying started, then it was joined by another, and another, until the entire pack was howling, a ghostly chorus that chilled Thomas's spine. It sounded like they were just at the end of the street.

"Noba, what the hell's going on?"

The auburn-haired girl smiled grimly. "Thomas, you'll have to study harder if you expect to ever get that degree. My full name is Abnoba. Perhaps that will help."

Thomas bit back his first instinct, which was to laugh at her. Abnoba was a Celtic goddess of the hunt, similar to Diana. A mistress of the forest, it was believed that she had also had connections to maternity or fertility. The idea that this slim young woman was the incarnation of an ancient mythological figure struck Thomas as more than a little deranged. *Okay, I'll just play along until I can get out of here,* he thought.

"So, those are your dogs?" he asked, smiling.

"No, they're his," Abnoba said, pointing down the alley toward a reddish-hued light, where the outline of a very tall humanoid was visible. As he strode toward them, the fog dissipated in front of him, reforming after his passage. On his head was a massive pair of antlers, silhouetted in the crimson glow. A huge sword hilt jutted over one shoulder. Thomas didn't even want to think about the blade it was attached to.

The figure stopped just before his features would have become visible. Now Thomas could see other shapes around him, canine forms swirling through the pale mist. Their eyes glowed an unearthly red, their speckled white bodies blending nearly perfectly with the fog. They trotted in between the man's legs, their chains clinking as they moved. The man (at least Thomas assumed that's what he was) raised his hand, and the entire pack moved as one, standing at readiness in a perfect line in front of him.

"That's—" Abnoba began.

"I know exactly who that is. Arawn, lord of the underworld in Celtic myth—" Thomas stopped, realizing that finishing his sentence could get him killed. As far as he knew, gods didn't like to be told they weren't real.

This can't be happening, it's got to be some kind of really weird trick they play on the tourists, he thought weakly. But the odors of leather and fur made a convincing argument that it most certainly was happening. Thomas didn't know why he was suddenly convinced that this was the actual god, and not just some leather-clad freak celebrating Samhain six months early, but somehow he knew that what he was looking at was the the real thing. *Perhaps because this is too ludicrous to be anything but the real thing, whatever that may be,* he thought.

Arawn said nothing, but pointed a leather-sheathed finger at Thomas.

"I know mortals do not participate in the hunt, my lord, but this was an accident. However, now that he is here, he will give you merry sport, I assure you," Abnoba said.

Sport? I'm going to be sport? The anger that rose in Thomas dispelled his initial fear and confusion. "Excuse me?" he said. "Look, I don't know exactly what kind of twisted games you folks play at night, but I'm not going—"

"If you wish to survive this night, then consider this anything but a game," Abnoba said. "You followed me, remember? Now you're in it. The hounds already have your scent, so you can't leave, even if you wanted to. Your only choice is to play."

"Play what?" Thomas asked, afraid he already knew the answer.

Abnoba smiled. "Come now, Thomas, surely you know your mythology better than that. Arawn loves to hunt. This time, we will be his quarry."

Thomas looked at her, than back at the panting hounds and their shadowy master. Was it his imagination, or had their teeth and claws suddenly grown larger? "You've got to be kidding," he said.

Abnoba shook her head. "I'm afraid not."

Thomas looked at her for a long moment, then chuckled. "Very funny. This is cute, it really is, but I'm leaving now." Shaking his head, Thomas spun on his heel, only to freeze as he heard a chorus of low growls from behind him. Abnoba stood beside him again.

"Take another step and they'll be all over you," she said.

Thomas looked back at the hounds, all of which were staring at him. "This is all really happening, isn't it?"

Abnoba nodded. "Yes, it really is."

"He's really going to hunt us down, isn't he?"

Again she nodded.

"But it's no contest, I mean, I certainly can't outrun a pack of hounds," Thomas protested.

"Not in this form, true. I will help with that," Abnoba said.

"Great, I feel so much better already," Thomas muttered.

"Of course, I could just leave you like you are . . ." Abnoba let her sentence trail off, an ominous look on her face.

"No, no, please, whatever you can do would be really appreciated," Thomas said, realizing the folly of biting the hand that could save him. "How long will we be hunted?"

"The hunt starts at midnight and lasts until dawn . . . or until we're captured," Abnoba said.

"Why can't he just go hunt a stag or something?"

Abnoba's smile nearly lit the dim street. "Oh he does,

but every so often Arawn desires more of a . . . challenge."

"And if we get caught?" Thomas asked with a sinking feeling.

"If we're caught, then the hounds will do what they do best, next to chasing their prey to ground," Abnoba said. "However, if the chase is exciting enough, Arawn has been known to spare the life of his victim."

Thomas looked at the grinning dogs, who were watching him like he was a walking beef brisket. "Great, that's what I needed to hear. Is that why you're still around?"

"That, and the fact that I'm immortal. We don't have to follow all the rules," Abnoba said.

"Ah. By the way, does he ever say anything?" Thomas asked, motioning towards Arawn.

Abnoba's face turned grave. "No mortal can hear the voice of Arawn and live."

"Oh." Thomas said, slowly backing away from the towering figure.

Off in the distance, a clock tower began tolling midnight. The pack tensed expectantly, awaiting the command from their master.

"Time to go," Abnoba said, turning and heading for what Thomas assumed was the other end of the street.

"Wait, what about the help you promised?" Thomas asked.

"Walk with me," Abnoba said, linking her arm through Thomas's. Although the fog was still as thick as ever, it didn't seem to affect her in the least.

At the end of Kirwan Lane, just off Quay Street, she turned to him. "Now, when the change happens, start running as fast as you can. Head across Wolfetone Bridge and up Henry Street to Newcastle toward the university. Got it?"

"Yes, but what—" was all Thomas had time to say before Abnoba leaned forward and kissed him. At that moment, had she asked, Thomas would have gladly headed back down the street to battle Arawn barehanded. However, as he soon discovered, that was no longer an option.

Convulsing, Thomas found himself hunched over on all fours, his whole body tingling. He looked down to see his arms lengthening, becoming narrow and sheathed in fine fur. He felt his legs readjusting themselves, with packed muscles that weren't there before growing and stretching. His head grew heavy for a moment, then his neck elongated and strengthened, adjusting to the weight. His eyes blurred, and he blinked several times, discovering that his sight was now partially obscured, as if he was looking at the world through a brown beer bottle. Twitching his ears, he realized that his senses of smell and hearing had become phenomenally acute. He stood up, hearing his feet (all four of them now) clip-clop on the stones. Looking down, he saw his hands and feet had turned into sturdy hooves.

What has happened to me? Thomas looked up at a shop window and got his answer.

The face of a noble stag stared back at him, crowned by a magnificent rack of antlers, and followed by a large sleek body. Thomas scarcely had time to admire his new look, for he heard Abnoba's voice telling him, "Run!" The pack all howled at once, and Thomas heard dozens of claws scrabbling on stone. A second later, the first of the hounds, all teeth and tongue and tail, exploded from the fog.

Galvanized into movement, he shot forward toward Wolfetone Bridge. His new body seemed to know what it was doing just fine, so he concentrated on keeping himself pointed in the right direction. *I suppose it wouldn't be quite the accomplishment to catch a stag that was staggering around like it was drunk,* Thomas thought. He hit the bridge and clattered across it, all too aware of the clamoring pack close behind him. *Where the hell is Abnoba?*

"Thomas, I'm right beside you." Thomas heard in his mind. *"No, don't look!"* she commanded.

But it was too late. As Thomas instinctively turned his head to find her, his massive body followed right along with him, cutting Abnoba off between him and the stone walls of the bridge. The hounds took advantage of their confusion to narrow the gap, and Thomas swore he could feel their breath on his flanks.

"Straighten out!" she thought at him.

"What the hell do you think I'm trying to do!" Thomas

wheeled himself back over and poured on the speed, rounding the corner and heading for Dominick Street Upriver. Abnoba bounded ahead of him, leaping effortlessly, or so it seemed. She was now keeping pace with him in the form of a graceful doe.

"Dammit, pay attention to where you're going!" she thought at him.

"Hey, it's not everyday I get turned into a stag and chased by supernatural hounds and a Celtic god, you know! Why don't you cut me a little slack!" Thomas shot back while looking ahead to make sure no one was in his way as the pair ran up Henry Street.

"Don't worry, no mortal can detect us now. The hunt is invisible to human eyes," Abnoba thought to him.

"Thank God. I'd hate to think of what might happen when the pubs closed," Thomas thought back.

"Save your concentration for running," Abnoba thought. Thomas didn't even reply, but instead stepped up the pace, drawing ahead of the barking pack.

They were now on the straightaway leading up to the Newcastle intersection, and Thomas found, once he got over the surprise of being turned into a large horned animal, that he was actually savoring the wind in his face and the feel of his new, powerful body as he covered twenty feet and more in a single leap. Although he would have thought that a stag's hooves wouldn't have been able to handle the stony road, Thomas was able to run with no pain at all. *I suppose that's one of the advantages of being transformed by a goddess.*

For a second, it seemed like the stag's body was running of its own accord with Thomas just tagging along for the ride. He smelled the myriad scents that made up the Irish night, from the rich grass and peat they ran past to the smell of cooking salmon and oysters from the pubs they had left behind. Despite the clamor of the hounds at his heels, his ears gathered every available sound from the darkness, from the gurgle of the River Corrib as it emptied into the lake to the rustle of the wind as it blew across the heath to the faint inimitable sound of a bagpipe jig. A feeling of antiquity washed over Thomas, the sense that he was participating in a ritual that stretched back to the dawn of time and perhaps earlier.

As the pair hit Newcastle Road, Thomas was seized with a sudden desire to leave the beaten paths. *"Hey Noba, follow me!"*

"Thomas, what are you doing?"

"Arawn wants a good hunt, doesn't he? Well, let's give him one!" With that Thomas leaped off the road and onto the soft loam of the Irish fields, Abnoba right beside. The pair of deer paralleled the road until they had passed the hospital and University of Galway, with Thomas casting a contemptuous look at the library building as they ran by.

Once outside Galway proper, they ran alongside the N59 road for a few minutes, then peeled off into the *Maigh Cuilin* region, an unspoiled landscape of gently rolling hills and fields.

"I hope you realize that the hounds will be able to run us down more easily out here," Abnoba thought to him.

"I don't care. One of the reasons I came to Ireland was to see the landscape, and I'll be damned if I'm going to die without experiencing it one last time." Thomas thought.

"I will say this, Thomas, I do admire your spirit," Abnoba thought.

"Thanks, just do me a favor and keep up," Thomas thought.

"The stag or man has not been born that can outrun me," Abnoba thought as she accelerated ahead of Thomas, who put on his own burst of speed to match. It seemed their hooves barely touched the soft grass as they flew across the fields to the hills beyond. The tireless hounds were still behind them, barking their delight at the chase.

As Thomas climbed the first hill, he noticed that his body was tiring a bit and he was breathing more heavily. *So much for supernatural endurance,* he thought. *I suppose Arawn, like Hades, eventually wins in the end.* That thought seemed to spur a greater anger in him. *Americans don't run from a threat. I've played by their rules long enough. It's time to change the game.*

At the top of the hill, Thomas skidded to a stop and

wheeled around. The moon bathed the land in soft white light, making the dark waters of the River Corrib sparkle and flash on its journey to the lake. The gentle hills and rolling fields looked as if they had been cast in silver, frozen forever in time. A few miles away, the lights of Galway twinkled as its inhabitants drank or danced or slept the night away. Thomas's breathing slowed as he took in the scene, filling his lungs one more time with the cool night air. He felt strangely calm, as if he had stopped fighting against this fate. *It is a good night to die,* he thought to himself.

With an angry snort, he lowered his antlers toward the approaching pack. He could see the dogs charging up the hill, and behind them Arawn, following on a gigantic black charger.

"Thomas, what are you doing?" came Abnoba's alarmed thought.

"I'm simply playing your game my way," Thomas answered. The hounds were almost cresting the hill, the leader opening a mouth that looked like a bottomless pit. A few more steps and the pack would be upon him. Thomas pawed the ground with his foreleg and made sure his hind legs were firmly planted so he couldn't be bowled over.

"Thomas, run! You can still escape!" Abnoba cried.

"No, I won't give him the satisfaction. If I am going to die, it will be on my terms, not his. I think this is as good a way as any," Thomas thought. The lead hounds spilled over the top of the hill and leaped for Thomas. With equal rage, he braced himself to meet the charge . . .

. . . Only to find himself instantly returned to his own human body, just in time to see the first hound flying through the air straight at him. Throwing up his arms, Thomas yelled in terror as the wiry dog slammed into him, bowling him over.

Off balance and rolling down the hill, Thomas clawed for a handhold to stop his descent. He landed face up with a hound of Arawn standing on his chest, its claws digging into his skin. The beast's hot breath stifled him. Its teeth looked as large as short swords.

"All right," he said, grimacing, "get it over with."

The dog's face came closer . . . and slobbered all over Thomas as it licked his cheek. The rest of the pack came pouring down the hill in an avalanche of fur and surrounded Thomas, tails wagging and tongues hanging out. It was only seconds before he was soaked to the skin, his face and neck nearly licked raw.

A piercing whistle cut through the night air, and as one all the hounds left Thomas where he lay. Raising his head, Thomas saw the pack regroup around Arawn, who inclined his head slightly toward Thomas, wheeled his horse around, and rode off into the fields, his hounds flitting around him like pale spectres in the moonlight.

Then Abnoba was standing over him, smiling. "My, my, my, don't you look a mess."

Thomas just lay there, staring at her in silence. "What?" she finally asked.

"I was never in any real danger, was I?"

"Not really, I wouldn't have allowed it. A dozen centuries or so quells the appetite for blood rather nicely. I don't want you to think we've all gone soft in our dotage, however. While Arawn can be a funny bird sometimes, he does respect courage, which you certainly showed tonight. You gave good sport, as I thought you would," Abnoba said. "What I didn't count on is that you would bring us so far out of town. Would you mind if I took you back? It would be quicker than walking."

"Sure, on one condition," Thomas said as he got to his feet. "Let's run back without a pack of hounds at our heels."

"Done," Abnoba said, her cloak rustling as she stepped closer to Thomas. This time, however, he initiated the kiss, pulling her close to him as he did so.

The familiar tingling came over him again as they broke apart. "I've always wanted to kiss a goddess," Thomas said. Then the change came over him and they were off again.

This time, without the sense of being hunted, Thomas reveled in the sensations that coursed through him. Together Abnoba and he circled around Galway, sometimes running at full speed, sometimes trotting, sometimes just lazily walking. Thomas even tried the local flora, and found out that while his body had changed, his tastes hadn't. Abnoba found his experiment very amusing. *I've never seen a deer laugh before,* he mused as he spit the mouthful of grass out.

After a few hours, they found themselves back in Galway, wandering up Cross street to Busker Brownes, where the whole evening had started.

"Stop here," Abnoba said. She looked at him for a moment, and then they were both back in their respective original bodies.

"Why does it take a kiss to transform me into a stag?" Thomas asked.

"It doesn't, it's just more fun that way," Abnoba said. She looked up at the stars for a moment. "It's been quite an evening, hasn't it, Thomas?"

"Yes, it has. I just wish I knew what parts were real," Thomas said.

"What do you mean?"

"Well, it's obvious you planned this from the beginning," Thomas said.

"No, I actually did spill my drink on you. What can I say, even gods aren't perfect all the time," Abnoba said. "But once I got to talking with you, I liked what I found."

"If that's true, then why did you lie to me?" Thomas asked.

"I didn't lie, I tricked you. A woman only tells the truth half the time, remember?" Abnoba smiled. "Besides, you shouldn't have been there in the first place. But there you were, so there was really no choice for anyone. And Arawn does not like his hunting to be spoiled, so I gave him what he wanted. Anyway, would you have really done your best if you hadn't believed your life was at stake? That wouldn't even have been any fun. And you're here now, whole and in one piece, so what are you complaining about? I mean, do you know what you just took part in?"

"Yes, I think I do," Thomas said. "The celebration of the hunt, the kinship between the hunter and his prey, the thrill of the chase, the fear of the pursued. The thanks from the hunter to the animal spirit for allowing the hunt to happen. By taking the place of the hunted, you understand and grow closer to it. All of that, and more."

"Well said. There might be hope for you as a literature student yet. Speaking of, I have a gift for you." Abnoba reached under her cloak and brought out a leaf-wrapped parcel, which she handed to Thomas. "Be careful of strange women spilling beer on you in the future." She leaned over and gave him a quick kiss, then started walking down the street.

"Wait! Will I ever see you again?" Thomas called after her.

Abnoba half-turned toward him, her smiling face gleaming silver in the moonlight. "I'm sure we'll run into each other again, Thomas. After all, it's a small town." And with that, she was gone.

Thomas stared at the spot where he last saw her for a long while. Only when the first rays of the rising sun spilled over the horizon did he remember the package in his hands. Carefully unwrapping it, he found a familiar book of poems, whole and undamaged. Opening the cover, he found a note written in silver on a freshly picked leaf.

"What is kipling?"

Knowledge is often a fragile thing, and the Guardian knows that only a few strong individuals can accept certain aspects of it. One Seeker has come for this special knowledge. The Master of the Archives nods to a man of middle years whose silence is as intense as his dark eyes. Only he among this group asked to see a possible future. The light from the Guide's fingers appears almost transparent, like a thought not yet finished. The man rises from the table and finds his gateway is an iron door shrouded in shadow. Beyond it are miles of subterranean concrete caverns where he learns of the:

PRECURSOR

by Matthew Woodring Stover

THE funny thing about storm sewers is how *loud* they are. You'd think, down under the streets there, yards of concrete and earth between you and the rumble of trucks and the snarling of car horns, that there'd be a cathedrallike hush—with the low vault of the curving roof overhead, and the way darkness before and behind seems to press in against the beam of your flashlight. You expect the odd skitter of rat claws on cement, the occasional plash of water drops; what you get is a sort of generalized thunder of rushing streams and heavy trucks, picked up faintly, maybe, at the source, but concentrated and echoed upon themselves, reflected from cement and channelled through miles of tunnel.

The sound wraps you up; you can't hear your footsteps, or your breathing, and it gets louder the longer you listen, until when you speak, you start with a shout and are shocked at the echoes. And then for a time the sewers seem quieter, but it builds again. The longer you let it, the louder it gets.

After an hour, we keep up a constant stream of conversation, even Duncan—it's the only way to keep the noise at bay.

Me, I'd prefer silence. At least I'd have a chance to hear something coming up behind me.

We walk.

Duncan holds his funky spotlight across his chest like a soldier in Basic; I keep the Nitro slung. Shay drifts along like a sleepwalker, eyes half-shut, her head cocked like a deer listening for wolves. We wander randomly; my watch tells me we've only been down here 90 minutes. I know better.

In my bones, I know we've been under the city for years.

Forever.

No way of telling where we are by now. There are metal signs bolted to the walls here and there, covered with glistening slime that reflects back a flashlight's beam. None of us bother to wipe one off.

It doesn't really matter where we are in relation to the city; the city over our heads has nothing to do with us. We might as well be on another planet. The sewers are warmer than the ground above, but not enough so to account for the sheen of seat that paints Duncan's face. He grins at me.

"Having fun yet, Harry?"

Shay stops at a branching tunnel. "It's been here," she says quietly. She points with her flashlight. "It went that way." She sets off in that direction without waiting to see if we follow. The back of my neck prickles as we go after her.

I stick as close by her shoulder as I could, and keep my thumb hooked behind the rifle's strap.

"Are you ever going to tell me what this thing is?" I murmur to Duncan. "I mean, you know, I'm down here walking through this stinking sewer and all you've got is a spotlight, and what the hell exactly are we looking for? You know?"

"Why, Harry!" Duncan says tightly. "I think you're starting to lose confidence in me."

"Duncan, Jesus Christ—"

"Actually, I was wondering what took you so long to ask. Still a bit shy with me, Harry? After all we've been through?"

I move closer to Shay. "Forget about it."

But the smothering noise gets to be too much for him, and he comes close to us to speak softly. The faint tremor in his voice doesn't do a lot for my nerves. "This is what I think. I think it's a troll."

In the chill winter afternoon, Duncan looked like he'd been waiting for a while; he leaned against his car with the ubiquitous dangling cigarette trailing lazy curls of smoke. He was a tall, slender man, with the looks and manner that come only from money. Old money. Clear blue eyes, glossy brown hair, perfect teeth, chiseled jaw and cheekbones: an easy face to hate. He was also astonishingly strong and swift for such a skinny man; he beat the snot out of me once a couple years ago, not long after we first met. Maybe I deserved it and maybe I didn't, but that's not the point. We both knew he could do it again any time. That's the point. That's what kept me from taking a poke at him damn near every time we met.

His car was some low-slung Italian upper-five-figures thing; his gray trenchcoat looked hand-tailored. I pulled my battered Mustang up next to him and climbed out.

"Duncan," I said in greeting.

"Harry." He sounded cool as ever, but he was pale, and new lines had carved themselves around his mouth.

I looked around. "Where's your Psychic Friends Network?"

He jerked a thumb over his shoulder at the dingy blues bar down the street. "In the can. Think she's on the rag."

I just shook my head. Answering would have only encouraged him.

Afternoon in the West Loop is a bleak and dirty time. We stood in the tangle of railroad tracks at the ass-end of Jefferson Street, at the barrier of oil-soaked timbers packed with blackened snow. Dead weeds poked through the soiled drifts along the tracks. It's a neighborhood of windowless warehouses and decaying factories and the constant rumble of the El and the freight trains; the slate-gray winter light draws your eye to the broken windows and the clumps of miscellaneous garbage. I turned up the collar of my overcoat and shivered.

"Why here?" I said. "Hell, *Uptown*'s less depressing."

He blew a cloud of smoke at me. "Yeah, but in Uptown somebody might be wondering why three nice folks like us are climbing down a manhole. Around here, you don't even get bums—excuse me, homeless persons. You still look like hell. You take that nap?"

I shook my head and waved away the cigarette smoke. "I couldn't sleep if I tried. I don't mind telling you this thing has me kind of spooked."

"Harry Pigeon, you are this century's great unrecognized master of understatement. Personally, I'm scared shitless," he said with an easy smile.

It never takes long for me to get tired of Duncan's crap. "So," I said heavily, "what's the plan? What did you do all day?"

"I'll show you." He opened the trunk of his expensive European whatever-it-was. Inside was something that looked vaguely like a homemade version of a flamethrower: a bulky backpack attached by cables to a three-foot-long black tube. There was an oversized pistol grip crudely welded about a third of the way down the tube, along with what looked like one of those circular wall switches that yuppies like, you know, the kind that can dim or raise the room lights? He said, "The real key to hunting is the proper weapon."

"That's a weapon?"

He nodded. "I had a friend put it together. If I'm altogether right, this'll stop your killer in its tracks."

"What do you mean, if you're 'altogether right'?"

"Well, I've never actually used one before. It's a carbon-arc light."

"You mean like a laser?"

"Not exactly. More like a spotlight."

"You're nuts," I told him.

I said it like I was sure I was right—but if I was sure, I wouldn't have met him there in the first place.

I wasn't too sure of anything anymore.

All I really knew was this:

Something hungry had come to Chicago.

At the rim of stark white pool of floodlight in Cabrini-Green, I'd watched a dog nuzzle at the headless corpses of three teenage boys; I'd watched it turn aside to lap at the sluggish puddle of blood that still leaked from their necks.

In the Lincoln Park Zoo, I'd watched flies walk across the open eyes of a pride of lions before flickering down to feed on the remnants of their guts spilled across the sand-colored stone.

In four days, a single Streets & Sanitation crew found the bloody heads of twenty-seven dogs.

A workman wandered away, I was told, from the city crew that cleaned and repaired the North/Clybourn subway station, seeking the darkness of the tunnels to smoke a little dope and make the night pass more swiftly. When he did not return, his coworkers searched for him and found only a red-spattered yellow safety vest and his carved pipe of pale marble.

A pair of severed legs held open the door of a small house in Marquette Park. We followed the wide-smeared trail of blood that marked where a middle-aged man had dragged himself, clawing into his dirty threadbare carpet, to die beneath a red, white, and black flag bearing a swastika. We found him huddled there as though seeking sanctuary at an altar.

Before dawn that morning, I'd been called to a new multiple homicide, at the pilings on the Chicago River bank beside Lower Wacker. Three men, two white, one black. A machine pistol—an Ingram Mac-10—was still clutched in a white hand at the end of a severed arm, and the ground was littered with shiny brass nine-millimeter casings. All three bodies had horrible gaping wounds in the torso, exposing torn and tangled bowels. Bits of leather and cloth from their coats had frozen into the wounds. The black man's head had been torn completely off; it lay wide-eyed a few feet away. One of the white men—not the one with the missing arm—had tried to crawl away from his killer; his guts trailed behind him and one of his thighs was flayed to the bone, hip to knee.

I'd tried to imagine what would make wounds like those while I struggled to keep the coffee in my stomach. A fire ax, maybe, or one of those three-pronged garden tiller rakes swung by Mr. Universe. Both of the men who still had their arms wore guns; one had a big automatic behind his belt and the grip of what looked like an old Chief's Special poked out of the other's jacket pocket.

The frost on the little swatch of grass where they lay had been melted in dozens of tiny disks, maybe an inch in diameter—melted by the heat of the flattened, spent nine-millimeter slugs that lay scattered at random around the bodies.

They'd hit something, and *bounced*.

Crime Scene found what looked like footprints, crushed into the frozen earth; they told me these couldn't really be footprints—whatever made those impressions had to weigh at least a thousand pounds.

I'd suddenly found myself conducting an investigation where my prime suspect was the Incredible Hulk.

This had gotten entirely out of control. Something drastic had to be done.

I did something drastic: I called Mike Duncan.

He and his partner—Chaeli Forbes—they're not cops. They're hunters.

Now in the bleak afternoon light, Duncan hefted his homemade spotlight and shrugged at me. "You saw those bullets on the ground. You have a better idea?"

"A spotlight. You're out of your mind." I went over to my Mustang, opened the door and pulled out the soft leather case containing my better idea. I handed it to Duncan. "I got to thinking about all that myself. Those Ingrams don't have all that hot a muzzle velocity."

He unzipped the case and looked inside. "Jesus Christ!" he said. "What is this damn thing, an elephant gun?"

"Exactly," I told him. "That's a .455 Nitro Express, belonged to my grandfather. A slug from this rifle would go straight through the engine block of that big-dick car of yours and still have enough left to take your balls off." I filled my coat pocket with a handful of the thick finger-length shells.

Duncan had the rifle out and was admiring it. He snapped the stock to his shoulder and squeezed off an imaginary shot. He whistled. "It's a beautiful gun, Harry, I'd never deny it." He handed it back to me. "It won't do you any damn good, but it's beautiful."

"You're just jealous."

"Don't say I didn't warn you." Duncan nodded at something over my shoulder. "Here comes Shay."

Tall and slender, cut from the same aristocratic mold as Duncan but young, frighteningly young. She came toward us on the street with a peculiar coltish grace, all knees and elbows but somehow controlled and effortlessly charming. The setting sun behind her transformed her fine, drifting red-gold hair into a shimmering halo about her pale heart-shaped face. She looked toward us as she approached, but there was no seeing in her eyes, only the bewildered questing of a jacklighted deer.

She mumbled something I couldn't quite make out—it sounded like *angry*—or maybe *hungry*.

"She's got him," Duncan said.

Her eyes were completely vacant. "Far below . . ." she murmured. "Beat the sun . . . concrete and water . . . tunnels and moss and rats and rock . . ."

Duncan nodded to himself and winked at me. "You ready for this?"

"I, ah . . ." I sighed. "I'm never gonna be ready for this."

"Then there's no reason to wait," Duncan said, lighting another cigarette with his perfect movie-star timing. He pulled a long prybar out of his car's trunk and levered up the manhole cover.

"Let's go."

"Okay, it's a troll," I say slowly, softly, trying to ignore the way even my lowest tone seems to ring back overloud from the concrete bounds of the sewer. "Let's say that's what it is. Where did it come from? What's it doing in Chicago?"

"Feeding." He shrugs. "Where it came from? Who knows? Northridge, California. San Francisco, maybe." His eyes glitter in the flashlight's glow. "Maybe Mexico City."

I stare at him. "But Chicago—there's never been earthquakes in Chicago . . ."

"Not recently." He turns his head so I can't see his face. "Ever hear of the New Madrid fault?"

I don't really want to think about this—not now, not down here.

"I think it might be a population-pressure thing," he says. "This series of murders—animal attacks, whatever you want to call them—you find this kind of stuff all the time, increasing in frequency and intensity in the quake zones. Look at LA, San Francisco, Mexico City—hell, look at China; look at Armenia, take your pick. They're like opening shocks, you might say, like what scientists call *precursors*—except the scientists are only talking about earth tremors. I think that maybe, if the, the, whatever they are, the trolls, breed up to a certain density, it triggers something—the earth opens, y'know; letting in the light of day, whatever. A die-off."

"You seem to know a lot about them."

"Reading is Fun-damental, Harry. There's extensive literature on the subject, you'd be surprised. Once you sift through all the crap, you find that the only thing that kills them is sunlight." He smiles weakly. "Turns them to stone, you know."

"Oh, God."

"Oh, yeah. You have to remember that basically, they're only animated stone to begin with—the touch of the sun destroys all kinds of night magic. Think of vampire stories, and fairy tales, and riding the night-mare until the cock crows and all that stuff."

"But, I mean, come *on*, Duncan—!"

He shrugs, half-embarrassed to be saying this out loud. "There's an account by a fella name of Nikos Makronos, who claims he encountered a troll living in the basement of a theater in Cyprus in 1932. He survived by tricking it up onto the stage and turning the theatre's main spotlight onto the thing."

"It was a carbon-arc?"

Duncan nods. "Used to be real popular."

"And that killed it?"

"Well, old Niko got away, didn't he? My guess is that it's something in the UV band that kills them. Carbonarcs put out a lot of UV."

"But did he kill it?"

Duncan grins at me, sweat gleaming on his face, his usually-perfect hair plastered to his forehead. "Harry, if I knew that, this'd hardly be any sport at all."

*   *   *

We pace an hour's length, maybe a day's—in the endlessly rumbling silence, I can't tell the difference. I've given up looking at my watch.

Shay stops suddenly; I bump into her and back off, muttering apologies that I don't think she hears. Her whole body's trembling. Her hand shakes—she points to a broad, ragged-edged patch of darkness on the mossy surface of the tunnel's wall a few yards ahead.

"Home," she says in a small voice that's eerily calm. "We're close to home."

Duncan gestures for us to wait and glides up along the walkway. He stops beside the dark patch, his back against the wall, his chest expanding and contracting with great, slow breaths. He fiddles with the knob on his spotlight; even over the constant sewer-rumble I can hear a crackling buzz as an eye-burning disk of blue-white light appears on the cement above him.

He fiddles a bit more and the fuzzy edges of the disk sharpen into perfect focus. He looks back at us with a tight smile, gives us a thumbs up, then swings smoothly around, bringing the spotlight to bear like a rifle, and disappears into the darkness.

I shake my head. "Is he crazy or what?"

Shay gives me a look that hurts my chest. "Aren't you going after him?"

I look at that ragged patch of darkness and try to swallow my heart. "I, uh, I don't know. I mean, he wanted us to wait. . . ."

"Harry, he doesn't even have a gun."

I lick my chapped lips, but it doesn't help; the driest thing in this whole maze of sewers is my tongue. "And leave you here alone?"

Those beautiful leaf-green eyes of hers fix on my face; I can feel them, even though I can't meet their gaze.

"I guess I'm not as crazy as he is," I mutter. She and I both know that *crazy* means *brave*. Still, somehow I force my hands to unsling the Nitro and I start moving toward the hole.

Duncan saves me: before I get halfway there, before I have to stand there and find out whether or not I can make myself walk into that darkness, I see the beam of the arclight coming from the hole, and he steps back onto the walkway and beckons to us, his habitual smile a little tighter than usual.

Before we reach him I can smell that smell—that one from the river beside Lower Wacker, that half-gagging musky, skunky smell—stronger here, I can feel it filling my lungs.

"Duncan, for Pete's sake!" I snarl. "What's in there? What'd you find?"

"Tunnels," he says softly. "Lots of them, going up, down, sideways. I was afraid I'd get lost."

Shay touches the rim of the ragged hole, stroked away bits of earth and stone. She says, "Oh."

I say, "That sounds like bad news. . . ."

"Oh, Michael . . ." she murmurs, "this tunnel . . . it wasn't dug by the one I've been following. . . ."

Duncan closes his eyes, and leans his head back against the slick cement wall.

For a while I can't seem to do anything but look at Duncan and feel bone-deep cold seeping in through my numb fingers and wrapping around my stomach. Up to now, I'd been doing a really good job of not thinking about the bodies by the river, about the man in Marquette Park, or the lions at the zoo.

Now I think about them, about claws and teeth, about what it would feel like when skin and muscle is ripped away from bone by blunt fingers. I think about the expression on the severed head by the river. I think about seeing that look in Shay's bright eyes.

I say, "Duncan, let's get out of here."

He looks at me. "And do what?"

"Go," I say. "Just go. For the love of *Christ*, Duncan! Didn't you hear her? There's more than one!"

"Yeah, I know, Harry. What's your point?"

I can't answer him. To answer him, I'd have to think about it, and I can't let myself do that.

Duncan draws himself up. "You can leave if you want. I'm going up there. I figure I only need one."

"For what?" I say desperately. "A head to hang on your stupid trophy wall?"

Shay murmurs, "To prove they exist."

Duncan cocks a finger and shoots her with it. "Exactly. Once we do that, we can leave the mopping up to your buddies on the force."

"What's wrong with you? You *want* to do this!"

"Reading, Harry." Duncan's eyes take on a faraway cast and his smile returns, faintly. "Ever read Hemingway? 'The Short Happy Life of Francis Macomber.' You'd like it, I think."

For an instant I fantasize drawing down on him with the Nitro, marching him back up into the open air at gunpoint—but I know, I just know it won't work. He'd face me down, the way he always does. And I can't let him go in there alone.

Not for the first time, I am reminded what a powerful force shame can be.

"All right, you prick. All right," I say, surrendering. "But let's get Shay out of here, at least. There was a manhole not too far back that way. We can take her up and come back here."

But now it was Shay shaking her head. She has her arms wrapped across her slender chest, holding onto herself to stop the trembling, and her face is sheet-pale in the glow from the flashlights. She says distantly, "You need me."

I begin to sputter. Duncan cuts me off. "She's right. It's a maze in there, a maze in Three-D. We need to find the nest—you know, wherever they've set up housekeeping. We need to find our way in . . . and we might need to find our way *out* in a sizable hurry. We'll never do it without her."

I guess, in the end, what makes the difference is that I still don't really believe in them, no matter what Duncan says. After a few seconds, I just shrug and slide the Nitro's strap higher onto my shoulder.

Duncan nods at me like a solemnly proud father, and leads us away into the darkness.

The earth of the tunnels is moist but not muddy, full of rocks that pick up the beams from the flashlights, some of them glittering like gems. The tunnels are easily big enough for even Duncan to stand upright—in some of them he can stretch his arm up to full extension and not reach the ceiling—and we can walk three abreast.

We can, but we don't.

We stick close together, Duncan leading and me behind, Shay in the middle, walking with her right hand brushing the soft earth beside us and murmuring directions. Occasional cross-tunnels open to the right or left, some sloping down, but most angling gently upward. We generally take the upward turns. That animal reek in here is thick and never fades; my nose can't adjust to it the way it does to ordinary smells. It's so potent that a deep breath can make me cough and earn me an exasperated warning look from Duncan.

There is no more conversation.

After a time we come to a crossing tunnel, and Duncan freezes. We copy him. He lifts a hand, his head tilted to listen intently. I can't hear anything—but when he starts fumbling for the rheostat on the arclight, I unsling the Nitro.

I feel a rhythmic vibration coming up through my boots. This time there is no pause for a cocky grin and a thumbs up: the beam bursts brilliantly from the arclight's barrel and Duncan swings around the corner and the creature hits him like a freight train.

I drop the flashlight when Duncan screams. The arclight's beam spins crazily and winks out. In the weakly rolling light of the dropped flash I can see something huge and gray, bigger than a bear, massive gorilla arm uplifted with blunt and bloody claws.

The Nitro goes off with a blinding flash and shattering roar, recoil slamming the stock against my shoulderjoint, knocking me stumbling backward. Shay is screaming, I'm screaming, the creature spins, knocked backward, falling. Afterimage blooms inside my eyes, wiping out most of my vision—movement, noise, the creature rises, looming over us, howling like a wounded dinosaur, a blurred glimpse of violet eyes the size of dinner plates and I yank on the second trigger.

Another flash and bang, and then only the sound of something heavy thumping away as I break the Nitro and scrabble in my pocket for more shells. I fumble them and they scatter across the floor, and I drop to my knees and paw after them until I finally realize that it doesn't matter, the thing's gone, because if it wasn't, I'd be dead already.

I kneel there on the floor of the tunnel, gasping "My God, my God," over and over, barely able to hear myself through the ringing in my ears.

Shay's voice comes to me faintly. "Harry, Harry, he's hurt! Harry, help me!"

I lurch to my feet and start to stumble toward her voice, until Duncan barks, "Don't be a bloody idiot, Pigeon! Reload your damned rifle, it could come back!"

This makes good sense to me, right now; I blink and rub my eyes, trying to erase the bright green flame that fills my vision. As it starts to fade, I manage to gather a handful of the shells, poke a couple into the Nitro's chambers and recover the flashlight, all the while listening to Duncan's preternaturally calm voice.

"Tighter," he says, "there. I can hold this one, but you'll have to tie off the arm. Take the laces from my boot—won't be needing that, not now. . . ."

"Oh, Michael," Shay says thickly as I come up to them. "Oh, my God, Michael—"

Duncan looks up at me with a sickly smile. "Hello, Harry. Wouldn't happen to have a Band-Aid, would you?"

The right leg of Duncan's trousers is torn away, along with a football-sized chunk of meat from his thigh. Shay had used his belt to tie a tourniquet just below his hip-joint, using the other flashlight as a tightener. Shay's furiously unlacing his boot, her breath coming in short, choppy gasps. He's using his left hand to block the armpit pressure-point of his right arm; the outside of his arm has been stripped to the pink-gleaming bone.

The earth around him is black with his blood.

"Have to apologize about the rifle," he says. "Good thing you brought it. Saved my life."

"Don't try to talk," I say numbly. "We'll get you out of here."

"I should bloody well hope so." His voice is thin with stiff-upper-lip strain. "Get it? Bloody well? I'm a big enough man to admit I was wrong. And, Harry, I want to thank you for not saying *I told you so*."

"Duncan, for once in your life, shut up, will you?"

"Listen, you have to take the light. I think it was working—I only grazed him, across the right shoulder, but I think it did something—you notice he only got me with his left."

The arclight lies beside him, dented and bent, bright streaks showing where claws had scored it. One of the cables ends in a glittering spray of wires.

"It's broken," I say hoarsely.

"Well, somebody'd better fix it, hadn't they?"

Shay had now gotten the lace around Duncan's upper arm. "I need something to tighten this with," she murmurs.

I dig into my breast pocket and come out with a transparent Bic ballpoint. "If we live through this," I say nonsensically, "I want that back."

He gives me a sickly smile. Shay only nods as she uses the pen to twist the tourniquet tight and ties it down with the excess lace.

Duncan releases the pressure-point and sags a little. He fumbles one-handed with the buckles on the backpack straps. "You'll need to . . . to splice that cable. Nothing fancy . . . just make sure it's a good connection. This is starting to hurt."

I bend down to help him with the buckles. He slaps at my hands. "Shay can do this . . . can't you?"

She nods. "I can do it, Michael."

"Get . . . the Dunhill out of my pocket. You can use it for light. Harry . . ." His teeth clench and cords stand out briefly in his neck. "Is this shock? Am I going into shock?"

"Shh, Duncan, don't worry," I tell him helplessly.

"Harry . . . you need to track the bastard . . . Not too far, just . . . see if you can find out how bad we, we hurt him. I want to know how bad we hurt him."

"All right," I say. "All right."

Shay has already gotten the straps loose; she lifts the backpack clear. Duncan grunts. "It's heavy," she says calmly. In the glow from my flashlight she looks pale and drawn, maybe a little shocky herself. No surprise there: I'm unsteady, too.

We get Duncan to lie down, and I strip off my overcoat to cover him. Shay sparks Duncan's lighter and sets it on the ground between them, for light as she works on the cable; her hands shake only a little as she begins twisting the wires together.

I shine the flashlight down the tunnel; the beam trembles in time with my heart. On the floor, only a few feet away, lies an arm as big as my leg.

"Oh," I say. "Oh, we hurt him, all right."

I creep toward it hesitantly; deep in some irrational part of my mind I'm expecting it to move, to dig its huge hooked claws into the earth and drag itself away, or somehow leap for my throat. I nudge it with the Nitro's barrel—this makes a crisp chinking sound, metal on stone.

"Bless you for a holy fool, Michael Duncan," I whisper.

I kneel beside it and look more closely, still not willing to touch it with my hand. The difference in texture is visible: halfway down the upper arm, the grainy granite-like stone gives way to gray-toned leather. At the shoulder joint a knob of what I guess had been bone protrudes, not the pink-gleaming yellow-white of normal bone, but like the surrounding flesh, it has the gray sandpaper look of granite.

When the impact of the Nitro's heavy slug knocked the creature down, it must have fallen on this arm, the shoulder made brittle stone by Duncan's arclight, and its own weight had snapped it off.

This will do for Duncan's proof. This half-stone arm could convince anybody from my captain to the Amazing Randi, and then Duncan can nail it up on his trophy wall for all I care. I'll be out of it.

It's heavy, or maybe I'm weak. I have to sling the rifle and lift the arm with both hands.

Even as I turn the sound begins, a howling roaring wail from the depths of the earth behind me that unstrings my knees and turns my blood to water. Then the voice is joined by others, a chorus of damned souls screaming in the lakes of Hell, but always that first voice rises above, and beyond, a cry of inhuman pain and rage, and I know that sound, I know it in my bones, it echoes back to the beginning of Time, to the cry of God when He cast His brightest angel out of Heaven.

The wail strikes the arm from my hands; I fall to my

knees and press my palms against my ears. When the cries trail off to deathly silence, I lift my head and meet Shay's wide and stricken eyes.

"We're going to die here, aren't we," she says with unnatural calm.

"No." Like an old man, I climb painfully to my feet. "I'll get you out of this, Shay. I swear to you I will." I drag the arm back to them and drop it beside Duncan.

His eyelids flutter faintly, and a ghost of his smile touches his lips. "We got him, Harry . . ."

"Yeah, something like that."

Shay stares at the arm. "My God," she breathes.

"Get that thing working, will you?"

She shakes herself and nods. "Almost got it. Strap me in."

"You? But—"

"Somebody has to carry Michael. He's too heavy for me, so I'll use the light. Just do it, Harry."

Duncan whispers, "Don't be . . . bloody idiots . . . just go—"

I pick up the backpack and begin to strap her in. The tunnels rumble with distant thunder and a far-off rushing sound, like a hurricane heard over the phone.

It gets louder.

Fast.

"They're coming," I say stupidly, fumbling with the buckles. My fingers feel thick and clumsy, like sausages tied onto my wrists.

Now I can feel the thunder through the earth; my imagination fills with huge violet eyes and thick muscles driving blunt hooked claws.

"There's nowhere to run," Shay tells me. "They're all around us."

I finally get the last buckle fixed. "Just fire that thing up," I say, raising my voice to be heard over the rush. *"Just do it!"*

I spring into the junction of the crossing tunnels, shining the flashlight along the barrel of the Nitro. I catch a glimpse of violet and fire one barrel blindly, closing my eyes against the muzzle-flash. Without even looking to see if I'd hit anything I spin and fire the other barrel along the tunnel at my back, then crack the Nitro and feed in two more shells like I've been doing it all my life.

I fire again and again and reload and then Shay is at my side, but the arclight isn't on and they are coming closer, I can smell them and see them now—great gray hulking shapes loping toward us, and as I fire I think, *My God, Duncan didn't tell us how to work the damned thing!*

Then a dazzling blue-white beam like the blade of a sword sizzles out and my ringing ears are battered by jagged howls of pain. Shay sweeps the arclight around like a flamethrower, and when my vision begins to clear, the tunnels are empty.

"Where?" I gasp. "Where?"

"They're still there," Shay whispers. She shines the arclight down one tunnel, then another. "They're hiding in the cross-ways. They're waiting for something. And . . ." She looks at me, and all hope is gone from her eyes. ". . . they're *digging.*"

There is nothing else she needs to say; I can see all too clearly what will happen as we try to make our way back to the sewers. The sudden explosion of earth from a tunnel wall and a howling creature tearing into us before we can bring our weapons to bear.

And that will be the end, except for the fall into oblivion with claws and teeth ripping at our flesh and cracking our bones.

"We'd better get moving," I tell her. "Our only chance is to be out of here before they can get in position."

From all around us there comes a humming, buzzing sound like a choir of monks beginning a wordless chant.

Shay shakes her head. "It's too late," she says. "What they were waiting for, it's here."

The humming increases until I can feel it vibrating in my skull. Shay points the arclight down the biggest of the tunnels; the beam stabs into the darkness and strikes something gigantic.

It comes toward us with deliberate speed, moving like a wall at a walking pace. It fills the tunnel from top to bottom and side to side, and the arclight doesn't seem to bother it at all. Something like legs extend before it, or maybe they are arms; it rocks slightly from side to side as it approaches, like a fat man crawling on hands and knees. I bring the Nitro to my shoulder and fire without bothering to aim—I can hardly miss. When I open my eyes again, it is still coming at the same lumbering crawl.

I reload the Nitro.

Shay says, "Why doesn't the light work?"

The thing's approach answers her question. As it comes closer we can see, clearly in the blue-white beam, the thick layer of mud and earth crusted over its body.

I say, "Get its hands, its arms. The mud might be coming off. At least we can slow it down."

It stops.

LITTLE BIRD, I WOULD HAVE PARLEY.

The Nitro slips from my numb fingers. Shay gasps.

"You heard it, too?" I ask her.

She nods. "In my head . . ."

"Yeah."

LITTLE BIRD, YOUR STONES STING ONLY, BUT YOUR SUNBLADE KILLS. MY ELDEST SON IS SLAIN, LITTLE BIRD.

I say, "Uh . . . I guess it's talking to me, huh?"

HE ALONE OF MY CHILDREN HAD THE AGE TO HUNT THE GREAT HUNT, AND YOU, LITTLE BIRD, ARE NOT YET LAWFUL PREY. I WILL NOT HAVE THEM CORRUPTED.

I look at Shay, then back at the creature. I lick my lips. "What's that mean?" I ask. "You're letting us go, or . . ."

I WILL TAKE THE BROWN HEAD. YOU AND YOUR FEMALE ARE NOT YET LAWFUL PREY.

"Duncan?" I say. I steal a glance over my shoulder. Duncan lies under my coat, his eyes closed. Shay grabs my arm. When I look back, the creature is closer.

HE IS PREY.

I say, "Uh . . ."

"Harry, we can't—we can't just leave him here!"

I say, "How is he prey, and we're not?"

YOU ARE PURE.

"So is he," I say, thinking: Pure bastard, maybe, but

pure nevertheless. Hysterical laughter crawls up my throat; I swallow hard to force it back down.

The creature comes closer yet. I can smell the age of it, that skunk-stench underlain with dust from millenial tombs. I think about picking up the Nitro, but why bother?

"What about the lions?" I say. "Or the dogs?"

THAT IS THE LESSER HUNT. THEY KNOW NOT GOOD FROM EVIL NOR THEIR RIGHT HANDS FROM THEIR LEFT. THEY KNOW NOT COURAGE FROM COWARDICE NOR LAW FROM CHAOS. THEY ARE ONLY FOOD.

"But Duncan—"

THE BROWN HEAD KILLS.

"Hell, *I* kill. I'm the one that killed your son."

THE BROWN HEAD KILLS TO ENLARGE HIM-SELF IN HIS MIND. THE BROWN HEAD CAME TO MY HOME TO DO THIS. WHY DID YOU COME, LITTLE BIRD?

"I'm no better than he is," I insist.

"For Christ's sake, Harry, don't *argue* with it!" Shay says with as close to a shriek as you can get and still whisper. "Are you *crazy*?"

The creature rocks forward a few more feet. Now I can see it clearly, huge and bloated, its head the size of a Volkswagen, arms like girders on a drawbridge. I keep thinking how it said I'm not lawful prey, yet.

I say, "Let me get this straight. You have some kind of *rules*?"

WE ARE THE HUNTERS OF GOD. OUR PREY IS THE DISEASED, THE CRIPPLED, THE WEAK.

"But not physically, right? Am I getting this? Like, you're talking about spiritually, or something."

WE ARE THE HUNTERS OF GOD.

"Well, guess what?" I say, standing up straighter and taking a deep breath. "I don't care. You can't have him."

BEGONE. I AM BEYOND CORRUPTION, AND I WILL HAVE HIM. BEGONE AND LIVE, LITTLE BIRD. STAY AND DIE.

Shay's grip on my arm becomes painful. I look down

at her for a moment, and her eyes plead with me, and I can't ask her to make this decision.

The humming is so loud I can barely think.

Finally, I say, "We're leaving."

Shay's hand drops away.

I say, "And we're taking him with us."

WHY WOULD YOU DIE FOR THE BROWN HEAD? For the first time, a note of querulousness crept into the creature's tone. THE BROWN HEAD IS NOT YOUR FRIEND. HE DESPISES YOU, AND YOU HATE HIM.

The creature was close enough to touch. I stood between its massive claws.

"I don't care," I say simply.

The creature makes a noise in my head that seems like a sigh.

I turn my back on the creature and take Shay's hand, so that neither of us will have to die alone. A moment later, when we find ourselves still breathing, we go over and I pick up Duncan in a fireman's carry. With Shay leading the way, we slowly walk out of the tunnels.

When the sewers open before us, I hear in my head one final message.

FARE YOU WELL, LITTLE BIRD. YOU ARE A TRUE KNIGHT.

It doesn't take long to find a manhole and to climb back into Chicago's winter night. Falling snow gleams yellow like dry bone around the streetlamps. We lay Duncan on the sidewalk, under my coat. It's then I realize I left the creature's arm down in the tunnel. I don't say anything about it, because God knows I'm not going back down there. Shay stays with Duncan when I head off to call an ambulance.

As I leave, she says to me, "Harry Pigeon, I think you're the bravest man I ever met."

I shrug, and turn away so she can't see the tears, but I don't argue. I don't tell her that what she calls my bravery comes from equal parts just doing what the city pays me for, and the conviction that if we'd been low enough to take its offer, those creatures would have fallen on us like an old building.

She thinks I'm brave, and I don't have the courage to correct her.

We sit on the hard, antiseptic plastic chairs in the waiting room at Cook County. I hold Shay's hand for a couple of hours until a grim-looking doctor comes out and tells us he doesn't know yet whether they'll be able to save Duncan's arm. He doesn't know. Nobody knows.

I've been sitting there all night, thinking about things nobody knows. Thinking about them, and writing this down on scrap paper with that Bic—I rescued it from the trash when the paramedics threw it away.

I was there, I saw those things, heard them, smelled their breath, and I don't really know what they are, or why they are.

And I don't know if there is some kind of natural population control at work, or if there's a war between those things and something else equally weird and deadly; if what's coming will be a reaction to those underground hunters—or if it's something they do *themselves*.

I keep thinking about this show I watched, about how primitive man used to hunt. We didn't stalk animals and spear them, especially not ones that were big enough to do us harm. We drove them, whole herds of them in a mass, off the nearest cliff—then took what we needed from the random pile of meat at the bottom.

You can believe me, or not. I don't have any proof to offer, nothing except my fear and my uncertainty. There's almost three million people in this city. I can't carry all of you out on my back. And I don't know how to convince you.

I don't know much of anything anymore.

But I know one thing:

I can take a fucking hint.

Can you?

The next Seeker must be strong enough to accept the knowledge awaiting him. The future is a pattern of what may be, not what must be, and humankind easily forgets its mistakes if not constantly reminded of them. The Master of the Archives points to a tall man with curly dark hair and serious eyes, sending a thick burnished thread of light to his forehead. Knowing the gravity of the situation he questions, the man rises slowly. His door is almost hidden by shadows. Passing through it, he enters the mists of the future and walks until he comes to a book lying open on a stand of charred olive wood. Opening the tome, he allows the pages to fall where they may. The entry is marked:

"DEAREST KITTY"

by *Brian M. Thomsen*

"Sometimes too many facts obscure the humanity of history"

—Regis H. Sinclair
(22nd century philosopher)

HELLO, Investigator QB7.
"Hello, Counselor."
How was your week?
Fine."
That is not what my readings suggest. You need not worry about showing any weakness. It is my job to help you during times of problem.
"Sorry."
No need to apologize. That is what I am here for. Everybody encounters rough spots over the course of their duties. That is why everyone requires counseling.
"Of course. I should have known better."
Sometimes we forget. Now what is your problem?

It was night.

A young girl puts down the book she was writing in and joins others around a table.

The room was crowded, nine people huddled around a small table, their faces illuminated by the light of a multipronged candle holder.

No light escaped from the room, black shades blocking windows, keeping the activities within invisible to the streets below.

The people spoke in hushed tones, chanting in Yiddish. Occasionally a smile broke out, joined by others from the group as meager gifts were handed around.

The people gave thanks in whispers, and shared smiles again . . . until the high-low wailing of a siren pierced the room from the streets below.

All was quiet as the group held its breath. The reassuring diminishment of the siren as the vehicle continued its journey away from their hiding place did little to restore the thin festive mood of their holiday celebration.

The group gave thanks again, this time silently, each in their own way.

You were in archives?
"Yes. Twentieth century AD. Things are a bit of a muddle there."
I apologize, but you have to admit things are functional. Complete 5D access to the sights and the sounds of the century. Just like being there.
"Yes . . . but shouldn't there be some sort of commentary, something to put things in perspective?"
That is unnecessary. It was all covered in your indoctrination. True, the cataloguing of individual events is a little imprecise in twentieth century listing, but from 2350 AD on, things are perfectly cross-referenced.
"Of course."
So you are bothered by a research problem.
"Not exactly."

He probably should have left well enough alone.
No one disputed the fact that it was a suicide. Even with the advances in cere-therapy, the occasional unfortunate opts out of the system and takes their own life.
As a peacekeeping investigator, he had seen dead bod-

ies before, all different sexes, races, social orders. It wasn't even that the body was tattooed that bothered him. Tattoos came and went with style and fashion, and though they weren't "in" this year, they might just be retro enough to be next year . . . but these didn't look like fashion tattoos. You probably wouldn't even notice them unless you were looking for them. There was one on the dead guy's hand, two triangles interposed on each other on the webbing twixt the thumb and index finger. The other was on the forearm and was just a series of numbers not unlike the bar-code that was dyed into the back of the heads of convicts for easy scanning.

Both looked like they were "home grown," what used to be called "jail-house style."

Suicides are a problem. They are infrequent and in the overall course of things don't really affect the status quo, but they are a problem and we are working on it and will solve it the same way we solved those inconveniences of the past like cancer, acne, and laziness.

"Of course."

Your role as a peacekeeping investigator is to ascertain that it was a suicide and not a homicide.

"I know. I wanted to be sure, so of course I examined the scene and recorded a holo of it for later investigations."

Later investigations?

"The scene had to be cleansed so as to not disturb civilians who might happen by."

Very wise.

"And the subject had a large collection of non-data files that had to be examined on an individual basis."

Antiques?

"Possibly. I thought that some of the correspondence might rule out outside foul play."

Perfect procedural judgment.

"Thank you."

It was cold and damp, and his stomach felt empty, as if it had been too many days since it had been adequately sated. His skin felt all crawly, and the presence of fleas could not be avoided, particularly around his nostrils and ears.

He opened his eyes and looked around. He was standing in front of a barrackslike structure with several others, the sounds of coughing and wheezing confirming that the maladies he was experiencing were common. He seemed to be in a compound with several other blank-faced individuals.

Everyone seemed to be waiting for something whose arrival they had given up hope on a long, long time ago.

A quick scan beyond the group and the barracks yielded a view of a barbedwire fence and a few industrial-style buildings.

A sign in the distance read Manzanar.

So you think he was a researcher.

"That is what the plethora of twentieth century bookmark citations seems to indicate."

I have no record of anyone assigned to deal with that period.

"Maybe it was his hobby."

It is self-destructive to engage in activities that lead to a feeling of depression. Perhaps we can conclude that this was his motivation for suicide.

"Perhaps . . ."

The poor depressed SOB had no living relatives . . . at all.

His neighbors thought of him as a loner. The landlady thought he had some religious hangups as well, and, in our age of universal ecumenicism, this should have been enough to make him certifiable had anyone cared or taken notice.

The religious barriers were taken down years ago when the powers that be realized that they no longer mattered. Having explored the galaxy from one end to the other (and finding nothing in the way of intelligent life) had more than driven home the oneness of the human race.

His room was done in "luddite hermit" with a few collected bundles of printed words (he thought they were called books), and a handwritten note that he wrongly assumed was a suicide note. If it was he didn't understand it.

It read "Remember the Shoah—Never Again."

There were also a few letters, primitive format, not data.

". . . but I don't think so."

This is good—we are finally now talking about you. That is why we are here.

"No, you don't understand. I went over his correspondence. There was nothing really personal about it. Most of them were just notices of some other civilians' deaths."

Civilians?

Yes. Eleven others. The most recent was dated less than a cycle ago and seemed to be written in the same hand as the note that we originally wrongly assumed was the suicide note.

Perhaps he was driven to suicide by the deaths of the other civilians. Perhaps they were friends of his.

"Death was a recurrent part of his research. My subsequent studies of the contents of his room via the holo recording told me that much."

One should not dwell on death. You know that from level three of your therapy.

"Of course."

The clothes felt like coarse pajamas and did little to shield the hairless and emaciated body from the cold. Everyone was wearing the same thing (except those who weren't wearing anything at all and were lying on the ground or in some freshly dug trenches).

It was the duty of the clothed ones to bury the naked ones with as little fuss as possible.

It was easier to do if one refused to notice that some of the bodies at hand had recently belonged to women and children.

It was always harder when the detail involved women and children, rather than other men who just yesterday might have been performing the same task here at Treblinka.

*   *   *

"His research made several bookmarks on the subject of 'the Shoah' "

The shoah?

"A legend from the twentieth century."

Oh.

"The Shoah" was one of those dark legends of the past that evil historians sometimes told children to give them nightmares. In reality it was just another one of those unfortunate massacres that were all too frequent in the dark ages of the twentieth century.

A lot of people died from 1900 to 2000. Case closed. Sure some of them belonged to the Jewish faith . . . but it couldn't have been anything personal. People got killed in wars. You sided with the loser, you lost.

In the great game of world powerplays there are no innocent bystanders.

It was nothing personal. The extreme length of the lists of casualties more than assured him of that.

There were even myths about death camps where a minor industry of genocide had been set up to eradicate the Jews, but this had to be unlikely. The Third Reich had a war to win. Why would it divert his resources to such things?

Besides, camps were everywhere, Poland, California, Germany, Canada.

Massacres took place in other places, too. Cambodia, Babi Yar, Haiti, Bosnia.

He knew that all of the casualty reports and death statistics had been saved.

A lot of people had died in the twentieth century, maybe more than their fair share during the thirties and forties . . . but it wasn't anything personal.

You fight in a war, you run the risk of dying.

If you got caught, you could be executed a number of ways—plastic bag over the head to save bullets, hanging, gas, and the good, old-fashioned firing squads.

Soldiers had to expect this, Jews and Gentiles alike.

"What were things like in the dark ages?"

Investigator QB7, I am surprised at you. You know this session is for counseling and that I have been spe-

cifically programmed to render such assistance that I
deem fit to preserve your personal stability and assure
your ongoing contribution to society.

"I know. I apologize."

You are forgiven. I understand that focused research
is a very necessary part of your duties, but I cannot
allow you to fall prone to an unhealthy obsession over
materials and matters that might become detrimental to
your long-term performance as a contributing member
of our great society.

"I understand."

I know you do. Everyone is prone to occasionally los-
ing focus. It is a requisite downside of the human condition. We are working on that problem on a long-term
basis.

In the meantime, I am here to help you. I am here
for you. Not as some database research associate, but as
a friend.

"Thank you."

The families had been in hiding in Amsterdam for
over a year now and tempers were beginning to flare.
The worst slumlord allocated more living space to his
tenants than these two families had to share.

They did not dare venture outside for fear of being
seen.

All of their friends (with the exception of their protec-
tors) had moved on and probably no longer thought
about them anymore.

The wireless occasionally yielded news from the front,
encouraging words from the Allies, and propaganda
from the Nazis (they hoped that it wasn't in reality the
reverse; they had no way of knowing as they were in
hiding).

The girl was always getting into trouble.

She was young, just leaving girlhood, and not really
wise to the way of the world.

She was frustrated at being the youngest, at being in
hiding, at being constantly hushed and yelled at.

Her name was Anne.

Day after day, for another twelve months of eternity,
they stayed together, cramped, hiding, until the door was

shattered by the police and they were taken away on the last transport westward from the Netherlands.

They were separated before they even reached the train station after having lived so close together for so many months.

The girl was in the boxcar before she realized that she had heard no warning before her capture—the dreaded high-low siren that she had always feared as the wailing of some grim reaper out to get her had never heralded the arrival of the Gestapo.

The question of what had obsessed the suicide began to obsess the investigator.

Of course, he had no trouble believing that we were all alike, shared in the same past, believed in the same future.

It was good.

It was right.

It was proper.

We move on.

We don't live in the past.

That is what history taught us.

The suicide had refused to buy into the collective, had not realized that everything was for the best, that we live in the candide of all possible worlds.

It began to bother the investigator as well.

He sought sleep therapy to get over the rough spots, but the questions didn't go away.

He began to do research.

QB7?
"Yes."
You missed yesterday's scheduled session. That is why I have insinuated myself into your laptop's program.
"I am sorry. It won't happen again."
I know. I have also downloaded the statistical abstracts from the Twentieth century that should help you with your research.
"Thank you."
You will have to finish your project in a timely manner, and under no circumstances can you miss another of our scheduled counseling sessions.
"I understand."

* * *

Yet another camp.

Poles, Jews, Russians laboring together under the harshest of conditions.

Something is said in Russian, and all hell breaks loose as the ill-fed workers storm the fences.

Machine guns cut down droves of the interred workers, but some get through and soon the guns are turned on the captors.

More die.

Some get through.

Everyone runs to the woods, away from the place called Sobibor.

6 million?
1.5 million children under the age of 15 (probable exaggeration).
5.1 million?
(Somebody named Hoess stated that 2 million were gassed at Auschwitz alone, 500,000 killed in other ways, Historians have concluded that this is a gross exaggeration)

You seem confused.

"The statistics on hand seem contradictory."

I am sorry. It was the best I could do.

"And I don't really understand how it all meshes with the materials from the suicide's apartment."

I will look into it . . . but now is the time for our talk. Are you sleeping better? Do you feel more rested?

"Yes, the additives you prescribed are working fine."

Arbeit Macht Frei.

Yet another camp, this one the aforementioned Auschwitz.

The body of a young girl named Rosa Robota hangs at the end of a rope. Her neck is unbroken; death by strangulation was slower and more painful.

The capos remembered her twisting in agony before she became dead weight.

The fire in the gas chamber had finally gone out

though the structure itself seemed beyond repair, Rosa's bomb having done its job.

They would have to increase the traffic through the other chambers in order to make their quota.

The capos averted their eyes.

No one really believed that they were showers.

Another train was pulling in, and there was work to be done.

No one asked about the young girl who had been hung, not even those who were sent down the path away from the compound and toward the showers.

Questions were always discouraged. This they had all learned.

5.86 million.
33,771 at Babi Yar outside of Kiev.
All prisoners at the camps were photographed.
There were not a million photographs in the archives.
Some were lost.

The girl from the crowded hiding place arrived in Auschwitz after the three-day journey from the Netherlands.

She was stripped and shaved and given a uniform like all the rest.

She was not immediately sent to the showers, but assigned a place on one of the three-level bunks in Barracks III, sharing the hard wooden pallet with four other new arrivals and a complement of lice and feces.

She became another blank face in the crowd, and did not last long.

Her book was left behind back in Amsterdam.

Back in a now empty room that had once been part of a hiding place known as the Secret Annex.

I am afraid that we do not recognize the documentary materials that you have discovered. They appear to be based on accounts that have been handed down orally over the centuries.

The investigator noted the footnotes that supplemented the statistics and censuses of the time.

Mass executions were not uncommon as a method of punishment or a means to rid a new society of its dangerous element.

China had its long march.

Cambodia had its killing fields.

He remembered seeing in one of his Classical Lit classes back in primary level a movie called "The Great Escape" where two thirds of the escapees were killed upon capture to serve as a deterrent to others.

Nothing personal.

People get killed in wars.

It's an unfortunate hazard.

The files will have to be sorted and set aside for further study should time permit.

"Can I still have access to the models I set up?"

Not once they have been absorbed for future sorting. You will then have to wait until the proper classifications have taken place.

"When will that be?"

The project properly archiving materials related to the twentieth century is 123 years away from scheduled completion, but recent updates indicate that that particular data function is running 23% behind schedule.

There has always been a tendency to romanticize the past.

Abraham Lincoln didn't really free the slaves.

Custer was not the last man standing at the Little Big Horn.

Cold Fusion wasn't discovered in a high school laboratory.

John J. Grubb did not come up with the first usable plan for world peace on his laptop on the way to the retirement home.

The Jews were not almost wiped out in World War II.

People like legends.

They like to exaggerate.

History has shown the world that.

Facts and numbers don't lie as long as you take into account the proper circumstances.

People were killed for a variety of reasons.

Sometimes mistakes were made, but they had to be within an acceptable margin of error.

The investigator soon tired of listening in on the twenty-ninth century symposium on the historical reevaluation of the previous millennium.

There was too much to absorb, and it didn't all seem to go together.

Maybe the truth was not in the data.

He needed a quiet place.

He needed to go back again.

He needed to retrace some steps.

"How much time do I have till I am off-line?"

Undetermined. Your files are being absorbed as we speak.

"Can I work with them until while they are in process?"

Agreed. Our session will resume after that.

He needed a quiet place to think, and retreated to the first of the models he examined.

Amsterdam.

The address was 263 Prinsengracht, and the building was deserted.

There were no more sirens, and people came and went down the street minding their own business.

No one stopped him as he entered the deserted building that used to house a company that packaged assorted jams.

The book case that had hidden the door to "the Secret Annex" had been torn off its hinges, and all furniture, cabinets, and drawers had been tossed long ago.

No one had bothered to clean up or restore order.

The investigator had felt the claustrophobia on the night of the Hanukkah celebration, but only now realized just how cramped these quarters really must have been for the nine who were in hiding.

Were they revolutionaries?

They had been here over two years, just hiding, nothing but waiting.

Revolutionaries never just sat around doing nothing, let

alone for two years while the entire world was blowing up around them.

He couldn't tell if the war was still going on. He didn't remember seeing any Nazis in the streets, but that didn't really mean anything.

Maybe the morning of the raid, August 4, 1944, wasn't that long ago.

Hc looked around at the cramped quarters, his keen eyes quickly becoming accustomed to the dark.

Under a pile of rubbish, he found a book.

It was the young girl's diary.

He picked it up, and began to read. *"Dearest Kitty,"* it began. He stayed there until he had read all that she had written, the entire diary of a very ordinary young girl who just happened to be Jewish.

This wasn't a list of casualties.

These hadn't been criminals or insurrectionists or prisoners of war.

They had been innocents, and they had been slaughtered, just because they were Jewish.

. . . and it was ancient history.

The room began to dissolve around him and the diary ceased to be, its data now part of the still-to-be-classified archives.

He was now in the shell of the models, his original holo of the suicide's room that housed the other relevant data.

The correspondence had indicated that he had gone by the name of Asher rather than by the more traditional professional classification that had become the norm of their ideal society.

Little by little the holo began to shimmer and fade as it too was archived.

The memories of Asher and his eleven other witnesses disappeared from the known world.

"It is all gone now."

I am sorry. Did you solve the problem?

"That it was a suicide and not a homicide? Yes. He was depressed. He was alone. He opted out."

How sad.

Do you wish some time off? You are overdue.

No, thank you.

Is there anything that we need to discuss about these matters? Are they behind you?

"I am ready to resume work."

That is good. I will monitor your vitals and reactals to make sure that you are in sync and notify you if anything needs to be brought to your attention.

"Thank you."

No thanks are necessary. You are a valued member of society and your well-being is a necessary part of the status quo.

It is for the best of the greater good.

There are some legends that do not withstand the test of time even though they should.

The investigator known as QB7 vowed to remember what had really taken place, what he had seen through the testimonies of the witnesses, and read in the primitive handwriting of one who had not survived.

The facts and statistical abstracts had not told the whole story, and somebody had to remember the rest.

The burden had passed from that lonely suicide named Asher and his eleven other witnesses to himself, and he hoped that he could withstand the burden.

He was the next witness. Soon another would have to be found . . . lest we forget.

"The greatest trick the devil ever pulled was convincing the world that he didn't exist"
　　　　—Unknown Twentieth Century philosopher

The Guardian of Light reaches out, pointing two fingers at the last Seeker in this group. The woman absorbs the golden spill, squares her shoulders, rises from her chair, and steps to a door that seems more shadow than substance. The corridor behind it is a long one, filled with seemingly endless turnoffs and many worn, splintered portals. The Seeker bypasses these, walking with determination until she reaches the hallway's end. A door stands opposing her, softly glowing like a dim star. She pushes through it, learning about the:

LAST KINGDOM

by Deborah Turner Harris
and Robert J. Harris

Then the fifth angel blew his trumpet, and I saw a star that had fallen from heaven on to the earth, and he was given the key to the shaft leading down to the Abyss.

—Revelation 9:1

THE Leader was growing tired. Increasingly these days he would speak of nothing except the past and emerged from the Bunker only at night to walk his dog in the withering gardens of the Chancellery. This served to fuel the whispered rumors that sunlight had grown too painful for his fading eyesight to bear. In a city where perpetual bombing had reduced the dwindling population to a shuddering band of troglodytes, he alone seemed willingly to embrace the dim atmosphere of his subterranean labyrinth. Already he was living in a tomb. In eight days' time he would be dead.

Fifty-five feet below ground, he sat alone in his sparsely furnished study, the candlelight flickering over the walls and sparking strange patterns off the many maps which were pinned there. The Leader had always liked maps, their fine detail and absorbing intricacy, and now they served as windows on to things large and far away: the crumbling boundaries of his Empire and the relentless advance of his foes. In the midst of the maps, thrusting them aside with its bulk and magnificence, hung Anton Graff's portrait of Frederick the Great. He had purchased the portrait ten years ago, and since then it had moved with him back and forth across Europe to decorate the study of each of his many headquarters. It had, at last, followed him here to his final citadel.

He sat back in his plain wooden chair and stared at the painting, searching the eyes of the imposing Prussian monarch for some secret, unspoken inspiration. Every evening during the previous month he had had his old friend, the good doctor, read to him from Thomas Carlyle's 'Life of Frederick the Great'. Beleaguered by an all but victorious alliance of his enemies, Frederick had written to his friend, the Marquis d'Argens, "In fine, my dear Marquis, we live in troublous times and desperate situations. I have all the properties of a stage hero: always in danger, always on the point of perishing!"

The Leader, too, was a consummate showman, and he meditated upon the sudden shift of alliances which had saved his predecessor from defeat. With the death of the American president ten days ago, there was every possibility of another such realignment before the final curtain fell on his own performance.

A discreet knock at the door failed to disturb the Leader's reverie. There was another knock, then the door opened and his valet cautiously peered in. Seeing his master awake, he was about to attract his attention by announcing a visitor, when he was shouldered brusquely out of the way by another man who entered the study and closed the door, shutting the valet outside.

At once something in the room changed. It was as though some alien, elemental force had invaded the enclosed air of the Bunker. The visitor flicked a switch on the wall, and the room was instantly filled with the harsh, artificial glare of the overhead light.

The Leader winced and squinted up at the man by the door. Unlooked-for relief and pathetic gratitude flared in his washed out eyes. "Himmelmann!" he gasped.

He removed his steel-framed spectacles and pushed

himself out of his chair. Moving unsteadily across the room, he raised a hand toward the tall, golden-haired newcomer. Himmelmann stiffened at the suggestion of a handshake, loath to indulge in physical contact with this body which was so clearly debilitated by illness and an excess of drugs. The Leader stopped short and confined his greeting to a smile and a nod.

Dispassionately Himmelmann noted the extent to which the other man's appearance had deteriorated since their last meeting. The Leader's eyes, which had once flashed like blue flame, were now as lifeless as glass. His complexion had taken on a yellowish tinge and there were spots of mustard and soup stains on his previously immaculate uniform. His posture was bowed, like that of a beggar, as though there were a terrible weight clinging to his back.

"Himmelmann, you've come at the right time," the Leader said, a feverish eagerness creeping into his tone. "I have plans, you see. We'll show them the war isn't over yet." He stretched a trembling hand toward one of the strategic maps which littered his desk.

Himmelmann removed his soft leather gloves and slipped them into the pocket of his mohair coat. He had purchased the coat in Paris, an irksome reminder of one of the many outposts the Empire had been forced to abandon. "The war is lost," he told the other man evenly.

The Leader's body seemed to shrivel even more, if such a thing were possible, the last of his hopes melting away like slivers of ice. "The generals!" he rasped, his fingers curling into a pair of bony fists. "They wouldn't listen to what I said. All they cared about—"

Himmelmann cut him off with a curt gesture. He had heard all of this before and had no time for it now. "The war has served its purpose," he went on. "You did, after all, find what I asked for."

The Leader uttered a weak laugh that was lost in the back of his throat. "Yes, yes, I did. I never thought we'd have to kill so many millions to find its guardian."

Himmelmann waved his hand dismissively. "Whatever stands in the way of the will must be swept aside. That is the natural order, is it not?"

The Leader automatically nodded his agreement as he had done so often during the many years of their acquaintance. Any doubts he might have entertained during Himmelmann's long absence were immediately banished by that voice, so firm and confident that the Leader could feel it reinvigorate him like a bracing tonic.

"Then let us not delay," Himmelmann concluded.

He raised a suggestive eyebrow, prompting the Leader to shuffle over to the safe, trailing his weak leg behind him. Replacing his glasses in order to read the numbers on the combination lock, he quickly opened the safe and lifted out a small, padlocked metal box which he placed on the table between himself and Himmelmann.

"The key, please," Himmelmann requested quietly, opening his left hand.

The Leader reached into the leather holster which was sewn inside his trousers and in which he normally carried a Walther 6.35 caliber pistol. He produced a shiny key which he handed over to Himmelmann. The golden-haired man removed the padlock and opened the box.

The object inside was concealed from sight by a green silk wrapping, upon which were sewn in black certain cabalistic letters of the Hebrew alphabet. The Leader reflexively curled his lip at the sight. Oblivious to the other man's discomfiture, Himmelmann used a finger and thumb to peel apart the layers of material and reveal what lay within.

There was something like elation in this face as he lifted the object from its silk wrappings and examined it in the naked light. The Leader had never before seen him display such undisguised emotion, and it was all the more unexpected in view of the humble nature of his prize.

It appeared to be a broken segment of a brass rod, no more than four inches in length. It was discolored with streaks of green and showed such evidence of corrosion that it would have been no surprise to see it crumble into dust under the pressure of Himmelman's fingers.

"In your darkest and most extravagant dreams," Himmelmann breathed, "you could not imagine how long I have sought this or how far I have traveled to obtain it."

"You said it was a key you were looking for," the Leader began.

"A key?" Himmelmann echoed. "Such a small word. It is the Key of Abaddon I have been seeking."

"I've never heard of it."

"Of course you haven't. Your mind has been occupied with lesser things. It is the key which unlocks the gateway of the Abyss, the great pit into which the fallen angels were cast at the dawn of time. They have been imprisoned there, nursing their hatred for eons, and this key is the only thing which can release them before the time ordained."

The Leader scowled. "It sounds like some primitive folk tale."

Himmelmann continued as though he were too absorbed in his triumph to be aware of the comment. "It was broken into three pieces countless centuries ago, and those pieces given into the care of certain priests to be guarded by them and their descendants. This is the first piece, and I have been closing in on the second."

He looked up as though recalling the Leader's presence. "You might have recovered that, too, with more wisdom—but it was not wisdom I chose you for."

The golden-haired man wrapped his hand around the metal fragment and at the same time folded up within himself that brief glimpse of his inner nature he had exposed to the Leader's gaze. He placed the object back in its container and fastened the padlock.

"Many of your countrymen believe that Armageddon is upon them," he said with a mocking tilt of his head. "This is hardly even a rehearsal."

"But what of the Empire?" The Leader asked in a near croak. "You promised me . . ."

"I promised you many things," Himmelmann responded, "but you know that I never promised you that they would last."

"You will take me from here, then, so that I can begin again?"

Himmelmann regarded him with the detachment of a surgeon. "The life of a fugitive is not for a man like you."

"But if they capture me, who knows what tortures they would practice upon me? Worse still, they might display me like a common criminal."

The Leader's lip began to quiver at this dreadful prospect.

There was no pity in Himmelmann's eyes as he regarded

the defeated figure before him. Such an emotion was inconceivable to him. Yet it would not suit his purposes for the Leader to grow too weak to bring the drama to its necessary conclusion. He leaned forward and placed his hands on the other man's shoulders. The Leader closed his eyes and immediately felt the pain and discomfort, which were his constant companions, ebbing gently away. A soothing, reassuring relaxation stole over him.

"You have done all that destiny requires of you," he heard Himmelmann's voice say. "All that is left is to write the final scene."

"I must not be taken alive," the Leader stated with the beginnings of new resolve. "That would be intolerable."

"No, you must not," Himmelmann agreed. He removed his hands and reached into his pocket. When the Leader opened his eyes, he saw a bottle of blue capsules on the table before him. He picked them up clumsily, like a man suddenly stricken with palsy.

"Are they poison?" he asked, gripping his arm in his other hand to steady it.

"Cyanide," Himmelmann replied. "One is all that you will require and the effect is virtually instantaneous. However, to be absolutely sure, I would advise that you shoot yourself through the right temple as you bite down on the capsule."

He picked up the metal box and started for the door.

"This is the end of everything, then," the Leader said in a voice that would have been inaudible to less sensitive ears.

Himmelmann looked back and smiled without mirth. "No," he said, "it is just the beginning."

He turned away and left the study, closing the door silently behind him. Passing once again the security checkpoints which marked the route to the surface, he emerged into the sunlight and the smoking ruins of the city.

His driver was waiting with the door of his staff car held open. All too soon it would be impossible for his plane to escape the city, yet Himmelmann paused for a moment to savor the taste of his triumph. He had hoped by now to have also obtained the second key, but it still remained to be found somewhere in the east. It would have been simpler if the Bolsheviks had succumbed to the Empire's armored might, but all was not lost.

Three years before, the gray-clad armies ground to a halt on the outskirts of the vast industrial cities, and blizzards as deadly as marching battalions had swept down on them. Himmelmann was never lacking in foresight, and he had arranged even then a secret meeting with the general secretary of the ruling elite, Joseph Vissarionovich Dzhugahsvili.

He called himself *The Man of Steel*, but Himmelmann had been disappointed at the modesty of his ambitions. Still, how much vision could one expect from the offspring of a cobbler and a washerwoman? At least, this pawn was not lacking in ruthlessness. He would require every ounce of it before Himmelmann was through with him.

After completing a last survey of the ruins, Himmelmann climbed into the car and signaled the driver to make speed. There was much work to be done.

One week later, the city was overrun by its vengeful enemies. Alone in his quarters with his wife of two days, the Leader put a gun to his own head. Biting down on a blue capsule, he pulled the trigger and the world ended for him.

For others, it went on.

One cold, bright day on the threshold of winter, two men occupied the flattened summit of the mountain. They had arranged to meet here in secret, and for the past hour they had been discussing a future that loomed over them as ominously as the mountain loomed over the unsuspecting landscape below.

One man was pacing restlessly in the background and chewing his lower lip. He was a handsome, well-muscled figure, but in spite of his evident vigor, his black overcoat was fastened tight against the icy wind that was buffeting him here on the height.

He was a man of destiny. At least that was how he thought of himself, and never more so than now. Such were the forces arrayed against him that only such a man would seek to overcome them. The decision that faced him was a momentous one, but he was determined not to shrink from it.

The other man was standing close to the edge inhaling

deeply on a half-smoked cigarette. Mere inches from the tips of his patent leather shoes, the cliff face plummeted sharply, but he did not appear to be concerned. Neither the cold nor the wind made any impression on him. He was toying casually with a silver cigarette case that reflected flashes of sunlight as he turned it between his fingers.

"You should be more careful," came the voice of the man in the black coat. "Those things will kill you, you know."

The smoking man did not look round. "I don't think so. I'm made of stronger stuff than that."

He took a final draw on his cigarette, then flipped it into the void beyond the brink of the precipice. He slipped the silver case into the pocket of his immaculately tailored suit and turned to face the other man.

"Have you had enough time to think?"

"Can you really do all that you promised, Westerlicht?" the man of destiny asked hesitantly.

"You have seen the danger posed to your people, both by their enemies, and by their own leaders whose sole concern is to further their own selfish interests," the man called Westerlicht stated impatiently. "Do you propose to change things by endlessly interrogating me? Do you truly doubt my word, or is it your own capabilities you are uncertain of?"

The man of destiny bristled at the suggestion of weakness. "I can do all that is expected of me," he asserted.

"That is good, because I expect much of you."

"You've made that clear. What isn't as clear is what exactly you want in return for your support."

Westerlicht almost smiled. "It is a small item, an antique of sorts. It has been kept hidden for a long time and it will not be easily surrendered by those who possess it."

"An *antique*?" the man of destiny repeated dubiously.

Westerlicht shrugged. "I suppose you can think of me as a collector. The item has sentimental value for me."

"You don't strike me as much of a sentimentalist."

"There are many things about me which would surprise you. Come here."

He gestured to his companion to join him. The man

in the black coat could hardly refuse and took two careful steps forward. Together they stood at the mountain's edge.

"You will attain all that you desire," Westerlicht promised, "as long as you have the stomach for it."

"What do you mean by that?" asked the man of destiny, flinching involuntarily as a gust of wind pressed against his back.

"I mean you know how the enemies of your people must be dealt with," Westerlicht answered. "There is no room for weakness here, no place for undeserved mercy."

"I know what to do," the other man affirmed, gaining a renewed sense of assurance from the steely tone of his companion's voice.

"Perhaps so, but are you a man of vision?"

"What do you mean?"

"We're here upon a mountain top. Tell me, what do you see?"

The man in the black coat looked down, to where a scattered handful of people milled about like insects among the paths and trees of the park below. He was so close to the edge now that the wind seemed to be pushing him forward, daring him to surrender himself to the merciless pull of gravity. He could not shake off the impression that it was only the force of Westerlicht's will that was keeping them both from toppling helplessly into the empty air below their feet.

"I can see we're very high up," he replied, marveling at the steadiness of his voice.

"You should be more farsighted," Westerlicht chided him. "I can see all the kingdoms of the world in their splendor."

"I'll settle for this one right here," said the man of destiny, "at least for the present."

"That's more like it," said Westerlicht, nodding approvingly. "You had best go now and continue your preparations."

The man of destiny stepped away from the edge with barely concealed relief.

Westerlicht pulled out his cigarette case, but before opening it he stopped to gaze into the polished surface. He saw Himmelmann's reflection staring back up at him.

The face was unlined by the passage of time, yet it still discomfited him to look upon his own features.

For a moment he was taken back to the subterranean hideaway where he had taken his leave of another leader of men decades below. He was struck by the contrast between that meeting in a manmade cave and this rendezvous high atop a cliff face with sunshine and clear mountain air all round. He tried to focus his mind on the fate this short-lived millennium had in store for it, but the recollection of the man-made cave faded only slowly. Perhaps that was itself the echo of an even older event that had failed to crystallize in his mind.

In an existence as long as his, there were so many memories that almost anything he experienced now could evoke one of them. It was more difficult sometimes to track down those things he wished to recall. He would often have to move by association from one segment of his past to another, as though following a delicate thread through a lightless maze. His own origins were now so distant in time, so overlaid with intervening events, that even to him they had become little more than a legend.

Behind Westerlicht's back, the man of destiny had halted before returning to his car.

"Has anyone ever said *no* to you?" he asked, abruptly interrupting the other's brief reverie.

Westerlicht rubbed his cheek with his forefinger. "Only once—and that was a long long time ago. Don't worry about a thing. I've done all this before."

The man of destiny's footsteps receded into the distance. As though prompted by a remote memory, Westerlicht put the cigarette case away without opening it, and took a deep breath. It was as though he could already sense the acrid smoke of destruction on the wind.

Below his feet, four great stone faces stared out over the landscape, each a colossal image of a past ruler of this particular kingdom. For a moment, Westerlicht wondered idly if they could see as far as he did. These kingdoms had always been his to offer to those who would follow him.

If all went as planned, this one would be the last.

ABOUT THE AUTHORS

Jane Lindskold's recent novel *Changer* is a contemporary fantasy which, like the story in this anthology, gives a new shape to old myths and legends. Other of her recent works include the novels *When the Gods Are Silent* and *Donnerjack* (in collaboration with Roger Zelazny). Some of her short fiction has appeared in *Black Cats and Broken Mirrors*, *Wizard Fantastic*, and *First Contact*. She resides in New Mexico with her husband, archeologist Jim Moore.

Josepha Sherman is a fantasy writer and folklorist whose latest novels are *Highlander: The Captive Soul* and *Son of Darkness*. Her most recent folklore volume is *Merlin's Kin: World Tale of the Hero Magicians*. Her short fiction has appeared in numerous anthologies, including *Battle Magic*, *Dinosaur Fantastic*, and *The Shimmering Door*. She lives in Riverdale, New York.

Dennis McKiernan is the best-selling fantasy author of *Eye of the Hunter*, *Caverns of Socrates*, and *The Dragonstone*. His latest work is the Hel's Crucible duology *Into the Forge* and *Into the Fire*. His short fantasy fiction has been collected in *Tales of Mithgar*, with other fiction of his appearing in *Olympus*, and *Elf Fantastic* and various other anthologies.

Kristine Kathryn Rusch has worked as an editor at such places as Pulphouse Publishing and most recently *The Magazine of Fantasy & Science Fiction*, though she is currently a full-time writer. Forthcoming novels include *The Black Throne* series. Her short fiction has recently appeared in *Once Upon a Crime, First Contact,* and *Black Cats and Broken Mirrors*. A winner of the World Fantasy Award, she lives in Oregon with her husband, author and editor Dean Wesley Smith.

Janet Pack lives in Lake Geneva, Wisconsin, with three black cats named Canth, Brika, and Syri. She writes, directs, and acts in radio ads for a local game store. She gives writing seminars, and speaks to schools and groups about reading and the writing profession. When not writing short stories and books, Janet sings classical, Renaissance, and Medieval music. During leisure time she composes songs, reads, collects rocks, exercises, skis, and paddles her kayak on Lake Geneva.

Richard Lee Byers worked for over a decade in an emergency psychiatric facility, then left the mental health field to become a writer. He is the author of *The Ebon Mask, On A Darkling Plain, Netherworld, Caravan of Shadows, Dark Fortune, Dead Time, The Vampire's Apprentice,* and several other novels. His short fiction has appeared in numerous other anthologies, including *Phobias, Confederacy of the Dead, Dante's Disciples, Superheroes,* and *Diagnosis: Terminal*. He lives in the Tampa Bay area, the setting for many of his stories.

Kristin Schwengel's work has appeared in the anthologies *Sword of Ice and Other Tales of Valdemar* and *Black Cats and Broken Mirrors*. She lives in Milwaukee, Wisconsin, where she works in a bookstore. She says, "My life is surrounded by books; I'm either selling them, reading them, or writing for them. Who could ask for anything more?"

Kevin T. Stein is author of *Brothers Majere* and the short story "The Hunt" in the *Dragonlance* series by

TSR. Kevin's other works include *The Fall of Magic* (as D.J. Heinrich), *Twisted Dragon,* and the *Guide to Larry Niven's Ringworld*. Kevin is a script consultant, and also has two screenplays optioned by a Hollywood production studio.

Robert Weinberg has spent the last thirty-five years ensuring that the thousands of pulp stories published in the first half of the century remain in print today. In his spare time, he writes in all genres of fiction, recently appearing in the anthologies *White House Horrors* and *David Copperfield's Tales of the Impossible*. He lives with his family in Oak Forest, Illinois.

Mickey Zucker Reichert is a pediatrician whose fourteen science fiction and fantasy novels include *The Legend of Nightfall, The Unknown Soldier,* and *The Renshai Trilogy*. Her most recent release from DAW Books is *The Children of Wrath*. Her short fiction has appeared in numerous anthologies, including *Battle Magic, Warrior Princesses,* and *Fantastic Alice*. Her claims to fame: she *has* performed brain surgery, and her parents *really are* rocket scientists.

Gary A. Braunbeck's stories have appeared in *Robert Bloch's Psychos, Once Upon a Crime,* and *The Conspiracy Files*. His occasional foray into the mystery genre is no less accomplished, having appeared in anthologies such as *Danger in D.C.* and *Cat Crimes Takes a Vacation*. His recent short story collection, *Things Left Behind,* received excellent critical notice and a nomination for the Bram Stoker Award. He lives in Columbus, Ohio.

Peter Schweighofer was West End Games' Senior Creative and Editorial Director. His writing credits include numerous books for West End's *Star Wars* Role-playing Game, including numerous articles for the Official *Star Wars* Adventure Journal. He ran the Journal for four years and edited *Tales from the Empire,* a collection of *Star Wars* short stories. Besides engaging in role-playing games, he enjoys dabbling in historical research and writing, focusing on ancient and Victorian Egypt. Before moving to the Pennsylvania frontier to work at West End, he worked for a small-town newspaper in suburban Connecticut.

Margaret Weis is the *New York Times* best-selling co-creator, with Tracy Hickman, of the World of Dragonlance, which now covers two trilogies, *Dragonlance Chronicles* and *Dragonlance Legends,* four books of short stories, and numerous novels. Other series, also written with Tracy Hickman, include the *Death Gate Cycle* and the science fiction epic *Star of the Guardian.* Her most recent series is the action adventure series featuring an intergalactic mercenary company, Mag Force 7, written with her husband, Don Perrin. Margaret and Don live in a converted barn near Lake Geneva, Wisconsin.

Ed Gorman's name is synonymous with some of the best dark suspense and mystery fiction being written today. His novels *Black River Falls, The Marilyn Tapes, Blood Red Moon,* and *First Lady* have all met with widespread critical acclaim and several foreign sales. His latest novel is *Daughter of Darkness,* available from DAW Books. He is also the Editorial Director of *Mystery Scene,* one of the top trade magazines of the mystery genre. He lives in Cedar Rapids, Iowa, with his wife, author Carol Gorman.

Robyn Fielder is a painter and writer who lives in Chicago, Illinois with her partner Matthew Woodring Stover and her man-eating Maine Coon cats, Aleister and Israel. Her paintings are featured in galleries in the Midwest and on the West Coast. She studies martial arts at the Degerberg Academy; Savate, the French martial art, and Degerberg Blend, a compound of approximately twenty-five martial arts from around the world. She is also an amateur marathon runner and an aspiring triathlete. She has been the recipient of an Award for Outstanding Achievement from NASA for research in black hole dynamics, and has been an award-winning equestrian. "The Wind at Tres Castillos" is her first short story. For more information, her web page is <http://www.para-net.com/~robyn_fielder>

When not writing, **Jean Rabe** feeds her goldfish, visits museums, and attends gaming conventions. A former newspaper reporter, she is the author of seven fantasy novels for TSR, Inc., including the *Dragonlance* Fifth Age Trilogy. She has written numerous fantasy and science fiction short stories, and she edits a BattleTech magazine for the FASA Corporation.

John Helfers is a writer and editor currently living in Green Bay, Wisconsin. His fiction has appeared in anthologies such as *Sword of Ice and Other Tales of Valdemar, The UFO Files,* and *Warrior Princesses,* among others. He is also the editor of the anthology *Black Cats and Broken Mirrors.* Future projects include attempting to coauthor several novels. In his spare time, what there is of it, he enjoys disk golf, inline skating, and role-playing games.

Matthew Woodring Stover's incredibly violent science fiction-adventure-fantasy-romance *Heroes Die* was published in 1998. He's also the author of the (merely) extremely violent heroic fantasies *Iron Dawn* and *Jericho Moon.* He was bitterly disappointed to find that the Science Fiction Book Club dual edition of his first two novels only carried a warning for explicit language. One wonders how much disemboweling, impalement, and general mayhem it takes to get an explicit *violence* warning. He has resolved to try harder in the future. For recreation, Matt runs marathons and competes as an amateur kickboxer. He lives in Chicago with his partner of nearly ten years, the noted painter and up-and-coming fantasy author Robyn Fielder. For more information, his web page is <http://www.para-net.com/~matthew_stover>

Brian Thomsen has been nominated for the Hugo and the Tucker Awards, and has had stories appear in *Alternate Generals* and *Sherlock Holmes in Orbit,* along with many others. Recently he co-edited the anthology

Mob Magic as well. Currently he is a freelance writer and editor living in Brooklyn, New York.

Deborah Turner Harris was raised in Florida and gained a doctorate in English Literature from Florida State University. She is the author of the *Mages of Garillon* trilogy and the saga of *Caledon,* a fantasy series inspired by the legends and history of Scotland. She has collaborated with Katherine Kurtz on the best-selling *Adept* series and on the recent novel *The Temple and the Stone*. She plays the guitar and Celtic harp, but her secret ambition is to be the bass player in an electric blues band. She lives in St. Andrews, Scotland, with her husband Robert and their three sons.

A native Scot, **Robert J. Harris** has in his time been a classics scholar, a bartender, and a film extra, but is perhaps best known as the inventor of the world's best-selling fantasy board game *Talisman*. He has sold short stories to several recent collections, and is currently working on a historical novel. His hobbies include gaming, fencing, and writing potted biographies of himself. He is also learning to play the harmonica badly, because he has discovered this is a sure-fire way of chasing his children out of the study.